MW00655059

LIGHT OF ORION

GUARDIANS OF ORION BOOK TWO

S. L. RICHARDSON

S. L. Richardson

www.slrichardson.com

Available in these formats:

ISBN: 978-1-7340644-2-1 (eBook)

ISBN: 978-1-7340644-3-8 (Paperback)

Cover Design: Natalie Narbonne at Original Book Cover Design - www.originalbookcoverdesign.com

Book Formatting: BooklyStyle

Editing: Rebekah Dodson

Published by Flasheila Press | Friendswood, Texas

~

To Dan, Lilly, Emily and Jack.
Never stop chasing your dreams...

PROLOGUE
SUMMER 1999

The birth of Anne, the nun from Mark of Orion.

T he air conditioner clicked on as she kneeled beside her simple wood framed bed. Cool air caressed her damp neck, exposed by her bent head. Her soft, aged hands were clasped together; her lips moved silently, reciting her evening prayers. From around her neck, a wooden crucifix dangled from a silver chain, touching the side of the mattress. She crossed herself with her fingertip and opened her dry eyes.

"Amen." Her hushed affirmation filled the quiet small room.

She exhaled, releasing her pent-up worries of the day. Stifling a groan as she straightened her knees, she stood and stretched her stiff back. She leaned over the bed where she'd lain for over forty years and pulled back the brown wool blanket uncovering the thin beige sheets. She'd long forgotten the comforts of a thick mattress, instead choosing to be grateful for the sagging one. Her forehead creased, realizing she should put new mattresses on the Convent's wish list.

She sat on the bed's edge and slid her feet out of her worn slippers, sliding them next to her bed, wanting to avoid the cold tile floor when she rose early in the morning. She settled on top of the sheet, relaxing as the vent's cool air pushed away the room's heat from a hot

1

summer's day. Saving money meant the Sisters' rooms stayed a balmy eighty degrees during the day, but their reward was the luxury of turning down the temperature at night. The corners of her lips lifted when chills ran along her skin under her white cotton shift.

Finally...

Her eyes fluttered closed, hissing air from the vent lulling her to sleep.

Creak.

She jerked awake as if she'd missed a step on the sidewalk. Had she been floating in a dream when she heard the high-pitched squeak? She waited, hoping to catch another errant sound.

Nothing, except the uptick of her beating heart.

Agnes, you old fool, things don't go bump in the night around here...

She clucked her tongue, rolled over, and faced her room, letting the refreshing cool air blow on her sticky back. A black leather bible, pages worn from countless turnings, lay open on her oak desk. A terry-cloth robe draped over her only luxury, a black vinyl office chair she'd bought to ease her pain. As Mother Superior, she spent too much time at her desk instead...

Slam.

She bolted upright. She hadn't been dreaming. The rusty iron gate in the cloister had opened and closed, but had someone come from inside or outside the courtyard? Her ears strained against the unnerving quiet as she shoved her feet into the slippers. Pulse pounding in her ears, she scrambled to don her robe before she rushed through the bedroom door.

Who'd venture out this late? Maybe a drifter wanting to spend the night on the cool grass.

The Convent's chapel was a dark cavern on her left as she entered the hallway. She glanced to her right, but the common room's night light displayed no unwanted shadows dancing on the walls. In front of her was a waist-high wall with ceiling high windows running the length of the building and an exit door in the middle. The daytime view of the cloister delighted onlookers regardless of which season decorated the landscape. But at night, moon's light illuminated the outline of the large white stone fountain nestled in the middle of the courtyard.

A faint cry from outside sent a shiver down her spine. Quick feet shuffled on the cement sidewalk lining the courtyard. Agnes's heartbeat galloped along with the stranger's running footsteps. She clutched the top of her robe as the footsteps grew closer.

Smack.

A white palm struck the window stark against the dark night. It moved, smearing across the glass toward the door. She squinted trying to make out the bent over dark shape dragging the hand along the window. Muffled sobs filtered through the window seams as the intruder crashed against the door and slid to the ground. Agnes couldn't move, her eyes transfixed to the bottom of the door, frozen by the fear of what lay slumped on the other side. She jumped at the hollow boom against the door. A sharp cry rang out followed by rapid, more insistent pounding.

"Help me." A woman's raspy voice called out, as if she knew Agnes stood a few feet away.

The urgent plea jolted Agnes out of her stupor. Her trembling hand reached for the knob, hesitated, then turned it ignoring her inner voice clanging of danger. Hot, muggy air hit her face, but a small body landed at her feet with a thud. She inhaled sharply as she took in the long stringy brown hair covering the woman's face. The stagnant night air rolled over them and brought a pungent odor that had Agnes throwing her hand up to cover her nose. An underlying smell mixed with stale body odor. Metallic... nauseating... blood. It splashed brightly, covering the skirt and hands of the limp body half inside her Convent.

What's happened to you?

A sensation that different eyes glared at her, scoured every inch like claws raked over her fragile skin. A cold sweat sprung, so vulnerable in the open doorway. Agnes dared to lift her head and frantically searched the shadows cloaking the courtyard, but her view was obscured by the dark masses of manicured shrubs and overflowing flowerbeds. Nothing moved, but the hairs prickling on her neck assured her something sinister was out there. Terror wound around her, clenching her insides as she shook the woman, while her eyes still scanned for the ominous trespasser blending into the dark.

"Wake up, child." Agnes's hand squeezed tighter on the unresponsive flesh. Her heart skipped a beat, blood rushed in her ears when she found what she'd feared. A dark shapeless form slithered around the base of the fountain. It grew bigger, spreading across the fountain like a cloud sweeping across the sky engulfing the sun while hatred poured out to her in waves. Agnes groped for her crucifix inside the robe and raised it at the rising evil looming across the disappearing fountain.

"Mother Superior?"

A strangled cry escaped from her throat as she jerked her head toward the voice. But concerned eyes met hers, not hateful ones.

"Sister Clare," she gasped.

Her eyes flicked back to the courtyard. She blinked a few times at the white fountain, now in full view, but her unease lingered along with the rigid hairs on her neck. She licked her lips and shook her head, trying to clear the tendrils of panic ensnaring her senses.

What's out there?

"Are you okay? I thought I heard pounding." Clare stepped closer, her eyes widening, now close enough to make out the body half inside the hallway.

"Who—"

"I don't know; but help me get her into my room... quickly."

A moan floated out from under the limp hair covering the woman's face while her body folded into itself. Agnes found the cause of the moan. The woman was heavily pregnant. Fresh blood bloomed over her skirt, spreading like a spilled can of red paint.

"Hurry!"

They each grabbed an arm, wrapped it around their necks and

half carted the pregnant woman onto Agnes's bed. Frightened blue eyes stared back as another wretched cry echoed; her body arched in pain; teeth gritted together. She fell back panting as blood seeped on the bed.

The woman latched on to Agnes's hand with a strength her condition didn't convey. "The baby—" she panted, "You have to help me!" A primal keening cut Agnes to the core as the woman suffered another wave of pain.

"Sister, call 911," Mother Superior called over her shoulder. Panic seized her senses, thinking of no way they could help this poor woman in time.

"No! No! Only you — no one else. No one else can know." Her hollowed out eyes blazed a desperation, tugging on strings that might snap. "Please. It's not supposed to be this way. I should be alive to protect her... guide her. But—" She cried out again, arching forward. "It'll be back soon." Her panting increased; tears leaked from the corner of her eyes. "I've no one and you—" she squeezed her hand harder. "You can protect her. Please..." The woman pulled her knees up, readying herself.

Stop... I can't help you...

Agnes stroked the woman's forehead, pushing the damp hair out of her face. Fear ricocheted through her old bones. "You need medical help," she glanced at the bloodstain growing on her bed, growing like her unwanted anxiety. "You're bleeding badly." The woman didn't answer, all-consuming fear and pain etched hard lines on her pale slick face.

"I'll go get towels and water." Clare dashed from the room.

Blue eyes opened and pierced Agnes again. "You don't understand. This baby is different." Another wave of pain hit. She groaned and fisted the sheets.

"Different... how?" Agnes murmured. Her eyes widened though her vision grayed around the edges. The woman's cries echoed off the walls, bombarding her from every direction. Agnes tried to slow her swirling chaotic thoughts, needing to make sense of why this poor soul wouldn't want more help than hers.

"I'm from a long line of women," she panted. "We're vessels — wardens of an ancient demon seed. If they find the truth... the secret... he'll come back into our world and —"

The woman reached for her skirt and pulled it back, revealing thin legs smeared with her own blood. Horror swept through Agnes as the woman's bloody hand moved from her leg and snatched the front of Agnes's robe, yanking her closer. Agnes gagged on the repulsive metallic smell— the lubricant for the pathway of life. She was too old, too tired to hear the demented story demanding her action. But the woman was heedless of Agnes's rioting emotions and uttered an ungodly, unholy tale that spurted out of her like a geyser releasing its pressure.

Agnes shook her head, dazed by the improbable words. "That can't be... it's not possible that a—" but the hot breath against her ear punctuated the woman's desperation, her terror and the reality of the baby's unimaginable ancient lineage and her frightful future.

The woman released her robe and gripped her womb. "She's coming!" She collapsed back on the pillow. So pale and slick with sheen, Agnes wasn't sure she had the strength to birth the baby. The woman pulled back her shirt, revealing her large taunt mound while her blue eyes became unfocused as if lost in another time.

"It's time..."

At the base of the woman's chest, a tiny glow illuminated through her skin, sparking like a flaming match. The woman closed her eyes as the small orb skimmed beneath her skin, riding up to the apex of her belly where it hovered for a moment. It shot down and struck the baby, illuminating it with a brilliant flash. The child arched as it received the orb.

Agnes pushed herself away from the bed.

No, no, no... this is wrong... this is unholy... I can't...

The womb went dark as did her mind except for the vivid image of the baby. The unborn child doomed to a task she didn't ask for... just like herself.

"Promise me."

Her raspy voice challenged Agnes, yet the nun's tongue was thick, unable to answer. Her panic and fear for this woman, her child and her incredible demand muddled any cohesive thought. How could she honor it and put the Convent in such terrible danger?

"Now... promise me!" she begged. Her head came off the pillow. Another scream reverberated as the dire request pressed upon Agnes, forcing her to make a promise she wasn't sure she could keep.

Sister Clare barged into the room and stopped short at the end of the bed, raising a hand to her mouth.

"I see its head!" Clare dropped to her knees and reached under the bloodied skirt. "Push!"

"Promise me!" the woman yelled as she bore down, straining to free the baby. Her sweat-streaked face scrunched up, and a primal cry tore from her lips.

"That's it! Keep pushing... it's coming!"

A new cry pierced her ears. The baby's outraged wails had Agnes staring at the foot of her bed. Clare placed the wailing infant on a towel. A sob clung in Agnes's throat when she saw the pink baby with a white pasty sheen nestled within a thin white towel. The woman fell back, her shallow breathing the only movement she made.

"It's a girl." Sister Clare announced bright eyed and breathless.

The infant's clenched fists and her mighty cries beckoned Agnes. A baby... a desire she'd given up the day she took her vows. Tears streamed down Clare's face as she handed the child to Agnes. She took the fragile bundle and wrapped the towel tighter around the baby. Time stopped as she held her: so perfect, so small, so innocent.

How could the wicked story be true?

"Promise me." The woman gasped, breaking her spell.

In that moment of maternal yearning, Agnes found her courage, her resolve. As Mother Superior, she couldn't refuse. She couldn't forsake this child, a gift from God. As these warring parts inside of her became one, this child became hers and with her life... she'd protect it.

"I promise," she uttered through barely moving lips.

"We have to call an ambulance. She won't stop bleeding. I don't know what to do," Sister Clare raised her hands covered with the woman's bright blood.

Agnes bent over her. "What's your name?" she whispered.

Colorless lips mumbled, "Hannah."

"Wait... the baby... what's her name?"

"Anne." Hannah's head fell to the side, hands releasing their grip on the sheets. Her wide vacant eyes stared at Agnes, but they held no fear, no pain, emptied of life by death's call.

Clare sobbed, her head bent over as she cradled her arms, rocking back and forth. She glanced up between her fallen strands of hair. "Is she dead?"

"Yes." Agnes's heart ripped in two for the poor soul laying on her bed... tormented bringing a helpless child into this cruel world.

A gasp from her doorway jolted her head up and she discovered the anxious, fear-stricken faces of nuns awakened from the night's bounty of helpless cries. The baby wiggled in her arms. Agnes couldn't believe what had happened or the turn her life just took.

"What do we do now?" a timid voice asked from the doorway.

Silence hung in the air as thick as the odor of death. She couldn't tell them everything. The knowledge was her burden.

A bitter cold swept across the room, as if she'd plunged into an icy pond. She was certain whatever she'd glimpsed chasing Hannah had entered her room. Agnes clutched the infant to her bosom. The bundle squirmed against her tight grasp as she dared to turn and confront the intruder.

There.

Hovering in the corner was a dirty mist with a set of blazing gold eyes boring at her with a hatred that took Agnes's breath away.

Oh, Lord help us!

Her body shook as the misty mass shimmied down the stark wall.

The wispy ends morphed into arms and legs, its head emerging with twisted curved horns erupting from its temples, while its white hard face glowed, framed in bright gold hair slicked back to its shoulders. He landed with a thud while his broad chest slashed with gold rumbled.

"Look what I found. A withering old nun clutching a babe and her cult of heretics." It's loathing for them suffocated her. Its intensity cuffed like a strait jacket, immobilizing her inside a prison of horror. "Give me the child and I'll not harm you." His hollow deep voice wasn't asking, and his hard arms reaching for her weren't leaving empty-handed.

"Go to the chapel, Sisters!" Agnes stepped back, feeling the crucifix between her and the baby.

"No!" Sister Clare jumped up and raised her crucifix at the demon. "We won't leave!" The demon swatted his hand at Clare, launching her body against the wall. Her eyes bulged as an unseen force held her by her throat, pinning her in place. She clawed at her throat, gasping for air. Two nuns rushed in and grabbed her legs, but another swipe from the demon flung them effortlessly aside.

Another nun charged the demon and raised her crucifix. He hissed at her; his face contorted in rage. "Our Father, who art in—" A crack split the air above the chaos, her prayer cut short by a vicious slap across her face. Her head snapped back as she dropped to the floor.

"Stop it!" Waves of anger overrode Agnes's fear. She had to fight this demon before he killed them. "You can't have this baby. She's not going with you. She's an innocent—"

He released Clare from the invisible force. She collapsed to the floor, struggling for air between her coughs and ragged breaths, her chest heaving beneath her shift.

"That abomination isn't an innocent, and neither was her mother or any of her kind. They kept him from us. But I've found the ancient one and you can't stop me from taking him—"

He knows...

9

A bright white light exploded in front of Agnes. The demon screeched as another flash threw him against the wall, cracking upon impact. Agnes's knees threatened to buckle as a glorious angel with silver hair and luminous white wings fanned out shielding her from the demon. She raised a red-hilt sword high.

"You should never have laid a hand on them. Death is your consequence."

The demon rose and peeled his lips back, its golden eyes narrowed as he unsheathed his sword. "I get to kill an angel, too? Oh... today is the finest of days!" He leaped into the air.

"Run!" The angel yelled before she jumped and met him mid-air. The collision cracked of thunder, their swords sizzled with gold and red electric currents, entwining like an enraged snake pit. The angel grunted.

"Go!"

Galvanized out of her stupor, Agnes lurched to the doorway while the others grabbed the wounded nuns. Still holding the baby to her chest, she dared a glance over her shoulder. The angel's crimson colored eyes flared at the demon, locked in a battle of death. The angel's sword ignited with a red bolt of energy as her powerful wings gave a mighty flap, sending them both through the ceiling. They disappeared, leaving no trace of destruction in their wake.

Agnes's lips trembled in a litany of prayer as the nuns followed her into the chapel. "Get the holy water! We'll fill the baptismal font!" She'd try the only thing she could think of that might protect the baby from the demon. It felt useless, ridiculous even, but what if it was the only choice they had?

The chapel's tile floor vibrated, the walls rumbled as the angel and demon crashed onto the courtyard. Blood pounded in Agnes's ears as she gazed out the window. The swaddled baby hovered in her arms over the granite font as it was filled with the precious water. The baby's face scrunched as agitated whimpers came from its rosebud lips.

"Shh... it'll be okay."

But would it?

Agnes ignored the chaos and dipped her thumb in the water. She moved it over to the baby's forehead, the few drops startling Anne. Agnes made the sign of the cross on Anne's dainty forehead and whispered a sacred prayer.

I'll dunk her if I have to.

"Watch out!" Agnes peered up, afraid the demon was inside, but it was the nun's witnessing the unfolding battle through the chapel's vast windows facing the courtyard. She froze, stunned by its clashing colors and powers between good and evil.

The demon hurled himself at the rising angel and swung his sword, but she ducked and swung her blade, slashing the demon's thigh. His shriek cut short as the angel twirled to miss his wild swing and sliced the demon across his neck. His golden head fell back, black blood erupting before the demon disappeared in a cloud of ash. The angel shoved her sword in the sheath held by her red belt. Her mouth lifted in a satisfied smile as she turned toward the windows.

Cries of joy and grateful sobs burst from the nuns as they collapsed to their knees. Relief coursed through Agnes's emotionally ravaged system. She brought Anne back to her chest.

I've witnessed a miracle; thank you, my Lord...

Her chin trembled as their savior angel glided into the chapel. A sense of peace washed over her as the angel approached her. The nuns crossed themselves, eyes glistening as she passed them, giving each a radiant smile. She stopped at Agnes and gazed at the baby with love that made the angel glow.

"Thank you, all of you, for protecting this child. Your actions tonight were courageous, worthy of the warrior angels that I fight alongside." The angel's hand fluttered across the baby's chest. She exhaled, nodding as she turned to the nuns. "But your work isn't finished. Anne still needs your protection, your love, and your silence. What happened here must never be spoken to anyone outside this room. She's in your care until the time is right for me to share her life's purpose and the sacrifices she will make.

"You have our word. We'll do whatever we need to do for Anne. Thank you for saving us tonight from that evil." The angel smiled, acknowledging the thankful murmurs around her.

"What... what's your name?" Mother Superior needed to know before she left.

The angel lifted her chin. "My name is Meira and I'm Anne's guardian angel. She'll come to know me, and I'll be watching over her and this Convent. Be at peace, Sisters." Her words melted into the air as she turned into a brilliant orb that flashed and disappeared, leaving the chapel bereft of a splendor it may never hold again. Only the deafening sound of silence remained.

"Sisters," Agnes scanned the group of nuns she cared for, nurtured and now must lead on this mission. "The young mother had no home and no family. She begged me to promise to raise her daughter here, with us, just as Meira has implored us to do. We'll love Anne, educate her, and she'll be a part of the Convent."

Agnes walked out of the chapel on legs moving of their volition. Turning into her bedroom, the air was thick with the stench of death, blood mixed with singed air from the electric storm created by their ominous visitors. Hurried footsteps followed her into the still room. She leaned over her bed. With a featherlight touch, she closed Hannah's eyelids over vacant blue eyes that no longer saw a world full of lurking evil out for her and her child.

"But what about the mother? What will we do with her—" the words trailed away, too heartbreaking to speak.

She sighed and closed her tired eyes. She felt the cool silver cross nestled between her and the infant and sent up a prayer for strength, wisdom and... forgiveness.

"We'll bury her in the crypt next to our sisters."

"But Mother—"

"It's the right thing to do. I made a deathbed promise to her, to Hannah."

And broke rules and some of my vows along the way...

"I'm asking a lot, maybe too much, but this wish I must honor. God brought her to our door."

"Why'd the demon come for the baby?" Clare's question hung heavy as Agnes struggled to answer it.

"That isn't for us to know, or Meira would've shared it. We're only tasked to protect Anne. The reasons why aren't for our souls to bear."

Forgive me, Sisters...

"I'll do it. I'll honor Meira and poor Hannah's wishes." Clare drew her shoulders back as she faced the doorway, eyeing each of the nuns.

They nodded in silent agreement, a few swiped tears from their cheeks while other drawn faces struggled to overcome the night's shocking events.

"Thank you." Overwhelmed emotions clogged Agnes's throat, but buoyed her heart.

Agnes found resolve among her fellow nuns as they bonded together on this fateful hot summer night. She wasn't sure of the path they'd take or if they'd accomplish it, but all her life's work had brought her to this moment. She had only one mission now. Protect this child, Anne, from the outside world and unknown demons that stalked her for their own malevolent intent.

Life's crooked paths are straight when realized in the rearview mirror...

God help us, for I fear we've not seen the last of this evil...

CHAPTER
ONE

OLIVIA

J iggling the pencil between her fingers, Olivia propped her head against the palm of her other hand. Her eyes glazed over as Ms. Thomas bombarded her ears with mindless facts about a British monarch. She shifted in her seat, glancing at the classroom clock. Only a few minutes had passed since the last time she'd checked.

"Am I boring you, Miss Drake?" Ms. Thomas's question startled her.

Oops. Guess I was too loud.

"No, ma'am." She sat up straighter. "Just frustrated the British queen allowed herself to get bullied by the nobles." A snicker behind her told Olivia she'd missed the point. Ms. Thomas crossed her arms as she stepped to the blackboard.

"We've been in school for a few weeks, and it's time to put Christmas break behind you and focus on school." She turned her back on the class and wrote on the blackboard with quick, hard strokes. "To help you refocus, each of you will write a five-page essay on a British queen and the noble you found to be her greatest neme-sis." A collective moan echoed around the room.

"Due on Monday," Ms. Thomas announced as she crossed a *"t"* with emphasis. A cacophony of protests erupted while Olivia slumped lower in her chair as her classmates' laser-guided anger hit her square in the back.

"Not all is lost," Ms. Thomas declared in an overly cheery tone. "Since it's Friday, you can work on your assignment now."

Heavy books thudded onto the desks as low rumblings filtered through the classroom.

Great. I don't have time for this. We're training with the Magi all weekend.

"Ms. Drake... A moment after class."

Olivia pressed her lips together, not trusting herself to respond. She flipped open the history textbook, but the words might as well have been in a foreign language. She skimmed the pages, hoping something grabbed her interest through her red haze.

Why does this woman ride me so hard? I'm not the only one bored in her class.

The school bell rang, too late to spare her now. Olivia stayed in her chair but didn't miss the daggers her classmates aimed at her. She stared right back, arching an eyebrow, not accepting their intimidation unlike the monarch that had brought on this mess.

Gathering her gear, she turned to Ms. Thomas, who sat behind her desk and watched Olivia's approach over the rim of her reading glasses. She took them off and tossed them on her tidy desk. Olivia braced herself for whatever happened next.

"Did you have a nice break?" Ms. Thomas asked.

That's not what I expected.

"Um... yeah. It was good... a little busy."

Understatement of the world.

The pause dragged out as Ms. Thomas studied Olivia. She sighed, then stood and pushed back her chair. She came around to the side of the desk, leaning her hip against it.

"Do you remember the conversation we had before school let out?" she challenged.

"Yes. You said you'd make me late for work if you caught me daydreaming." Olivia huffed.

Be nice...

"Yes, but I also stated you're one of my best students. And I meant it." Ms. Thomas scoffed and cocked her head. "It's difficult teaching history to teenagers so fixated on the present. Facts and events about a time long ago" — she shook her head — "seem insignificant compared to their troubles or wants of the here and now." Her chin lifted toward the empty classroom. "I'd love nothing better than to take these kids back in time. They'd soon discover that the complications of figuring out their place in life and within their families has changed little." Ms. Thomas gazed over Olivia's shoulder as if caught in a fleeting memory.

Hello... who you talkin' about?

Her focus quickly returned to Olivia. "But you always pick up the intricacies of history better than most of my students. For instance, your comment about the queen. That wasn't where the lecture was heading, but you understood what was taking place around her. That's a valuable quality, but it's how I recognized you weren't listening. Being present in the now is just as important as figuring the future... or the past."

Olivia sagged inside with her tidbit.

"I'm not here to punish you."

Kinda feels like it...

"I'm here to get your attention. Something is distracting you." Her brown eyes softened as she stepped forward. Olivia reached up and twisted her dragonfly earring under her long, dark blond hair, unsure where this was headed.

"I may not be your favorite teacher or anyone you'd consider confiding in, but... my door is always open."

Ms. Thomas could have knocked Olivia over with a feather. She'd never have guessed this prim and proper teacher would offer her an ear or shoulder. But, more seriously, someone spotted a change in her behavior. She needed to be more careful.

"Thanks for your concern, but I'm fine. I need to get back into the rhythm is all." Olivia shrugged her shoulders. "You know how it is after school breaks." She smiled, but it felt more like a grimace.

Disappointment flickered across Ms. Thomas's face before she pasted on her own attempt at a smile. "Yes. I know how it is." She shifted around and returned to her chair.

"Well, goodbye."

Ms. Thomas crossed her arms, settling onto her seat. Olivia stepped toward the door —

"Olivia."

Almost made it...

She twisted and faced her teacher.

"Those who cannot remember the past are condemned to repeat it," she stated.

"Winston Churchill," Olivia answered with authority.

Ms. Thomas shook her head. "George Santayana. Churchill made it famous."

Olivia gave a half-hearted wave and left the room. Her brow furrowed as she strode through the school's wide hallway.

That was the weirdest exchange ever. Why'd she tell me —

She spotted a flash of red hair before being pushed in her shoulder, knocking her into the metal lockers.

"That's for causing us to have extra homework," sneered Ryan.

"What are you worried about? Shouldn't be tough for you to pick out the bully," Olivia sneered. She readied herself, clenching her fists when Ryan stepped closer. Next thing she knew, she was staring into a very familiar back.

"Hey! Back off," Zach threatened, standing between her and Ryan. The hallway buzz had stopped, hoping to glimpse the first punch.

"Oh, look who stepped in for his girlfriend." Ryan shoved Zach's chest. "You a big tough guy now?" He leaned in, daring Zach to react.

Zach shoved Ryan in return. "Get out of my face." The scuffle ended before it had a chance to begin when Olivia pushed her way between them. Ryan blinked, surprised by her strength, and stumbled back into his group of fellow thugs.

Olivia glared at Zach. "I don't need you to fight my battles." She spun and pointed her finger at Ryan. "And you, touch me again, and you'll be sorry." Olivia rolled her eyes, disgusted with each of them, and marched away from the *ooooos* of the crowd.

"Liv!"

She ignored Zach as she stormed down the hallway, dismissing the petty bystanders.

How dare he step in front of me. I'm not a damsel in distress.

She pushed open the exit door and sent it colliding with the building. Fresh air washed over her heated body. She ignored Zach calling her name from the doorway, and picked up the pace until she reached her car. Olivia opened the driver's door and tossed her backpack in the passenger's seat, continuing to grumble under her breath about what idiots they were.

She steered for the lot's exit, hopeful she'd still make it to Cuppa Joe's on time. Glancing in the rear-view mirror, a gust of wind caught Zach's brown hair. He was still standing in the doorway with his hands on his hips.

Good... hope he's pissed off too.

Olivia didn't like being mad at Zach, but she needed to set him straight about his new-found Tarzan act.

I'm a Guardian of Orion and wielder of kick-ass weapons.

I'm not the same girl you fell for.

I can stand up for myself just fine, thank you very much...

Zach Paxton.

CHAPTER
TWO

OLIVIA

Pulling into her dimly lit driveway, Olivia slammed her SUV into park. She gathered her gear then stepped out into the crisp desert air. She welcomed winter's kiss on her cheeks. Between her irritation at Zach and her cranked up metabolism, she was in a perpetual state of hot. She'd better get used to it soon, or she'd melt during the Vegas summer.

Showing just enough restraint not to slam the front door behind her, Olivia set her backpack on the foyer bench and inhaled the cinnamon scented air.

Home...

Her sanctuary...

That is, until her dad returned a month ago and smashed her world wide open. With any luck, her parents were asleep upstairs... together. *Ugh.* She still wasn't comfortable with her dad, Conner, in their lives. He was a Godsend with how he helped Mom heal and land on her feet after her horrific car accident after Christmas. But the resentment and heartache Olivia directed at him for twelve long years when he had abandoned them didn't disappear overnight. She tried her best to be polite, to consider topics safe for both of them, but the barriers she erected needed to be broken if she wanted his help with being a guardian of Orion and a demon slayer.

A soft thump sounded at her feet. Thunder's purring greeted her while he brushed himself against her shins.

"Hello kit-kitty." She rubbed his ears while his large green eyes peered at her in the filtered light from a small living room lamp left on for her return. She stroked a hand over his arched back, smoothing his long gray fur. His tail waved as his loud purr filled the quiet.

"Hungry?" she guessed. "I sure am."

"Then let's have a snack." Olivia jumped at the deep voice speaking from the stairwell. Long strides brought his great shadowy frame down the stairs. His blue eyes scanned her as he walked past, turning the corner for the kitchen.

She jabbed a lock of hair behind her ear, resigning herself to follow him. Light cast from the open fridge as her dad bent inside and rummaged for food. Closing the door, he placed provolone cheese, turkey and wheat bread on the counter.

He raised his eyebrow. "A sandwich sounded good. Want one?"

Her stomach growled in reply, making them both smile. He built the sandwiches with efficiency while Olivia grabbed a water bottle from the pantry. She plopped onto the barstool and drank the refreshing liquid in deep gulps. The cool water quenched her thirst while giving her something to do besides stare at her Dad. He handed her a hefty sandwich.

"Thanks."

"Welcome." He took a big bite, jaw muscles worked as he chewed voraciously, readying to take another.

She sat in silence, letting the sounds of eating fill the void instead of false platitudes. She didn't know how to start those conversations with him. There were so many things to ask, but questions could bring conflict, so it was simpler to keep distance between them.

Chicken...

"You off to meet the Magi?"

She finished her bite and swallowed, hoping the snarky reply sitting on the end of her tongue disappeared with the chunk of food.

"Yes. I'm trying to go every night with Zach and Sergio." Her stomach fluttered at the thought of seeing Zach after the scene at school. She set the unfinished sandwich on the napkin. "In fact, I better get moving. Thanks for the snack." She strode to the stairs, but a large hand grabbed her shoulder.

Jeez, he's quiet for a powerful guy

"Wait... uh... how's training with the Magi?"

Olivia exhaled then turned to face him. Concerned lines etched the corners around blue eyes matching hers. She placed her hands on her hips.

"It's fine, I guess." She shook her head. "It's hard. I mean... I knew it would be hard work, but this training is crazy—"

"So, Melchior is being his militant self," Dad cracked a smile.

"That's one way of putting it," she scoffed. "But I like Melchior pushing me." She lifted her chin, squaring her shoulders. "I love it! Learning about weapons and hand-to-hand combat... it's so exciting. There's so much more to master. Sometimes, I just want to remain there and not come home—" Olivia stopped the words rushing out of her before adding something she'd regret. But a tightness loosened in her chest at having unloaded what had been building inside for the past weeks.

"Well, that would break your mom's heart."

Bubble popper.

"I remember having those same feelings too, but you have to return to this world. Building and strengthening your senses in these surroundings will make you a better hunter. You'll fight the demons here, not in the land of the Magi. When the school year is over, it'll be easier for you to disappear for chunks of time and train longer if that's your goal."

Grudgingly, Olivia acknowledged he was right, but it didn't sit well with him being the messenger. She turned to the staircase, leaving his words hanging between them.

Ask him...

She huffed and twisted toward the man, her father, who she replaced as a guardian, standing with his hands stuffed in his pockets.

"Do you miss it? I mean..." She faltered. "The training and fighting—"

"Every day. It was my life, my purpose, for over twenty years. But it's not my time anymore. It's your time now." Dad grinned at her. "Besides, I'm back home with you and Mom. It's what I wished, for so long... to be here with the two of you."

She bit her cheek and stepped away; not wanting to listen to his newfound bliss in her home.

"Livvy..."

She paused and closed her eyes.

"I'm here to help you, if you'll let me. My dad hung back at first, letting me find my feet. But later he taught me tricks and told me about his fights or what to search for when hunting." He hesitated and propped up against the wall. "Those interactions helped with my confidence more than anything. I'd hoped to pass on the same wisdoms to you."

A slow burn grew in her gut.

"As wonderful as it was for you with your dad, I'm not ready for that." Her hands gripped the staircase rail as she leaned toward him. She bit her lip, struggling for the right words. "I realize you want to help me. And maybe one day I'll be able to accept your return as easily as Mom. But now, I need space. It's still challenging for me... you being here and this... this—"

"Guardianship?"

"Yes," she confided. Dad stood only a few feet away, but the distance between them felt like miles.

You're holding back... not him.

"I understand." He waved toward her room. "Better get going before Melchior comes here and grabs you," he added, a little too light-hearted.

"Night... and thanks." Olivia raced up the stairs, and Thunder's soft scamper followed her. While her dad's words echoed in her head, nervous excitement ignited at the thought of training. She knew she was being stubborn with her dad. Sergio and Zach were so excited by the stories shared by their parents. A pang of petty jealousy would find its mark, but that was her own fault. She promised herself to work on their relationship. But how? If he shared his encounters and skills with her would this be the best place to start? Grasping the tricks used by her lineage was a definite bonus.

It's your time now...

Thunder jumped on the bed and curled up on her teal furry blanket tossed across the middle. He gave her a lazy blink; his purrs were soothing to her. He'd be in the same spot when she returned. She chuckled as she changed into black yoga pants, long sleeved t-shirt, and running shoes.

"It is my time, Thunder," Olivia asserted fiercely to the cat. He flicked his tail as if he approved.

She glanced at the two feathers in the mason jar on her crowded desk; one stiff, black, menacing, and the other soft, white, ethereal. After Manny had died, she'd wanted to burn them both. But keeping them reminded her of the good and evil colliding in her life. They were a constant warning that both angels entered her bedroom. She ran a finger over the contrary edges, sending a shiver down her spine.

Ugh... is that an omen or just my nerves?

Stay alert...

Olivia removed the polished brown talisman from her jean's pocket. Her warm damp fingers closed over it creating instant heat inside her hand. Closing her eyes, she envisioned Orion and engaged with the surging energy emanating from in her mark. A blue sizzling web widened in front of her; another world opening on the other side. With a huge grin on her face, she stepped through in greedy anticipation of the next lesson.

CHAPTER
THREE

OLIVIA

The sizzling web closed behind her. Olivia stood alone on the massive gray stone bridge and stared at the most brilliant sight that still took her breath away. When she'd come here the first time, her impression was she had portaled to an ancient world and faced an old medieval castle built into the rock face of a steep cliff. The granite gorge burst with lush greenery.

But she'd been wrong. This was the home of the Magi. Their noble church honored the God they loved. They'd carved out, beneath the building and into the cliffs, winding hallways leading to training rooms and passageways she'd yet been shown.

Olivia absorbed its stunning architecture, especially its white tipped spires with a huge Rose window centered above three separate arched wooden double-doors. She strode towards the entrance across the long wide bridge that created a plaza in front of the gray stone church. Thundering waters flowed beneath the two-arched bridge, matching her pounding heart. Zach claimed it was a hundred and fifty feet from the bridge to the ravine. She wasn't certain, but when she'd dared to peer over the edge, her stomach fluttered at the dizzy height. Tall, radiant white marble angel statues lined each side of the bridge's walkway. Some held instruments, others held their hands in prayer; all gazed up into the cloudless blue sky with adoration carved on their faces.

The heavy wooden door opened before Olivia reached the handle. She jumped back, as Melchior's imposing frame dominated the entrance.

"Come. Zach and Sergio have started their lesson." He stepped aside and let the door close behind her. He pointed to the rear of the chapel before his powerful strides headed in that direction.

"Hello to you, too," she mumbled to his muscular back. She scowled as she trotted to keep up with his hurried pace. The vaulted ceiling gave the church an openness, but the wide room wasn't as deep as one would assume. Rows of worn wooden pews lined each side of the aisles and faced the stark back wall where a simple, large cross carved from dark wood hung, commanding attention.

"Hello Olivia," Melchior called over his shoulder, his striking silver hair in a stubby ponytail. He stopped to the right of the hanging cross; his hand paused on the rough white wall. As his bright blue eyes passed over her, he paused with a furrowed brow.

"Did something happen today?" Melchior's low rich voice was laced with concern.

Olivia's heart skipped a beat, still unsettled by the fact he could sense her emotions. She didn't want to come off as whiny or scared, so she kept her run-in with Ryan and Zach to herself. She lifted her chin and hooked her hair behind her ear. "Just irritated with school. I'm ready to go."

He scanned her again then pushed against the wall. Seams appeared, forming the shape of a door. Cool, moist air hissed through the cracks and over her until a shadowy entrance came into view. Lined with rugged stones of various dark shades and shapes, Melchior engulfed the corridor as he swept his arm forward for her to go ahead. The air grew cooler the farther they walked into the mountain behind the church. There were other passageways branching off on each side, but she'd remain on the main path until Melchior said otherwise. She pursed her lips as her fingertips skimmed over the rough hallway.

"How can the walls be damp when this place isn't real?" Olivia glanced at her glistening fingers.

"Oh, but this world exists... in our dimension. The Earth is exquisite in her complex beauty. We want to revel in her majesty when we come to our home." The awe in his voice wasn't lost on Olivia, but she stopped short and faced him.

"You live on Earth, too?"

He chuckled, a smile broke across his chiseled face, but sadness then settled in his eyes. "The memories from the orb I gave you are mine and from past guardians living all over the world during different times." He nudged her forward. "But we'll get to that later when we unlock those treasures when we teach you to meditate."

Olivia let the news sink in as she advanced in silence. Their tucked away memories she'd received that fateful night at the Valley of Fire were inaccessible even though she'd tried to unlock them on many occasions. It was like searching for something stirring beneath the surface she couldn't reach... elusive yet beckoning her to keep seeking.

"But to answer your question, Olivia. You need to train, fight, and analyze in the same environment and circumstances as on Earth. Even though there aren't any city streets in our world, we can recreate them by portal."

Whoa... that's freaking cool...

"If we didn't teach in an actual setting, then we failed to prepare you when your day comes."

"To battle demons." Olivia's stomach shot to her floor.

"Yes... and more."

"What—" She hesitated.

He held up his hand. "Be patient. We'll show you and the boys in due time." He nudged her again. "They're starting."

Argh...

Olivia rushed ahead and set the cryptic message aside to unpack later. The excited murmurings floated up the corridor which ended in a large rectangular area the size of her school's gym. The walls were covered in panels of mirrors except the long wall on her left. It was padded floor-to-ceiling and various sizes of round targets and human shapes suspended at different heights in front of it. The opposite wall had shelves packed with weapons of all types and sizes: swords, bows, spears, knives, axes and others she didn't know their names. The far end had an area of wall-to-wall cushioned mats.

Hope Melchior doesn't think I'm wrestling him...

Thawp... clang. Olivia's attention shifted to Sergio and Zach. Each stood a short distance away from their targets with Caspar and Balthazar behind them, arms crossed. She walked toward them, careful not to create any noise to distract them.

"Stop," Caspar commanded. The boys dropped their arms and faced him but acknowledged her in the process. Zach frowned and Sergio only lifted his chin, his lips pressed together.

Not happy campers...

"Welcome Olivia," Caspar swept an arm for her to join them. The slight accent in his voice elongated his words, almost formal in his pronunciation.

She threw her shoulders back and approached the boys. They each held a large metal star with four sharp points. More lay at their feet while others were stuck to the targets or on the floor. Her heart fluttered as Caspar laid one in her palm; cool and deadly.

"These are Shuriken or throwing stars." He had a stack in his caramel colored left hand and a single in his right. "These little beauties won't kill any demons, but it can harm them or add a distraction. Let me show you. Hold it like a disc, thumb on top. Work on feeling as if the blade slips out of your hand, instead of flinging the stars at the target. Tense your fingers and wrist slightly at the moment of release." Caspar tossed the star with ease, striking a bullseye.

"Cool," Olivia marveled.

"Okay, now don't stand flat footed either. Rock forward by moving your body along with the throwing action." He grinned as he handed her a few more stars. "Let's give it a go, shall we... nice and easy."

He stepped behind her. Olivia lifted the star and tossed it as he'd shown. It hit above the target, but at least it stuck. She grabbed the next one between her moist fingers and let it fly, but it fell short of the mark with a clang. Wiping her damp hand down her leg, she tried again. This one held firm but landed wide. She practiced and improved each time. Determined to strike the target's center, she released her last star.

"Yes!" Olivia pumped her fist as it struck near where she'd aimed. A thrill of excitement whipped through her as she turned to Caspar, who grinned with approval. She glanced at Sergio and Zach's targets, and saw they'd gotten better, too.

"Good," Melchior proclaimed. "Now, take your bucket and gather the Shuriken."

"Nice job, Liv," Zach made his way over to her. Olivia nodded, but let the clanging sounds of metal-on-metal hide her silence and her flushing reaction to his clean forest smell. She threw another one in, irritated with herself.

"I can't wait till we get our own weapons and fight for real," Sergio's eyes narrowed as he scanned the wall of weapons.

Olivia tilted her head. "You're sure... you're ready to do this?" she swept her arm around the room. "To become a guardian and hunt demons?"

She waited for Sergio's reply. He'd been distant since Manny's death and his moods swung from detached to anger. She never knew which Sergio would appear. He finally glared at Olivia and Zach with a dark intensity.

"That all changed when they murdered Manny," he jeered. He stalked off toward the Magi, his bucket swinging next to him.

"I don't like that. That's not how he talks. He was so nervous before, now he wants to be Rambo." Olivia bit her lip. Sergio was hiding something from her... she could feel it.

Zach shook his head as they headed in the same direction. "Me either, but he's still raw from losing Manny."

"There's more—"

"Liv, about today—"

"Let's move to the Endurance Room," Melchior commanded.

Phew...

"Later, we'll work with throwing knives." Melchior pulled a sleek metal knife off the shelf. Not much bigger than the length of her hand, it had a circular hole at the top, leading down to a lethal point.

"We saw Agora's eye explode when Zemira threw one, when they were protecting us at Red Rock." Zach glanced over at Olivia.

I hope I get to see Zemira again... that was a perfect strike. I need to —

"Yeah, and her blood sprayed on me," Sergio shivered in revolution. His flat golden-rimmed eyes stared at the knives. "I want a little payback."

Balthazar clamped Sergio's shoulder. "It's not about revenge, my friend," his deep voice rumbled while his thick beard moved in sync. "It's about defending yourself and protecting others."

Sergio's lips thinned; his attention didn't waver from the knives.

Olivia would rather throw another bucket of stars, but she knew Melchior was right. She embraced how her body was stronger. Every day she was more in tuned, more poised and confident with herself and her surroundings. The hardest part was being patient when she was afraid there was a demon lurking around the next corner.

Guess I'm no different from Sergio...

Olivia followed the boys, but sensed movement behind her. Turning, she watched Caspar reach inside a bucket and come up with a handful of Shuriken. His wavy black hair fanned back from his face as he ran towards them, releasing the stars in quick secession, striking each target's center. Olivia sucked in a quick breath when the last star embedded in the eye of a human target.

"Showoff," bellowed Balthazar, hands cupping his mouth.

Caspar clamped a hand on each boy's shoulders, grinning like he'd won first place. "Today we started five feet from the target. One day you'll accomplish what I just did."

"That's what I'm talkin' about," chimed Sergio.

Olivia glanced back at the targets, nodding in approval.

Definitely... and soon.

I have to prove I'm just as worthy as they are.

CHAPTER
FOUR

OLIVIA

A beeping nudged Olivia out of her deep sleep. Squinting against the morning sunlight, she rolled over towards her nightstand and fumbled for her phone. She moaned when she read the text message.

Hi,
Can I come over before practice?
Want to talk to you about yesterday.
Z

She flopped back against the pillow and flung her arm over her eyes. Dealing with Zach was not how she wanted to start her day, but it was better to get it over with and move on than letting her feelings distract her.

Okay... give me an hour.

That gave Olivia enough time to wake up and figure out of a plan on breaking the news to Zach. Deep down, it tore her up to realize how much she'd miss him; his touch, his sensitivity, his strength. But she had to do the guardianship on her own... and so did Zach.

Sounds good... thanks.

Olivia tossed back her comforter and headed for her bathroom. A hot shower would help clear the cobwebs and revive her body for what lay in front of her. A thrill of excitement zipped through her... training all day with the Magi. She wondered what they'd learn today. She hoped to work more on her telekinetic powers. As the invigorating spray hit her body, she thought of the possibilities instead of dwelling on Zach.

Hushed voices drifted to Olivia as she entered the sunny kitchen. Her parents faced each other, talking over the rims of their coffee cups. Mom's face lit up when she noticed Olivia. She set her mug on the counter and came over for a hug. No matter how angry or frustrated she got with her mom, she'd never deny herself the gift of her affection. Almost losing her in a car accident last Christmas had been a living nightmare. The thought of Mom dying...

Long arms, too skinny for Olivia's liking, encircled her. "Good morning, sweetie," Mom's husky voice enveloped her like the hug as cool lips planted a kiss on Olivia's cheek.

"Morning." Olivia gave her a squeeze before releasing her.

Dad raised his coffee cup at Olivia. "Hi." He waved at her before he took another sip.

"I've got eggs and fruit ready." She pointed at the barstools as she moved toward the stove. "Sit—"

"I'll get it—"

"Honey, please. Stop fretting over me. It feels good making you breakfast again," she showed off her warm smile and eyes sparkling with pleasure.

"Okay... if it makes you happy, I'm for it." Olivia beamed back at her.

Dad walked by her and topped off his coffee. He brought a

steaming cup for her to the counter and placed the liquid gold in front of her. But his other hand skimmed parallel with it, pausing next to the mug. A slender metal bar materialized beneath it. A flush of adrenaline rushed through her body when she realized it was a thin switchblade with an ivory handle studded with a few brass pins cradled between its square silver edges. She jerked back in her seat.

"What's this?" Her brow furrowed. "I mean, I know it's a stiletto, but why are you showing me this?"

Mom set the cheesy eggs plate next to the blade like it was the most natural thing to do.

"We wanted you to have protection on you until... well... you get your weapons," Mom's gaze dropped to the knife. "I've always had one stashed in the car, my purse and in my nightstand."

"Really?" Olivia's eyebrows shot up.

Dad picked it up and flipped it over, resting his thumb on a small brass pin.

"This pin is the lock. Slid it down to unlock the blade." His thumb moved up to the larger brass stud.

"Press this button and the stiletto will deploy." The spring snapped, ejecting a sleek silver blade. The overhead kitchen light gleamed against its polished metal surface. He placed his palm on the blade and pushed it back into the handle. He passed it to her, but Olivia hesitated.

"Try it," Dad's calm voice and cool blue eyes reassured her.

Olivia's stomach fluttered as she reached for the unusual gift. Her fingers wrapped around the cold, light-weight stiletto, brushing her dad's warm palm. She drew it closer and examined the simple, yet elegant ivory handle that didn't look so intimidating. She slid her thumb down the lock and pressed the button. The blade's quick release made her body tense. It tingled in her hand as she marveled at the steel's translucent effect against the light. She closed it with ease and lay it beside her coffee cup.

"This isn't a weapon you can buy at a store. The steel is not forged in this world, specifically created to fight and kill demons. Aim for the heart. That will kill them. Because of its unique make, it won't pop on metal detectors." Dad tapped the ivory handle before stepping backward.

"What's it made—"

"That's not important right now," her fierce cocoa colored eyes bore into hers. "Keep this with you. Slip it into your boot, purse, backpack... you know... in case you might need it." Mom's voice hitched as she peered back at the blade.

"Wow. This is a bit intense before my morning coffee, but okay... I get it." Olivia cast a glance between her parents, releasing a pent-up breath. "Thanks."

"You're welcome." Mom patted her hand. "Now eat," she urged, beaming like it was perfectly normal to give a magical weapon while serving scrambled eggs.

This is the strangest breakfast... ever.

Olivia swallowed the last bite when the doorbell rang. She nudged the plate aside and seized the blade with a jittery hand. The ivory handle cooled her fingertips as she slipped it into her jacket's pocket. Dad headed for the foyer, allowing her a minute to gather her thoughts before she faced Zach.

Hearing footsteps on the tile floor, Olivia turned to find Zach's emerald eyes hopeful, like a pooch wanting out of the doghouse. He invariably caused her stomach to do a little flip, but she had to put her feelings aside and be honest with him about his over vigilant behavior because those green eyes couldn't shield him from her ire anymore.

"Hey," he handed her a white lunch bag. "Breakfast tacos in case—"

Olivia took the sack and put it on the counter. "Thanks, but Mom made me eggs." Her belly tightened as everyone stared at her. "I'm ready. Let's go meet the Magi."

Waving goodbye, she opened the sliding glass door and walked into the back yard. The stark leafless trees and brown grass didn't help her disposition. She zipped up her fleece to guard against the brisk breeze even though the sun warmed her face. She heard the door slide closed behind her.

"Liv, I'm sorry about yesterday at school. Ryan pushes my buttons and—"

She spun around and raised her chin. "Look, Ryan pushes my buttons, too. He's a slimy jerk, but I was handling it just fine before you rode in on your white horse." Zach shoved his hands in his pockets. His lips thinned as she stepped closer. "Here's the problem. This isn't the first time you've tried to intervene for me or protect me during training with the Magi." She stopped in front of him, never breaking eye contact.

"I just don't want you to get hurt." Zach gazed over her shoulder, sadness floating across his grim face. "I don't know what I'd do if something happened to you." His voice was thick and scarcely above a whisper.

Olivia's mutinous arms ached to hug him, but she couldn't do that. Not if she needed him to change and accept the depth of her conviction. Instead, her hand grasped her jacket above her heart.

"That's why I must train hard, even harder than you. But that can't happen if you are trying to protect me or volunteer for me... or step up against a bully—"

"You're right, Liv," he shook his head. "I wasn't thinking it through... it's kind of a gut-level reaction. Insulting you is the last thing I'd ever want to do. You amaze me with what you've accomplished and how fast you learn new skills." He lifted his hand and moved it toward her hair, but she stepped away, leaving it frozen mid-air.

Olivia's chest ached as the words tumbled out of her. "I think we need to slow down our personal relationship. With so much time and energy being devoted to the guardianship and practice with the Magi, we should focus on remaining just friends. Maybe you wouldn't feel so protective of me—"

Zach flinched as if she'd struck him. "Really... so that's how you want to play this?" he stepped backward. "I see where you're coming from, but don't blame your insecurities on me. I may have been a little overprotective, but the real reason you're forcing me away is you're afraid of commitment," he pointed back at the house. "Daddy issues and all..." Zach stormed past her.

Olivia spun with her mouth hanging open.

"What did you just say to me?"

Zach yanked the talisman from his jean pocket. "You heard me. That you have Daddy issues. He left you when you were little and now, you're scared to get too close to anyone... afraid you'll be hurt again— but I tore down those walls, didn't I? Scared you. So... go ahead... stay independent!"

I can't believe he just said that...

How dare he say that I have Daddy issues!

She clenched her hands into fists while her eyes narrowed and threw daggers at him. "That's not fair! I'm only trying to keep us safe... and clear-headed."

"Right." Zach scoffed. "I told you I get it, Olivia. Sad part is you don't." His green web crackled open, and he stepped through without looking back. She blinked as the portal disappeared, leaving the back-yard quiet and her stunned by his stinging words and total dismal.

She jerked her talisman from her pocket, its heat cradled in her damp grip.

Mr. Perfect just can't be wrong...

That's why he turned on me and wouldn't listen...

Well, he's not getting away with that attitude...

She pulled up her portal with no effort and stepped through the blue sizzling webbing.

But an annoying little voice inside her head told Olivia he might be right.

And that fueled her anger even more.

37

CHAPTER
FIVE

LUCIFER

L ounging on his black stone dragon throne, Lucifer gazed upon
his serpent's pool. Ripples broke the surface with Tannin's lazy
strokes as he glided the perimeter of its murky home. He admired
how this enormous creature patiently stalked for a vibrant color, then
launched its mass at the unknowing prey, striking quickly, and
slipped back into its dark, deep abyss.

Lucifer's next move would be just as calculating; kidnap the
guardian and return to the Realms with his victim, leaving no trace of
his deed. He must take the girl and learn of her guardianship powers
and the Mar of Sin's secrets before implementing the next stage of his
plan. Drumming his fingers against the dark claw arm rest, he waited
for his Princes of the Seven Realms to arrive. He had to make certain
they all remained in line and set the trap for the traitor in his midst.

His fist slammed down, wishing he had the betrayer's neck
between his huge hands. Which one dared to think he could take his
place as ruler of Hell? He had his suspicions but needed to be sure
before he took out a trusted comrade: a leader of one of his Seven
Realms inside Hell. Zar would never have been inspired to snatch the
girl on his own, even if he thought it might impress Delilah. No.
Instead a lapdog, caught in someone's web of deception. But Zar paid
the price for his disobedience with his sight. Eyes ripped from their

sockets by the mountain mutant's vicious whips slashing with precision and no mercy. Zar's only worth now found in the snail trail he'd leave, leading to his traitorous ally.

A slim hand ending in long, black claws trailed over his arm and down his thigh, squeezing it before she came around and stood in front of him. His nostrils flared as Delilah's other hand caressed his chest. Her flaming red hair and suggestive green eyes lit a fire in his belly. Lucifer yanked her onto his lap for a hard kiss.

"Hello to you, too," she teased, nipping his ear as she drew herself closer and surrounded him in her glorious hair.

"Come here to distract me, Delilah?" he growled, running his hand the length of her spine.

Her throaty laugh echoed in his ear. "Just a friendly reminder of what's waiting for you when this meeting is over." She pressed harder against him.

"There's plenty of time for celebration, you greedy girl." He nipped her bottom lip then removed her from his lap. She slipped to the side of the throne, but he caught her sly smile reminding him of the Lessors with a human's soul within their grasps.

Tsk, tsk... Playing me for a fool?
We shall see...

Lucifer's vision narrowed. His thick, black blood surged in his veins as the imposing double doors swung open, revealing the Princes of the Seven Realms. He leaned forward and scrutinized each one, strutting across the long thick glass walkway. Water lapped over the sides of the pool, as the serpent paralleled their approach, awakened by their vibrant colors. The distinct colors from each of the Seven Realms flooded through the gigantic arched windows lining each side of Lucifer's Throne Room. A kaleidoscope of color, ignited by power and evil, emanated from each Realm.

The Princes stopped below the steep steps leading to his throne. They faced him while their shrewd eyes darted to Delilah but revealed nothing of their lurking thoughts. He stared each one in the eye, receiving a bow in return.

Pure power.

Pure submission.

Except for the devious betrayer...

"Princes of the Seven Realms, Masters of the Deadly Sins, I called you here today to remind you of a story. One we know so well; one we chose freely. But now this familiar story has a new ending. One I'm sure you'll enjoy much better."

They glanced at each other, their curiosities piqued and primed.

"But first, let me introduce you to our newest guest. This is Delilah." He picked up her hand and nipped her knuckles, keeping it within his grasp. Her body hummed through his hand as she basked in her moment of false power. "She's brought with her a gift literally from the heavens above. If you look closer, you may recognize her from our earlier time in Heaven. She was a guardian angel with the Green Kingdom of Kindness. You remember that place, Leviathan? Culturing that virtue to enhance the souls of those wretched humans?"

"I do," Leviathan, Prince of the Green Realm of Envy snarled, his neon green eyes flared when he glared at Delilah.

"Well, Delilah came to us not too long ago in the same manner we did," Lucifer scanned their guarded faces, "through the same chasm we were forced into after our defeat."

"Master, how is that possible? We've been here—"

"Forever. Yes, I know Beelzebub—" the Prince of the Gold Realm of Pride bowed his head, "—by the hands of St Michael and all the Angels." He slammed his hand against the throne's arm, sending a vibration through the stone. He eased back against the throne, a thump from deep within echoed beneath him. "But I digress. Delilah fell through the same chasm because *Goooodd* — left it open."

Murmurs rolled between them. Confusion etched on their marble-like faces. Lucifer held up his hand, quieting them.

"He left it open to tempt the weak Angels that stayed with Him. He told them it would stay open if they wished to come here, testing their free will. But no one until Delilah has shown the courage to join us. She came here to share the secret of how to open the portal and how to close it. Or should I say, who can do this for us. God, in his infinite wisdom—" he paused at the snarks and chuckles from the Lords "—has given a girl and two boys this power. Why? I don't know, and I don't care. My goal is to get one of them here, find out the secret and then, once the portal is open, we wage war. We'll kill or force every angel through the portal, turning them into one of us. We'll destroy every human soul and lay waste to Heaven. We'll kill them all, including *Gooooddddd*, and reside in the new Kingdoms of Heaven and the Realms of Hell and then turn our attention to Earth." Lucifer yelled, his tirade ricocheting off the stone walls.

"And finally kill the humans," shrieked Berith, pulling his red fire emblazon sword from his belt raising it as if striking the sky. Excited war cries erupted as others raised their weapons, eager for battle.

Once again, Lucifer held up his hand. Berith's long, straight black hair, flat face, slits for eyes burning with red irises within their inky orbs. Two pair of jet-black wings, slashed with red, erupted behind him. But his cry was not alone. Three other beasts' heads were attached around Berith's head: a lion with an ebony black mane, a black ox with razor shape horns, and an eagle black, except his red beak. His Cherubim display mighty when consumed with red fiery anger.

"Berith, Prince of the Red Realm of Wrath, you're a fierce warrior. I'd expect nothing less from your vindictive enthusiasm."

Lucifer's massive form unfolded from the dragon throne, stalking down each step while the fires that lined the staircase grew as he passed until he stood on the last one.

"We've been here for too long, trapped in this dimension of Hell created for us. An eternity spent, building an Army of Damned, turning human souls—brought here by the Lessors— because their sins ruled over them, darkening their souls. Our army languishes away deep in the bulging mountains, begging for release... and release we will— onto mankind." More roars of approvals fed Lucifer's desire to share his new vision.

"But we've lost our focus. We've stopped planning for how to bring war to the Heavens. Instead, we wait for the end of times, when we could wage war again."

He took the last step, letting their excited cries fuel the rage surging in his body. His lip peeled back in a sneer.

"If we start war on our terms, we can surprise our enemies, destroy them and rule over the humans on Earth." Lucifer's chest heaved with excitement exhilarated to be finally sharing his new plans.

Lucifer walked over and stood in front of a gorgeous woman with long, curly dark brown hair framing her hot pink irises floating in their black pools. He plunked a strand of hot pink hair flowing around each of her high set horns. He rubbed it between his fingers and leaned in, watching a sultry wicked smile play on her exquisite light brown face. Her curvaceous body, adorned in nothing but a hot pink electric webbing, crackled from head to toe.

"Asmodeus, Prince of the Magenta Realm of Lust—Igniter of unrestrained sexual desires. Imagine your Realm on Earth, dedicated to only lustful desires and pleasures... mankind using each other as objects for their perversions. They'd spend their entire lifetime in your Realm, never leaving your den, feasting upon the very sin you incite." He drew her body closer; pulling her at the small of her back.

"I'd say it sounded like my kind of Hell on Earth," she confessed breathlessly into his face while her body vibrated against his. "I'll go get that nasty little girl right now. My Fallen will have her spilling her secrets in no time." Six Seraphim wings expanded behind her, ready to take flight.

"I have no doubt she'd break at your hands." He chuckled, running his other hand down her excited face. "But, sadly, we aren't quite ready for this step. Our armies aren't massive enough to defeat Heaven and control Earth."

"What can we do, Master?" demanded Sonneillon, Prince of the Blue Realm of Greed, who was handsome with his short, spiked white hair and cobalt blue eyes blazing with greedy wants. He struck his fist against his blue-marbled bare chest. "I'm ready for your every need."

Lucifer clasped his shoulder, nodding at him in appreciation. Sonneillon bowed and stepped back, folding back his blue Seraphim wings.

"What about you Astaroth, Prince of the Purple Realm of Sloth and you Gressil, Prince of the Orange Realm of Gluttony? Are you ready to do whatever I ask of you to fulfill our destiny?" he proposed, reaching the last two of his Lords.

"Always at your service, Master," hissed Astaroth. A purple forked tongue flicked out of his black lipped mouth. The purple snake coiled around Astaroth's neck gazed at Lucifer, shaking its purple rattle as if in approval.

"You know I love to indulge in anything you need." Gressil's bright orange eyes lit up as she cracked her electric orange whip high overhead. Water surged over the pool's edge, Tannin tracking the whip's path until the end snapped on the stone floor out of his reach.

Lucifer strode back to the staircase. Their unwavering approval fed his hunger... his drive to rule Heaven and Earth. Exhilaration and power coursed through him, emboldening him in his mission. He faced them, his body thrumming, morphing, becoming larger and taller; his skin turning into dark armor of scales and spikes- fierce, intimating... deadly.

"Princes... the seven strongest and most loyal of the Fallen." He stared at their adoring faces. "Go back and tell your Realms that war is coming soon. Tell the Fallen and Lessors they're to use their full force on the humans." He withdrew his great broadsword, thrusting it into the air. "We must have the filthy abomination turned away from good, and use their own deadly sins to corrupt themselves and those around them so that when we attack Earth—" his chest heaved, and spittle shot from his black mouth, "—these dark souls are ready to help us fight, kill and conquer until we have absolute and complete control of mankind!" He roared, lifting his hands out from his sides, head dropping back in complete adulation.

The Princes frenzied cries were music to his ears; food for his black soul.

"Go." He basked in this sublime moment. He hadn't felt this way since the uprising. But this war will be different. He's not that Angel standing before God; naïve in assuming God would listen to him, his most trusted Angel, about how humans would be their utter downfall.

No... this war is different.

I will not fail this time.

CHAPTER
SIX

DARK
PRINCE

The arrogance of Lucifer; his ego so fiercely blind, his mind so weak, his body so smitten with the flamed-hair beguiler. The Prince had listened in complete horror as Lucifer unraveled his new master plan of war and kingdom... so ludicrous and grandiose! Why would *we* prefer to lord over humans, make them our playthings or slaves? Our mission to massacre them all, decimating them, should never change.

You know you must stop him... the Fallen are the only ones meant to live.

The Prince's lips peeled back, baring his sharp teeth.

You are stronger than him now. Lucifer can't defeat you. We are one... invincible.

The sinister voice pounded his senses and fueled his fury at Lucifer's traitorous profession. He clenched his fists; breathing quickened as the ancient soul's mantras bombarded every passageway in his mind.

Set us free! Reveal to the others your power. Kill Lucifer. Rip him apart before their eyes and feed him to his beloved serpent who would feast on him like the mindless beast it is.

He flung his chair against the wall, scattering blackened wood throughout the room.

"It is too soon." The Prince's nostrils flared as he fought for control of himself over the relentless voice. "I must first discover the secrets of the portal. Find out how I can use it to conquer Heaven after I do away with Lucifer. Only then can I put our plan in motion."

Yes... Soon, very soon... and all this will be yours...

Those rhythmic words wrapped around him, soothing his charged-up nerves. The vivid, burning colors of Hell played before him through the window. He observed the colored lava of the Seven Realms, each flowing into the black lava river; evil vibrant beauty collided and boiled until it churned black around Lucifer's fortress.

"He will ruin it... ruin it all," he hissed against the glass. "But I won't let him." As he gazed at the Realms and let their ominous beauty consume his thoughts, an idea formed he both loathed and adored. One corner of his mouth lifted as the simple perfection of the solution cleared away any doubt and lack of control.

"What better way to demolish Lucifer's obscene paradise than to poison the wicked seed?" he murmured to his reflection, blurred on the murky windows.

No. Do not conspire with—

"Shut up! I tire of your abuse. I'm the one in control and will free you when I'm ready. I understand now what I must do, even though it sickens me. But you will come to realize, this is how we get the girl before Lucifer and tumble his kingdom around him at the same time.

It is too dangerous—you can only trust me...

"And you must trust me. She's the secret, whether we like it or not."

The Prince formulated his new deception, repeated it over and over until the soul could no longer find fault, silencing his voice. He strode from his room with renewed purpose to reel in his unsuspecting prey.

CHAPTER
SEVEN

ZAR

Blackness surrounded Zar, smothering him in its bleak and unforgiving darkness, pressing against his mind, body, and vacant soul. His fingernails gouged into the black lacquer armrest as he sat facing the Realm of Envy. Exploding pools of green seeped into a river of molten green lava, feeding the churning black lake surrounding Lucifer's tower. When he had stared before at the Lessors dropping the black human souls into the green pool, then freed by the Fallen in their new tortuous bodies, it had always filled him with pride and motivation to turn more humans against themselves. But he relegated those visions to painful memories. Now his existence was consumed by opaque nothingness, as lonely and oppressive as his blindness.

His hand glided over to the sharp blade of his sword laying useless on his lap. The edge of the steel cut his finger, leaving a trail of slick black blood as he moved up to the hilt. His pale hand, mapped with green veins, gripped the handle. Zar's mind played before him the practice sessions from his past with other Fallen. The clash of metal, the sharp clang in the air, detecting his adversary's fear of their looming defeat. His superior talents were highlighted by his opponents lacking the devious skills necessary to beat him.

Loosening the grip, his hand dropped while his head fell back against the hard chair. He'd never stare down an enemy again, or gaze at the glorious colors of Hell, instead doomed to an inky blackness for eternity.

Just as Lucifer had wanted.

Zar's body had been slow to heal from the mutant's tortuous beating he'd taken while Leviathan brutalized his mind. A quiver snaked over his skin as he remembered the whip tearing his flesh to shreds, peeling back layers and exposing his muscle, his oily blood exploding all around him. His body tried desperately to repair itself before another slash came across his damaged flesh. But the beast had been relentless in pace and ferocity.

Zar's hands flew over his ears. Leviathan's last words kept chant-ing, repeating—

Are you with us or against us?

While shaming him by exposing his weakness for Delilah.

He shook his head, desperate to halt the barrage of words, needing the humiliating memory to end.

Then the final strike: tearing his eyes from their sockets. The instant white-hot pain, blood pouring out over his face followed by complete and utter darkness.

"Stop!" he cried out, needing to end this self-torture, but the echo in his empty chamber taunted him with his own painful plea.

His head collapsed forward into his hands; fingers entwined in his platinum hair. Not a true Fallen anymore. Instead hollow, numb and useless.

All because of her.

Delilah.

He'd been suckered into her lies, her plan for them fighting Lucifer together, achieving control together, reigning over all-together, being... together.

Together.

Never. It would always be her with Lucifer and Zar along for the ride, used for as long as he would let them.

Such. A. Fool.

When he answered Leviathan- *I'm with you,* Zar meant it. He may be blind, but he was not stupid. He had nothing but time while he healed to contemplate about how to handle Delilah. His wish to crush her skull sometimes clouded his true desire. He wanted to reveal her lies in front of Lucifer and the Princes and then kill her.

It calmed him to formulate a plan, generating possibilities of the perfect scenario, one he could walk away from in one piece. He didn't need to lose another—

"Zar?"

The knock on his door shot a bolt of adrenaline through his body.

"Zar... are you in there?"

Her voice poured over him like gasoline on his exposed wounds, igniting them, inflaming his hate. How dare she come here? He crushed his lips together, stopping the cruel words on the tip of his tongue from spewing at her.

"I know you're in there. You haven't left your room in weeks." She pounded on the door. "Let me in... please."

If I kill you it's your own fault.

"It's open," he muttered, his voice as dead as he felt.

The door opened, scraping along the stone floor. His body froze as her scent... her essence slammed into him; her heat, her power, her dark beauty. Worse, it all mingled with Lucifer's evil dominant musk, creating a pungent odor overwhelming him, gagging him. He sucked in a sharp breath, not daring to show any weakness.

"What do you want, Delilah?" He kept his face turned away from her. "Come to gaze upon my black eyeless pits?" he sneered.

She closed the door, pausing before her light footsteps brought her to his side along with a subtle whiff of fear.

"Hi to you, too." A hint of sarcasm laced her voice. "I thought you'd like a visit from a friend. I brought news to cheer you up and a gift." She stepped in front of him. The swishing of a dress ignited a memory of her in a red dress, enhancing her flame-red hair. His body tensed so tight, if he moved, parts of him might break and fall away.

"I brought you this," her cheery voice announced. Her warm

hand laced around his. He fought the urge to yank it away before she placed a smooth staff in his hand. "It's a walking stick. It can help you get around or use for a weapon."

His hand ran the length of the metal, touching the grooves and divots like a tree branch. Clutching the staff, he heaved it at the window. Delilah gasped as it crashed and landed on the floor with a loud clang.

"Why did you—?" Her dress swished when she stepped away from him.

"Did you really think bringing me a weak human staff would cheer me up? You imagine me shuffling around the Realms clinking in the hallways announcing—*Here comes Zar... make way for the blind and useless.*" He launched from the chair, following her scent, pushing her back against the wall.

"You don't know me very well... *my friend*," The corner of his upper lip lifted. "Not very well at all." He stepped back, not trusting himself to not throttle her long neck. Her heavy breathing mixed with his as he backed away until the back of his legs touched his bed. He sat, needing distance and a chance to regain control of his rioting emotions.

"I didn't mean to upset you. I was just trying—"

"To make up for getting me beaten?" The air whirled in front of him as she landed, wings ruffling behind her.

"How dare you! I helped you and, if you care to remember, I almost got caught, too." She pushed her finger into his shoulder. "I didn't know about those nasty friends of hers or the brother playing superhero because we didn't talk before the Fallen brought you to Lucifer. I thought he was going to toss me into that inky, murky pool and be gobbled up by his pet serpent." Her furious words rolled right over him. As much as he hated it, she saved him from death.

"Well, if you weren't always shacked up with Lucifer, I could have found you and spilled the beans before Berith cornered me about Silth and why he couldn't find him." He bellowed back in her face.

She huffed and turned away. The dress rustled as she paced the floor in front of him; the sound grated on his nerves. She huffed again before the bed sagged next to him. Her long nails clicked against each other as she sat in silence.

"I didn't come here to fight with you," her voiced strained, trying to sound pleasant. "I'm here to give you the staff and share some news. Believe me or not, I'm on shaky ground with Lucifer. At times, I sense him staring at me when I turn my back. A flick of hostility or suspicion will strike me between my shoulders. I ignore it, while a shiver threatens to spread down my spine, but since our attempt to get Olivia failed, I fear he suspects I was a part of the plan."

"Well... you were," he smirked.

"Thanks for stating the obvious." Her sigh ruffled his hair. "Anyway, Lucifer had a team meeting. He told the Princes about the girl and how he would use her knowledge to carry out his renewed world vision to start a war and create his dominance over Heaven *and* Earth."

"Do I even care about his grandiose plans?"

She ignored him, oblivious to his sarcasm. "He wants to charge Heaven, defeat everyone there. No change. But during the attack on Heaven, he plans to unleash the Lessors and the damned on Earth and kill or capture *the saved* as he calls them. He'll keep the evil humans alive and have them fight the saved humans. They would use these corrupt humans and the captured for their pleasure after the war. The Princes are to unleash their Fallen and Lessors onto the humans now and change as many as possible so when we attack, they'll be in place. He said the Princes could build their Realms on Earth, living in eternal bliss, watching mankind kill and brutalize each other for their entertainment."

"That's new," he snorted. "What happened to kill them all and be done with it? How did the Princes receive his revised plan?"

"Asmodeus and Beelzebub are completely on board. Berith wasn't a fan because he wants to kill any and everything, but the others? I think they had reservations but played along with him."

Zar couldn't imagine the Princes even entertaining this concept. Eradication of the humans was the premise of everything they carried out in Hell. What would this mean for him and the plan he built?

Delilah grabbed his hand, her fingers entwining with his like scalding tentacles. He pushed away his repulsion, needing to deceive her as much as she did him.

"I still believe we can rule," she ventured. "If we somehow undermine Lucifer's new world vision so the Princes don't like it or trust him anymore, maybe we can start an internal power play between them and pick up the pieces. This is why I need you to help me figure out our next move. We must look at it from every possible angle, so we don't make any mistakes," she pleaded, squeezing his hand tighter.

He shifted to face her, letting her get a close and personal look at his black sockets.

"All right, I'll help you, but if it goes south again, you might as well jump into Tannin's pool before I push you to your death." He spoke with all the malice he had inside him.

Which is what you deserve, Delilah.

She drew in a sharp breath, certain her dainty nostrils flared at his threat. The bed lifted next to him, sensing her eyes glaring at the top of his head.

"I'll come by more often, saying I'm taking you for walks or whatever. We can talk then. I understand why you're still mad, but I haven't lost my trust in you."

Well, I've lost mine in you.

Delilah's confident stride stopped at the door. "See you soon," She left, taking her insufferable essence with her.

Zar let out a pent-up breath. Did Lucifer divulge this new vision of his world order or is she feeding him more lies to set a trap?

"She's a piece of work, isn't she?" A contemptuous voice muttered from the dark corner.

Zar flinched, unnerved he hadn't sensed his entrance. Had he been there long?

"You have no idea." Zar's disgust tainted his words. "What brings you here, Master?"

"I came to see if you wanted to spar. You don't need your eyes to weld a sword. But to my surprise, I heard her voice as the portal opened, but she was already leaving." He chuckled. "I see she brought you a staff."

"Yeah, she says I could use it as a weapon too."

"Anything else?"

Here we go.

"She wants to plot against Lucifer."

His laughter rumbled as his hard steps came closer.

"I'm beginning to like Delilah," Leviathan slapped his massive hand on his shoulder.

That thinking almost got me killed.

And it might get you killed, too.

CHAPTER
EIGHT

ZACH

The Shuriken twirled toward the lone oak tree, sunlight glinting off the shiny metal, but the star whirled past the target. Zach stretched out his hand, lifting another star from the bench. He launched another spinning star over the open field, but it struck the bark below the mark. He huffed and dropped his arm to his side. Fed up, he turned and marched over the spongy grass. His water jug's strap dangled from a wooden corral fence post as tall as him. He yanked it off and chugged the cool water, trying to soothe his hot frustration. Zach jammed the cap down and slung the strap back over the post. He propped his forearm against the rough wood and banged his sweaty forehead against it.

Why can't I hit my target anymore?

He kicked the post, glaring down at the lush green grass butting up against brown hard-packed dirt inside the paddock. A gentle breeze cooled his damp t-shirt. He sighed, knowing he needed to relax to concentrate on improving his techniques, not on his regrets about Olivia.

Two weeks passed since their confrontation in her backyard. She seldom looked at him — never talked to him — and her contrite politeness for Zach in the Magi's presence drove him crazy. After a few days of her not returning his texts, he'd given up and relegated himself to watching her from afar which didn't seem to faze her ability to train at all. She shifted the dagger's path when Melchior threw them at her, and her stars hit the bullseye with deadly accuracy. So, he decided two could play that game.

And it's killing me.

I can't get her out of my head.

He booted the post again.

Real slick, telling her she has Daddy issues.

Zach knew Olivia struggled with her emotions for her dad, but Zach never intended to broach the subject. But he'd struck back when she called him out on his boorish behavior. She nailed his act, too, and it stung. His misguided protective reactions harmed their relationship, but he hadn't worked up the guts to tell her why it happened.

Cody's death.

A nudge against the top of his head startled him as a white furry horse's hoof contrasted against the brown dirt in his vision. He jerked his head up only to have a black muzzle nudge him anew. Zach found himself face-to-face with a great white horse staring at him with golden brown eyes.

"Where did you come from?" Zach whispered at the magnificent creature.

Zach ran his hand over the prickly fuzz of its muzzle, stretched up over its upright ears, and brushed down the side of its long silky mane. His hand stilled as broad white wings erupting from its shoulders, fanning out and catching the breeze. Its nostrils snorted hot air into Zach's face while its hoof clopped at the soil.

"All right—sorry I stopped," Zach chuckled, continuing his stroke while mesmerized by the white iridescent feathers dancing in the breeze. "What could this be?"

Zach whipped his head around as more horses galloped across the grassy field. He gasped at their range of beauty: white, cream, brown, chestnut, gray, black and some a mix of colors. The band leaped over the fence; puffs of dust clouds bloomed with their graceful landings.

"You can close your mouth now," snickered Caspar behind him.

Zach pressed his lips together still staring at the paddock. They nudged each other as they wandered along the fence line, but their ears perked up at Caspar's quick whistle. Zach admired their luminescent wings glistening in the sunlight as they trotted over and fanned out, each neighed for Caspar's attention.

"There must be a least twelve of them," speculated Zach. He ran his other hand over the nose of a chestnut, with luminous orange eyes, who'd joined the white. "Are you what I think you are?"

"If you think Pegasus, you're correct. Fifteen here... more throughout the valley. This is the place they come to meet with us. They've become very curious about the three of you, and some have decided to present themselves." A black nose nudged a suede tan pouch hanging from Caspar's hip. He laughed, backing away from the eager teeth looking to relieve him of his pouch.

"Come here." Caspar waved to Zach. The creatures pawed at the ground, whinnying with excitement as Caspar produced glittering small blocks from his pouch. "You'll make friends quickly with these."

"Sugar cubes?" Caspar dumped a pile of cubes into his outstretched hand. They vied for their place in front of Zach. He placed one in his flat palm, lifting it to the chestnut. Its nuzzling lips tickled before the sugar cube disappeared behind the nimble lips. It nudged his hand for more.

"Greedy Gus," Zach chuckled, moving over to the white one.

"Oh ya... they love sugar." Caspar beamed while he scratched the ear of a huge gray.

Lost in awe of their majestic beauty, some tension eased in Zach's shoulders.

"Ya know, you'll get to ride one if it chooses you," said Caspar as casually as if he mentioned the grass was green. For the second time, Zach's mouth dropped open.

"What! How? Can I—"

"Hold on a minute." He raised his hand at Zach "Pegasus are wild, free-roaming creatures and most never take on a rider. But the fact they showed up during your training means you've piqued their interest."

Zach's heart sank as he fed his last sugar cube to the chestnut. A tingle zipped through his palm before he stroked its nose.

"Don't look too hard or you'll be disappointed," he mumbled. The Pegasus snorted and shook its head, then backed away from the fence. It trotted to the others, who had their wings spread out as if they were sunning themselves.

Knew it.

Zach rubbed the back of his neck, palm still tingling. He gazed at the chestnut, hoping against hope he would pick Zach. Caspar laid a hand on his shoulder.

"Do they each have a name?" Zach's voice hitched.

"Yes. They'll tell the rider." Zach scrunched his face, turning his head only to have his forehead poked by Caspar's brown finger. "You'll hear it in there. They'll link with you during flight and battle... you'll be as one. But the Pegasus aren't the only creatures living here. There are other kinds that may choose you."

Zach felt like his breath had gotten all bottled up inside as he imagined himself on the back off the chestnut, hands entwined in its silky yard of mane, soaring the vast blue sky.

"Like what?" he asked, licking his lips. Caspar's mischievous grin and twinkling eyes offered him hope.

"We'll see who comes poking around, but first you have to get over yourself."

Caspar might as well have tossed a bucket of ice water on his face. A whinnying came from the paddock, like an exclamation point on Caspar's blunt remark.

"See, even the Pegasus think so," Caspar chuckled, clapping Zach's back. "Right now, your mind and body are opposite the Pegasus. Wild and free—" Caspar pointed at the paddock "—locked up and bound," he pointed to Zach's forehead and then his heart. "Clear up your emotions or you'll never be ready to fully take on the guardianship. You might get hurt or those around you because your head and heart aren't one."

Zach winced at the full blow of the words he feared most.

"Don't you think I get that? It's what keeps me up at night... the thought of losing someone else I care about because I couldn't save them like... like Cody," his chest heaved, strangling out his friend's name, rarely uttered. "What if I make the wrong decision with Olivia or Sergio and—"

"Let Cody go." Long fingers clasped Zach's neck, sending warmth over his shoulders and down his back. "Find forgiveness for yourself. A good place to start is by telling Olivia and Sergio." Zach tried to pull away, but Caspar held him in place with a firm hand and firmer eyes. "Did you ever consider they have fears as big as yours and don't know what to do with those feelings either?" He gave his neck a squeeze. "Your honesty would help them and also clarify some of this... overprotectiveness towards Olivia?"

"Hey, I never told—"

"Your emotions are clear to me. Words don't always need to be spoken for thoughts to be understood. We're linked." Casper thumped the Orion mark below Zach's collar bone. Zach slumped and glanced at Pegasus. "Remember?"

How could I ever forget?

"I have no wish to be in your head... it's a little too crazy in there for me." His accent on *crazy* made Zach smile. "But your friends, your fellow guardians... you're in this together. Yet you're not talking to each other about your experiences. Each more focused on their own training instead of functioning as a team." He paused until Zach focused back on him. "The guardianship isn't meant to be carried out alone."

"You're right," Zach swallowed hard. "I'll talk to them. Thanks," he acknowledged, a little lighter now having Caspar's guidance.

The Pegasus pumped their wings, lifting them over the fence, with their long tails flowing behind them, and into the tranquil sky. Zach yearned for their freedom with every fiber trembling in his body. He waited there until they were disappearing dots, wondering if he'd ever see the chestnut again.

"Come on." Caspar surveyed the pile of Shuriken on the bench. "You've got some work to do."

CHAPTER
NINE

OLIVIA

The parking garage's elevator car shuddered and jerked as it slowed to a stop. Olivia stared at her distorted reflection in the shiny metal doors covered with smudges and fingerprints. The G button lit up on the panel, chiming her arrival. The doors slid open, the odors of exhaust and motor oil assaulting her. She stepped out onto the concrete; the doors dinging as they closed behind her. Gray concrete pillars were center points, with cars and trucks parked in their rows. The echo of her footsteps crossing the cement sent her the eerie message that she'd been one of the last shoppers.

She'd wandered the massive shopping mall looking for the perfect birthday present for her Mom. Her confrontation with Zach a few days ago lingered and distracted her, leaving her unsure about the gift ideas she'd examined: a scarf too busy, a candle too cliché, a shirt too plain. She glimpsed at the small yellow bag swinging from her wrist, satisfied she'd made the perfect choice. A small jewelry box, nestled at the bottom, contained a pair of gold, teardrop earrings, each with a modest oval Abalone shell dangling at the bottom. The mix of blues and greens would contrast beautifully against her Mom's dark, sun-kissed hair.

Her keys jingled as she pulled them out of her purse. The overhead light reflected off the stiletto's ivory handle propped against her wallet. It still weirded her out that her parents wanted her to carry it, but her training with the Magi gave her confidence about using the weapon. She hurried, thinking she might have time for a quick session with them before she hit the sack.

Olivia found the cement pillar posted with the row where she'd parked. Pressing the remote, her headlights flashed a few cars ahead. She quickened her pace, eager to get home.

She faltered as the hairs raised up on her neck and arms. Her heartbeat thumped, her mark burning against her flesh. She reached the front bumper of her backed-in car and resisted the urge to look over her shoulder. If she could just get inside —

From the corner of her eye, a shadowy figure emerged from the side of a pillar. The harsh florescent lighting played off his faded black jacket, its hood shrouding his features. His quick fluid movements had him next to her before she reached the door. Her clammy hand tightened around her keys, but one key jutted out between her two white- knuckled fingers. His dirty hand whipped out, clamping on to her bicep.

"Give me your bag, girlie." His rank breath assailed her while his other hand snaked toward her mom's gift. Olivia twisted back to avoid him.

I don't think so.

"Get your hands off me!" She yanked back, sensing a rising power course through her. Heat spread across her chest, sending a tingling down her arms to her hands. Blue electric current lashed out from her fingertips, hitting him across the chest and racing over his black jacket. The crackling lattice traveled over his body, encasing him.

"What the—" he yelped. He struggled to move, but she held him in her spidery web. She sent another current out like a wave, sending him flying across the cement. He crashed against the far pillar and landed in a heap. She took a few steps towards him, ready for his next move.

He rose on his elbows and shook his head. His hood had fallen back, revealing sunken eyes staring at her, his gaunt face filled with surprise. He moved his feet, like a dog on a tile floor, until they found traction. He stumbled up, cradling his arm, and ran away, not looking back.

"And keep running!" she taunted, her voice amplified in the cavernous parking garage. She crackled with energy, excited by her strength and courage. Her feet stayed planted until his footsteps faded away.

"How 'bout that?" she smirked to herself. "Wait till I tell the boys about this."

But all her bravado faded when her mark burned hotter against her skin. She froze, her eyes scanning the shadows, seeking the hidden demon. It must have been lurking with the mugger, like the coffee shop demon with Ryan.

Olivia sensed it before she saw it, alerted by the tingling between her shoulder blades. She turned her head, catching a flash of blue heading towards her. She twisted away, but not before the bolt sliced her bicep. Hot pain ripped through her arm. She thrust her arms out, blue light exploding from her hands. The demon was midair, leaping towards her when the charge hit his legs. The force sent him cart-wheeling back, landing on the cement with a thud.

Blood stained her sleeve, but the bleeding had slowed. Her skin stretched together, sealing the wound while the sliced muscle below fused back as one. A tendril of fear hit her core, fighting her first demon.

With no time for fear, she raced to her car, but a white-hot bolt of pain pierced the back of her thigh. She fell against her car's hood, crying out, her purse and gift bag scattering on the ground. She reached back and found the demon's knife embedded in her leg. The pain had her gasping for air when she pulled it out. Dropping the knife, her hand slapped over on the wound. Blood rushed through her fingertips as her palm pressed on the hole gapping in her thigh. Fire burned deep inside, straight to her bone.

The demon leaped on her, grabbed her hair, and yanked her head back. Sulfur and ash assaulted her. He flipped her on her back, her scalp screaming for release. She hissed as her thigh hit the grill of her car. The demon was only inches from her face.

He had black eyes with bright blue pupils, his black skin stretched tight across the sneer on his face. Jet black hair stood up in spikes ended in bright blue tips, surrounding two black twisted horns. His body was rock hard, pressing against her.

"What human tricks have you learned?" He dug his claws into her scalp harder, slamming her head against the hood. Olivia cried out as a piercing pain radiated over her head. "Have you learned some kind of unknown magic? It won't work on me." He growled as his eyes roamed over her.

"Get off of me!" She shrieked. "They're not tricks, demon." She grabbed his wrists, pulsing fiery energy through them. He screamed as blue light crackled up his arms. He released her jumping back. His eyes narrowed while his lips peeled back.

"You'll pay for that, you filth." He spat at her.

Olivia rolled off the hood onto the cement, jarring her injured leg. He approached her, cackling, his stench making her gag. She scrambled for the scattered contents of her purse, but the demon's claw grabbed her ankle. She kicked back with her free leg, feeling the satisfying thud of her boot making contact. Finding the stiletto against her tire, her hand lunged for it. Her dragon eye ring flashed as her sweaty hand clutched the handle. The demon punched her battered thigh. Her vision sparkled with bright lights. She cried out, pain as she'd never felt before surged through her thigh.

"Did I hurt you?" His malicious laugh spiked an outrage inside her.

She summoned her strength through the pain of her leg wound, not healing like her arm. Her thumb found the buttons on the handle. The sharp blade snapped into place. She twisted, the demon looming above her, his own wicked dagger raised above his head. She thrust up, grunting, as she shoved the blade deep into his heart.

His howl ricocheted off the walls while surprise painted across his face. He fell forward, exploding into ash and oil. It cascaded all over her, his black blood falling on her like fat splats of rain. She turned her face, dry heaving under her car, as dark gray ash landed around her like snow.

A car beeped in the next row. She couldn't let someone see her in this condition. Pulling herself up by the car handle, the blood and ash disappeared around her, taking the hideous sulfur odor with it. She opened the car door and threw in her gift bag and what was left inside her purse. Olivia heaved herself inside, gritting as the back of her thigh hit the seat, blood still oozing from her wound.

She slammed the door closed as her vision tunneled. Leaning her sweaty forehead against the cool steering wheel, she tried to take some deep breaths. Passing out wasn't an option. She had to get home.

A red SUV crept into view and slowed down in front of her car. The driver leaned out his window, craning his neck, scanning her car until he locked eyes with Olivia.

Did he see or hear something?

Olivia gave him a thumbs up with more of a grimace than a smile. He waved back. With his curiosity satisfied, he drove down the row, tail lights gone as he turned away.

Her numb fingers found her phone still inside her purse. A cold seeped into her bones as she found the last number, she'd ever thought she'd call. Her body shook uncontrollably, the phone heavy against her ear. Her dad's voice came to her as if traveling down a long tunnel.

This isn't good.

Michael...

"Dad, a demon... jumped me." She tried to talk, but her tongue turned thick in her mouth, her body so heavy. She ignored his explosive reply as she kept trying to talk. "I'm at..." but her world tilted. She fell over sideways onto the passenger seat, the phone sliding from her fingers.

A flash of blue lit up the passenger window. She prayed it wasn't another demon before her world slipped into a black void.

CHAPTER
TEN

SERGIO

The green webbing sizzled around Sergio as he stepped through his portal. The green hue in his bedroom faded when the portal closed, leaving him alone in the dark bedroom. Closing his eyes, he inhaled as he flopped on his bed. He raised his fists and slammed them down on the mattress. He hated coming back from training when they should stay and learn. Putting on a show by going to school meant nothing to him. Neither did guarding the secrets of the Fallen's portal. His pulse quickened as he imagined going on a hunt for demons and killing them with the ax tucked away deep in his closet. That was his only purpose in life.

Revenge for Manny's death.

He launched himself off the bed, needing some food to appease his growling stomach. He opened his bedroom door to a dim hallway leading into the living room. The rustle of the carpet where he stepped sounded like he was beating drums to his sensitive hearing. These heightened senses invigorated him and made him realize he was the predator, not the prey.

The kitchen smelled of lemon cleaner as he approached the counter. He flipped the wall switch, turning on the soft lights under the cabinets. Sergio sent a silent thank you to his mom for leaving a covered dinner plate for him. He peeled back the plastic wrap, exposing his favorite white enchiladas. His mouth watered as he placed the plate inside the microwave. He grabbed a few cookies from the glass jar next to the refrigerator. The food turned in circles, steam expanding the cellophane. He shoved in a few more cookies, opening the microwave when it dinged. Standing at the counter, fork in hand, he shoveled in his first bite, moaning in delight when the spices hit his tongue.

The fork paused halfway to his mouth when his parents' bedroom door opened. He finished chewing, but kept his head down. His dad's musky scent drifted over, announcing which parent would pepper him with questions. The food turned flavorless, but he chewed, giving him an excuse to not talk.

"*Hola, mijo,*" Dad spoke quietly, pulling out a white wooden chair at the kitchen table. Sergio cringed as it scraped across the tile, sounding like nails on a chalkboard. Dad slipped into the seat, folding his hands on the table, acting as if he had all the time in the world.

Great... another man to man talk.

"*Hola,* Papa," Sergio put the plate in the dishwasher, but didn't move to the kitchen table, preferring some breathing room.

"How was training?" His tone was calm, but Dad's shrewd eyes were upon him.

"Fine." Sergio's clipped response was sharper than he'd intended. A strained silence fell between them.

"What weapon did you work with today?" Dad inquired in the same calm tone.

"Chakrams." A tingle of excitement zipped through Sergio. "They're super cool. Balthazar took us out to an area where they grew green sugar cane. He had a stack of them laying on a table. They didn't look impressive. How dangerous could a metal hollowed-out Frisbee be to a demon? But then he twirled it on his finger, the saw-like teeth around the edges blurred. He flicked his wrist, and it whizzed through the air, cutting the cane in half. Bal explained that the cane was similar to human bone. My jaw dropped when he told us that. It's wicked!" He pushed away from the counter. "We then tried it. It's a lot harder than it looks, but I'm improving. My goal is to master them."

"They're cool all right, but I never used them. Bal is a patient teacher. You'll master it under him." Dad spoke with a smile in his voice. "Your sword ceremony is coming up soon."

"Ya, they said in the next few days. I'm so stoked for it. I don't know why we have to wait so long." He paced behind the counter; his body restless, almost twitchy.

"Sit down, Sergio," Dad waved to the seat across from him. Sergio rubbed the back of his neck as he walked to the chair. He plopped down, preparing himself for Dad's lecture.

"I'm proud of the seriousness you're taking, and how excited you are to learn, but this training is like nothing else you've ever done. It takes time. Be patient—"

"But I don't want to be patient. I want to learn now. I don't want to do anything else. All I want to do is train and not mess around with school. It's a waste of time." He huffed, slamming his hand down on the table. Sergio glanced away from his father, sensing he was pushing his dad's limits.

"That's quite a few wants, but let me share with you some needs. It's more than just swinging a sword around. Much more. You're the protector of a secret that would change the world if discovered. That means you need to be mentally and physically strong." Dad pointing at him. "I know you feel like Superman right now, but your body and mind need to rest to stay sharp and focused. These late nights—"

"Are you putting a training curfew on me now?" Sergio drummed his fingers on the table. "The Magi let me stay."

"Did you ever consider they're pushing you on purpose? Testing you to find your limits or to cause you to face your own demons? Do you want to break before you even begin?"

Sergio popped out of the chair, but Dad's firm hand grabbed his arm. Sergio turned and stared over his shoulder.

"Look at me, Sergio." Dad voiced a harsh command. "Manny's been gone for a few weeks—"

"Twenty-three days." A stabbing pain ripped through Sergio's heart.

"Yes," Dad exhaled. "The worst twenty-three days of my life." His voice hitched, throat muscles working up and down. "It will take us a long time to heal from his loss. But if you don't set your anger free, your training will be a waste of time and you'll never be the guardian of your destiny." Dad stabbed his finger into Sergio's chest.

"I will never forgive those that killed him," he admitted. "They took him from us—" Sergio's throat clogged.

Dad's powerful arms wrapped around him. Sergio sagged against him, gripping the back of his shirt. He couldn't cry, wouldn't fall apart. Not now. He had to contain this pain driving him. Would the Magi take the guardianship from him? That must never happen.

"I'm sorry I yelled at you." Sergio pulled away from his Dad. "I guess I'm more tired than I think."

"Please *mijo*, you've nothing to apologize for." Large, warm hands cradled his face. "I love you," he whispered.

"I love you too, Papa." He turned for his room. "Night."

"Good night."

Sergio had to get to his room. He rushed through the door, closing it a little too hard. Falling to his knees in front of his closet, he slid the door open. His hot, eager hands pushed aside a pair of boots and an old baseball bag, seeking a black canvas backpack in the back corner, hidden under an old fleece blanket. Blood pounded in his ears as his hands wrapped around the strap, freeing it from its secret hiding place. His hands, itching to hold the contents, pulled the zipper.

The scent hit him before he saw it. A stale oily odor, like what he'd imagined Hell would reek of. His fingers gripped the ax handle, always surprised it was still as hot as the day he brought it home. The warmth snaked up his arm. Its glowing red handle whispered to a part of him, and he wasn't sure he wanted to shut down. He laid the ax across his lap as the memories of Manny's death flooded him and crushed him, until he thought he couldn't breathe.

How could he let Manny go? He didn't know how. Sometimes

the anger was easier than the sorrow, threatening to swallow him whole. So his fury stayed while he envisioned all the unique ways, he'd exact his revenge. The platinum haired demon, the one they called Zar, remained first on his kill list. That's what Manny would do. Nothing would have stood in his brother's way.

What about Gabriel? He failed you.

Sergio shook his head, hating the wicked voice whispering Gabriel's name. His phone vibrated in his pocket, but he didn't answer it. It started again. He growled and yanked the phone out. Zach's face flashed at him.

This better be important.

"Hey," Sergio retorted, not hiding his irritation. "What's—"

"A demon attacked Olivia."

"What!"

Zach kept talking. "She's at her house. I'm on my way there."

"Okay, I'll be right over." But the phone line had gone dead.

Sergio's heart pounded as he quickly hid the ax back in his closet.

Please let her be okay... please let her be okay...

He scrambled up and threw his door open. He ran across the living room, through the kitchen and pounded on his parents' bedroom door.

"Dad! Olivia's hurt"—the door flung open— "by a demon. She's at her house—"

"Go to the car, I'll be right there." He disappeared back inside. Sergio raced to the garage, his breathing heavy. His Dad was right behind him.

Please let her be okay... Please let her be okay...

"She'll be fine, Sergio. I promise."

They jumped into his dad's car and tore off down the road. Fear snaked inside Sergio, twisting his guts into knots as nightmarish images of what might have happened to Olivia bombarded him.

Please... I can't lose Olivia, too.

CHAPTER
ELEVEN

OLIVIA

Interwoven images flashed in Olivia's mind, making it difficult to grasp whether they were painfully real or haunting dreams.

Warm hands pressing on my wound, then another burst of blue light.

Mom crying while Dad hovers over me, calling my name.

Melchior crashing through a door.

Zach brushing his lips on my forehead.

Sergio's big brown eyes stark against his pale face.

A deep aching fire in my thigh.

Olivia woke to light streaming through her blinds and deep purring by her ear. She laid on her stomach, trying to clear her fuzzy brain. Grimacing at the sour taste in her mouth, she wondered if she'd been sick all night. She tried rolling over, but her throbbing thigh stopped her. Something was laying on her hair.

"Wait, honey. Don't move," Mom crooned. The mattress sagged as her mom's gentle hand rubbed her back. "Shoo, Thunder." He stepped onto her other pillow; his purrs no less comforting.

"What happened? I feel like crap and my leg is killing me." Olivia pushed her hair from her face.

"Last night, a demon—"

Adrenaline shot through Olivia. The memories of fighting the blue demon crystalized. Her spark of panic subsided, realizing she was resting on her soft bed, not the gritty concrete from the parking garage. She squeezed her eyes shut, wanting to erase the picture show going off in her head.

"You're okay now, safe at home." Mom planted a kiss on her head. The bedroom door opened, followed by quick footsteps. Dad squatted next to her; his tired blue eyes bright with tears.

"Livvy." He placed his warm hand on the back of her head. "You scared us to death last night."

"Yeah, well... you should have been there," she croaked out. "I figured I was a goner." She tried to laugh, but it fell flat.

"I want to roll over." She sucked air through her teeth when her leg jostled, but once it settled, the ache subsided. Mom offered her a glass of water. She gulped it, relishing the cool liquid washing away the dryness in her throat. Her parent's intense stare was tough to miss over the glass's rim. She handed the empty glass back to her Mom.

"Thanks." She smiled, her eyes darting between them.

"I don't know if you remember much about last night, but upset people packed your room." Dad divulged. "Some are still downstairs. I'll contact the rest of the calvary." No sooner had he mentioned it when a luminous blue light flared. Michael stepped out of the portal, his wings retracting behind him. An enormous grin broke out across his face.

"Thanks be to God." He leaned over, placing his hand on her thigh. An instantaneous warm balm seeped through to her wound. Olivia sighed, smiling back at him. He moved his hand to her arm, releasing the same sensation. "You are healing well, my friend."

Footsteps pounded up the stairs before Zach and Sergio busted through her door. Melchior scowled like a grizzly bear stalking in behind them. Chaos broke out as the boys peppered her with questions, then everyone started talking at the same time. The boys sat on each side of the bed, bouncing the mattress.

"Jeez, enough already." Olivia placed her hands over her ears. "I can't answer you all at once. I'll just tell you what happened first."

Olivia's hands gripped the blanket laying across her lap. She picked at the fuzz while she shuffled the jagged memories into the right order. Exhaling, she started with the mugger and then the demon. She focused on her hands, letting the story tumble out as matter of fact as she could. Her stomached knotted when she flashed on the demon's evil delight, readying to bury his knife into her chest.

"The last thing I remember is seeing a blue light out the car window and thinking another demon had returned to finish the job." She raised her eyes and scanned the room. Some faces stunned and wide-eyed; others flushed with anger.

"That was me. You called for me." Michael's eyes glowed as a muscle twitched in his jaw. "Those were my hands on your wounds. I brought you home through the portal. Your dad had his medicine bag, so we treated you here." He raked his fingers through his gray hair.

Olivia glanced at her dad. He grinned, rocking back on his feet. She speculated what else he could do or if he had whipped out those acupuncture needles, too. The idea made her shudder, but she'd do anything to get back on her feet.

"Can you recall any specifics about the knife the demon threw at you?" Michael gazed intently at her, creating a nervous tension inside her.

Olivia closed her eyes, trying to visualize the weapon.

"I didn't get a good look, but the handle was small and thin with a ring on top. I yanked it out and tossed it, wanting it out of me. I was more worried about finding my knife before he jumped me again." She eyed her parents. "The stiletto saved my life. I want three more of those bad-boys. I guess it wasn't such a weird gift after all." Her nervous laugh released some of her tension.

"Have you seen that kind of knife before?" The men exchanged quick, worried glances, but Olivia caught it.

This can't be good.

"It sounds like a throwing knife, common use for them, but they laced this one with a poison." Melchior's voice was as tight as his body

73

language. "That's rare for a demon. I brought a serum to fight the spread. That's why your leg didn't heal fast like your arm."

"And why it felt like molten lava burning inside of my leg." Olivia lifted her shirt sleeve and found a faint pink line on the side of her arm. She flexed her muscles with no discomfort. "When will I be ready to train again?"

"Soon," Melchior nodded at her, but she felt no solace in his vague answer.

"Why didn't you tell us you were at the mall?" Mom tilted her head, confusion flashing in her big eyes.

A flush crept up Olivia's neck. "I got off work early because I wanted to buy you a birthday present. The mall was busy, but I lost track of time. I never thought..."

"Sergio and I have done errands by ourselves, assuming it's fine too." Zach reassured her. "Don't beat yourself up over this."

"We're just glad you're okay. I knew you'd kick demon butt. This could have happened to any of us. This is why we have to train more." Sergio's hand slapped down on the mattress, glancing over at Melchior. The room stilled at his outburst.

Michael crossed his arms, his eyes churning a dark blue. "You might be right, Sergio." His soothing voice held an edge. "There's been a shift in the Underworld. More Lessors—"

"What's a Lessor?" Sergio spurted.

Michael stared at Melchior, who bowed his head back in return. "It's time." Michael's confidence should have soothed Olivia, yet her heart skipped a beat.

"Balthazar and Caspar need to be here. Let's go downstairs where there's more room, if Olivia is up for it." All eyes converged on her.

"Yeah, my bedroom isn't big enough for the Magi." She smirked.

Before she could blink, Michael gingerly picked her up and cradled her in his arms. A whoosh of peace washed over her.

"The girls would be so jealous if they saw me now." She winked at him. His chest rumbled as he winked back at her.

The bedroom emptied as they followed Michael downstairs. A

bright gold light faded, leaving the remaining Magi standing in the den. Relief washed away their worried looks when they set eyes on Olivia.

"Thatta girl. No demon's poison going to take you down." Caspar jested in his musical lilt. Bal, the quiet one, only shared a half-grin.

Michael placed Olivia on the couch and then moved to the kitchen. She shifted, trying to get comfortable. "Everyone... stop staring at me. I'm fine," she grumbled.

Dad raised an eyebrow. "Good luck with that." He and Mom sat on the counter barstools while Zach and Sergio plopped onto the couch next to her... still staring at her.

Whatever...

Melchior stepped forward. "When you accepted the orb, it came with our memories, along with those of past guardians, connected to the world of the guardianship. You saw snippets of these when we released the orb inside you. Your personal and private thoughts are yours. We do not wish to infringe on your free will, but the link we share allows us to be more in tuned to your emotions. Your bodies have responded well to the orb as it enhanced your strength, senses, and healing abilities." Melchior scanned over Olivia, sparking a tingling in her chest. "But these memories have remained sealed. Releasing them all at once would overwhelm you. There's too much, good and bad, to take at once. In the past, we have opened them later to correspond with stages of your training." Olivia caught Dad nodding out of the corner of her eye while her mom clutched his hand.

"It's time to show you the beauty of Heaven and the horrors of Hell," Melchior moved to stand over Olivia.

"What?" Sergio squeaked.

"Seriously?" Zach blurted out as his brows shot into his forehead.

Olivia's mouth hung open, but nothing came out. She couldn't even begin to comprehend what she'd learn.

"Will we see the Fall, too?" Zach raked his hand through his hair.

"No. That's for another day." Sadness flickering in Melchior's eyes.

Caspar and Balthazar moved in front of Zach and Sergio. Melchior kneeled next to Olivia and raised his hand over her mark, as did the other Magi.

"Open your mind," Melchior laid his hand on her, engulfing the mark. Her head flung back, eyes closed, as a bright light exploded behind her lids. Beauty like no other unraveled before her. A scene of vibrant, colorful lights glowed on a canvas of an eternal white landscape. These lights centered on a lone mountain with an infinite number of overlapping sheer columns surrounding it. Glorious, luminous Angels floated through it all. Each a distinctive gender and skin color, displaying various hues on their wings or bodies.

Olivia's throat tightened, and tears rolled down her cheeks as she absorbed the serene, unfathomable majesty of Heaven.

"In Heaven, there's a hierarchy of Angels," Melchior's calm, smoothing voice echoed in her head. "There are nine Choirs of Angels, each separated into three Triads inside this hierarchy. The first Triad comprised of the Seraphim, Cherubim, and Thrones...the highest of all Angels and closest to God. The second Triad are the Dominions, Virtues, and Powers. The help fulfill God's plan in the universe. The third Triad are the Principalities, Archangels and Guardian Angels. They interact and serve humanity closely. Each of the nine choirs has its role in Heaven serving God. You'll discover these roles during your guardianship. But for now, realize the Angels serve you through their heavenly hierarchy."

Olivia tried to imagine how it all worked with the Angels roles so uniquely organized to better help humans to live a richer, fuller life. She was so thankful and incredibly humbled by their devotion to man.

"Within in Heaven, there are also the Kingdoms of the Seven Heavenly virtues: Humility, Charity, Chastity, Temperance, Forgiveness, Kindness, and Diligence." Reverence echoed in his voice. "These virtues represent the different colors chosen for us. God enhanced each angel with one of these virtues. They radiate the color of that kingdom. Their charge is to encourage mankind to live by these virtues in aiding them to turn away from sin. When the Fall of Lucifer happened, a third of the Angels from all choirs followed him and were swept down into the Mar of Sin."

The landscape changed from a dazzling beauty to a horrendous darkness. She gasped at the enormous black stone tower rising from a circular moat swirling with opaque black lava. Surrounding the black tower were seven massive areas, each vibrating with the same colors from Heaven, but it radiated with a cold, unrelenting malice. A smaller tower reigned within each section with various heights of black stone buildings surrounding it. These colors blanketed the buildings while an enormous pool boiled, its colorful lava flowing into the black moat. She felt suffocated by the heat and the evil rising from Hell. Her hands covered her ears, desperate to shut out the desolate moans and shrill wails invading her head. Flying demons dropped black orbs into pools bubbling with colored lava. Her stomach heaved as she watched one disappear into a swirling pool of gold, only to have a human form rise, dripping in gold.

Hell faded from her sight, but her mind was numb from what she'd had exposed to. A weight settled on her shoulders, but a sense of awe settled in her heart.

Your burden, your blessing.

I understand now, Mom.

Melchior stood up, but his concerned gaze never left hers. "The Fallen twisted these heavenly virtues. They use them to fan the flame of sin... the Seven Deadly sins as you know them. Pride, Greed, Lust, Gluttony, Wrath, Envy, and Sloth. Lucifer calls these Realms instead of Kingdoms. Each has a Prince who implements Lucifer's evil decree. The Choir of Angels remained as it was in Heaven, as did the Triad hierarchy. They also kept the angelic gifts of their choir. But the lower Triad repels Lucifer because of their constant contact with mankind, whom he despises and blames for the Fall. The top two Triads refer to themselves as the Fallen. The last Triad, he calls the

Lessors. They are what you consider demons. Their job is to turn humans from God, through their own deadly sins. When a human dies, the Lessors bring the soul to Hell." Melchior's stoic gaze clouded with sadness.

Michael's face tightened with pain and sorrow, breaking Olivia's heart.

"Is that the black orb I saw dropped in the gold pool?" Olivia held her breath, appalled at the actions of the evil underbelly working against mankind.

"Yes. The Lessors drop them in the pool of sin which drove them during their time on Earth. When they climb out, they have re-assumed their bodies, becoming part of the Damned. They will exist in eternal Hell, serving Lucifer," Melchior's voice hardened.

A horrific sorrow overcame Olivia at the thought of being a soul damned to Hell and Lucifer's whims.

"We're seeing an increase in Lessors, and even Fallen, lurking around man. More battles are happening between the Angels and Fallen every day. Lucifer is testing the waters for something," Michael stressed, scanning the room.

"Is that what you think happened to me?" A cold dread washed over Olivia.

"Yes, I do."

"How were the Magi able to see into Hell?" Olivia's mind spun with more questions.

"That's enough for one day," answered Caspar crisply.

"We'll have the weapons ceremony when Olivia finishes healing. Training will increase as will your knowledge of the guardianship." Balthazar's deep voice reverberated. He stepped forward, looming over them. "We'll push you harder, stretch you further, and demand your focused attention. Whatever Lucifer is up to has shortened our time line. Our goal is the next time you encounter a Lessor, it will be on your first hunt."

"Can you do this, give us all you have?" Melchior's request challenged the trio.

"Yes!" They chimed in, and Sergio raised a small fist pump in victory. But when Sergio glanced at Olivia, something more than excitement skirted across his eyes that she couldn't quite place.

"Good. Let's begin." Caspar raised his hand, opening his green portal. Crisp air rushed in as the stone bridge laid before them. The boys waved goodbye as they stepped through the web.

Melchior glanced back, nodding to her. "Rest, Olivia."

The portal closed, leaving behind a faintly singed odor. A spike of jealousy hit her, but she knew it was temporary. She was going tomorrow, and no one was stopping her.

Especially after my trip through Hell.

CHAPTER
TWELVE

DELILAH

L ucifer's enormous bed dominated his oppressive bedroom, a hellish cage framed by three mirrored walls. Delilah sat ramrod straight, her fingertips gliding over the silky, black bedding. Mocked by her reflections in the garish mirrors, she couldn't escape the sight of her flaming hair, or wide eyes, dreading his return.

This is what you asked for.

She lurched off the bed, fleeing the madness that happened between those sheets. At first, their interludes together were exhilarating and powerful. Now, even though pleasure passed between them, anxiety consumed her, fearing his next move—her last. Seeking refuge, she walked to the large picture window overlooking the Realms of Hell. From the top floor of the tower, Delilah had a bird's-eye view of the place she dreamed of ruling. She rubbed her hands over the sleeves of her black cat-suit, warding off the worry about her position becoming more precarious every day. Fear must not undermine her determination to hold firm while she implemented her plan.

She paced in front of the window, stalked by her reflections like an eager shadow. Her eyes darted to the ominous bedroom door. She felt trapped, taunted by her mimicking movements. Repulsion shot through her at the memories of Lucifer standing in the middle of the room, basking in his evil beauty and power. He demanded she join in his grandiose self-praise.

She always complied.

But a twisted part of her admired his unabashed self-adoration, his complete and utter control of everything and everyone around him. She played a dangerous game, desiring to outwit and destroy this ultimate evil. The repercussions of failure? Her life.

Delilah replayed Lucifer's recent meeting with the Princes, their every reaction monitored by her. Who to use for her benefit? Who to entice with her traitorous whisperings?

She paused when his heavy footsteps approached the door. Would he simply point to the bed, or would she leave with him? A dark thrill zipped down her spine as the possibilities excited, yet terrified her. Would he use her for his pleasure or lead her to her death?

Stay calm...

Distract his suspicions.

The door handle clicked. She adopted her serene mask, hoping it hid her festering angst. Lucifer's massive body filled the doorway, bumping up her heart rate. His dangerous allure alive in every step he took towards her.

"Good... you are up, my beauty." His arm slid around her, pulling her close. He nuzzled her hair and inhaled. "You smell like fire and my bed," he murmured in her ear. Moaning against him, her hands ran up his hard chest. She stared up into his black eyes swimming in red fiery pools.

"I just got up—lazy from our night together." A sly smile stretched her full lips. "I was hoping to fly to the different Realms with you. There's so much recent activity. It thrills me envisioning the new Damned for your growing army."

A groan rumbled in his chest, but he pulled away and grabbed her hand. "Maybe later. I've dealings in the Throne Room. I'm sure you'll find something to do."

"Of course." Her stomach churned at the thought of being close to Tannin's pool. He pulled her towards the door, relieved as they walked past the bed. She caught their movements in the mirrors, her body small and vulnerable compared to him.

He stopped, glancing back at her, his face an unreadable piece of marble.

"Like visiting a friend of yours?"

"Who would that be?"

"Zar."

She froze. Her heart pounded so loud she was sure he'd hear it.

Careful of a trap...

She tossed her head back in coy laughter. "Him? Yes, I go visit his pitiful existence on occasion." She shrugged, running her hand down his arm that could whip out and strike her like a snake. "I figured if I showed myself as still his friend, he might share with me if he or anyone else has plans to grab that insipid girl again." Her hand slid into his, the heat almost scalding her. "I'm sorry I didn't share my unfruitful talks. You know everything that goes on, so I assumed the visits were of little importance." Her thumb stroked over his as she maintained eye contact.

"You disappoint me, Delilah. Assume nothing with me again." His hands squeezed harder with every word. "You'll tell me everything you do from now on."

Fear licked at her as she bowed her head. He released her hands, threw open the door and walked out, his long strides echoing down the hallway. She leaned against the door frame, not trusting her jelly-filled legs to not collapse beneath her. She blew out a quick series of breaths, trying to get control of herself. It was more important than ever to put her plan into motion. Her eyes narrowed down the empty hallway that still breathed of his scent.

Time is running out.

～

Delilah liked the tight fit of her black attire and that her undeniable beauty turned heads. She reveled in the sense of power it gave her.

She also understood others gossiped behind her back. But it made no difference to her. She had a list of people in her head she'd kill the second she was in charge.

Leviathan, Saxem, his sniveling aide, that evil serpent...

She raised her hand to knock on Zar's door, but it flew open, leaving her face to face with the first person on her list.

Hope I wasn't talking out loud.

"Leviathan, always a pleasure." She squeezed by him, having no interest in the contempt he held for her in his neon green eyes.

"Lucifer know you're here?" he smirked, crossing his arms over his barrel chest.

She threw a smirk back at him. "Of course, he does. I tell him everything." She laughed at the audaciousness of her statement. "Does he know *you* are here?"

It was his turn to laugh. "I, unlike you, are not his caged plaything." He glanced past her to Zar. "Practice what we worked on today." And with that, he shut the door, tossing one last caustic glare at Delilah.

Leviathan's barb hit a little too close to home. She punched her fist at the door, wishing it landed on his smug face.

She exhaled through her nose, turning towards Zar. He sat in his chair where she always found him, his repulsive eyeless face staring out the window. He'd changed after his beating. He acted suspicious of her visits, pulled away from her when she came near, and said little when they talked. It irritated her, forced her to work harder than she wanted to until he would begrudgingly interact with her. She was wondering if he was worth the effort.

"What are you practicing with Leviathan?" She stood next to him, sharing the view of the hypnotic colors of Realms.

"How to fight using my other senses," he mumbled, still ignoring her presence next to him.

She inspected him closer, noticing the dried black blood on his chin and his ripped shirt.

"That's an improvement from sitting here all day. Must feel good to fight again." She chose not to inform him that he looked worst for the wear.

"Don't be foolish. I'm just his punching bag," he sneered, his head snapping to her. It still shocked her every time she viewed his scarred black pits, stark on his white face. Even eyeless, she suspected he saw her somehow, and he wasn't missing a thing. But his action conveyed he was too busy with his pity party to dig too deep, choosing to shield himself in anger and bitterness. But she didn't care how Zar behaved as long as he helped her achieve her goals. She'd played his silly game until it was time to rid herself of him.

"I'll never fight like I did before I lost my sight."

Eye roll...

"Well, you're not the only one used as a punching bag. I've had Lucifer's brutal hands disgrace me one too many times. You have no idea the tightrope I'm walking with him. One minute, he's consumed with me, the next minute... he's vile and inflicts pain." Her body tensed, recalling a vicious blow.

"Need I state the obvious, Delilah? He's evil incarnate. If you think he truly cares about you... you're crazy. I told you... you're in over your head," he scoffed, facing back out the window.

She raised her hands, aching to rake her fingernails down his ridiculous face. He was wrong. Their relationship was unique. She had an effect on Lucifer. She saw how he feasted upon her. The craving in his eyes, his secret thoughts he professed only to her, and how they plotted their future together. Zar didn't want to understand, still wrapped in his petty jealousy. She turned from him and paced the dusty stone floor, wanting to scream in frustration on dealing with such a selfish, rude, indulgent—

"We could use that to our advantage," Zar's lips barely moved.

"What do you mean?" Her ears perked up.

"Drop hints about how Lucifer's behavior has become erratic, more paranoid about the Princes. Mention how he talks about devious ways he wants to draw the traitors out into the open and destroy them. Or... how every day, he determines it's a different

Prince betraying him, convincing himself he won't need any of them anymore once his new world vision has come to life." He paused, tapping his finger to his lips. "One of the Princes will take the bait and want to rock Lucifer's boat."

"Or tell Lucifer and that's the end of me." Her stomach twisted as the visions of her death flashed before her. "We have to be very careful who we choose." She laid a hand on Zar's shoulder.

"The Princes are extremely loyal to him, even though Lucifer's iron-fist of tyranny through terror, punishment, and domination has been inflicted upon them personally. His drastic change in our core beliefs will cast enough doubt that one Prince might just be willing to take the risk. Lucifer is beating the drums of war. Someone might conclude it's the perfect time for a mutiny." Zar rubbed his chin.

"We just need one Prince to inspire another, and another..." Delilah's eyes gleamed with excitement, daring to imagine this might work. "But who?"

"Yes, that is the question." Zar drummed his black fingernails on his chair.

"Definitely not your dread-lock, dueling buddy, Leviathan." She snorted. Visualizing him made her blood boil. "He'd never have the guts to challenge Lucifer."

Zar chuckled. "Right... or Beelzebub or Asmodeus or even Berith. They may not be thrilled with this new vision of the future, but their devotion to Lucifer is unwavering."

"That leaves only three. It's against Astaroth's lazy nature to go against Lucifer. He just does what he's told. That leaves Gressil, Prince of Gluttony and Sonneillon, Prince of Greed." Delilah mused. She didn't like either choice.

"I suspect Sonneillon is our best bet." He stood, clasping his hands behind his back. "Gressil wants more of everything, but only what's right in front of her voracious orange eyes."

"But Sonneillon... he likes power... feeds on it." Delilah vibrated with excitement. "He'd see this as an opportunity and won't be afraid to get a little dirty."

"Exactly," Zar exclaimed. "He might contemplate your whisper-ings, if well placed. He's our weak link."

"I like it. We need to watch him. Seek a way inside his Realm and inner circle and find the kink in his grubby, ambitious armor." A sly smile crept across her face.

"I might know a way."

"How—"

"Leave me, Delilah. I need to think and you distract me too much." Zar's lips thinned into a hard line.

Oh, do I?

She acted on impulse as she approached him. She darted forward and kissed Zar on his hard mouth. His body stiffened.

"Thank you," she murmured, letting her chaste kiss linger on his lips. She sauntered to the door and out to the hallway, leaving Zar like the marble statue he pretended to be.

For the first time since Zar's failed attempt to snatch Conner's irksome daughter, Delilah had a real glimmer of hope for her plan to take out Lucifer. If they started a war inside of Hell, she'd pick up the pieces from the disarray and land on top.

If Sonneillon takes the bait.

CHAPTER
THIRTEEN

ZAR

Delilah's visits were unwelcome and exhausting. He despised how it threw him into a state of inner turmoil. At first, Zar wanted to kill her. Just the thought of her sent him into a rage. He'd fantasize about it as they roamed the tower, her mundane words droning on in his head. But as her incessant visits continued, he learned to push away her musky smell mingling with Lucifer's scent, driving him to distraction. Her touch no longer seared his skin and her voice stopped grating on his nerves. He functioned this way... until she kissed him.

Zar lost track of time, standing there after she'd left. He rather she had slapped him, stabbed him or lit him on fire then to have kissed his lips. It was a quick kiss, but it was lethal. That simple gesture shattered the wall he'd built full of icy rage and hate to protect himself in his fractured life. But those emotions melted and pooled at his feet, leaving him stripped of all defenses. He had no one to blame but himself.

No matter how hard Zar tried to indict Delilah for his torture, loathe her for being with Lucifer, or dream of imposing a brutal revenge, he recognized in that moment it was futile.

Realization struck him like a lightning bolt.

Delilah's kiss was all he'd ever wanted for as long as he could remember, going back to when he first met her before the Fall. And now he had to figure out how to protect himself from her again, because a new jarring madness had settled inside of him. One that could lead to his death.

Zar stood in his room's open door way in Lucifer's tower, letting the vibrations and sensations of his surroundings lay a path out before him. Ever since his eyes were stripped from his face, his hearing, smell, touch and taste had become hyper-sensitive. He couldn't *see* what was around him, but he could *sense* it, building a mental map borne of moving, humming static. Forms and areas came to life, over-laying his memories of familiar places. He took the staff Delilah gave him on his daily walks. To those who observed Zar, he appeared the blind fool, tapping his way around the tower. But *they* were the fools. The Fallen saw what they wanted. Their perceptions fit right into his plan. They made the grave mistake of underestimating him and he'd use this to his advantage.

The long, curved hallway led to a winding stone staircase to other rooms in the tower and the Main Hall on the bottom floor. The heat in the hallway grew ending in a large arched floor to ceiling window overlooking the Realm of Envy. Mixed with the cries of the Damned was the gurgling of lava. Before his whipping, he jumped from the ledge and flew to his destination, but he dare not show that ability.

One day soon.

Instead, Zar turned right and entered the curved staircase. He pressed himself against the wall, going down the stairs. The rough stone grazed across his shoulders. As he neared the bottom, a cacophony of muffled voices, steel meeting steel, grunts, and cheers for those fighting, echoed in the Main Hall. A couple of Fallen ran past him up the stairs. Lustful energy exuded from their husky laugh-ter. He scoffed. They never noticed him, in their zeal for one another.

Invisible.

The Main Hall pulsed with violence, centering around the deep, wide pit in the center. Seven massive entrances, like spokes on a wheel, led to seven bridges, one to each of the different Realms.

Most Fallen never used the bridges, preferring to fly. But once a week, the Lessors fought matches against each other in the black pit. Some battled for fun and glory. For others, it was a punishment given by one of the Fallen. The fights were always brutal. Death wasn't always the outcome unless they deemed it as punishment. The crowd preferred the battles where the Lessors could each heal enough to continue to fight until submission by an opponent. They sought Lessors and Fallen from different Realms to satisfy their like-minded desires. Zar wasn't interested in either. He came searching for Asura.

Zar skirted the edges of the massive hall. He was either ignored or heckled by those around him. Their jeers rolled off his back. His focus on finding her in the crowd. He was sure of Asura's presence here, watching the pit's festivities.

He knew the moment Asura found him. The intensity of her gaze was undeniable, like being in the crosshairs of a predator. Zar stayed against the wall, both hands holding his walking stick in front of him. His senses laid out how the Fallen parted for Asura as she moved towards him. He'd never forget her black polished marble skin cracked, with swirls of gold. Her long mane of gold hair in fine braids sizzled like a hundred, thin deadly whips. Her snake skin black armor fit her like a second skin with a gold curved sword hanging from her hip. Six black feathered wings enhanced her beauty and stature among the Fallen. A Seraphim, highest rank of the Fallen, second to Beelzebub in the Realm of Pride.

"What brings you here, Zar?" Asura's voice was as smooth as silk. "A little dangerous for you, isn't it?"

Zar sensed her curiosity, but his black pits didn't repulse her like the others who passed by him.

"My room has gotten tiresome and too quiet. I thought I'd come and hear the noise of a ravenous crowd again." He shrugged. "Maybe overhear the whispers of the Fallen's latest conquests."

"Ha," she scoffed. "I thought Lucifer's toy was keeping you up-to-date during your daily walks. I'm told she is always whispering in your ear." An ugly sneer marred her face. "I don't understand what

Lucifer sees in that whore. She's not a real Fallen, no matter what story she tries to sell. He's a fool, caught in her deceitful lies." She spat.

Zar raised his eyebrows. "Is that jealousy I detect, or is your pride hurt that he's not yours anymore?"

The icy steel edge of her blade pressed on his neck.

Her breath was a hot blast, scorching his ear. "I should kill you right here. Lucifer means nothing to me. Sonneillon is my mate." He didn't need to see her to know her eyes were fiery gold sparks.

The room had whipped up into a frenzy as the battle neared its end. The crowd's screeches and clang of metal added to the fevered volume of the room. No one paid them any attention.

A lazy smile stretched across Zar's face. "My apologies, Asura. I meant no harm. But it is good to find where your true allegiance lays." He slipped his fingers over her hand on the blade's handle. She pulled back, sheathing her knife.

"I'll ask you one more time. What do you want?" She cocked her head to the side. "I could feel you seeking me out in the hall. I know when someone wants something from me." Asura's talon fingernail slowly slid down his face, stopping as his throat.

His black heart kicked up a notch with her talon set to rip his throat open. "You're correct I came here seeking your attention. Delilah does whispers in my ear the most interesting details about her and Lucifer." The pressure on his neck increased. "Come now... you misunderstand me. I only meant about his plans and who he thinks is with him," he paused, leaning into her ear, "And who is against him."

Her sharp intake of breath was all he needed to validate his deduction about Sonneillon. His greedy nature was indeed his downfall.

"Tell me more or I'll—"

"What? Rip out my throat?" Zar smirked.

A Lessor emerged airborne behind Asura, broken and bloodied, into the crowd. The winner hovered above the pit, accepting the crescendo of raucous cheers. The Fallen disbanded, most flying back to their Realms.

Neither uttered a word, only their harsh breathing was audible as they each sought to control their emotions.

"I'll tell you more, but not here... not today. There are many eyes who have witnessed us together," Zar said. She growled as she removed her nail from his throat. "We can meet under the guise of you teaching me to ride a Degasus. We'll have more privacy there."

Her white-hot anger was mixed with an air of uncertainty as she glanced around them. Asura backed away without responding to his suggestion. Six black wings spread from her back. She took flight toward the glowing gold entrance without looking back.

An uneasy prickling rose on his neck as he stared eyeless out into the emptying hall.

What exactly is Asura uncertain of?

Me, Lucifer, or her mate.

And what will she do about it?

CHAPTER
FOURTEEN

LUCIFER

The Realms churned with greater activity as the Fallen led the Damned back into the mountains, thrusting them into their gelatinous holding area until it was time for release, and for war. Lucifer's shrewd eyes missed nothing as he soared above his kingdom. A sneer crossed his face at the Lessors, who gave him a wide berth, their precious cargo locked in their black talons. Even though they followed him in the Fall, Lucifer had complete disdain for their insignificant purpose as Guardian Angels, helping pitiful humans experience a way of life closer to God.

Disgusting...

After the Fall, Lucifer changed their names to reflect their place in his hierarchy. As Lessors, they retained close contact with man, turning their souls to sin. They had their purpose, but they reeked of humans. And he hated them for it.

He observed a Lessor release a black orb into the swirling purple pool of the Sloth Realm. The black orb morphed into a burned black man with purple swirls down his back and legs. Another lazy man who spent his days lying around wasting his life.

Bet he never thought his laziness would land him in Hell.

Two Fallen heaved him over the pool's side, leaving him cradled against other Damned, discarded in a pile. A Fallen wielding a three-prong purple whip cracked the air, landing on the new arrival's back. His scream pierced the air along with the others, forcing them into motion. Lucifer chuckled at how the whip's unmerciful lashes motivated the Damned to migrate towards their mountain destination. Lucifer himself was fond of whips and their ability to persuade yet horrify in the same chilling point.

He flew through the enormous retractable double doors in the Throne Room's roof. Lucifer retracted his six wings when he landed near the pool's edge, the lair of his beloved serpent, Tannin. The water slapped the pool's edges as Tannin skimmed the surface. Lucifer stretched out his hand. Tannin ran its spike laden scales under the outstretched hand of Lucifer.

Yes, my pet, soon... I'm hungry, too.

Lucifer walked toward his towering dragon throne. Its monstrous body with enormous bat-like wings personified Lucifer's evil domination for those who dare oppose him. He reached the steps, but paused as the heavy entrance doors opened behind him. Beelzebub and Asura strode inside with three Damned in tow. Two of Beelzebub's Fallen soldiers brought up the rear. Tannin's shiny black scales shimmered along the surface next to them, mirroring their advancement to the throne. Lucifer's eyes narrowed as they approached. It wasn't Beelzebub that intrigued him, but his former companion, Asura. They stopped in front of him, bowing low.

"Beelzebub, I do not remember requesting your presence, but I forgive you since you brought the most lethal temptress, Asura, with you." Lucifer grabbed her hand, inhaling her intoxicating scent. His tongue slowly flicked across each knuckle as his eyes dared hers to ignore the dormant flames they shared for each other. "Will Sonneillon be joining us too?" Turning her hand over, he studied her palm, its golden streaks extending to her fingers.

Oh, the things these hands could do.

"No, my Lord," she murmured. He kissed her palm, igniting a gold fire through them.

Was that for anger and lust?

"Good," Lucifer's chuckled. "He'd spoil the occasion. I'm sure he wouldn't appreciate me sending him away while I partake in your... company."

Lucifer glimpsed her hardening face before she bowed to him again. He released her hand, intrigued even more by her. He glanced over her shoulder at the Damned, who were prostrate before him. Raising an eyebrow, he turned to Beelzebub.

"A gift from our Realm to please either you or your serpent." Beelzebub waved toward the pool. Lucifer pushed between them and stopped at the first Damned. He jerked him up to his feet. Awe filled gold eyes stared back at him.

"Master," he wailed.

"Welcome to Hell." Lucifer hissed. He thrust his sharp talon fingernails into its rib cage. Lucifer slashed, gutting the wailing creature. Black blood spurted and oozed over his hand. The Damned fell to the floor, surprise etched on its face. The room smelled of sulfur as Lucifer lifted the damned over his head. He relished the oily blood dripping on his head, rolling down his face. A triumphant cry escaped his mouth as he launched the body into the murky pool. Tannin broke the surface, devouring the meal in one bite before slipping back to the murky depths.

"I needed that." Lucifer smirked, glancing at the two remaining victims frozen with a guard's sword pointed at their backs. "I'll get to them in a moment."

Lucifer faced Beelzebub and Asura. He licked his bloody lips, then spat on the floor. Oily blood trickled down the white marble skin of his chest. His heart pumped an excited beat from the thrill of the quick kill. He'd need more than two docile Damned to quench his blood lust.

"So, tell me... what's the true purpose of your visit?" He glanced between the two of them. "I sense it's more than enjoyment for me and my serpent. Is it not?"

Beelzebub took a step forward, not daring to look away. "No, my

Lord. As always, your instincts are correct. Asura and I have come on a grave matter. A traitor is plotting against you—."

A rumble of laughter built in Lucifer's chest, bursting into a maniacal cackle, surprising his guests. But underneath the glee, rage boiled. Lucifer wiped his mouth with the back of his hand when his laughter subsided. No sound echoed, or wave splashed in the room, heavy with uncertainty of his next move.

"Do you think I don't know one of my Princes is an impostor?" His voice was so menacing, Beelzebub went perfectly still. Lucifer stepped closer. "How dare one of my inner circle invoke this loathsome betrayal? After everything I've done... the trust and power I gave them because of their loyalty to me!"

Lucifer's full fury unleashed as his body transformed into black scales of armor, growing three times as big as those before him. Beelzebub and Asura stepped away from the muffled sobs of the trembling Damned. He grabbed the next one off the floor with one hand, his talons piercing her sides. The woman with gold hair screamed, trapped in his grasp.

"Don't you think I want to squeeze this betrayer—make him spill the vile lies he's spread about me. And after all I've done, freeing us from the clutches of God and his horrid creation!" Lucifer's voiced boomed across the room. He squeezed the woman until she fell limp and threw her high into the air, nearing the ceiling. Tannin broke the surface with a roar erupting from its opened jaws. The full glorious length of him met the woman in mid-air, snapping his mouth closed while his black eyes rolled back in his head. Waves splashed over the edge when he slipped back into the depths.

Lucifer snatched the last damned off the floor. Her shrill scream only added fuel to his blazing fire. Beelzebub and Asura rocked back and forth in anticipation, but cast a wary eye. His massive body moved in front of them, the ground vibrating with each of his steps.

You should fear me.

He snatched the last Damned writhing on the floor. Ripping off its head, more black blood ejected in the air, like a fountain, squirting over Beelzebub and Asura. Both snarled in delight as blood rained down on them.

"I want to roll the head of my traitor across the ground in front of my faithful Princes so they can see the lifeless eyes of the one who dared to presume he could fool me... rule instead of me?" Lucifer bellowed as he rolled the woman's head toward them, landing at their feet. He threw the body like a rock, skipping across the pool into the gaping mouth of Tannin.

Lucifer's chest heaved. His bloodied hands lay clenched at his sides. He inhaled through his nostrils, reclaiming control. His body lost its scales, returning to its white hard surface. He searched the remaining sets of eyes. All intent on him. He commanded their complete attention.

Lucifer walked past them, up the steps to his throne. For the first time, he saw Delilah next to the throne. Her wide green eyes stared at him, her bosom rising and falling. He patted her hand before he sat on his throne.

"Don't worry, Delilah. I know you'll never betray me," Lucifer proclaimed loud enough for the others to hear. He smirked, gazing back to the Fallen who had yet to move.

"Beelzebub and Asura. Thank you for your gifts today. It seems I needed to blow off a little steam." They both bowed slightly, never breaking eye contact.

"As for the traitor, it's none of your concern. I will personally take care of this deceiver." He released an irritated sigh. "Is there anything else?"

"No, my Lord."

"Then leave me." They bowed low and turned to leave.

"Beelzebub?" Lucifer called out. He paused, turning back to Lucifer.

"Yes, my Lord?"

"Get that gold head out of my sight. Maybe your Hell hounds would like to fight over it?" Lucifer sneered at him.

"They will indeed, my Lord." He grabbed it by its hair. Its

macabre mouth open, skin shredded at the neck. It swung at Beelze-bub's side, while Tannin stalking swim escorted them to the pool's end. The red guards closed the door behind them with a loud click.

"What was that—" Delilah shut her mouth as Lucifer lifted his hand in a sign of silence.

"Not now. I need to think." He waved her away. "Go back to my room and wait for me." Delilah headed to the staircase door behind his throne. Quick footsteps struck the stone floor as she scurried away from him.

Lucifer lounged back against the throne, his long arms laying over the heavy arm rests. He grasped to control the rage seething inside of him. Each day became harder to contain his desire to storm Heaven and wage war against his eternal enemies. The mere idea of it threat-ened to release eons of pent-up revenge and hate. But control these emotions he must. He first had to capture the girl and then root out the traitor. He couldn't move forward with his plan until he destroyed the one plotting against him.

A low rumbling stirred beneath his chair. A deep vibration connected with the core of his being. He stroked the stone claw where his hand rested. The throne rumbled in response.

Go back to sleep, Abaddon. Your time nears.

CHAPTER
FIFTEEN

OLIVIA

Zach and Sergio were throwing knives at the mannequins when Olivia arrived at the Magi's training room. They both had great aim and were hitting the center of the mannequins with regular success.

"Welcome, Olivia," Balthazar's deep voice resounded behind her. She turned, finding Balthazar smiling at her, his black skin creased around his eyes. He ran his hand down the length of his beard. "You look well."

"I'm good as new. These angelic healing powers are amazing. My old knee injury from soccer has healed, too." Olivia did a quick knee bend. "I couldn't have done that before without it hurting, but not anymore. Super cool." She smiled back up at him.

"Your healing powers should have been quicker, but the poison slowed it. You'll carry salve with you, in case it happens again," Balthazar declared.

"Zach and Sergio." He waved them over. They set the knives on the table and jogged to join her.

"Hey." Sergio wiped his damp forehead with the back of his hand.

"Glad you're back," Zach offered. "You gave us quite a scare." Sergio grimaced in agreement, but his attention was on Balthazar.

"Ya," Olivia snorted. "You and me both." She nudged Sergio. "You guys are awesome with the throwing knives. Proud of you both." Her eyes flickered over to Zach. A smile spread on his lips, but an invisible barrier separated them. He had called and come over while she recovered. She sensed his hesitation when he was near. She was thankful he was honoring their *working* relationship, and she tried to convince herself she felt good about it. But if she was honest with herself, she missed her *personal* relationship with Zach. He made her laugh and feel comfortable in her skin. He understood her faults and didn't judge her for them.

You're your own worst enemy...

"Follow me. Caspar and Melchior are waiting for us." Balthazar walked out the door, leaving them to follow. Instead of turning to go back to the church, he headed deeper into the hallway. Olivia followed his broad back down a stone circular staircase heading underneath the church to its levels beneath the bridge. It was wide enough for two people across, but they stayed single file, winding their way to an area Olivia had never seen. Cool air drifted up from their destination, but not stale as she was expecting. Light filtered up from the bottom of the staircase. Balthazar had an aura as if he'd stepped out into the sunshine, but then he disappeared in the light. Olivia's damp palm skimmed the stone wall as she cautiously approached the glowing bottom.

Olivia gaped; her foot paused over the last step. Sergio bumped into her followed by Zach as she absorbed the extraordinary room before her: majestic, stunning, unparalleled to anything she could have ever imagined.

"Wow," murmured Zach.

"You can close your mouths now," Melchior chuckled. Olivia slammed hers shut as she approached the Magi. "Welcome to the Weapons Room."

They'd entered a towering square room surrounded with stain glass windows, casting their color schemes across the gleaming tile floor. Encased inside was a white-walled circular room supported by huge, ornate arches. A shimmering film cascaded down each arched entrance, like a waterfall, distorting what lies behind it. Olivia was awash with a luminous light, but no heat radiated over her.

"They don't have weapons rooms like this in any video games I play." Sergio's voice reflected the same awe coursing through Olivia.

"Me neither." Zach snorted. "I've seen these stained-glass windows from over the bridge, but I never imagined this inside under the church."

Caspar grinned at the trio. "Enter." His hand parted the liquid-like film as if he had swept open an incandescent curtain. "We must not keep our guest waiting... or you." His voice was laced with excitement.

Olivia cautiously walked through the entrance, a current passed over her, igniting her senses and tingles creeping along her skin. A circular fire pit blazed in the middle of the room. Steep steps surrounded the pit, leading to its soaring white flames. Suspended from the high ceiling in front of the walls between the arches, were clear cabinets containing a menagerie of weapons: swords, daggers, whips, hammers, bows, axes and more. Each weapon twinkled with its own vibrant color reflecting into the room. Olivia imagined this was what it looked like when a rainbow speared a diamond.

"Wow." Olivia turned full circle, absorbing the room's phenomenal, yet deadly, display.

Michael, Gabriel, and Raphael, sheathed in their sleek white armor, stood majestically in front of the towering white flames. Each held a long, white satin bag at their side. Olivia's heart thudded as a strange yearning for the bag Michael held engulfed her. She walked toward him, almost without will. Whatever was inside called to her.

Olivia glanced at Zach and Sergio. Their faces held the same intensity toward the bags as she did. She stopped in front of Michael, the bag only an arm's length away. She vibrated with anticipation. A deep need beckoned for whatever the bag held. Melchior stopped behind her. For a moment, it took Olivia back to the Valley of Fire when she'd received the orb from Melchior. She stood up straighter, knowing this would be another defining moment in her journey.

"What do you think of our Weapons Room?" Gabriel asked, his golden-tipped wings glistening against the fire light.

"It's absolutely incredible," beamed Sergio. "Where did the weapons all come from? Why are they here?" Sergio spread his arms out wide.

"These weapons are here for you, for those who came before you, and those who will follow you," said Raphael, the sword hanging at his hip surged with a green wave from silver hilt to its pointed end.

Awash with a sense of calm and clarity, Olivia harnessed this within her. Michael raked his eyes over Olivia, Zach and Sergio. A shadow of sadness crossed his face as he gazed at them.

"After the Fall, a period of mourning set among the Angels. Lucifer had swept away a third of their comrades into the desolate abyss. Lucifer's ominous promises of war and revenge echoed from inside the abyss while he fell to his treacherous destiny. As much as the Heavenly hierarchy wanted to ignore his evil decree, we had to prepare for war. The Angelic Choir of the Powers, keepers of history and the Heavenly warriors, were tasked with making weapons to match what Lucifer created with evil and hate. A river of molten steel flowed through the Power's order. The Angelic warriors worked tirelessly creating weapons of all types for their fellow brethren." Michael paused as if reliving that tangible moment in time.

"But there was another mission given to the Powers known only by a sacred few. They forged a sword for each Guardian to wield in their battle against Lucifer. They poured the steel, combining one feather from an Angel along with a drop of their blood. Once held by the guardian, they become one; infused with the characteristics of the Angel's powers to enhance the Guardian's strength and capabilities."

The Archangels removed the satin cloth, which fluttered to the floor. Olivia eyes widen at the glorious sword Michael held in his hand. The grip and blade gleamed with polished silver as a cobalt blue jewel, embedded in the hilt's pommel, burned with a flame as if it were its soul. The bottom of the ornate hilt glowed with the same blue flame inside small angel wings sweeping out from each side. Seven small blue orbs trailed down from the hilt, on each side of the blade.

"This sword has my feather and my blood. It's named after the Angel who forged it for you. Her name is Sandalphon, Angel of Power." Michael bent over and blew across the blade. Fiery blue script erupted on the polished silver, dancing across the blade as if handwritten by the sharp tip of a delicate feather.

"While the blade forges in her hands, Sandalphon chanted the ancient language of the Angels into molten steel with my name and yours, sealing it together for eternity." The scroll disappeared, leaving no trace of the ancient writing.

"I am Michael, from the Choir of the Archangels, of the Blue Kingdom of Charity, Wielder of Fire, Warrior of God, and Protector of Man. I give you this sword to honor you, Olivia, and thank you for your courage to fight for our freedom... the freedom of mankind, and to abolish the evil bent upon both of our annihilations."

Michael's last words echoed in the room. She felt the weight of all eyes upon her.

"Olivia, step forward and receive your sword."

She stepped with trembling legs and grasped the silver hilt, lifting it off of Michael's outstretched hands. Olivia's heart leapt, overwhelmed by the sensation of finding a treasure, once lost, was finally home. Both her hands looked small holding the sword, but it was lighter than she'd expected. She gasped as the sword crackled with a blue flame, as if it too surged with excitement. The smooth blue jewel, with a triangle engraved on it, burned brighter at the hilt as her grip tightened. An electric charge zipped through her hands, up her arms and then surged through her body, uniting with something deep inside of her, settling like a dormant fire waiting for her to stoke the flames to life. Her eyes snapped to Michael. His eyes glowed with the same blue, gazing at her with pride, love and strength. Speechless as she grappled with the gravity of this gift.

Gabriel presented his sword to Sergio. "Nisroc, Angel of Freedom, forged your sword." The sword gleamed from tip to end with polished gold. Three large translucent golden triangles, with a line through the triangle's tip, crackled at the top and bottom of the hilt and another in the pommel. Each sizzled with an inner current, igniting another to course the length of the blade.

"I am Gabriel, from the choir of Archangels, of the Gold Kingdom of Humility, Welder of Air, Messenger of God, Protector of Man. I give you this sword to honor you, Sergio, and thank you for your courage to fight for our freedom... the freedom of mankind, and to abolish the evil bent upon both of our annihilations."

Sergio took the sword, igniting the current flowing within the gold blade. His face lit up in a smile Olivia hadn't seen that big since before Manny's death.

Raphael raised the sword before Zach. "Machidiel, Angel of Courage forged this sword." Zach's silver blade was wider than Olivia's with a deep groove running the length of the blade. The grip had stripes of green feeding into the triangle jewel at the top of the hilt and larger jewel at the bottom. Spikes of green glowing in the metal surrounded the jewel, forming a swirling cross guard. The jewels glowed with a wavelike motion with an upside-down triangle engraved in it. The wave of energy pulsed through the length of the silver blade.

"I am Raphael, from the Choir of Archangels, of the Green Kingdom of Kindness, Healer for God, Wielder of Water, Protector of Man." Raphael placed the silver sword in Zach's hands. "I give you this sword to honor you, Zach, and thank you for your courage to fight for our freedom... the freedom of mankind, and to abolish the evil bent upon both of our annihilations."

The room became silent as the guardians gazed upon the weapons given to them by the Archangels, each lost in their thoughts and of what their futures held.

Responsibility for the Mar of Sin.

Protector of Orion's secrets.

Death to the Fallen.

"I don't know what to say. It's spectacular." Olivia beamed as her chest heaved, needing more air as the reality of the guardianship hit home.

"Thank you, Michael. I'll do everything in my power to stop Lucifer and the Fallen."

"This is all we ask of you, in this burden and blessing." Olivia gasped at similar phrasing of Michael's words, but before she could say more, he turned away and walked up the fire pit's steps. Gabriel and Raphael joined him at the top. The white flames behind them illuminated their wings and armor, enhancing how dazzling, yet powerful Archangels are.

"Peace be with you." Gabriel called out.

The Magi bowed, splaying their hands across their hearts. The Archangels turned and walked into the fire, disappearing inside the tall hissing flame.

"Whoa," gushed Sergio.

"Is the fire pit a portal?" asked Zach.

"It is for any Angel who wishes to appear here. But it's not meant for us or for you." Balthazar warned. Olivia didn't ask why. She had no desire to incinerate in a white flame.

Sergio and Zach joined her, brandishing their swords. Olivia couldn't tear her eyes from the sword still firmly in her grip.

"Machidiel. I love the name and what it stands for." Excitement shone on Zach's face as he held the sword in front of him, watching the green light play across it.

"I can't believe they made this for me... for us!" Sergio touched the sword's current, but it didn't spark, continuing to flow. "Nisroc." Sergio stood back and gave the sword a few swift strikes in the air. A hard glint of satisfaction burned in his eyes. "I can't wait to use it."

Caspar clamped a hand on Sergio's shoulder. "You have much to learn before you will go on your first hunt." Caspar's words were spoken to Sergio, but she knew he meant it for all of them.

"When can we train with them?" Zach's exuberance overflowed as he ran his finger over the blade.

"Now. We'll begin with basic skills," Melchior instructed. "But first, you will need this. Follow me." They followed him to the back of the room where three cabinets hung with folded black clothes.

"Each of have your own armor you must wear when you hunt. The Powers created this for your protection. They designed it to absorb the power behind a strike and to stop the intrusion of a weapon, similar to a bullet-proof vest. You may still feel some pain and the mesh covering your face is the most vulnerable. Connect to it with your talisman as you do when you portal and say 'armor on.'"

Olivia thought of the stone in her pocket. "Armor on." The talisman heated, quickening her pulse. The scaly black garment hovered off the shelf and unwrapped before her. She froze when it rushed to her and wrapped the material around her body, forming to her as if she'd dipped herself into a liquid pool of metal. Every part of her was covered from the hood around her head to her feet. A fine mesh covered her face, but her vision wasn't encumbered, nor was her breathing. Her heart thumped a frantic beat as it waited to succumb to the crush of the armor, but that sensation didn't arise.

"The armor is now yours and knows your call. It has now molded to your body and will adjust as you grow and become stronger. You don't need to be here to call for it, because it works through the talisman's portal. When you're finished with your armor, say 'armor off' and it will disrobe and come back here, waiting for your call." When Olivia remained in her stunned silence, Melchior crossed his arms, lifting an eyebrow. "Well?"

"This is kick-ass," she blurted.

Melchior's chuckle sparked one of her own, releasing the tension from the ceremony's intensity. "No truer words spoken."

"Yea, but honestly, it's overwhelming having a sword made just for me and black armor swarm my body." Olivia glanced at her armor covered hand grasping her sword.

Melchior laid a heavy hand on her shoulder. "That is a magnificent sword worthy of its mighty owner. You were made for this. Are you ready?"

Olivia swallowed past the lump in her throat. "Yes, I'm ready."

Melchior's eyes sparkled before he turned and left her to follow him. She paused, struck by how her future was now forged forever in the reality of armor, metal, and fellowship.

CHAPTER
SIXTEEN

SERGIO

Clang.
Grunt.

Sergio's arms vibrated from the clash of steel against steel. His shoulders ached as he strained against Balthazar's blade. He pushed and dropped into his ready stance. His armor stretched as he brought his sword's hilt even with his stomach. Sweat trickled down his back as his thick, hair lay damp across his forehead. Sergio blocked out the bright room, concentrating on Balthazar brandishing his sword, glowing gold swirls, from the grip to the blade's tip.

Balthazar's eyes narrowed as he spun to his left, bringing his sword up high. Sergio moved to his right, bracing himself for contact. He moved his sword to block the strike. Balthazar's upper lip peeled back, revealing his white teeth, gleaming against his black beard. His sword came down, stopping inches from Sergio's side, a devastating blow had he followed through, Sergio's block a split-second too late.

"Good." Balthazar's deep voice boomed. He put his feet together, bringing his pommel even with his lower stomach. Sergio mimicked the move; his golden triangle crackled, poised in front of his heart. Holding eye contact, they bowed to each other.

"How is that good?" Sergio complained, sheathing his sword. "I'm a dead man." He grabbed the grip, yanking it up halfway from the sheath, then shoved it back inside. His nostrils flared as he exhaled a deep breath. He wanted so badly to catch Balthazar off guard.

Balthazar grinned, placing his large hand on Sergio's shoulder. "You did well because you anticipated where I'd strike. You moved, but your body and sword didn't share the same timing. This is why we practice." He squeezed Sergio's shoulder. "It has only been a few weeks. Being frustrated with yourself will not make your learning any easier. Come."

Sergio followed him to the suspended shelves that housed the Guardians armor. Balthazar didn't say much, but his body language spoke volumes. Sergio envied his powerful body, graceful stride and the quiet confidence he exuded. He wanted to be more like him...

Except meaner and deadlier....

"Armor off." The armor unwrapped itself from Sergio's body and lay folded on the shelf. The fresh air felt good against his damp clothes, but it didn't ease his frustrations. He laid his sword across the shelf and took a drink from his water bottle. He closed his eyes, rejoicing as the icy water washed away the dryness in his mouth.

Sergio sensed the ever-present weight of Balthazar's eyes upon him, searching for what, he didn't know. His pulse kicked up, constantly working to hide his thoughts about the ax and his deep desires to use it. He imagined it as a force field surrounding both his squirreled away backpack and the imaginary black box, hiding the emotions he kept to himself. Sergio set the bottle down and faced his mentor.

"Holding bitterness in your heart is an acid eating away at the gifts we have given you." Balthazar chided quietly, pinning Sergio with his intense stare.

Crash goes the force field.

"My brother is dead because a Fallen killed him. It's hard not to be bitter." Sergio crossed his arms, thrusting out his jaw. A white-hot inner heat rose, having nothing to do with the sword lesson. "They didn't have to kill him. We were no match for them. But they like killing! So the red Fallen killed Manny just because he could... and then—he laughed!" Sergio yelled as the fire pit's white flames flared toward the vaulted ceiling. He stabbed his finger at his sword. "They will pay!"

Sergio's chest heaved; his last words echoed around the room. Balthazar cocked his head at him.

"Does it feel good to get that off your chest... uncork the bottle and say it out loud?"

"Yes," Sergio sneered. "And I mean it."

Balthazar took a step, backing him up against the shelf. His eyes bore into him combining with the sharp anger rolling off of Bal, but disappointment settled on his face.

"Then you will not live long enough to fulfill your destiny. Set the burden of your guilty feelings free, or either you, or someone you care for, will pay the heavy price."

It was as if Bal had pushed him off a cliff. He stared at back in disbelief.

You don't know what you're talking about!

"I'll let no one I love get hurt again." Sergio struck his fist into his hand.

"Then lay your brother's death to rest and let's get to work."

Balthazar walked away, leaving Sergio staring at his broad back.

The warm sun beat on Sergio's already flushed face. He couldn't believe Balthazar expected him to forget about Manny. It was so unfair. Manny was his brother, and he could never set Manny free. Sergio fed off his memory, keeping his hatred at a low simmer, as motivation to learn all he needed to kill demons. Sergio progressed well developing his skills. Balthazar even acknowledged as much, but he would not take his advice on letting Manny go. He knew what he needed to do to accomplish his goals.

Sergio's feet trampled the grass as he hurried to catch up to Balthazar. The breeze cooled his damp neck, releasing some of his tension. He stopped next to his mentor, who gazed out into the open field leading to rolling lush mountains. The faraway cry of birds and the roaring river next to the church added a sense of enchantment to this mystical land of the Magi. Sergio loved the freedom and power he had when he came here. It aroused his very being.

"We are moving to the next level of your telekinetic powers." Balthazar shifted to acknowledge Sergio's arrival. "Every Angel has an element they can command: air, water, fire or earth. Gabriel and I became one with air, as will you."

Sergio's jaw dropped. "Well, that's cool. But how do I do that? Just ask the air to move and it will?" he snorted.

"Something like that," he replied more seriously than Sergio would've expected. Balthazar closed his eyes, inhaled a deep breath and released it turning to Sergio. "It is difficult, and will take great concentration on your part."

Balthazar raised his hands in front of him, palms out. The hair on Sergio's arms lifted as the air swirled around their feet. A turbulent golden cloud materialized in front of each of Balthazar's palms. Multitudes of long, golden opaque needles the size of pencils appeared and extended from the cloud, vibrating in mid-air. When he shoved his hands out in front of him, the needles rocketed into the air. They darted across the field and struck the grass, like a strafing run from a war plane. Micro explosions sounded as clumps of grass and mud flew into the air, leaving holes the size of bowling balls.

"Whoa..."

Balthazar slapped his hands together, then flung his arms out to each side. The surrounding air collapsed before exploding out into a shock wave. The rushing wind flattened the grass across the field, steamrolling it to its roots. Sergio imagined the Fallen shredded by the air needles and thrown aside as if rag dolls. The rushing river soon replaced the roaring sound of wind.

Balthazar turned to face him. "The spikes of air can strike the heart of the demons, killing them. The air wave knocks them, or anything else coming towards you, back."

Sergio's heart hammered with excitement as he considered all the possibilities of using the air around him as a weapon. "That's freaking amazing! I wanna learn the air spike. I'd kill so many—"

"That skill may not be yours. You have limited use of the air because you're human. Only one ability will form. You can use it in tandem with your telekinetic ability to put people or objects into an inanimate state."

Sergio's shoulders slumped, deflated like his air weapon dreams. "Well, that sucks."

Balthazar crossed his arms. "It's better to excel at one special gift then be mediocre at a few."

A breeze ruffled Sergio's hair as if it chastising him for his greedy thoughts, but the burst of air stilled. Sergio glanced at his hands, wondering how he could ever command something so uncontrollable.

One is better than none...

"So how do I know my gift?"

Balthazar scanned the sky and the surrounding field. "The element will show you." He stepped next to Sergio. "The potential to create a weapon or manipulate the air is endless. To get started, first concentrate on your mark."

Sergio searched for his connection with the mark in his mind. "Let it feel alive, like you've awakened the orb beneath your skin." Balthazar's calm voice floated over him as he imagined the orb glowing shooting out electric impulses into the mark. The seven dots tingled, hot against his skin.

"Open your hands and spread them out in front of you. Think of the air moving between them, circling around your fingers." A sensation emerged as if butterfly wings fluttering against his palms. His eyes widened as a gold cloud developed with a brighter gold sphere glowing inside of it. The air swirled around him, flattening his shirt against him. He sucked in eager breathes, watching the sphere grow.

"Now set it free!" Balthazar commanded.

Sergio lifted his arms, launching the sphere like an arching basketball. Landing with a thud, the sphere expanded before exploding in a mound of grass and mud.

"Yes!" Sergio shouted, giving himself a fist pump doing a little dance. "That was awesome! Did you see that explosion? What's that called?" Sergio's enthusiasm faded when Balthazar's stone face stared at the small hole.

"You created an air bomb, a compressed ball of air force that explodes on impact." Balthazar's intensity stopped Sergio cold. "At full ability, it's a powerful weapon not to be used lightly"

Sergio glanced at his puny hole, nudging the grass with top of his sneakers. "I guess my sphere was a dud." He sighed.

Balthazar shook his head. "You connected with your element, and the air showed you what you can manipulate. That is what you asked of it. But this ability will take much discipline and oneness with self to reach its full potential."

"I can do that. It's only practice." Sergio threw his arms in the air. "I'm here every day working harder than anyone else. I'm getting stronger and better with the weapons, so I will master this, too," he said, pointing to the churned-up hole.

"There's a part of you that isn't ready for this element. This isn't about strength or practice. To master the air, it has to flow through the fiber of your being. Your mind must stay clear and focused. Your heart must be strong and pure. But your focus is on the past... on pain, and you're clutching it too close. For what purpose? It's easier to stay mad than forgive. Only you carry the emotional baggage you choose to lug around, so don't be surprised when the burden gets too heavy and you fall."

Once again, Sergio was left watching Balthazar's departure. He kicked a clump of grass, and another until he faced the hole. It wasn't very impressive next to what Balthazar could do, but Sergio didn't care. He'd harness the air for what he needed in battle. Besides, his sword was what he wanted to use in battle.

You need this ability—

Not if I have to give up Manny—

He squished a clump of grass into the hole, covering up his first effort like he was trying to cover up his thirst for revenge.

CHAPTER
SEVENTEEN

ZACH

The turbulent river cut its way through the menagerie of colored granite, creating a rugged canyon with lush greenery expanding at the rim. The church towered above Zach and Caspar, the stone bridge casting its shadow across them. Zach thrived in the wilderness. The rough edges and soft beauty matched the dichotomy of his own inner emotional landscape, striving to flourish in its vast diversity.

"Feel your mark; search for the orb's power vibrating beneath it." Caspar's soothing lilt purred within him, encouraging him to become one with the orb.

Zach's mark tingled to life, sending a wave of energy over his arms and into his open hands. A jolt of excitement rocked through him as a cyclone of green water swirled between his palms. As the water cyclone grew, the inside of Zach's hands glowed a darker shade of green.

"Call upon the water from the river. Ask it to join you, to become one with your cyclone." Caspar moved behind Zach. "Don't be afraid to ride its rolling force."

A trickle of sweat rolled down his back. His vision tunneled on the river, its edges beating against the grassy banks. He beckoned the water to merge with his cyclone and unveil its powerful beauty to him. Zach's eyes widened as a small water funnel emerged from the water's edge. It spun like a green snake towards his hands, coming closer until it collided with his cyclone like a ball breaking a window. It morphed into a twister inside his hands.

"Set it free!" shouted Caspar.

Energy released from his arms through his hands as he threw it back at the churning river. Zach gasped as the cyclone split into small green spinning half-moon shapes. It sped towards the riverbank until it slammed into the rock and grass, shredding it into an earthy whirl, raining into the water. Caspar's excited *whoop* matched Zach's while his chest shuttered with exerted energy.

"Did I really do that?" Zach spun, looking at his hands.

Caspar clasped Zach's shoulder, shaking him with enthusiasm. "Yes, you did. And a splendid job at that." Caspar's youthful grin stretched across his tanned face. "Well done, child of water."

Zach's head jerked up toward the bridge as encouraging shouts showered down upon him. Sergio and Olivia gave each other a high five as Balthazar and Melchior beamed at him. Zach waved his hand, his face flushed with the excitement of harnessing his angelic abilities, more than he ever thought possible. His cheering gallery moved out of sight, but the moment was forever burned in his memory.

"The water has shown you the ability to cut down what lays in your path. With practice, you will create slices as big as boomerangs cutting off a demon's head. Your mastery will lead to slicing buildings or larger objects, too." Caspar moved beside him, crossing his arms as they gazed at the small field of carnage laying on the bank.

"What if there's no water? Can I still generate a cyclone?" Zack asked.

"Yes. Your body's sweat or spit can initiate the combining of droplets of water in the air."

Zach gazed at the river, following the churning waters downstream as it broke around large rocks in its path. His body froze as the memory of the lifeless form of a blond-haired boy being pulled away from him in the rapids. His feelings of triumph were shattered. Grief and helplessness flooded him as Cody's body slipped from sight, pulled under by the powerful forces of nature.

Zach slammed his eyes shut, willing the image away to stop his tears from forming. Nausea rolled over him, threatening to chop him at the knees. Caspar's firm hand gripped his arms, gently shaking him.

"What is it?" Caspar implored. "Tell me."

Zach opened his eyes, knowing he couldn't hide the pain and misery deep within him. "I just had a flashback of Cody floating away from me," he said, choking on his own words.

"I see." Compassion filled Caspar's eyes as warmth traveled up Zach's arms. "Sit with me."

Zach plopped down, his legs a wobbling mess. His vision shifted to the safe green grass in front of him, not wanting the water to pull up any more painful memories.

"Your mother told me of this accident. It was a tragedy, but not your fault."

Zach's muscled tensed, his teeth grinding together.

She doesn't know everything... no one does.

"The canoe capsized, yes? And Cody hit his head on a rock in the rapids?" Caspar paused when Zach didn't answer him. "Is there more?"

Zach's throat worked up and down while guilt soaked him like a sudden thunderstorm. He tried to gather enough spit to talk.

"No matter how many times I play it out, I'm responsible for his death. I should have never taken him out on the river." He turned to Casper, and his body heaved with his burden. "And now, I have the ability to control water." Zach scoffed, shaking his head. "It's ironically cruel."

"Do your friends know about Cody?"

"No, but I need to tell them. It's messed me up with how I treat Olivia. I have this compulsion to protect her, and it's pissed her off. She pushed away from me, when we had become so close. I deserved it, acting like an over-bearing jerk. She's incredible, like no one I've ever met. There was this instant connection to her before all this craziness started." Zach hung his head between his knees.

"I think you need to tell them. Be honest with them, so they'll understand your actions better. Olivia and Sergio each have shared their burdens with you. It's time you do the same. You're not meant to carry this heavy load on our own." Caspar stood up, wiping off his black pants. "I'm going to the training room. Stay here. Let the fresh air clear your head before we spar."

Caspar slipped away before Zach responded. He stretched out on the grass. Puffy clouds floated across the crystal-clear blue skies. He thought about Caspar's words, willing them to loosen his body's tension. Caspar was right, but it scared him what Olivia and Sergio might think of him if he told them a friend died on his watch. Would they trust him again or look at him the same way? His Dad certainly struggled with it, so why should they be any different? He'd worked hard to pick up his mangled confidence and slap himself back together. Was he ready to open himself up and be vulnerable again?

The thought of it made him feel sick. Zach slammed his fist into the soft ground. He couldn't do it; not yet. Flinging his arm over his eyes, it disgusted him, but he wasn't ready. He needed to wait a little longer. Let them see how strong he was, let them grow tighter as a unit and understand his vital place in the guardianship.

He exhaled, sending his fears out into the air. The cool breeze ruffled his hair as the sun's course shifted the bridge's shadows. His eyes grew heavy as the surrounding nature lulled his senses.

Just one more minute and I'll go...

Zach's lungs gasped for more air as he raced in darkness across the hard desert ground. Olivia's screams filled his head when the burning gold web opened. Sergio kicked up dust, running in front of him. A high screech pierced his ears. Sharp feathers assaulted him as ash filled his lungs, besieging him in the chaotic blackness. His arms flew to his face, while he struggled to run against the battering wings. Zach was so close. He couldn't let them take Olivia... he couldn't lose her, too.

A sizzle broke through the thumping of flapping wings. Panic struck his core. His hands scrambled to find the dagger at his hip. He grabbed the grip, pulled it out, striking out to hit anything in his way. Angry howls were his reward. The desert terrain peeked through the black wings. Zach charged towards the opening, swinging at will. He broke free, sheathing his dagger while he ran at the web. He tried to connect with his mark, willing the water cyclone between his hands, but a Fallen shoved him in the back and sent him sprawling to the dusty ground. Black wings flew to the webbing, gliding inside its inky abyss.

Zach rose, desperate to reach her, but he was too late. Olivia lay limp over a Fallen's shoulder as it stepped through the webbing. The cyclone whirled in his hands. He set it free, launching it at the closing portal. But it disappeared, the blades circling through the desert air.

No, No, No!

Sergio screamed into the night sky as his air bomb disintegrated where the portal once stood.

Zach jack-knifed off the grass. Blinking his eyes, the bright sun startled him. He hung his head in relief, realizing he'd been dreaming. He slowed his breathing while he grasped to remember the fading vision.

What he'd witnessed before the portal closed hit him like a sucker punch.

Zar, with eyeless black pits, was grinning at him with Olivia draped over his shoulder.

Not again... not him...

CHAPTER
EIGHTEEN

CAMILLA

I t was a warm spring day in the desert valley, so Camilla took advantage of it. She basked in the morning's warmth on a porch lounge chair. The palm trees rustled in the breeze as the sun reflected off the pool. She absorbed the peaceful surroundings, needing the serenity for what lay ahead for her today.

Gabriel.

She closed her eyes and lifted her face, willing the sun's warm rays to melt the cold apprehension in her stomach. After weeks of worry and denial about her granddaughter Lucia and the ominous mark on her chest, Camilla realized she was more concerned about Gabriel's thoughts of her then the safety of Lucia.

She covered her mouth as shame sliced through her. Nothing was more important than Lucia. She'd made a promise to herself on that fateful day ten years ago...

Two shiny new bikes, helmets hanging from the handlebars, rested on kickstands in the garage. Spring was in the air, so Camilla had bought the twins the gifts in hopes her grand babies would join her on rides.

"Sergio, Lucia... Vamos, por favor!" Camilla called from the kitchen.

Two brown-headed skinny kids ran out from the hallway, yelling at each other.

"I told you to stay out of my room! But no! You go in there and smash my Lego airplane!" Sergio sneered at his sister.

"I'm sorry!" Tears streamed from Lucia's big puppy-dog brown eyes. "I thought it would fly..."

"You're so stupid! Lego's don't—"

"Sergio! Don't call your sister stupid." Camilla spoke calmly, trying to diffuse their fighting. "We don't use that word in this house."

"Abuela! She broke my new Lego—"

"I heard, but it's no excuse for calling her names."

Sergio crossed his gangly arms. "Sorry," he mumbled.

Camilla sighed, knowing he could do better. She hoped the bikes would cease their bickering.

"I have a surprise for both of you. Follow me." She stepped into the tidy garage. Camilla waved her hand toward the bikes. Lucia squealed with delight, but Sergio's foul mood clung to him as he approached his blue bike. He ran his hands over the black vinyl seat, then put both hands on the handles. His eyes darted to Camilla as he threw his leg over and sat on the seat. A faint smile creased his face.

"Abuela! Abuela! Muchas gracias!" Lucia jumped up and down in front of her purple bike. "Can we go for a ride now! Por Favor!" Lucia's hands flew into a praying position, her tear-streaked face pleading.

"Sergio?" Abuela arched an eyebrow.

He stepped off the bike, shoving his hands in his pocket. "Muchas gracias, Abuela, but I don't feel like it right now." His face was grim, his back to his sister. "Maybe later."

"All right." He walked by, giving her a brief hug. The door closed behind him, but Lucia didn't seem fazed by her brother anymore. She was on her bike, helmet on, with a toothy smile in place.

"Let's go!" Lucia pleaded. She flipped up her kickstand and

headed for the driveway. Camilla got on her peddle pusher and squeezed the clown horn, inciting a giggle from Lucia.

"Abuela! That's silly!" Camilla squeezed it again, rewarded with an eye roll. She grinned as her heart swelled looking over at her grand-daughter. She peddled out to Lucia.

"Rules: no crossing the street without me, stay close, and look both ways."

"Si, Si, Abuela. I'm not a baby. Can we go now?"

Camilla chuckled, and they set off down the quiet street. They rode around the block and found the path through the small park in the middle of their neighborhood. Lucia's constant chatter floated back to Camilla, but she only caught a few words. She didn't worry about it, enjoying this moment with Lucia. She wished Sergio had come along but understood his desire to fix his Legos. Glancing down, she noticed her untied shoelace. She stopped and stepped off.

"Lucia! Alto!" But the purple bike kept moving towards the street, Lucia's chatting fading with her.

The world slowed as Camilla saw what Lucia couldn't. A white sedan squealed around the corner at the same time Lucia entered the street.

"Lucia!" Camilla screamed, but it was lost in the screech of slam-ming brakes. Camilla scrambled to her feet; her heart lodged in her throat as a cruel nightmare played out before her eyes.

The driver hadn't seen Lucia in time. The hood hit Lucia, sending her airborne. She hit the pavement and lay limp like a rag doll.

"No!" Camilla's gut-wrenching cry pierced the air. She couldn't catch her breath as her wobbly legs took too long to get to her grand-daughter. A woman jumped out of the car, hands to her face, frozen at her car door.

Camilla dropped next to Lucia. Blood ran from her lip, eyes shut on her pale face.

"I didn't see her... came from nowhere... Oh my God!" the woman sobbed.

Camilla's head snapped back. She wanted to rake her nails down the hysterical woman's face. "Call 9 1 1!" Camilla yelled.

The woman backed up, nodding. A man jogged towards her as she bent over to cradle Lucia. She needed to hold her as Lucia's face became blurry through her tears.

I'm so sorry, Lucia. It's all my fault.

A sob rocked her as she wrapped her hands under Lucia's shoulders.

"Stop! Don't move her." The man laid his hand on Camilla's shoulder. Her eyes lifted to the stranger and followed his to Lucia's twisted legs.

Camilla heard the faint sound of a wailing siren as her world crashed in around her.

The porch door slid open, interrupting her tortured memory. She hastily wiped away her errant tear.

"Mama. Lucia and I are back from the gym. I need to run a few errands. Okay?" Javier peered at her with his hand on his hip.

"*Si.*" She waved as he disappeared back into the house.

Unfolding herself from the patio chair, she inhaled a cleansing breath, lifting her chin, determined to do right by Lucia. She slid the door closed behind her; thankful the house was quiet. No one can know what she was doing. Not yet. She headed for the hallway, praying this was the redemption she needed for herself.

Camilla opened her bedroom door. The room was bright, filled with family photos and colorful knickknacks from her world travels. Various types and sizes of crosses adorned the wall above her headboard. Lucia sat in her bright pink wheelchair in the middle of a colorful Bohemian styled rug. She greeted Camilla with a tentative smile.

"Is today the day?" Hope filled Lucia's gaze. Camilla nodded her head, trying to conceal her apprehension in meeting with Gabriel. Lucia pumped her fist, heedless of her abuela's apprehension.

Camilla's eyes slid across Lucia's workout t-shirt: *I'M SO GLAM I SWEAT GLITTER.* She chuckled, admiring her grand-daughter's spunk. She sat on the white bedspread next to the wheelchair.

"Remember what we talked about? You can't share this with anyone... at least until Gabriel gives us guidance." Camilla reached across and grabbed her hand. "He'll know what to do."

"I promise. It feels weird not telling Mom and Dad, but hiding the mark hasn't been too bad." Lucia shrugged. "I'll do whatever you two decide."

"*Bueno*, Lucia." Camilla rose and went over to her rustic wooden dresser. Her hand trembled as it reached for the smooth ceramic knob and pulled the drawer open. She pushed aside old shirts, searching until her fingers found the porcelain box.

No turning back...

Camilla pulled the box out, holding it like a delicate egg. The bed barely indented as her petite body sat back down. Its hinges creaked when she lifted the rectangular white lid with gold trim. Camilla's chest ached with a longing she'd put behind her long ago. She took out a small luminous gold-tipped white feather. Lucia's eyes grew wider, her mouth opened with a gasp.

"Abuela... it's beautiful."

The edges fluttered as she laid it inside Lucia's cupped hands. "Gabriel pulled this feather from his wing and gave it to me the last time we met... along with this." Camilla also plucked out a translucent gold triangle. It fit perfectly inside her palm. She marveled at how the middle still glowed after all this time. There had been many nights where the pull of the medallion was hard to resist, but she denied herself, knowing it would only rip open old wounds.

But she had no choice now.

"This jewel was in the hilt of my sword named Cassiel, after the Angel who forged it for me. It connected me with Gabriel's strengths. I can use it to summon him." Camilla whispered, lost in those memories.

Please still work.

"Shall we try together?" Lucia's eager nod sent her ponytail bobbing behind her. Camilla put the feather back in the box and set it down. Her pulse raced in anticipation as she put Lucia's hand over the jewel nestled in her palm.

"Gabriel," Camilla's voice cracked. "Please come to me. I need your help." Camilla implored into the room, but it remained silent. Her heart did a slow roll as her fear came to life.

He doesn't forgive me.

Camilla swallowed past the lump in her throat. "Please—Gabriel, Lucia needs—"

The air filled with a static electricity. A dark-haired man wearing white armor emerged from a gold flash. Gabriel's gold tipped wings closed behind him, his feet planted wide. His gold tiger-like eyes always drew Camilla, now laser beams on her, filled with caution, laced with concern. His face softened when he saw Lucia. He stepped toward her, placing his long-fingered hand under her chin. Lucia eyes, the size of saucers, gazed back at him.

"Lucia. It's an honor to meet you, my brave girl." He smiled down at her, radiating soothing warmth throughout the room.

Lucia's jaw dropped. "No... no, the honor is all mine," she stammered.

His body tensed as he faced Camilla. She'd reveled when he'd stared at her the same way, but his sharp eyes were not of those from times long ago. He scanned the room, brow furrowed as he shifted his feet.

"Camilla." Her heart galloped, hearing her name spoken by him. "Why do you call me? You and the child aren't in danger." He cocked his head and narrowed his eyes. "Is this a trick to get me here, using your granddaughter—"

"She bares the mark of Orion." Camilla grabbed Lucia's hand. "I found it a month ago when she was attacked by a demon in her room."

Gabriel's head swiveled to Lucia. "Show me, child," he commanded.

Lucia pulled down the neck of her t-shirt, exposing the seven dots. Gabriel bent closer, his finger grazing over the raised mark.

"How can this be?" Gabriel marveled. "There is only one in each line." He stood, touching Lucia's cheek with his fleeting hand. "Who else knows?"

"Manuel. He was there when a sloth demon attacked." Camilla stopped trying to control her quivering voice. "He killed it with my old switchblade, made from steel by the Powers, that I gave him as a present. He saved us both." Lucia squeezed Camilla's hand. "I asked him not to say anything until after I had... uhm... talked to you. But he was killed not long after."

Gabriel laid his hand upon Camilla's shoulder. A much-needed warmth surged through her as Gabriel's face filled with compassion, dropping his guarded mask. She swallowed the small sob threatening to escape.

"I didn't make it in time to save him. I'm sorry..." Gabriel hesitated, as if he wanted to say more, but instead stepped back. "Lucia's mark is a mystery to me, and that is God's way. I'll seek answers and return with what I find. In the meantime, keep a careful watch over her." He paused, looking between them. "Do you have your weapons, Camilla?"

"Yes. One is under my pillow. The rest are hidden here in my bedroom."

"Choose one for her." Gabriel's stern words left no room for argument. "Show her how to use it."

Lucia's grip tightened, but Camilla didn't flinch. She welcomed the pain and the excited vibration zinging down her back. Memories of a young female warrior surfaced, feeding her confidence.

"Peace be with you."

"And also, with you," they replied in unison, but Gabriel disappeared in a flash of gold.

CHAPTER
NINETEEN

ZAR

Primal screams and tormented moans echoed in Zar's head, crowding out any other sound around him. His skin crawled with every step he took closer to the ominous mountain. The hiss of flowing lava, crackling with life, was more inviting for him to enter than the gaping mountain's entrance. The last time he was inside one of Hell's mountains, the mutant had whipped him to near death. But he kept taking the next step, fighting off his torturous memories. Asura waited. Her evil presence... her malice, a life force pulsating within the mountain's core. If she got a whiff of his fear, then jumping into the lava would be a more desirable demise.

Delilah hesitated, her talons digging into his arm. An instant flush of apprehension pulsed from her before she could hide it behind her diabolical mask.

"Aw, you sense her, too. She's magnificent, isn't she?" Zar couldn't help poking at Delilah. Goading her was certainly more fun than obsessing about what he'd find inside the mountain. "I don't know if you've heard the whisperings, but Lucifer and Asura were once an item... quite an item, as I recall. He cast her aside, but his appetites are ever changing."

Delilah snarled in his ear. "Now is not a wise time to taunt me. I could lead you to the cliff and push you off, and you'd never know until your skin sizzled in the lava. Besides, it doesn't matter what they were in the past," Delilah boasted with an elongated hiss. "I'm with him now, not her." Her pace increased, but it wasn't the reason Zar's heart raced.

The walls...

"My, so testy today. Someone not get their morning kiss?" Zar, fueled by his panicked state, landed another jab. Her hold on Lucifer was slipping if his senses were correct. Her attempts to push the plan forward stunk of desperation, not confidence. He also detected a fresh scent on Delilah. Should he be concerned, or did Lucifer bring it to her?

"That's none of your concern," her nails dug deeper. "You stay focused on Asura and Sonneillon, and I'll take care of Lucifer."

Bullseye.

"You need to retract your talons. My arm is not her face." Delilah's head swiveled towards him, and her jealousy was palatable. "Asura will use your weakness to her advantage, so you'd better shove it away or pay the consequences. She'll cut you in two and leave before your body hits the ground. Regardless, I'm here to learn to fly a Degasus and you were kind enough to help me. That's the story. You're along for the ride, nothing more."

Zar didn't know what had changed or how she did it, but Delilah was sashaying with red-hot confidence by the time they approached the cavernous entrance. Asura's wings flew open, halting their progress.

"Why did you bring... her? This lesson—" Asura sneered "—is only for you."

Ohhh... I feel a hellcat fight in the air.

Zar resisted the temptation to rub his hands together in delight. Instead, he inclined his head toward Asura. "I haven't acquainted myself much with the outdoors since my... punishment. She offered her assistance... so—ah," he paused, extending his hand between them. "My manners have escaped me. Asura... Delilah, our newest Fallen."

Zar was certain Delilah's smug smile was perfectly affixed.

Asura sounded like she was choking. "I saw you the other day, cowering behind Lucifer's throne. So disappointing to find the nasty rumor was true. Must have been quite a spectacle for you to see Lucifer in his full glory... and fury. It doesn't take much motivation for him to make someone a treat for Tannin. Anyway, welcome to Hell." Her eyes roamed a scathing trail up and down Delilah's body. "I'm sure you've found everything to your liking. How is he? Does he still like to have his—"

"Well, now that we've finished introductions, how about we go inside and get started?" Zar's nudge forward opposed the voice screaming to run in his head.

Asura turned and strutted into the cave, her halo of golden braids gobbled up by the darkness. Delilah's anger spurred her into the entrance, pulling him with her. She wasn't mindful any more of his balance or her surroundings, only the seething hatred for her new nemesis. But he grasped what was lighting the tunnel walls and what lay inside.

Delilah gasped, her surroundings cutting through her angry haze. She stopped; her musky scent now mingled with fear.

"The walls are alive. What is this place?" she muttered. "It moves in waves with the colors of the Realms." This tunnel differed from Leviathan's mountain. No souls wailed, instead faint animal sounds, not in pain, only in grunting movement.

"This is where the beasts of Hell are housed. They're released by the Fallen as needed for their purposes." A shiver coursed from Delilah to Zar.

"Are you coming or not?" Asura's yell echoed off the churning walls from deep within the cavern.

"Right behind you!" Delilah replied with a vicious sneer on her face. She practically dragged him through the tunnel, but he paid no attention as he mapped the undulating gelatinous walls.

Zar sensed the opening into the massive pit, similar to the other mountain. No tangy odor of fear or hate, nor the thunderous voices with their malevolent cries of pain and torture. Instead, whooshing wings and horse's neighing greeted them at the tunnel's end. A flash of heat washed over him as one flew past.

"They're spectacular!" professed Delilah.

"Indeed." Zar remembered the Pegasus, one of many types of majestic creatures of Heaven. During their exodus, the escaping Fallen drove or rode these and other beasts into the abyss.

"These are my pride and joy." Asura raised her arms. "Degasus—wings, manes, and tails of flames carrying the flagship colors for their Realm. Fearless in flight, we'll ride them when we go to war."

Zar envisioned it and yearned for their power beneath him. Asura grabbed him around the waist and pulled him forward, yanking him from his thoughts. The rocky ground fell away, replaced by air rushing over him in his free-fall to the pit below. He unfolded his wings; the dormant feathers charged with exhilarating pulses. He relished the soaring moment until he sensed the pit's stone floor closing in under him. He landed hard on his feet, stumbling, but was determined not to fall in front of the watchful occupants.

Delilah settled beside him and reached for his arm, but he pushed it away. He walked a few feet away, absorbing the sounds raining down of the Degasus in flight. An ache for the freedom burned, wanting this fearless beast as his eyes and shield for him in battle.

"Speak now, while only the Degasus can listen," Asura's impatience were laced in her words.

Let the games begin...

"You've known me from the beginning. You, a mighty Seraphim, one of the highest and most powerful Angels of all. Me—" Zar splayed his hand across his chest "—but a humble Dominion, stuck in the middle, tasked to guide the lower Choirs of Angels and humanity with the guidance of higher Choirs. I always turned to you for help because our thoughts were similar in the way we each viewed our world." He walked back toward them, wings retracted, his sensory map making his stride more confident. "Together, we heard Lucifer's call and followed him in rebellion. We revel in our place here, free to chase our own desires, and drive God's abomination to their sins. Every soul I damn is a victory for me... and for Lucifer. You understand me well, Asura, therefore I dared to call upon you and entrust you with our concerns." He stopped, his back to Delilah, concentrating only on Asura.

Zar sensed a subtle shift in her attitude, an understanding of his words, accepting the bridge it built between them.

"Go on," Asura's confident voice encouraged him. She retracted her wings, a sign of her relaxing her guard. Delilah was smart enough to do the same.

"But Lucifer is changing from the leader he was before. He has changed the vision we agreed upon, the one we've consumed ourselves with since we came here. He now wants humans as his playthings... to punish at will in creating a Hell on Earth *with* mankind. We are supposed to destroy man, wipe him from Earth and rule Heaven and Hell." Zar let his anger and betrayal burn in his voice. He turned, including Delilah with a swept of his arm. "She is the brunt of Lucifer's delusional ranting. He believes his Princes, sometimes one or all of them, are plotting against him. Every day a new paranoid suspicion arises. Some might be true, but most are figments of his deranged imagination." He paused, his chest rising and falling. "For instance, it was you and Sonneillon's idea to have me kidnap the girl."

The heat of Asura's anger punched at him, swirling gold on her body as her six wings burst from behind her. "Lucifer said no such thing. He'd never think I or—"

"He has said it to me many times and then beat me while cursing your name." Delilah stated. "When I told him about the open abyss and the guardians, it shifted his mindset. He no longer wants just a war with Heaven and Earth, he craves to rule it all... without any of the Princes if they don't comply with his vision." She swallowed quickly. "He knows not everyone agrees, and that some dare to even doubt. It's turned him into an erratic paranoid leader, willing to kill anyone he thinks is in his way."

"How do I know her story is true? Just because she says the words, doesn't make it so." Asura sneered at Delilah, hate burning in her golden eyes. "You weave lies, not truth. Why would I ever trust you?"

"You saw for yourself how he tore apart the Damned you brought him, the veiled threat he sent both of you. Trust your own eyes and ears if you don't trust mine." Delilah threw down a gauntlet, daring Asura to deny what she saw.

"There is a traitor! I also think you poison him with your words of fantasy and fan discord among his Princes. I should kill you now and free him of his forked-tongue whore." Asura snarled at her, pacing in front of them.

"Killing her will not stop Lucifer's madness. His reasoning is warped. He believes only what fits his new vision. I have told him it was my idea to grab the girl, but he won't listen—"

"Was it Zar... your idea? Or did you have help?" Asura pointed at Delilah.

"I am responsible. I thought it would please Lucifer—" he lifted his head a little higher "—that I might gain more respect and attention from... Delilah."

Asura's incredulous laugh erupted into the air. Zar's nostrils flared at her insult, but he didn't react. "Really, Zar? You got whipped and cut blind over a woman?" Asura shoved him in the shoulder as her snicker faded. "But that is your nature, isn't it?"

"The punishment for my envy was just. But that sin doesn't drive me anymore. Concern for my life and that of Hell has taken its place. I think Lucifer will get us all killed if *we* don't stop him."

"By we, I assume you mean Sonneillon." Asura crossed her arms.

"And any Princes wise enough in following your mate." Zar let his words hang between them, hoping she'd understand his underlying meaning.

Asura turned, her pounding footsteps walking away from him.

She whistled; its pitch rising to the Degasus. Four hooves landed, its snorting and wings beating blended in a powerful tune. The heat emanating from its body was like a moth to a flame for him.

"Whistle, Zar, and we'll see if one comes to you." she commanded.

Excitement whipped through him. Zar licked his lips and pursed them, releasing a loud steady tone up into the mountain walls. He willed a Degasus to hear his call.

He turned as a thunderous galloping charged at him. Its wings in full flame; its tail and mane a swirl of fire. His heart pounded, but he dared not move. The Degasus stopped inches from him; its nostrils blowing scorching air upon him as the dust cloud swirled at his feet. He lifted his face, letting the beast decide if his pitiless sockets still made him worthy.

Asura whispered hushed words to the creature. "He's from the Realm of Wrath. His red flames match the fire he sees in you. They were forged with us in the same fire during the Fall. Their flames cannot burn us. He's chosen you. If you're a deserving rider, he'll share his name."

Zar moved forward, but Asura's hand landed on his chest. "The words you speak today. They are treasonous, inciting war against Lucifer and the Fallen who stand with him."

"They are. Which leaves you with a decision to make. Will you die for your vision or for one that might kill you during a tantrum, or worse, for a world you don't believe is our future? You are a ferocious, female Seraphim. Don't let the males impede your destiny."

Zar sidestepped her. He grabbed a chunk of flaming mane, weaving it between his fingers. Flames licked over his hand and wound around it, connecting them together. He leapt onto its back as it pawed against the ground.

"Don't get in my way either." She slapped its flank.

He turned away from Asura and Delilah, glaring at each other, their distrust seething between them. Better than having it aimed at him.

Freedom lashed at him as the Degasus galloped for a moment and then took flight. He clung to its mane, his thighs squeezed against its side. But he knew the beast would never throw him.

Cydanos.

The word burst inside his head, spiking the pulse rushing in his ears. The Degasus shared its name with him.

Fire, fury, and fearlessness connected them in mind and spirit.

Fly... Cydanos... fly!

CHAPTER
TWENTY

OLIVIA

Closing the front door behind her, Olivia dropped her backpack on the foyer bench. She started up the stairs but paused when she glimpsed her dad standing by the den window. The afternoon light outlined his handsome profile, a cup of coffee dwarfed in one large hand, the other tucked in his front jean pocket. But it wasn't his dapper pose giving her pause, it was the adoration etched across his face. He had the look of someone who could stand in that spot forever, feasting his eyes upon whatever fed his soul. Curious, she stepped towards the den, her shoes slapping against the rust-colored tile.

Dad's gaze turned to her, peeling away from what held his interest. His cheeks creased with his pearly white grin. It was the same smile she had trusted as a little girl, but now she greeted it with a hint of caution.

"Hi. How was school?" His eyes flickered to the window before he moved to the kitchen.

"It was fine. Same old thing. Everybody's getting spring fever and talking about graduation. All I want is more training time with the Magi and to stay with them on the weekends." She slipped onto the barstool, eyeing the banana in the fruit bowl. "Not your normal teenage girl's dream."

He cocked his head. "You could ask them. It's intense practice, but you're ready for it." He opened the refrigerator door. "Hungry? I can make a snack?" His voice rumbled from inside, sliding open the lunch meat drawer.

"Sounds great. Thanks." She giggled as he emerged from behind the door, arms loaded with a loaf of bread, sandwich makings, and a square Tupperware. "I'm thinking when you asked me if I want to eat, it's really because your stomach was growling."

Dad's eyebrows wiggled as he laid his bounty on the countertop. "Mom made her salsa this morning. I won't get in trouble if we break into it because *you're* hungry." He flashed a conspirator's grin and opened a cabinet, pulling out a bag of tortilla chips. Olivia's mouth salivated in anticipation of the spicy salsa hitting her tongue. Dad tore the bag open and placed it and the salsa filled Tupperware in front of her. Her greedy fingers found a chip, scooped into the salsa and popped it in her mouth. She closed her eyes, rewarded with the flavor she'd hoped for.

"That's so yummy!" Olivia dipped her chip in for another bite.

"I could put this on everything I eat," Dad proclaimed with his mouth full. He scooped again, coming out with a dripping mound. He closed the distance, shoving it in his mouth, as a red splat hit the counter. She grinned at him, lost in the mundane moment of eating. He opened the bread and began making sandwiches like it was an everyday occurrence.

Olivia's chip paused halfway to her mouth, and it dawned on her. They hadn't shared a snack in years before his return last Christmas. Now they ate a meal together every day. Coffee and cheesy eggs were ready each morning before school. When she came home, either the delicious smells of dinner greeted her, or a full plate waited for her in the microwave. Had enough time gone by where she'd grown comfortable with this routine and his place in it? She put the chip in her mouth, slowly chewing as she contemplated her insight.

Dad's eyes glanced over his shoulder again. Satisfied, he turned back and built the sandwiches with efficiency.

"What's got your attention out the window?" Olivia asked, wiping her hands on a napkin.

"Your Mom's been pestering me about working in her garden. I gave in, so we bought cucumber, tomato, and pepper plants. I dug the holes, but she insisted on planting them herself." He slapped the bread on top of the turkey. "Next she wants to attack her herb garden. You know how she is about that. Whispering to them, making sure the crystals and stones are placed just so." He anxiously glanced over again and slid the hefty sandwich toward Olivia. "I better go get—"

"Mom is fine. Let her be... it makes her happy." Dad's shoulders sagged. He grabbed his sandwich and took a huge bite. His jaw muscles flexed, chomping on what he really wanted to say.

"Can I ask you something?" Olivia glanced up from her sandwich, nervous about taking the first real step in opening up with him.

"Anything." He turned his back on the kitchen window, raising his brow.

Olivia didn't know where to start. She'd avoided any deep talks since receiving the orb, only skimming the surface about killing demons or his favorite weapons. But she had one burning question that needed answering. She pushed away the half-eaten sandwich.

"Why didn't you ever call me?" She watched the conflicting emotions play over his face until he finished his bite. He scratched his bearded chin and leaned against the gleaming counter.

"I've been waiting for this question, wondering how I could answer it, so you'd understand." He exhaled sharply. "I guess I'll backup to when the trouble started. I was on a hunting mission. I found a demon in an alley behind the Strip. We battled, and I killed it. But another demon had seen the fight. They may have been traveling in a pair or it was just bad luck, but I was compromised. It disappeared before I could kill it. I was afraid to go home for fear it had linked with me or try to track me. I couldn't have it find me here and harm you or Mom. So, the next day I left in a panic. There was no easy explanation to you for what had happened. I was devastated, but Melchior, Michael, Javier, and Rachel all agreed it was the best way to keep you safe. Javier kept me up to date, and Mom and I talked, like when you hurt your knee, but it was dangerous. We knew the guardianship would reunite us, so we waited until that time arrived."

Olivia's ears pounded with the beat of her racing pulse. She closed her eyes, breathing through her nose, and exhaled, puffing out her cheeks. When she opened them, she saw hope in his guarded eyes, but she didn't see truth in them. She slipped off the stool, not breaking eye contact. "That's a clever story, Dad, and there might even be some facts in it. But I'm not a naive girl willing to believe your story. I'm a warrior and I sense your deceit. Angels could have protected a meeting or a phone call between us."

"Olivia... I couldn't risk—"

"Liar." She fingered the talisman in her pocket. "Please say nothing more. Why you're choosing your pride over telling me the truth is your choice." She shook her head in disgust, sick to her stomach. "I thought we were past the lies... apparently not."

She raised her hand, calling up her portal. Crushing disappointment was all she felt as she turned her back and stepped through the blue swirl of lights.

"Wait! I'm sorry—"

Her mom stared through the sliding glass door, brows bunched together, as her eyes darted between them.

Let him tell her. I'm done...

Olivia walked into the Weapons Room. The huge white fire from the center pit heated her icy skin. Her footsteps echoed off the walls as she made her way to the hanging cabinet holding her weapons. She ignored her dagger and the throwing stars and zeroed in on the silver sword. A flame grew inside the blue jewel, a signal that the connection between it and her orb had ignited. She grasped the handle and pulled it off the shelf. Her heart pounded as angry unshed tears burned in her eyes. The power of the sword coursed through her arm, yet a part of her didn't want to have this call to guardianship. Its force had ruled over her dad, blinding him to truth, tempting him to lose sight of his daughter and his place as a father.

I don't want this to ruin my life, rule my dreams...

"What are your dreams?"

Olivia turned and raised her sword, taking a warrior stance. Her heart skipped as she recognized the angel standing in the white flames who had spoken to her.

"Zemira. How did you know what I was thinking?" She lowered her sword, relaxing her posture.

Zemira lifted her chin as she walked out of the flames, magnificently highlighting the gold swirling in her white armor. She took the steps one at a time, watching Olivia with her golden eye. Her other socket was milky white, marred by three slashes across the side of her face. "You were mumbling to yourself. But we were once linked. There was a time when I watched over you, before you became a guardian."

Olivia's faced scrunched in confusion until it hit her. "You were my Guardian Angel."

"Yes." Her smiled, softening her face. "And I'm honored that Michael has shared your secret with me, and that I'm allowed to meet with you." She stopped in front of Olivia, her feathers glowing in the back light of the pit's flames. "You, my child, are so incredibly brave to take on Lucifer and his Fallen."

Olivia glanced at her sword. For the first time, it was heavy in her hand. "I don't feel brave. I'm burdened by this." She raised it, turning it back and forth. "This guardianship has caused so much pain, has generated lies and betrayal in my family. I don't know if I want to be a part of this anymore."

"You are not your father. Your hurt was a great sadness for me, but you grew up strong, smart and faithful because of the love in your home. Your mother adores you. Your dad put her in an indelible situation, and she chose love. She loves him despite the guardianship, his faults... his sins."

Olivia turned away in disgust. "She made that choice, and we were happy. But now, when I asked him why he left, he wouldn't share the truth. He tried to sell me some line about a demon seeing him fight, but that's not enough to leave his family. I wanted to believe that there would finally be honesty between us, but he ruined it today. How can I not look at this sword and train with Melchior and wonder if I'll make those mistakes? Will I hurt people I love because of this decision I've made?"

"You are human, and you will make poor decisions and you might even hurt some people along the way, but that happens even if you aren't a guardian. Life is not black and white, neither are some choices we make. That's why we have to learn forgiveness." Her gentle voice contrasted with her intensity. "If we seek forgiveness, we must decide to give it first."

The blue stone in Olivia's sword glowed with a fire burning brighter, calling to the yearning inside her. "I don't want to be like him," she stressed. "And I'm afraid the guardianship will turn me." She raised her eyes to Zemira. "Can you tell me what happened?"

Zemira gazed at her with love and patience. "I hope you believe me when I say I do not know everything—"

Olivia huffed. "See—"

She raised her hand. "Even if I did, it isn't my story to tell. But whatever happened to your father must have been catastrophic, leaving him and your mother with a decision he never wanted to make. He made his choice to leave out of love for you. They both sacrificed for you and your safety. If he's not sharing the truth, maybe he's still protecting you."

"I don't want or need his protection anymore. I need his honesty." Olivia's throat closed up as her frustration mounted.

"It will come, when he can face whatever it is that happened." Zemira put a hand on Olivia's shoulder. Warmth flowed from her long fingers, easing her anger. "But let us not dwell on this. I'm here to spar with you. I hear you are very adept with the throwing stars, too." She touched the strap across her chest.

A smile spread over Olivia's face. "Yes. Ever since I saw you take out the demon's eye, I wanted to learn. I'd like to practice my sword because I'll be using it the most."

"Then let's begin." Zemira drew her blade. Olivia gasped, ducking and stepping to her right as the golden sword sliced the air above her. She straightened, raising her weapon.

"What was that for?" she asked, wide-eyed, her body shocked with adrenaline. She raised her sword, ready to fight. "You almost took off my head!"

Zemira laughed as she circled around her. "Lesson number one. When holding your weapon, always be alert, even in friendly company." Her face turned to stone.

She kept Zemira in front of her, watching for any hint of attack. "Is that what happened to you... your scar?" Olivia swung her blade, slicing at the side of the angel. She blocked the motion with her sword.

"Yes, I kept it to remind me to stay alert, because an ambush can come from anywhere at any time. It is the coward's favorite move."

Olivia didn't have time to ponder her message as they sparred. It wasn't until later, lying in bed when she replayed her words, wondering what friend had betrayed Zemira. Only one event came to mind.

The Fall.

When Angels turned upon Angels.

The greatest betrayal of all.

CHAPTER
TWENTY-ONE

ZACH

Man, Sergio makes a lot of racket.

Zach cracked a smile, perched on the tree branch concealed in the darkness. The tree bark's rough ridges pressed into his back as he steadied himself. Pine scent mingled with the earthy ground cover decaying on the forest floor. Water rushed with the current of the ravine's river, but it couldn't disguise the crunch of the dead undergrowth from Sergio's footsteps. Zach's sensitive hearing picked up his position about twenty feet behind him. Zach gazed at the outline of the old trees as Sergio moved closer. He was as clear as when he tried on his dad's night vision goggles on a camping trip.

Is this how creatures of the night see in their world?

I like it.

Sergio paused beneath him. Zach's body vibrated with excitement as he readied himself to pounce. He swiveled, but a golden ball brightened the dark forest heading for the tree. Zach jumped off the branch as it exploded next to him, sending large splinters of wood raining down on him. He hit the spongy earth and rolled to his left.

Good move... let's get it on.

Raising his hands, Zach punched a wave of air at Sergio. It lifted him up and knocking him on his back. He sprinted toward Sergio, but he was already launching himself in Zach's direction.

141

Sergio threw out his hand. An energy wave tazed Zach, freezing him in his spot, allowing Sergio to tackle him around the waist. Air whooshed out of his lungs when landed on his back. Sergio straddled him. Zach sucked air into his lungs, right before Sergio plowed his fist into his jaw. His teeth slammed shut, and stars erupted before his eyes. Zach's body jerked back to life in time to deflect the next blow. Sergio growled, staring at him with eyes too bright with excitement.

Zach leaned up, landing with a powerful punch on Sergio's face.

"Aw—" He howled while toppling off of Zach. He scrambled to his feet just in time to see Sergio holding a throwing star in his hand. Zach jumped to the left. The spinning glint of silver whizzed past his head, missing him by inches.

"Sergio! Wait!"

Another one whizzed by as Zach ran and dove behind a tree. He lifted his palm, calling upon the water. A swirling green vortex emerged. Sergio's footsteps closed in along with his heavy breathing. He jumped up and released the green energy at the ground in Sergio's path. It splintered, creating spinning green water spikes, hitting the earth in a strafing pattern. Large clumps of wet grass and dirt exploded in front of Sergio, who stopped and turned his back to the shower of muddy earth. Zach ran through the debris, driving into Sergio's back with his shoulders, sending them both to the ground. He grunted as Zach put his hand on the side of his face, pushing it against the musty under brush.

"What are you thinking tossing throwing stars at me? Are you crazy! You could have hit me!" Zach seethed through clenched teeth.

"Shut up and get off of me!" He threw an elbow, but Zach jumped off before it landed. Sergio raised himself up, covered in mud and clumps of dirt. He turned his head, but his eyes didn't waver from Zach's. "I was told to track and find a demon. So, I fought like you were a demon. You got a problem with that?" He spat next to him, wiping his mouth over his sleeve.

"I do, as a matter of fact. It was to track and find... not kill. What gives?" Zach ran his forearm across his face, wiping the muck from his eyes. "We're training to kill the enemy, not each other."

"Well, I'm tired of training. I'm tired of having to hold back. You may not be ready, but I am!" Sergio rushed at him, but he held his ground when Sergio stopped inches from his face. "I've got more reason to fight than you. You don't know what it's like to lose someone you love."

Blood roared in Zach's ears as he shoved him away. "You think you own misery and pain because Manny died? Well, you don't! I lost someone I loved too and I'm not trying to destroy everything in sight."

"Who did you lose, Zach?"

The boys both jumped, turning their heads. "What are you doing here?" Sergio's brow scrunched together.

"You guys lit up the forest like a firework show, so I thought I'd see what you were doing to each other and save you from the Magi. They're not pleased with your act. And in case you're wondering, if I were a demon, you'd be dead." Olivia turned and raised her hand. A stream of blue flames blasted the ground in front of her. She folded her arms, scowling at both of them. "So, answer the question, Zach. Who did you lose?"

Both sets of eyes locked on his. He scrubbed his face, then ran his fingers through his wet hair. He fisted the ends behind his head and released a sigh filled with anxiety yet relief. Slumping his shoulders, he tried to form the words that had been locked up so tightly inside of him. But they dried up along with his fledgling courage. He paced in front of them, fighting his rising panic and tongue-tied mouth.

This could go so bad...

"Zach? You can tell us," Olivia's soft voice urged, stepping closer.

God help me...

Here it goes...

He stopped and swallowed, scanning their faces. He had to get this off his chest... consequences be damned.

"His name was Cody, and he'd been my best friend since I can

143

remember. We did everything together... scouts, played ball... you name it. Cody was a little wild and crazy. He was a risk taker where I'm not. Life was an adventure to him. We did stupid stuff I never would have done on my own. Not drugs or booze, just having fun... pulling pranks... pushing each other with our competitiveness... do something more extreme than the other." Zach cleared the lump in his throat while trying to calm his racing heart. His hand rubbed the back of his neck, then let his hand fall and slap his thigh.

"The summer before we moved here, we went on a camping trip along the Colorado River with our dads and a few other guys. We'd had an awesome time canoeing the river in the mornings until we reached the next campsite. We'd then hike and tell stories around the fire after dinner. Cody had this infectious gut laugh. I can still see him, his face bright in the firelight, slapping my back after he shared a story about my puking after getting off a spinning carnival ride." Zach chuckled even though a sob lay at the base of his throat.

"If you don't want to talk—" Sergio offered with a softer face Zach hadn't seen in a while.

He shook his head. "Thanks, but I need to get this off my chest. I should have done it before now." He glanced over at Olivia, who chewed on her bottom lip. She stood close to him, the whites of her eyes startling against the darkness. He wanted to grab her hand and steal some strength from her. Instead he slipped his dirty hands into his pockets.

Please understand...

"On the last night, Cody nudged me awake. He wanted to sneak out before dawn and take the smaller canoe out on the river. He said there was this cool place to watch the sunrise. I thought about saying no, but that was impossible with Cody. We got dressed, snuck out, and slipped the canoe into the river. I was assuming we were going back upstream, but he said it was downstream. I shrugged, but I should have known he was up to something. We floated along, watching the sun rise over the canyon's top. I told him we better head back, but he said just a little further. That's when I heard the

144

change in the river; the rushing it makes as it travels over rocks, speeding up with the current sucking around the smooth edges. He'd wanted to ride the rapids without the helmet, or life vests. I tried to paddle against it, but the current was too strong. He started laughing that laugh of his, but things got out of hand real quick. The canoe careened over a dip, hit a rock and the next thing I knew, we were tipping. Cody sat in the bow in front of me. The last thing I saw before I hit the water was Cody falling in and his head smacking a wide rock lurking at the surface. I came up, sputtering his name. For a second, I saw his hair and yellow t-shirt, but then he was gone. I yelled and tried to catch him, but the current has a path of its own. I shouted his name until I was hoarse, half drowning myself in the process. The river finally spit me out, cut and bruised, but alive. I don't know how long I was there on the shore before my dad found me. Search and Rescue later found Cody downstream." A numbness settled over Zach, as he tried to work up enough spit to swallow.

"That must have been a nightmare for you." Olivia placed her hand on his forearm. "But it wasn't your fault."

He shook his head, shame rolling through him. "I should have done something more—"

"I understand your anger"—Sergio's rough whisper cut the thick forest air—"the pain. It hurts so bad sometimes you can't breathe."

"Yeah, but my guilt and worry were impeding my training and how I treated you guys. I'm sorry." He let go of a shuttering breath, nodding at his friends. "I know this doesn't make my overprotective behavior okay, but at least now you can better understand it." He turned to Olivia. "I'm working on it, I swear."

"Thank you, and thanks for telling us. We'll work harder as a team... talk more with each other. But I can take care of myself. I'm just as skilled as you are. And I think smarter by the looks of the forest." She smiled and reached for their hands. "Let's go back. The Magi have something they want to teach us."

"Come on, boy scout. We'll take our lumps together, after I

change my clothes." Sergio smirked before he headed through the trees.

Olivia followed him, leaving Zach last in line, hanging back on the walk to the church. He pressed together his lips, still grappling for control of his emotions, but the load he'd been lugging around was lighter, even if the dirty last piece of truth hadn't come to the surface.

That is for me to bear...

Alone...

CHAPTER
TWENTY-TWO

OLIVIA

C aspar led the guardians through an unfamiliar shadowy hallway. The arched entrance in front of them glowed with a filtered light dancing on the ceiling. An exotic smell drifted to Olivia from the unseen room. Its heady scent tickled her nose along with a faint memory of having smelled it before today.

Zach and Sergio followed in step behind her. They'd washed their faces and hands, but their clothes showed the effects of their escapade in the forest. Zach's heartbreaking story about Cody's accident lingered in her thoughts. More puzzle pieces snapped together concerning Zach's protective behavior, leaving her torn between giving their relationship a chance or continuing to keep her distance. She missed him and was tired of ignoring the constant attraction she had for him. She figured her best plan was to give him the opportunity to pull his own weight, allowing her room to train as an equal, not a damsel in distress.

I'm rooting for you, Zach

"Did they tell you what they'll teach us?" Zach whispered from behind. His voice echoed around the cramped hallway.

She glanced back and shrugged. "Melchior didn't say. He just told me to get you guys from the forest and meet Caspar by the lower entrance."

Caspar stopped before the doorway. Olivia strained to see around him, but the mysterious room remained hidden. He turned and grinned, his black hair falling across his shoulders.

"Enter, my friends, and take a seat where you please." He stepped aside, sweeping his hand in front of him. Olivia entered a dim windowless room, with sparse, unusual decor. Melchior and Bal sat cross-legged, each on an oversized, jewel-colored velvet pillow resting on top of a burgundy hued Persian rug. It filled the space of the intimate setting. A single swirl of smoke drifted from a metal bowl with a carved out scrolled lid. It nestled between various sized burning candles. Flames flickered from wall sconces, casting an eerie light. Olivia skimmed her tongue across her lips as she lowered herself onto a plump sapphire pillow. She ran her hands over the plush material, trying to ease the pace of her racing pulse.

Bal nodded after Sergio and Zach had settled onto their pillows. His golden eyes gleamed against the candlelight, gazing at each of the room's occupants.

"Welcome to my room... my sanctuary. I come here to quiet my thoughts and become one with my mind, body and spirit. This oneness is vital when I meditate and seek the evil one in his... sanctuary." His deep voice rumbled. Goosebumps ran over Olivia's flesh.

"The evil one. Do you mean the devil?" Sergio leaned forward, waiting for the answer to his question.

"Yes. His name is Lucifer, as he was called before their Fall." Bal's grim face turned toward his fellow Magi. "He was a Seraphim. The most supreme of all Angels and closest to God. His betrayal and lies filled our minds with thoughts of entitled knowledge and power we had no place knowing. The three of us were initially jealous of God's creation of man. My love and adoration for God and his kingdom was too selfish to share with an imperfect human race. It left me open to Lucifer's forked tongue. I have no one to blame but myself for my actions." Bal sagged as if the admission was too heavy for his broad shoulders to bear.

"When Lucifer declared war, and the battle began, the three of us stood next to each other and readied our swords," Melchior said. "As the Angels rushed toward us, the veil of hate and jealousy lifted from my eyes, and in my heart, I realized I couldn't draw blood because of Lucifer's warped vision. I sheathed my sword and took flight. I glanced behind me and found Bal and Caspar had followed. We flew toward God's light. I knew I had to beg forgiveness and fight for Him. My soul was racked with pain as I saw my beloved friends fall in the battle raging below us. I had forsaken them and God. When I landed before Him, I fell prostrate... grief stricken and ashamed." Melchior's voice broke, and his chin quivered in the candlelight.

Caspar waved his hand at Bal and Melchior. "You see, we were Cherubim, a high Choir of Angels below the Seraphim... the highest of all Angels. Our task... our duty... was to magnify the holiness and power of God and serve as a visible reminder of his glory, and to guard His throne. Lucifer poisoned us with lies, saying we deserved to have full knowledge like God, and should feel betrayed, just like he did. But in our free will, we committed an unforgivable sin. Bal, Melchior, and I lay mute at His feet, not daring to draw God's attention away from battle. No evil neared the throne, or we would have fought them. The horrid fight ensued, but Lucifer never had a chance. In his cowardice, he swept as many Angels and heavenly creatures as he could into the Mar of Sin. Their horrible cries still echo in my ears." Caspar's soothing accent turned stilted and hoarse.

"God told us to rise." Olivia's heart hammered as her eyes turned and locked with Bal's as he spoke. "He said in our moment of free will, we had irrevocably rejected Him and His reign by aligning with Lucifer. There would be no repentance for him and the Fallen after their descent through the Mar of Sin's portal to Hell. Numb in my horror, I wanted to shatter in my shame, but He showed us mercy instead of death. He told us because we didn't strike against our fellow Angels and came to Him, we would not be damned, though our actions weren't without consequences. He made us guardians of the Mar of Sin and gave us the secrets of Orion. He charged us to start a human lineage of three guardians. They, too, would protect humans from evil and be the only ones who could open and close the portal. We would live for eternity on Earth and train here, in this sacred place... in this dimension. But—" Bal stopped as if frozen in a different time.

Olivia felt suspended, as if an invisible force held her from falling off a cliff.

"We would share our angelic essence with the guardians through an orb. A bright light struck me. An immense pain ravaged my back. I fell to my knees, welcoming the agony as punishment for my betrayal. When the light faded, I knew my wings were gone, but He left a mark on my chest... all our chests."

"The mark of Orion," muttered Zach.

"Indeed," Melchior pulled off his tunic. "I panted on my knees, devastated by the loss, but held no malice for my just penance. When I peered up, Michael, Gabriel, and Raphael stood before us, bloodied and anguished from the fight. God nodded to them. I froze as Michael presented his sword in front of me. He wiped his hand across the blade. The blood of the treasonous Angels dripped, marring the iridescent floor. He raised his glistening hand and struck the mark. It burned and hissed. I arched my scarred back against the insult of their blood mixing with the seven dots. Before he walked away, Michael gazed at me with a kindness I didn't deserve. God said we bore this mark for two reasons. To brand us as hunters of evil and to bond us with them. We will teach you how to link with the Fallen."

Olivia's brow scrunched, and her stomach flipped. "Linked by blood... blood of the Fallen? Evil—"

"Evil doesn't reside in you," Caspar replied. "Lucifer created a link to himself, a light of fire he seared upon his mutinous angels as they fought, binding them to him, corrupting their mind, invading their blood. We'd fled before he laid his link. He must have sensed the end was near and didn't want to lose any of his Angels. Through the blood, we became linked with them and Lucifer. He's unaware of this and of our part in the Mar of Sin. Set your fears aside."

Olivia glanced at her fellow guardians. Sergio was pale, staring at a point beyond Bal. Zach turned to her, his eyes wide while a hand raked through his hair.

"How do we do this... link thing... and not get caught?" Zach asked.

"It is quite simple, yet a delicate balance between linking and staying linked, which you do not want to do. Right now, you will only tap into it by initiating your first connection by peeling back the curtain of Hell."

"What!" Zach's mouth fell open.

"No!" Sergio put his hands on his head.

"Wait!" Melchior raised his hand. "You know it through your memories, so don't let the horrors distract you. Be clear and focused because this is the fastest way to find the portal to Hell and sear your mark with the Fallen through your initiation."

"You will not be alone on this journey," Bal reassured, raising up his palms. "We'll guide you. But you must do as we say. You only need to glimpse into Hell and your mark will flair and set the link. You'll use this meditative doorway later when it's time to look upon Lucifer."

"We will spy on the devil?" Sergio's voice squeaked.

"It's part of your duties when your meditative skills are ready."

"What if they see us?" Olivia scratched the mark through her shirt.

"Your journey won't be in person, but in mind," Bal pointed to his forehead. "They won't notice you, because they're part of a—"

"Hive," Zach muttered.

"Yes." Melchior's affirmation hung like the thin haze along the ceiling.

The Magi stood, their hand each clutching a pillow. They walked to their disciple and sat in front of them. Melchior's blue eyes bore into Olivia's as he grabbed her sweaty hands. "I'm here, Olivia. Have no fear. Listen to Balthazar's instructions and I will help you with the rest."

She nodded, pulling his courage through their grasp. She'd never wanted to see Hell again after they had released those wretched memories.

Now, I will see it for myself...

Melchior squeezed her hand. "Those visions never get unseen, but there's too much beauty in this world and the next to let it stain your mind and spirit. You'll learn to balance—"

"My burden and my blessing," concluded Olivia.

He grinned at her and relaxed his hands.

Balthazar cleared his throat. "The first thing you must do is clear your mind and relax your body. Close your eyes, listen to my voice, and create a blank slate before you. Breathe in through your nose, count to five. Exhale through your mouth while squeezing your stomach, forcing your lungs to push out all the air."

Olivia did as Bal told her. Each time her mind shut out more thoughts which calmed her anxious body.

"Think of your mark and see it before you in your mind's eye. Focus on the first star, on your left, in the belt while you tap into the orb's energy." Bal's rich voice flowed over her as Orion lay poised in front of her closed eyelids. "Let the star blaze before you and visualize it opening just like your portal to us."

"I'm your anchor, Olivia," Melchior's voice sounded hollow, like talking through a long tunnel.

Olivia concentrated on the steady slow rise and fall of breathing as the star grew larger. The same spot on the mark against her chest tingled as the portal's electric blue ends crackled before her.

"You know this place. Let the memories be your shield." Melchior's voice pierced through the cacophony flooding through the opening. Mournful wails and sharp shrieks mixed with the gurgle of churning lava played a chaotic soundtrack. Heat slapped at her while the stench of sulfur and smoke threatened to spike her heart rate.

They can't get me... Lucifer can't see...

Trust the memories.

"Set yourself free... go through... now." Melchior's sharp voice urged.

Olivia sent herself free through the portal as if she was jumping off a bluff into the ocean, except no serene water tossed below her. Overcome with hate and suffering, a darkness pulled her into the hissing lava. She fought for control of her emotions and to hold on tight to the calm she needed to pass this test. Her mark erupted in hot pain as it absorbed the evil madness of this place.

A Lessor flew past her, its frayed wings moving the thick suffocating air over her. It dove, aimed at the red boiling pool of lava, clutching a black orb in its gnarled talons. More Lessors dive bombed around her ready to drop their corrupted precious loads. Her anger rose as she thought about how they manipulated the humans—

"Olivia. Turn away and return through the portal." Melchior squeezed her hands. "Now."

She fought the urge to strike out at a Lessor and the powerful draw of Lucifer's link with the Fallen. She pulled herself back, like snapping a rubber band, and watched the blue circular opening close in on itself. Snapping her eyes open, she found Melchior inches from her face. Her chest heaved as the visions from Hell branded her. She released his hands and dropped her head inside them, her hot palms cradling her forehead.

"Welcome back. Here." Melchior tapped her hand with a cool, wet glass. She chugged down the water, easing her parched throat.

"That was intense," Olivia handed back the glass. "I felt this pull toward a vast darkness that wanted to swallow me and Lessors were flying around so close, it moved the air. My mark burned as soon as I jumped through into Hell."

"These are normal experiences. Your body is safe behind the portal, but your mind and spirit are vulnerable, especially when you're first developing the skill. You did good and will be ready to hunt soon." Melchior patted her knee and rose. "I think we're done for tonight. Rest."

Olivia stood, releasing a shaky breath. She turned and met the stares of Sergio and Zach. Zach mouthed 'wow' to her. Sergio's eyes had a darker gaze, as if he wasn't fully together from his trip to Hell.

I don't know if I am either... something awakened under my mark...

Swirling dark and sinister like the air changing before a storm.

Did Lucifer's link now lurk within her, nipping at her heels or was she strong enough to fight against this evil with her sword and her heart?

CHAPTER
TWENTY-THREE

OLIVIA

Her bedroom had only a faint light coming through the blind's wooden slats, leaving lines across her bed's comforter, but Olivia's angelic vision lit her room like a black and white movie. Two eyes stared at her from her bed. There was a soft purring mixed with the swish of his bushy tail. She walked over and sat down on the bed, her body feeling as heavy as the sagging of her mattress. Thunder stood up and arched his back before he sauntered over to her lap. His purr filled the space like a loud motorboat. She stroked his fur with a shaky hand, her nerves letting go of her impressionable trip to Hell.

"Hello, Thunder cat. You won't believe what I did tonight," Olivia confided to her pet. His half-open green eyes blinked at her as he laid his big body across her. She chuckled at her cat, understanding Thunder had crossed paths with what resides in Hell, having had his own run in with a Fallen over Christmas break. "I'm sure you took a swipe at him before he shoved you in the closet." He blinked at her again before he nestled his head on top of her calves.

Was it Zar you tangled with Kit-kitty?

She glanced at the mason jar on her desk where two feathers crisscrossed each other, their plumes hanging over the sides. One feather was white and pure, its ends so delicate, they fluttered with any subtle disturbance of air. The other feather, inky-black and stiff, resembling a menacing weapon, rather than a tool for flight. Olivia recognized similar feathers tonight on the Lessors as they zoomed around her, eager to drop their cherished cargo into the pool of lava. A flare of anger surged to the surface when she reflected about the soul each one of them gripped. What had that soul done in its life so horrific that eternal damnation was its destiny?

Murder, hate, greed or was it simply turning away from God?

A shiver ran down her spine at the idea of living there for eternity.

No thank you.

She exhaled, ignoring the urge to call Zach or Sergio. Washing away the day's sweat and grim in the shower and the steam clearing her head sounded like a better plan, but she couldn't take her eyes off the black feather. Could she find out who it belonged to and who had broken the sanctity of her room if she meditated while holding it? Curiosity about its owner plagued her. Why they had left it? Was it a beacon for future travels or a warning for her? Her pulse quickened, eager to hunt down the demon. Did she dare?

Yes.

She scooted to the end of the bed, Thunder jumping off in a whirl of gray fluff. She stood, stretching her hand across the dark, her angelic vision zeroing in on the black streak stabbing into the jar. Her fingers grazed the spiky ends when she heard footsteps treading up the stairs. She paused, her shoulders tensed, knowing the face behind the gait.

"Livvy?" Dad's knuckles rapped softly on the door.

She closed her eyes, half hoping he would go away if she didn't answer it, but she knew better than that. Olivia opened it just enough to show her face. Thunder skirted through the opening and raced downstairs.

Lucky cat.

"Mom and I are searching for a movie to watch. Want to join us?" His eyebrows arched as he ended his plea on an upbeat note. Her mouth watered at the smell of popcorn, but that wasn't sufficient to entice her to be in the same room with her dad. They hadn't broken the ice since their last argument about why he didn't contact her and now wasn't the time to open that can of worms.

"Thanks, but I'm jumping in the shower and going to bed." She closed the door, but a brown boot nudged in first.

"Wait. I was hoping you'd be willing to talk. You were right—"

"Dad." She yanked it wide open, challenging his stoic and unreadable face head on, too tired to care about the consequences. She let go of the doorknob and folded her arms. "Ya know... now is not a good time. We learned meditation tonight, so me and my mark got sealed with Hell. I've had my fill of confrontation for one day." Her jaw thrust out, daring him to push her.

His foot slid from the door jamb, his face softening. "Yep. That's a tough one. You'll go on a hunt soon. We can talk in the morning when you're rested." He stepped away with his mouth turned down.

"Maybe..."

"Well... goodnight then."

"Night." Olivia closed the door before he could sneak his boot in again. His footsteps weren't as light going downstairs, and it irritated her.

Olivia stepped out of her bathroom, refreshed by the hot shower, ready to crawl into bed. She threw back the fluffy comforter, hoping her dreams weren't filled with Lessors and murky black orbs. On the desk, a movement caught her eye. The wispy ends of the white feather danced with the stirring air. She didn't linger long on it, instead shifting to the black feather unmoving next to it. She stilled, fighting the urge to pick up the ominous feather washed.

Can I find out who it belongs to?

She took a tentative step, her hand once again poised to draw a feather from the jar. She inched toward it, tension brewing in her stomach. She pulled her hand back, distracted by the picture of her,

Zach and Sergio taken the day after they received the orb at the Valley of Fire. Should she tell them her plan?

Nope. I can do this on my own.

No matter how desperate she was to find answers, inadvertently linking herself to a demon would make her vulnerable to their attack or even death. The white feather's ends quivered beside the black one, as if reaching out to Olivia. Her hand darted out and plucked the white feather from the jar.

It's time I find out who this belongs to... could it be Zemira's?

She twirled it between her fingers, Zemira coming to mind. Her shoulders relaxed, thinking about the warrior angel. Laying the feather on her nightstand, Olivia open the drawer and removed a long lighter. She pushed the button, igniting the flame, and lowered it to the candle jar, lighting the three wicks. Fire light flickered, followed by a thin line of black smoke. The faint scent of eucalyptus and mint rose from the pale green candle. Excitement grew in her like the budding flames.

Zemira will be so surprised...

Feeling better than she had all day, Olivia snatched the feather and plopped on her bed. Crossing her legs, she closed her eyes, and started the ritual Bal showed them of breathing and clearing her mind. She let the stillness of the room and the scent of the candle calm her... centering her as she clasped the feather's pointed end. Running her fingertips up the feather's soft row, she brought to life the orb's energy under her mark. A sensation tingled from her fingers to her mark. She exhaled and set it free.

Here I go...

The black void in her head erupted with her blue portal opening from the center. Her body vibrated while heat crept up her neck, exhilarated to surprise her friend.

But the curtain of Heaven did not part.

Nor was she staring at Zemira.

CHAPTER
TWENTY-FOUR

DELILAH

Her heels struck like an exclamation point with each step she took in Zar's gloomy room. The red fires from the Realm of Wrath played along her body as she strode toward the window. The view of the black looming mountains and bubbling red pool did nothing to keep her irritation in check. She reached the window and pounded her fist against the thick glass, the thuds mixing with the harsh, violent roars from the damned and their captives. The sounds usually pounded in harmony with her wicked heart, but not today... and less often.

Delilah hissed and spun around, stomping across the dingy floor for another round of pacing. Zar pushed his limits with her. He'd set up this meeting, and now left her hanging... waiting. His careless attitude towards her was wearing thin. Their next steps were critical, or she'd find herself on the serpent's lunch menu.

I bet he's with her...

How dare he make me wait while they fly or scheme together...

Conner did the same... pushed me aside for his simpering wife.

Her nostrils flared as she inhaled the stale air from his essence. She despised her inferior old-self, and to think she was behaving the same way... waiting on a simpleton. She paused when the door flung open, bouncing off the wall. Zar stormed inside the room, ash trailing behind him infused, with the scent of her.

She crossed her arms, a sneer emerging on her hard face. "Where have you been? I don't like waiting, especially when I know you were with her. Yet, you have the audacity to make me wait while the two of you—"

He turned, his black pits disarming her. "Yes, I was with Asura, but it wasn't to *see* her. I rode Cydanos. I realize this is painful for you to believe, but you're not my only priority. Learning to fight again and ride are what's most important in my miserable life. It helps me think clearer, push away the clutter of your insistent babble about Lucifer and how rotten your world is with him. If you don't like it, then you're welcome to leave."

He unbuckled his belt, the dangling sword clanking against the hard floor when he tossed it aside.

"Are you a fool or just stupid? There'll be no more visits with your precious Asura and her flying demons if we get killed!" Delilah marched over and thumped him on the chest. "You better put me, and our plans, first, or so help me—"

"What... God? You're no longer on his help list. You've made your bed... literally... with the devil, so don't threaten me or come to my room whining that you're not getting enough attention." He turned his back on her and walked to the red-hued window. He leaned his head against the glass, shoulders slumping as his body sagged.

His callous words found the vulnerable chink in her armor. She wasn't aligned with God anymore, and her recent alliances were as slippery and shifting as the serpent who haunted her dreams. Juggling Zar's and Lucifer's ever-changing moods was exhausting, but she had to keep her eye on the prize and beat them both.

"You're right. I'm not with God... by choice. And yes... I'm in bed with Lucifer, but you're my partner in this game plan. I don't have any other distractions like you. So, the only way to burn my pent-up energy is to stalk the Realms and plot my vengeance against Conner. His betrayal of the vow he swore to me to stay away from his family and his denial of our love, churns and burns inside of me like the pools for the Damned. I'll never forgive him, and I must get my revenge soon or—

Who's here?

Delilah's head jerked behind her. She searched for the presence she sensed had invaded her privacy. Nothing lurked in the dark recesses of the room, but an unfamiliar faint scent not found in this world tickled her nose.

What is that smell? How—

"Or what? You'll go mad. Please... you—"

"Sshhh," she hissed.

She sniffed the air again, but the whiff was gone, along with the prickling on her neck of eyes upon her. "Someone was here."

Zar rushed in front of her. She'd love to harass him about the fact that his stiffened body blocked her from the unknown intruder.

Your actions give you away.

He turned and faced her, relaxing as his hand slid from the dagger at his hip. "I don't sense anyone. Are you sure—"

"Yes. I'm certain. Eyes were on me, and a fresh scent drifted into the room... fragrance from Earth," Delilah said, scanning the area again.

"Well, that's impossible. Nobody has that capability, so once again, your imagination runs wild." He scoffed at her. "You need a hobby. Something besides me and Lucifer." He walked away and plopped down on his bed. He laid his head on the pillow as he flopped his dirty boots onto the bed.

She narrowed her eyes. "I'm working on it," she mumbled.

"What?" Zar put his hands behind his head, once again, displaying his indifference to her.

"Nothing." She waltzed over to the side of the bed. "So, what has you so riled up?" She cocked her head. "Asura deny your advances?"

She snickered, pushing his boots over so she could sit down. His dusty boot nudged her lower back, leaving a dirty mark on her red silky shirt.

"That's so droll, Delilah. Sonneillon is her mate. It would be suicide for me to seduce her." His face turned hard. "Besides. No one will have me now."

Hmmm... I don't know about that.

She wiped away the dirt smudge, grinning at herself. "Well, if it's companionship you desire, I'm sure when you're crowned Prince of the Seven Realms, you'll have all the salacious company you've ever wanted."

Delilah's body stilled as Zar slowly rose at the waist until he was so close, she saw the scars lining his eye sockets. "You mean Ruler of the Seven Realms, right?" His hot breath wafted over her face, his anger and distrust washing over her.

Careful...

She closed the inches between them and placed a light kiss on his lips. His body jerked and leaned forward, but she pulled away.

"You're right. Ruler has a better ring to it." She patted his boots, then wiped her hand across the bed. "Shall we discuss our next step in the plan? We have to get Asura to convince Sonneillon that Lucifer is cracking and—"

"Leave me. I want quiet so I can think. I'm in no mood for your plans and schemes. Come tomorrow, before I ride, and we will talk more then."

Delilah seethed inside, standing up. "All right, but I'm ready to move forward, with or without you." She made her way to the door, careful not to pound her heels against the floor.

Oh... I wish he still had eyes to rip out.

He grunted as she twisted the knob, squeezing it inside her feverish hand. She closed the door behind her, body vibrating with his arrogance and the unnerving occurrence in his room. Delilah regarded each direction of the hallway. Which way should she go?

Lucifer or Plan B...

One side of her mouth lifted in satisfaction as she threw her shoulders back and stepped to the left.

Hello Plan B...

CHAPTER
TWENTY-FIVE

OLIVIA

I did something wrong...
  That was not Zemira...
Oh, God... what if the demon saw me?

Tremors shook Olivia's body. Her heartbeat thrashed in her ears as her eyes shifted around her dark bedroom, its walls pressing in on her, squeezing against her while she struggled to take a deep breath. She inhaled through her nose and glanced at the white feather she gripped between her fingertips. What she had once considered an innocuous treasure, now embodied evil like its quill mate in the mason jar.

Olivia raised the feather for a closer look, her heavy breathing ruffling the ends. Her gut was certain it belonged to an angel... her guardian angel. She'd seen similar ones on the glorious wings of Zemira and the Archangels. She shook her head, trying to clear the ill effects of her unintended trip to Hell, and replayed the few seconds of her meditation before she'd snapped back to her room. When the warm light she'd expected didn't greet her, she'd instinctively sensed something was wrong. A red-flickering oppressive chamber reeking of smoke and sulfur assaulted her through the opening portal. She'd just seen Hell, drenched in its horrendous odor.

Was I still linked, or did I mess up?

Olivia closed her eyes and concentrated on the snippets of spoken words dripping with malice.

Plan my revenge against Conner...

Betrayal of vow to stay away from his family...

Denial of our love.

Olivia's eyes flew open as realization punched a blow straight to her heart. She leaned forward and rocked, her long hair covering her face, draping Olivia inside her horror and disbelief. Where only moments before terror held her in its grip, now an instant fire ignited, fueled by full weight of her father's utter and complete betrayal. Its flames roared at his deceit, disregarding what had been good and pure in his life... his family.

She jumped off her bed and yanked opened the door. Hateful words coursed inside her mind as she ran down the stairs, reckless in her desire to confront and shred her father. When she rounded the foyer's corner, her parents were standing. Her father's stance braced, his body tense as if realizing a fight was brewing. Mom was still, but her eyes widened as she watched Olivia's approach. Olivia's gaze was locked on the man whose ability to wreak havoc and pain in her life had no bounds.

Barreling into the den, Olivia stopped inches in front of him, stabbing the feather at the space between them. Her other hand itched to deck him, but she wouldn't lower herself to that level again.

"Who does this belong to?" She seethed; her lips peeled back. "Who!" She shouted.

His brow scrunched as he glanced at it, before coming back to hers. "I don't—"

"God... can't you even answer one question honestly? Just for once I—"

His pupils narrowed to pinpricks. "I've seen lots of white feathers in my time. I don't recognize that particular *one.*"

"I bet you have seen a lot." She scoffed. "Am I supposed to assume you've never gone into my room? To refresh your memory, it lays in the jar next to the black demon feather. Look familiar now?" She shoved it closer to his face.

"Okay..." his eyebrows shot up.

"What's wrong, Olivia? Your hand is shaking," Mom grabbed Olivia's arm.

She snatched it away and stepped back, glaring at her parents. "This feather was lying on my pillow when I went back upstairs the morning you left. I never thought much about where it came from or why it was there. I assumed it was part of a Christmas present I never got because you ditched us. Mom never mentioned it." She waved the feather between them. "A part of me hated it and many times I went to throw it away, but I couldn't. You know why? That little girl inside of me couldn't let it go because it was the last Christmas present I'd ever get." Mom inhaled sharply while Dad's beard grew darker on his paling face.

"Honey, when I saw it, I'd hoped an angel left it to comfort you. I didn't bring it up because I was waiting for you to ask, but you never did," Mom's voiced cracked, her hands clasped together, turning her knuckles white.

"Funny you should say that." She cocked her head. "Today, we did mediation for the first time and I got the unwelcome pleasure of staring into Hell. So, when I finished my shower, an idea occurred to me when I saw the feather. I wanted to erase that horrid memory and replace it with a better one." The words rushed out of her. "Zemira told me she was my guardian angel before Michael. I believed it must be from her. It made perfect sense."

Mom scooted around the coffee table and tugged on Olivia's arm. "You need to sit down and take a moment to get hold of yourself."

She pushed her mom's hand away, her vision tunneling on her father. "I'm fine, Mom." She could sense her mom's eyes on her back as she approached him. He remained glued to the same spot, wary blue eyes never leaving hers.

"I lit a candle and laid the feather in my lap. I did everything right, so imagine my surprise when the portal opened, and I don't see

166

Zemira. Instead, I'm back in Hell for a nanosecond looking at a female demon with fiery red hair talking about you and getting her revenge because you broke your vow and returned to your family. Why is the demon saying you denied her love?"

It was like a bomb blew up in the den. A second of doomed quiet and then chaos ensued. Mom rushed next to her yelling, "What! What did you say?" while Dad grabbed Olivia's arms and yanked her closer. "Did you hear her name?" Veins corded in his neck; his face flushed. "Did you?"

"Yes, I heard her name!" Fury punched through her voice. "Delilah!"

Everything about Dad's reaction was she'd given him the blow she'd yearned to land earlier. His mouth fell open while his eyes glazed over as if he didn't see Olivia anymore. Stiff hands slid down Olivia's arms; his body collapsed on the couch. Mom dropped to her knees in front of him, clutching his thighs. She squeezed them, leaning into his face.

"What does this mean? I don't understand, Conner! How can this be real?" Mom's chest heaved, her watery eyes gazed up at him, desperate for an answer. "She couldn't have seen—"

"Yes, she could have," his voice strained, as if he barely had the energy to speak. His gaze turned to Olivia, eyes rippling in pain. "If Delilah did the unimaginable... why do that? She's started something so cataclysmic... over what... me?" His head collapsed into his hands. "This is all my fault."

The shock of his response cooled her anger, sensing that her discovery was not only new to her, but to him as well. "Who's Delilah, Dad? What has she done? I need to know! Tell me... I can't stand these lies any longer." Olivia held her breath, waiting for the next revelation to send her world into another tailspin.

Will this ever end?

For a moment, Olivia wondered if he'd answer her, but Mom's hoarse whisper killed the silence.

"Tell her, Conner... tell her about Delilah. It's okay. We're a family again. We'll face this together." Mom pulled on Dad's hands, making him look at her. "I love you."

He choked down a sob and took Mom's face in his hands. "I don't deserve you, Stella." He leaned his forehead against hers. Olivia's stomach knotted as she steeled herself against their alliance, once again feeling like an outsider in their tangled love story.

"Dad..."

He stood up, bringing Mom with him. Mom turned her gaze to Olivia. "Before he tells you, I want you to understand that it was our intention to tell you this before my accident. Events unraveled so fast after that and I was recovering... well... the truth slipped away from us. I hoped the past would stay buried now that you were the guardian instead of your dad. But, in all honesty, I was a coward. My hope was for you to never learn the ugly secrets of our marriage. My shame or embarrassment for my part in it, was selfish and I'm sorry for the hurt it's caused you. I only ask one thing. That you try to find forgiveness... for both of us."

Her mom's words stunned Olivia. She lifted her chin and stared at her dad, who's gaze held shame, and a glimmer of grief.

"You may wonder why you don't have memories of Delilah or much of me." He licked his lips. "When you received the orb, memories of the Magi and past guardians are given to you, but those have to do with the guardianship, not our personal lives or struggles. That's too much information and those emotions are to be kept private. They release the collective memory over time to help you become a better fighter and understand the guardians of the past. It won't be long before they free them."

"We guessed that much; the Magi confirmed it." Olivia waved her hand in front of her. "Go on."

"Delilah was my guardian angel before Michael. Unbeknownst to me, Delilah had developed a bond with me that bordered on obsession when I reflect on it. When she was told to step aside for Michael, she was irate, unhinged by the thought of losing me. Secretly, she didn't let go. She'd come and check on me without Michael's or my knowledge. Even after I married your mom, she still peeked into my life, becoming more despondent as my world grew without her. But there was a period in our marriage that became very difficult for us. After you, we tried to have another child, but"—Connor shook his head—"we dealt with the pain and disappointment apart instead of together. I'd leave to train or hunt way too much. Your mom kept blaming herself, becoming depressed, so we withdrew from each other even more. Our only bright light was you." His eyes watered; throat working up and down.

"It was during this time Delilah came back into our lives." Mom's face was a careful mask, but anger simmered beneath the surface.

"Yes. She'd find me alone and soothe me with her angelic powers. I begged her to seek Stella and offer her the same comfort. Delilah told me she'd do it, but never did. I should have known"— he raked his hand through his hair—"I... I developed feelings for her... it was wrong. Then disaster struck when she found me in the middle of a battle. I had to tell her enough to satisfy her curiosity. I told her I was a demon hunter and the Mar of Sin was a portal. She doesn't know about the Magi, the other guardians, or any of the Mar of Sin's secrets. But it scared me that she'd push to find out more, so I gave her what she wanted hoping to keep her thoughts... preoccupied."

Olivia recoiled and scrunched up her face, "That's disgusting and horrible and—"

"I'm a monster. I know."

Olivia closed her mouth and jerked away. She started pacing the floor.

"I've sinned against God and my marriage. I bear that burden every day. After it happened, I was mortified, disgusted with myself. I tried to ignore her and tell her it was wrong, but she developed this fantasy that we'd be together, and I'd leave my family. I told her never, and she became enraged. That's when she threatened me. If I didn't leave you and Mom, she'd share what she learned with... Lucifer."

"What! That's crazy." It was Olivia's turn to crumble on to the couch, bile rising in her throat. "That's why you left? Because she blackmailed you!"

"When you asked me a few days ago about why I left, it was all true, except it was Delilah who saw me, not a second demon."

"Well, your half-truths were too late by then." Olivia threw her hands up, mind blown by this whole situation. "Just because you two have *finally* told me the truth, doesn't mean it's any a less bitter pill to swallow." Olivia pointed at her mom. "And you stood by him... after all that?" She raised her hand. "Don't answer. You obviously did and shared in his lies." Heat rose on Olivia's chest, creeping up her face. "So, because of your despicable actions, Delilah is now exacting her revenge?"

"It would seem so. If she went through the Mar of Sin"—he choked on the last words—"then we have to assume she's told Lucifer what she knows, which puts you, Zach, and Sergio in grave danger."

Olivia launched herself off the couch, sickened by her father. "That's just great! You're the one blazing the trail of lies, while everyone else gets caught up in your wake and pays the price. Well, I'm not lying or covering for either of you anymore. You can break the news to Michael and the Magi, because now I've got to tell my fellow guardians that because of you, Hell knows about us and *we* will suffer the consequences." She took a step back. "Thanks."

She turned and ran upstairs into her room, slamming the door behind her. She wanted to explode or punch something as she stalked across the carpet. Large silver scissors gleamed next to the black feather. Grabbing the handles, she strode into her bathroom and stared in the mirror.

How could he do that?

Forgive him... I despise him...

I'm not weak like him...

Her eyes flickered over her hair. She reached up and grabbed a long, wavy lock her dad had loved so much. Resolve washed over her as she took the scissors and cut her hair above the shoulders. She raised her hand in front of her, clutching the shorn piece, and felt...

Free.

The corner of her mouth lifted higher with each section she snipped. A fresh sense of self surfaced; of shedding away a part of her that had weighed down her spirit... her freedom. The harsh snapping of the blades resounded like claps, mixing with her excited breathing. It didn't take long before the clumps of hair covered the tile floor like dead leaves fanned around the trunk of a tree. She shook her head, delighted by the lightweight hair; the shearing of a mental burden. Staring back at herself in the mirror, stood a young woman freed of the last shackle that bound her.

The need for my father's validation...

I'll never crave that ever again.

CHAPTER
TWENTY-SIX

ZAR

The pit is alive...
I feel it...
I like it.

The vibration of the Damned's cries pounded within Zar, escalating his heart rate hammering inside him. He raised his sword, readying it as he anticipated his opponent's next move. The memory of the Realm of Envy's pit layout forever seared in his mind; the uneven gravel floor crunching beneath his boots as he made his way to the pole's dangling chains. Macabre green membranes glowed and moved, encased inside the steep circular walls of the black rock. The tunnel, which the beast stomped from to elicit his punishment, was to his right with its dark entrance crackling like a static rain, dictating how his world was now illuminated to him. Color left his life when his eyes were ripped from him, replaced with hues of gray and black. But color didn't matter anymore, and neither did his vison. Losing his natural sight was a daily reminder of the choices and mistakes of his past, directing the decisions of his present and future.

I'm a Fallen...
Made for the dark... not the light...
I'm not broken... I'm more resilient than ever.

Leviathan's rib cage raised up and down; the tribal markings across his chest and down his arms coursed with an energy matching his opponent. A grin stretched over his black face as he continued circling Zar.

"Your skills improve with each session. I'm impressed," Leviathan quipped as he appraised Zar with keen eyes and a warrior's lithe stance. "But you still have a long way to go before you beat me."

He sensed the subtle shift of Leviathan's feet; the shadows across his six wings shifted as the feathers prepared for flight, along with the smug gleam in his eyes that victory was within reach.

Gotcha...

Zar launched to his left, then twirled in the air, coming down behind his teacher. With as much force and power as he could muster, he planted his feet into his back. Leviathan, committed to his forward attack from the air, couldn't correct his path in time, grunted from the hit. Zar grabbed a hold of his dreadlocks and sent an electrical charge through the twisted black hair, then over his body. Leviathan hit the ground first with him crouched on his back. Gravel and dust flew up around them as Zar tightened his grip and yanked back Leviathan's head. He thrust his sword under his black chin and bent down close to his ear.

"You were saying?" Zar sneered, exhilarated at having bested his Realm Prince and mentor. But the thrill shifted to unease. The hard skin on his back tingled, his feathers ruffled with the sense of being watched by a new presence in the pit. Foreboding shot through him; Zar's muscles tightened as his head turned up, seeking the unwelcomed visitor from above.

"Then you better get off my back before I—"

"Well done, Zar. It's been a long time since I've seen Leviathan's face shoved in the ground," came a voice raining down, chuckling at his own words.

Lucifer jumped off the lip of the pit's jagged edge, his six enormous wings erupting behind him. He spiraled down in a lazy circle to the elation of its occupants. Their wails and shrieks deafening as Lucifer skimmed the wall's edges as if his wings were reaching out and touching the Damned trapped in their membrane prison. Leviathan shoved Zar's shoulder as they rose from the ground. His glare promised he would pay for besting him in front of their Master. Zar dusted himself off while a ripple of apprehension washed over him.

What's he doing here?

Zar's focus perceived Lucifer's gentle and pretentious descent. He rarely came inside any of the Realm's pits, disgusted by the Damned even though his life's work brought them here.

Why are you putting on a show for us? Is this flaunting for me, Leviathan... or the Damned?

Lucifer glided to a landing without stirring the dusty floor. Strutting with his wings still expanded behind him, he grinned from ear to ear. Zar raised his guard, his hand still tight on the sword. He sensed Leviathan's body tensing, his feet shifting to a wider stance as Lucifer's wings had yet to retract. When he stopped before them, he chuckled as his black soulless eyes roamed over them.

"My, you two must still have the thrill of a good fight raging in your veins if you're wary of my approach," Lucifer's massive wings retracted at a slow pace.

Leviathan bowed his head and Zar followed suit. "Master, I'm honored by your presence in the Realm of Envy's Pit. It's been some time since you've graced us—"

"Too long, indeed," he bellowed, tilting his head up to the pit. "My blood stirs near the Damned. I feed off their... dark, wild energy. I need their depraved spirits at their peak, for the time of their purpose is nearing. What better way to excite them than to have their Master come to their... home?" The Damned pounded their feet, the membrane thinning, moving like a bag full of agitated snakes. He raised his hands and closed his eyes, absorbing the frantic adulation. "But my visit here is two-fold."

Zar resisted the desire to step back as the benevolent cloak for his audience slipped away, revealing the unpredictable and maniacal Lucifer that he was more unnervingly familiar with... on all levels.

"Delilah informs me of your daily training with Leviathan and with... what's the Degasus's name?" Lucifer tilted his head like an interested lover, but the fire holding his black pupils burned brighter.

"Cydanos," replied Zar cautiously.

"Aw, yes... well, they're magnificent, intelligent beasts... curious." Lucifer let the offense hang while he moved to Leviathan. "Your skills as a teacher are much appreciated, but no longer needed. You've got a Realm vital to my plans. Have your Fallen ready." His voice rumbled with excitement, yet was laced with an undeniable threat.

"We'll not fail you," Leviathan bowed low, a darkness shadowing his features before his long locks concealed it. His hand remained clenched tucked at his side.

"Zar. Come with me." Lucifer turned his back on them, knowing he would obey his order. He sheathed his sword. Leviathan whose face was now a cool mask watched him take flight. The cries erupted again as he followed Lucifer to the top. But there was no lazy path this time, his wings disappearing quickly over the pit's edge. Zar reached the top and entered the undulating light show of the tunnel, playing along Lucifer's wings like shattered moonlight on a rippling black lake. His flight in a direct line for his tower... and away from the Damned he abhorred.

What does he want... and what's the rush?

Zar flew into the massive metal doors opened on one side of the Throne Room's roof. They dwarfed him as he passed through, wondering why the doors were open today. His pulse quickened, his body alert in case his Master unleashed one of his unpredictable moods on him. When he landed, his wings snapped closed as he strode toward Lucifer, who stood with his hands behind his back, watching Tannin's sleek body breaking through the inky water's surface.

"He's beautiful, isn't he?" he murmured as Zar stopped beside him. The behemoth glided across the water as if it knew it was being admired.

"He is... unless you're his next meal." Zar smirked.

Lucifer nodded. "But deserving if I make it so." He turned toward him, making a slow examination from head to toe. "You seem to be recovering well from your punishment. Having your eyes ripped out has given you a deeper strength... a darker fire. Stripped that insipid softness holding you back from your potential."

"I'm glad you notice a difference. I have only wanted to please you"—Zar bowed his head— "and bring demise to mankind."

"You've done well and proven me wise when I gave you my feather, claiming your place as one of my chosen." They both turned to the lethal black feather at the top of Zar's wing; glowing with a darkness unlike any of his others. Zar pushed his shoulder back, expanding his lungs with a deep, satisfying breath.

"It is my bigger honor, my Lord."

Lucifer leaned in closer, his eyes churning with an evil light. "But never assume again it will save your life. You've used that advantage. Disobey me again and I will pluck it out and toss you limb by limb to my serpent. Understood?"

"Completely," Zar replied, not wavering in his stance.

"Good. Then I can rely on you to carry out your next mission." Lucifer paced in front of the pool, his movements exciting the serpent. "Change is in the air, but not of my making. A loathsome, vicious energy prowls within my Realms. Forces working against me... undermining me with their plotting. This insidious force is unknown... maddening, as I can't locate its source. It is linked with these foul guardians, I know it. That's why I require you, and only you, to find these other guardians. You have seen them. I need to learn more about them. Who trains them, what their powers are, and what are their plans?"

"But I no longer have my sight—"

Lucifer's crack of harsh laughter echoed in the empty massive hall. "Your sight is better than ever. You have deeper sight, which is why I want you to use this to root out the traitor."

He stopped pacing and walked past Zar, his boots slapping in the water lapping over the pool's edge. "Leviathan will not take kindly to the student beating the master. Be on guard with him."

"I'll find the answers you seek."

"I'm sure you will. Your life depends on it."

Zar's thick blood pounded in his veins, excited to be tapped for this secret mission even though his life was in danger.

My life is always in danger.

"There's one more thing." Lucifer stopped at the foot of the stairs leading to his throne. Zar lifted his head, sensing the dragon's face chiseled into the granite. The hairs on his neck rose, feeling like the dragon stared at him with a malicious regard.

"Anything."

A smile stretched across Lucifer's hard features. "Delilah."

Zar tried to hide the spike of anxiety zipping through him. He remained silent, not wanting to step into an unforeseen trap when he'd gotten so close to Lucifer again.

"Our beautiful Fallen is not all that she portrays on the surface. There has been an unfamiliar smell on her. Not that I care who she throws herself at out of my bed," he scoffed, "but I believe she may seek a new alliance... someone whom she can better manipulate than, say... me. I know she comes to you and guides you through the Realms, whispering in your ear. Is she sharing her secrets with you?"

Oh no... he is setting a trap.

"Her mindless gossip of what she sees around us holds no secrets. She does not understand my sight. I put up with her droning to enhance the perception that I'm not as strong as I was. It's an advantage to me to have the Fallen underestimate me."

"Very devious of you. Good. Pass along anything of interest you discover from her."

Zar nodded at him, not wishing to speak more than needed.

"The time will come soon, where she must prove herself. I'm tiring of her and I need the information she's keeping from me. Unfortunately, she holds the key to these guardians, so I've devised a way for her to reveal her true intentions. Be on guard... she'll run to you for help." Lucifer turned and ascended the stairs. He waved his hand at him. "Leave me now."

He backed away, making his way for the tall arched doors on the other side of the pool.

"And Zar."

Zar stopped and glanced over his shoulder.

"Do not let your love for Delilah get you killed."

His jaw clenched, the muscle flexing in his temple. All of his troubles began when he saw her that fateful day in the park.

I should have strangled her like I wanted to, but no.

I had to say hi.

Idiot.

CHAPTER
TWENTY-SEVEN

MELCHIOR

S *ilence...*
Deafening in its weight of the future untold...

Melchior leaned back against the pew, worn smooth from sitting in the same spot for... too long. He exhaled deeply as he gazed at the large wooden cross engulfing his vision. There was peace for him in these quiet times; a place where he corrected his course through prayer and solitude. But an unease nagged at him of late, and he couldn't discern the source even in these moments. It was like waiting for a sliver of glass to work its way out when all he wanted to do was slice his finger open and pull it out himself. Whatever was the cause, it would come to light in God's time, not his.

You've learned this lesson, Mel... stop fighting it.

Powerful muscles rippled as he stood and walked to the door leading to the passageway behind the hanging cross. Cool air washed over him when he entered, and more followed, traversing the dim corridor he knew so well. The stone staircase ahead of him beckoned with a soft glow illuminating the ancient archway. Some of his uneasiness ebbed away when he rushed down the stairs to the Weapons Room. This was a place where he understood his role and performed his duties with all the honor he possessed. He slipped through the shimmering veil and gazed around the room, scanning the translucent shelves full of weapons made for the Guardians. The white flames licked at the tall ceiling within the massive pit. He closed his eyes and took a deep breath, preparing for the visitor's arrival from within the fire.

Why did Michael want to meet me today? Is Olivia—

The flames crackled, heat flaring, announcing the visitor. Melchior's body tensed and his eyes opened as he stepped into a wider stance. His right hand moved up and touched the blue steel handle of the dagger resting at his hip. His brow creased at his unusual reaction.

You need to relax...

Michael emerged through the flame's blazes, unscathed by the fire, yet his intensity matched the blaze surrounding him. He dashed down the wide granite steps. Melchior slid his hand from his side, but nervous energy ran up his spine. Michael's quick footsteps echoed as he approached with his hand outstretched. Their hands met in the middle, gripping each other's forearm in the familiar greeting.

"Peace be with you, my friend," Michael's deep voice rumbled.

"And also, with you," Melchior raised his other hand to clasp his shoulder. "To what do I owe the honor of your visit today?"

Michael's blue eyes sparked; his hand slipped from Melchior's forearm. His wings fluttered as if a shiver ran through them, stirring the blue tips. "I have grave news to share that will bring dire consequences for our young guardians."

A heat flushed through Melchior. "What has happened? Has Lucifer—"

Michael shook his head. "It's about Conner and the lies kept hidden. Let's walk."

Melchior's fists bunched at his side; his breathing harsh in his ears. He turned and fell in line with Michael while Melchior braced himself for whatever dire news was coming.

"Does this have to do with why he left his family? I knew he was keeping secrets from me... I should have pushed—"

"Mel. It doesn't matter. You can't perceive all they do or feel. A part of them stays private from us... it is only fair to give them this one piece of space when we ask for so much in return. All the guardians have kept their secrets. Their humanity demands it. Conner is no different, but his mistake might have the highest cost." Michael's jaw twitched as he scanned the armor-ladened walls surrounding them until his eyes settled on its prize.

Melchior followed his gaze and walked over to the shelf. His long fingers circled around the grip of Sandalphon and lifted Olivia's sword. He handed it to Michael, igniting the flame inside of the blue jewel nestled at the hilt. He turned the sword over, nodding at the masterpiece.

"Sandalphon created a beauty for our girl," Melchior sensed Michael's need for another moment before sharing his unwanted news.

"Indeed. Zemira tells me she's a fine and nimble swordsman. She will need the full capacity of all her skills." Michael's heavy sigh blew across the blade, igniting the ancient scroll embedded in the shining silver metal. Nodding, he laid it back on the shelf before turning to Melchior.

"This begins with Delilah, Conner's guardian angel, before I took her place." Michael unraveled the twisted story of Conner and Delilah's forbidden love, her threats causing him to leave, and what happened upon his return. Melchior's heart sunk, and knots of dread tightened with each fateful word. Michael revealed what Olivia saw in her ill-fated meditation, followed by the fight between her and her parents.

"Now we must face the unimaginable truth that Delilah took the fall into the Mar of Sin, survived it as well as her encounter with whoever she met on the other side. We also have to assume she divulged what she knows to Lucifer. This changes everything for Olivia, Zach, and Sergio."

Melchior clenched his teeth together, keeping his heated words locked inside while the seriousness of the disaster churned within him. What he wanted to do was confront Conner, but it would only create a greater conflict he didn't have the time nor the energy to spend repairing it. Besides, who was he to judge stupidity when he was Heaven's greatest fool. He ran his fingers through his thick silver mane, trying not to tear it out in frustration. Michael's watchful eyes were upon him, but Melchior turned away and paced around the pit's flickering flames lighting his way. His mind created potential solutions while it searched for clues that he missed about Conner.

The Archangel hadn't moved, his hands behind his back, tracking Melchior with steely blue eyes. When Melchior returned to the spot, he had a firm grip on his turbulent emotions.

Michael raised his brows. "Well..."

Melchior faced his mentor and friend, bound by a sacred link created on that fateful day in Heaven. They faced a trial, but this time on the same side, challenging the rise of their mutual enemy together.

"I suspect Delilah has an unlikely ally and his name is Zar. They were both from the Green Kingdom of Kindness and were close, if memory serves, before the Fall. Somehow, they've reconnected and became a diabolic duo. It explains why he and his thugs jumped the kids. I'm not so sure Delilah has divulged to Lucifer all she learned. She'd be of no use to him if she lost her leverage. If she was desperate enough to become a Fallen, then she has a devious plan and is playing a very dangerous game."

"I agree with you. She and Zar would make a deceitful, nasty team."

Melchior nodded, his mind swirling with possibilities. "This also explains the uptick in demon activity you've noticed. It makes sense if Lucifer felt he had an upper hand in knowing about the Mar of Sin without our knowledge, but he doesn't know all its secrets. The kids haven't even been told yet. The real question is, what is he doing with this information... whatever she shared with him? Did it whet his appetite to increase the war between Angels and Fallen or has it escalated his plan?"

"To carry out his threat..."

"To destroy Heaven."

Michael laid his hand on Melchior's shoulder. "We'll not let that happen, my friend. Our newest guardians are ready for the rest of their responsibilities."

Melchior returned the gesture, feeding on the peace and confidence exuding from him. "They go on their first hunt tonight. Then we'll reveal the secrets they will bear."

"You and the Magi have served the Heavens and guardians well and without pause. You're prepared for what lies ahead." Michael's hand slipped from his shoulder, nodding as he turned and walked up the steps and into the flames from which he came.

CHAPTER
TWENTY-EIGHT

ZACH

L iv's text message last night was short... and cryptic.

Meet me at 9 at Cuppa Joes. Don't train until we talk.

Zach wanted to ask her more, but decided a simple *okay* was a better plan. He'd tossed and turned all night wondering why she wanted to talk in person before their morning training session.

Did I do something wrong?

Is Liv still upset with me and Sergio?

What if she wants me to quit because of Cody?

The unsettling scenarios he'd created, combined with the lack of sleep, left him with a morning fog. No amount of angelic powers overcame an aching heart.

Zach first swung by and picked up Sergio. Hurrying towards the truck, Sergio's jet-black hair was longer than usual, falling across his forehead onto his brows. He climbed into the cab, his shadowed eyes glancing his way before turning to look out the windshield.

"Hey," Zach scanned his friend's wiry body. "You know why Olivia wants to meet us?"

Sergio shook his head. "Nope. Unless it's to lecture us about our duel in the forest last night. Olivia has a mind of her own."

Zach shook his head and pulled away from the curb. Didn't he know that for a fact? He missed her... the Liv that changed his life before the guardianship, but ever since their fight in her backyard—

"Uh, about last night. I'm sorry I was a jerk and I'm sorry about your friend." Sergio soft voice echoed inside the truck's cabin.

Zach glanced over, finding Sergio's relaxed and sincere brown eyes staring at him. Zach realized he missed this part of Sergio, too. Since Manny's death, a crust of hard bitterness had covered him. Zach needed to find a way to break through to both of his friends before they lost themselves... and their essence.

How much have I changed? Have I hardened like them, too?

"Thanks, man. And don't worry about last night. I'm sure if you had wanted to hit me with the throwing stars, I'd have the scar to prove it," Zach smirked.

"Damn straight." Sergio cracked a smile before settling back in his seat.

They rode in silence the rest of the way; Sergio keeping his own counsel while he worked on calming his nerves. He parked his truck in the front row, the bright morning sun reflecting off the glass windows, obscuring his view as he scanned for Liv. His stomach twisted as he turned off the truck's rumbling engine. They jumped out, Sergio reaching the entrance door first. The bells jingled as they walked through the door. Rich aromas of ground coffee laced with the enticing smell of baked goodies sent rumbles through his empty stomach. The cafe was half-full. Murmurs and the whirl of the coffee machine mixed with his pounding pulse.

Get a hold of yourself. She's fine—

He hesitated when he caught sight of Liv behind the counter.

Wow...

It was all his stunned mind came up with when the bolt of stone-cold attraction struck him.

Gone was Olivia's mane of dark-blond hair. Now its blunt ends brushed against the top of her shoulders, framing her face in strands of loose waves. Her striking eyes looked larger, her lips fuller, her jaw line sharper. He'd thought her long hair had accentuated her beauty, but he was wrong. It hid it.

My goose is cooked.

Zach took a step, but his shoe caught a chair leg, causing a loud clatter against the floor. He flushed as he untangled his foot and shoved it back under the table. When he looked up, she was staring at him, a smile tugging at the corner of her lips. He smiled back, but he hoped the heat he felt wasn't blazing in his eyes like it was in his heart.

"Finally, chica!" Sergio's cry of approval widened her smile. "Muy bueno!"

Zach reached the counter as Sergio grasped her chin, turning her head from side to side. "Although, whoever cut it needs glasses." He chuckled when she swatted his hand away.

"I did it last night... time for a change." Her eyes deflated along with her playful mood. She tilted her head, turning to Zach. "Hi."

"Hi," Zach cleared his throat. "Hair looks fine"—his mind went blank—"Better for battles."

Seriously dude... you're an idiot.

He stifled his groan, his armpits breaking out in a sweat. Sergio snickering didn't help. Zach turned his attention to the menu wall behind her, his insides slowly dying.

"You guys want some coffee?"

"Sure," Sergio pipped up. "And a chocolate chip muffin, too. I'm starving." He nudged Zach.

"That'd be great," he replied, nodding like a bobblehead.

Olivia returned with two to-go cups and two fat muffins. Joe emerged from the hallway, staring at them as he walked behind the counter.

"Hey, guys." He turned to Olivia. "Ready for your break?"

"Yep. I'm going out back for a little sunshine. Come with me?" She raised an eyebrow at Sergio and Zach. They nodded and grabbed Olivia's offerings.

Sergio had half the muffin in his mouth when he mumbled some nonsense. Zach took a swig of coffee, hoping the caffeine would knock some sense back into him.

"What did you say?"

"Remind me to use your *better for battles* line the next time I meet a cute girl, Boy Scout." Sergio grinned at Zach before he inhaled the rest of the muffin.

"Funny. Just move it." Zach nudged Sergio toward the hallway where Olivia had already disappeared. Zach pushed open the back door, relishing the cool air on his flushed face. She sat on her bumper, her faced tilted up toward the sun. She opened her eyes when they stopped in front of her. The shorter hair made her eyes look bigger, but it didn't disguise the dark smudges beneath them.

"Thanks for coming." She hooked her hair behind an ear, exposing the four dainty earrings running up the lobe. "I did something last night after we left the Magi that I shouldn't have, but I'm glad I did." She stood up, crossing her arms.

Sergio's brow furrowed. "Okay. What did you do?"

"Remember the white feather in the jar? I've always been curious about where it came from, so I... uh... did meditation to find the owner." Olivia paused, twisting the silver dragonfly earring between her fingers.

Zach leaned forward, not liking where this was going. "Did you find them?"

She exhaled. "Yep. And it wasn't good. Turns out it belongs to an angel named Delilah; my dad's first Guardian Angel turned lover."

Coffee sprayed from Sergio's mouth over the asphalt, his eyes bulging. "What!" He wiped his hand across his face. "What do you mean lover?"

"Wait. Start from the beginning." Zach's jaw clenched tighter as she unraveled the events: Delilah and Zar, the argument with her parents, her father's betrayal, and the potential danger it posed. By the time she finished, the muffin weighed like cement brick in his stomach

"So, I cut my hair. I was pissed off. It was that or shred my bed

187

comforter." She started pacing, hands clenched at her sides. "I'm so sorry my dad has put us in jeopardy. I still can't believe—"

"Don't worry about us, Liv. This isn't your fault. At least we now have knowledge of what we're facing. We can have an upper hand on Lucifer." Zach gazed past her shoulder, musing over the possibilities.

Olivia stood up, placing her hands on her hips. "How? If he knows—"

"We don't have any idea what Delilah told him. This way, we prepare for the worst, so we're ready for another possible attack," Zach crossed his arms, frustrated she was fighting him.

"What about Zar? Do you think he saw you?" Sergio sneered.

Olivia pinched the bridge of her nose. "No, his back was to me. I only saw Delilah. But I think this means they're a team."

"Zar is mine. He's the reason Manny—"

"Stop it, Sergio." Olivia pointed a finger at him and then Zach. "Both of you"—her finger dropped—"and me, too." She shook her head like she was berating herself. "We haven't been acting as a team. I did something foolish last night that could have gotten me caught or even killed. And you two weren't training in the forest... you were fighting each other like enemies, not teammates. I need to trust you both and you need to trust me. We aren't a team, a guardianship, if we continue to act alone, being reckless because we think we are smarter, stronger... invincible. Sergio"—she faced him—"you have got to let go of your anger. It's clouding your—"

"Don't you dare tell me to let Manny go—"

"I said anger, not Manny. They're different, but you're making them the same."

Sergio stepped back, running his hands through his hair. "I try, but my blood boils—"

"Then your blood will spill." Their heads jerked at Zach. "And ours too if we aren't careful. Our first hunt is tonight. We have to be laser-focused. The Fallen have fought with Angels throughout time and are still alive. Our skills and powers are new. We're infantile compared to them. We can't ever forget that." Zach glared at Olivia and Sergio, daring them to fight back.

Sergio growled, his head fell forward, but Liv stared at him with eyes he hadn't seen in a long time... unguarded.

"Okay... on that note, I better get back to work." She set off across the lot. "I'll see you later... and happy hunting," Olivia called out over her shoulder.

Zach scoffed. "You, too."

Sergio didn't reply, instead headed for the front of the building. He rolled his eyes and followed Sergio, understanding it would be an uncomfortable ride home with his irritated passenger. He threw his coffee cup in the dumpster, his need for caffeine gone after Liv's story. Zach turned the corner, happy with at least one outcome.

Her wall is down... let's hope it stays that way.

CHAPTER
TWENTY-NINE

OLIVIA

From light to dark.
From prey to hunter.

The portal closed behind Olivia, leaving the air singed in its wake. Her heart drummed an excited beat as she scanned the surroundings of the gloomy street located a few blocks from the downtown neon lights of Vegas. Nothing was glamorous about the cinder block buildings boasting tired graffiti and barred windows. Bass music thumped through the still air from a bar across the street. A couple stumbled out the metal front door, creaking shut behind them. They leaned against the building's wall, entangled in each other. Husky laughter floated as they staggered away from the bar, soon lost when they turned the dark street corner.

Her nostrils flared at the insult of booze and rotting garbage coming from the narrow alley next to her. Even though she was invisible with her angelic shield around her, she walked with caution on the uneven sidewalk. Olivia's senses were humming, all focused for any signal from her mark that a demon was near.

My first hunt...

The black, sleek armor Olivia had worn during her training moved like a second skin, barely a whisper as her feet tread in light, quick strides. The early morning hours were quieter here than the hustle and bustle of frenzied downtown, giving her a better chance to find a lone demon. She turned down the opposite street corner, her back skimmed across the rough building. A breeze licked at the sweat on her neck, lifting her hair... and the skin of her mark.

She froze.

Where are you?

Two figures emerged from the shadows a block down the street. Shoulders hunched, they hustled through the light from a street post and back into dim night. But it was just enough to see the shadow lurking behind them casting an orange hue.

Gluttony.

Olivia smirked and pushed herself away from the wall. Energy whipped through her as she ran across the street, not wanting to lose her prey. The familiar burn of Orion increased, but she now found the sensation reassuring. She unsheathed Sandalphon, readying her sword. Blood pumped in her ears. She rushed to the corner the figures had just vacated, focusing on her task at hand. The two men stopped halfway down the street, one leaning inside the driver's side window of a car. The other's head, face shrouded with a hoodie, swiveled and scanned the deserted street. Her target hung back closer to the building. It's smoke-like wispy strands floated above the sidewalk, orange eye sockets trained upon the men. The driver and man's rapid hand movements didn't distract her like it appeared to with the demon.

Good... got you now.

Olivia trotted down the sidewalk, her two hands raised the sword. Her eyes widen when the demon's turned its blazing orange globes to her. She remembered the first time a demon connected with her, terrifying her with his malicious intent in the cafe, but she wasn't the same scared, defenseless girl. She was a trained demon slayer, guardian of Orion, and she wouldn't be defeated.

The demon transformed as she charged it, going from a smoky apparition to a black-clad amazon. Three horns dipped in orange matched the color weaving through her white hair and talon fingertips.

"What is this?" The she-demon's lips peeled back, revealing sharp black teeth. Its head jerked, taking quick sniffs. "You dare to approach me... who are you, filthy human girl?" she yanked her sword from its sheath. The blade sparked with balls of electricity, its crackle splitting the night's air.

"My name doesn't matter, unless it's the last word you want to hear before you die!" Olivia matched the demon hatred, stopping within striking distance.

"Then here's mine. Baluk!" The she-demon's name roared from her dark cavernous mouth. She spread her feet and bent her knees, her orange eyes assessing her adversary.

A quick burst of a police car siren split the air. The men took off, chased by one cop who exited the patrol car. For a moment, Olivia thought they would burst through their dimension, but they turned between the buildings, swallowed up by the alley. The sedan's engine roared to life, tires screeching as it peeled away from the curb. The driver sped down the street, the police car turned around and gave chase.

Startled by the erupting chaos, it caught Olivia off guard when the demon leaped into the air, her pitch-black wings spread wide. Baluk descended with a piercing screech, her sword raised high. Time slowed even though Olivia had little time to react. She spun and lunged away, but Baluk's sword slashed across her calf. Pain erupted in her leg, but the armor held firm. Baluk hissed, bringing the sword up again. Its sizzling as frightening as its owner. Olivia turned and sprayed blue flames at the demon. Baluk howled and closed her wings around her, deflecting the fire like a shield.

"No human has this power!" Baluk lowered her wings and tossed an orange glob at Olivia's feet. She leapt into the air before it exploded. Olivia threw her body in front of the energy wave, driving her toward Baluk. Surprise registered on the demon's face, freezing her long enough to give Olivia an open shot. She reached for her throwing knife tucked at her hip and threw it at the demon. The sleek blue handle hit its mark, lodged in the demon's eye. Its talons clawed for the blade, but Olivia swung her sword as she landed. Her cry of triumph overpowered Baluk's nightmarish squeals. The weapon slashed through the demon's neck, her head flew into the air, silenced. Black blood erupted from the severed neck like an inky fountain, spurting with the last beat of its heart. The orange demon exploded into ash and disappeared, taking the pungent streaks of oily blood with her.

Olivia dropped Sandalphon to her side, her harsh breathing now the only sound she heard.

I did it... I really did it!

Adrenaline coursed through her. She bent over and retrieved her knife. Her throbbing calf grabbed her attention. Running her hand over the sleek armor, she found a slight indent, but the ache beneath was subsiding. Olivia closed her eyes, relieved that it hadn't been worse. She stood and opened her portal, elated she'd step through a victor in her first hunt. Her heart skipped a beat as the Weapon's Room blossomed before her.

But did the same hold true for Zach and Sergio?

Olivia stepped through the portal, greeted by Melchior's intimidating body blocking her way. He crossed his arms over his barrel chest and stared at her. Olivia's brow creased, wondering if she had done something wrong, but a smile spread across his face. He nodded his head, a twinkle glinted in his eyes.

"Well done, Olivia. Baluk was a worthy rival. Your reaction was slow in the beginning but riding the pressure wave was a great recovery." Melchior placed his hand on Olivia's shoulder, his long fingers giving her a squeeze.

"Thank you." She flushed with her simple reply. He patted her shoulder and his brief nod told her it'd been enough.

"Are Zach and Sergio back?" She lifted on her tiptoes, trying to spy her friends.

Melchior's face turned sober. "Zach has returned unharmed, but we await Sergio. Bal is linked with him, so I dare not intrude."

Olivia's stomach flipped when Melchior stepped aside, and Zach came into view. He stood next to Caspar talking in a hushed tone, but everything about his stance screamed confident warrior. His short hair was slick with sweat, his body taunt and sure. Zach glanced at her, the corner of his mouth lifting, showing off the dimple in his cheek. She felt a brick in her wall crumble when his emerald eyes didn't waver from hers, only darkening with intensity the closer she got to him. The tug for him she tried to deny herself couldn't be disguised in this moment of raw emotion. She stopped in front of him, noticing the fading angry lash on his jawline. Olivia reached up, and with a feather-like touch, ran her finger over the mark. His jaw clinched beneath it; nostrils flaring at her examination.

"I hope the demon paid dearly for this." Olivia's hand fell to her side, but her fingertip tingled where it had grazed Zach's skin.

"With his life."

Caspar cleared his throat. Olivia turned to find an amused look on his face. "I take it your hunt was successful?" He raised an eyebrow, cocking his head.

She narrowed her eyes but grinned back instead of stomping on his foot. "Yes. A demon from Gluttony Realm inciting two drug dealers. She got the first lick in, but it's the last one that matters. What about you, Zach?"

"Lust. Pimp pushing minors. Sometimes I wish we could take out who the demons are attached to... two birds with one stone."

"That's a hard feeling to deny, but you must not interfere with their free will. Sometimes when they are freed from the demon's influences, they're able to fight the evil choking them and turn away." Caspar stared at Olivia and Zach. "You need to concentrate on the positive, or the negative will create a darkness in you too."

Dad's betrayal has certainly left a black hole in me.

Sergio's gold portal flared in the room, diverting Olivia's attention from Zach and Caspar's words hitting a little too close to home. Sergio stormed through the opening, chest heaving, still clutching his sword, Nisroc. He fell to his knees and dropped his weapon. He clutched his rib cage. Bal was upon him, but he batted him away.

"I'm fine. Just need to get out... *armor off.*" He sighed in relief. The armor folded itself and rested on the floor next to him.

Olivia took a step, but Caspar's long fingers wrapped around her arm. "Give him a moment."

Her shoulders sagged, but Caspar was right. Sergio didn't need anyone but Bal. Sergio's sweat-soaked shirt was plastered to his chest. He hissed when Bal touched his side but nodded in answer to his murmurings. When he rose, she tugged on her arm, easily freeing it from Caspar's hold. She ran over, Zach close behind, noting the tension radiating between Bal and Sergio.

"I'm not bleeding... his hammer hit me just right is all." Sergio didn't look at them but must have sensed their approach. Irritation flared along with a spark of hurt.

What has made you so hard? Is it still Manny or something more?

She placed her hand on his arm. "Hey... what—"

He glared at her with hooded eyes, pulling away. "I'm good. Don't worry about me. I killed that blood thirsty demon—no problem. He just got around me is all. One down—"

"You were careless when you entered the alley." Bal's golden eyes churned even though his expression was unreadable. Sergio's face turned to stone, diverting his eyes from his mentor. "Your biggest advantage is your element of surprise. If you lose that, they get the jump on you. We have lost past guardians because of this. You're not invincible."

"I got the demon. Can you at least give me that?"

"Yes. You succeeded in your mission. Now that your first slaying is behind you, I hope next time you leave your emotions here and let your mind and skills do the fighting."

Sergio's lips pressed into a hard line. He exhaled through his nose and returned Bal's stare. "Ya... I'll work on that." Sergio glanced at Olivia and Zach. "You guys get hit?"

"Calf."

"Jaw."

Bal ran his hand over his beard. "Then I guess we have our first battle scars. Come on. Let's go get you something to eat."

Olivia scoffed, knowing she had more than external scars from today. An internal battle raged inside her, with no clear victor in sight.

Zach.

Is the wall worth building again or am I ready to let you back in?

I'd rather fight another demon than figure out this mess.

Careful what you wish...

CHAPTER
THIRTY

CAMILLA

S he paced over the colorful rug, further wearing a path created over many years of worrying about the ones she loved. Sometimes sleepless nights drove her out of her lonely bed. But other times, when Javier was on a hunt, she'd pray for his protection and for his safe return. It was all there was left for her to do. Camilla stopped and studied herself in the dresser's mirror. If she was honest with herself, there were occasions when the yearning to do battle cut deep inside her. She longed for a sense of vitality again in the face of her enemy. She missed it: the purpose, the challenge, the adrenaline of the hunt... and the kill. She shook her head, chiding herself for these selfish thoughts. Her pride had always been her downfall.

Camilla moved to her nightstand and picked up the silver-framed photo of her precious grandchildren, Sergio and Lucia. She ran her finger over Sergio's happy-go-lucky face.

I miss your sweet smile, nieto...

Her grandson had changed when Manny died in his arms. He lost his innocence that horrible night and a hardness... a darkness, settled in its place. Tonight, he would go on his first hunt, taking up the mantle from the generations before him. Camilla's chest filled with pride, but her heart squeezed with worry. Her finger fluttered over Lucia, tracing to the wheelchair she sat so regally upon, comfortable in her own skin. Camilla lifted her hand away and created a fist.

How can Lucia be a guardian? I can't send her into battle—

A loud knock on her door startled her. "*Si?*" Camilla returned the frame back to its place, sending a prayer up for her grandchildren.

"It's me. Can I come in?" Javier's voice didn't sound like he was asking. She glanced at the crosses above her bed before turning to face her son.

"Of course, *mi hijo.*"

The door swung open. When he stepped inside, Javier's edgy presence crackled the air. His jaw set in a hard line, determination glinting in his eyes. Camilla had seen this same look on him before he left on a hunt. The demeanor so similar to when he'd confront her on her failings as a parent... and a wife.

So, I'm the prey tonight...

"I need to ask you a question and I want an honest answer. No protecting anyone. Just the truth," his voice deceptively calm, unlike the coiled anger simmering beneath the surface.

Dawning came swift.

He knows...

She raised her chin along with an eyebrow, replying with only a nod. He stepped closer, but she held her ground, not flinching from his scathing stare.

"Lucia? Come here please."

Camilla's stomach dropped. She clasped her hands together, hoping to hide their trembling. "Javier—" was all she could say before Lucia wheeled into the room, her face pale under light brown skin. Her eyes widened as if sending a silent plea to Camilla. "*Abuela...* I'm—"

"Pull your shirt over, Lucia."

"Papa—"

"Now, *por favor.*" Camilla and Javier watched Lucia stretch the t-shirt collar, exposing her raised mark of Orion. Javier's nostrils flared when he focused on his mama. "Did you know Lucia was a guardian? Don't insult me with what I can see with my own eyes."

Camilla's mind raced with a myriad of replies, but she could only give one answer if for no other reason than to protect her grand-daughter. "Yes. I discovered her mark the night Sergio received his orb... when a Sloth demon attacked her in her room." Javier's body tensed; his face turned to stone. "I saw the mark on her shoulder when I held her. Her nightgown had slipped to the side."

"A Lessor?" Javier asked, his voice strained.

"Yes, I believed I'd been protecting her—" Camilla stopped, understanding her reasonings fell on deaf ears.

Javier ran his hands down his face, lips pressed together as if holding in back the flood gate of rushing words. "Manny drove by the house on his way home. He stopped to check on us and heard Lucia's screams. He barged inside and killed it with an angelic blade of mine I had given him."

"What!" Javier leaned in with murder in his eyes. "How could you keep this from me? You should have told—"

A heat rose on Camilla's chest, creeping up her face. "I needed to think. I was scared for Lucia! And you were with Sergio. I didn't understand how there could be another guardian. I wanted to ask Gabriel first, but—"

"But what, Mama? I'm her papa—"

"Manny died." Camilla's heart ripped open, spilling out a white-hot pain. The anguish fueled an anger, hurling her over its scorching flames. But now, the agony pummeled her with grief and stripped her bare. "So, I kept quiet, and we met with Gabriel."

Please forgive me...

Javier backed away as if she'd slapped him. "Gabriel... Lucia has met him? I—he told you not to tell me?" He placed a hand over his heart.

"No... no." Camilla shook her head and reached for Javier's arm, but he jerked away. He paced across the same strip of rug she'd vacated in what seemed so long ago. "He said to tell you and that he'd look for answers, but he hasn't shared his findings with me. Please don't be mad at Lucia. I asked for her silence."

Javier stopped and faced her. His mouth twisted in an ugly sneer. "Lucia is mine, not yours! You had no right to hide this from me and Sophia. She and Sergio are all we have left"—pain rippled over his face — "and yet you try to separate us... control over what you had no business doing."

"Papa," Lucia sobbed, "stop, please!"

"Once again, it comes back to you and your web of lies. I assumed that behavior was in the past. When Papa died... and you were almost taken from me that same night, I prayed your days of secrets were over... you'd learned your lesson, but no—no." Javier pointed his finger at her. "You're incapable of change."

Camilla remained silent, absorbing his anger and disappointment because he was right. "*Lo siento... por favor, perdoname.* Javier—" The rest became lodged in her throat as she watched Javier's eyes turn flat.

"Don't beg forgiveness from me... not now."

"Papa. Are you going to ask me how I feel about this?" Lucia cried. "How I want this instead of your anger at Abuela, who's only trying to help me?"

Javier turned to her. His eyebrows rose as if he'd forgotten she was in the room. "I don't think you understand, *hija.* How can you battle demons from a wheelchair? You don't stand a chance against the Fallen." He kneeled in front of Lucia, as she chewed on her bottom lip. A tear slipped down her face. "I can't lose you, too."

"That's not fair, Papa," Lucia grabbed a fistful of shirt above her heart. "If God has chosen me, who are you to doubt him?"

A gold flash brightened the room. Relief flooded Camilla when Gabriel appeared close to her. Javier rose and gaped at Gabriel like a man who'd been crushed by the weight of life's sorrows. He took two long strides and let Gabriel gather him in his arms. Camilla released a sob, realizing her son may never seek her solace again.

"Why?" Javier's unshed tears made the golden flecks in his eyes look like shards of gold glass.

Gabriel stared him in the eye. "Because for your children... two will become one."

∾

Lucia

Is that how he sees me... a cripple... unworthy of guardianship?

An abrupt silence swallowed the room. Gabriel's announcement left everyone stunned, especially Lucia. She gazed upon her papa, the man who'd sworn she could be and do whatever she wanted in life. A pressure settled on her chest as his truth crushed her to the core. She reeled from his revelation, blindsided by his lack of faith in her and God's choice. Had he always, deep down, felt this way, but only told her what he thought she dreamed to hear? She noticed a shift inside her, a shying away from the man she'd adored. She shrank back into her wheelchair, its leather seat cold and binding.

Papa pulled away from Gabriel's embrace. "Two will become one... I don't understand?" His shoulder's slumped like his lungs had deflated. She heard Abuela gasp through the trembling hand at her mouth.

How can Sergio and I become one?

Gabriel's bright golden gaze found Lucia's. Her eyebrows lifted in a silent plea as she tried to swallow through the painful tightness in her throat. But in his eyes, in that moment, she saw the confidence he had for her, not the fear she found in Papa.

"Your children are twins... connected in a way that only they understand. Even though they've lived different lives, their bond is unbreakable and a gift to them. Because of this unity, they're to share the responsibilities of the guardianship. Whatever weaknesses and burdens they carry in this world will strengthen them as they become one on this journey." Gabriel's smile spread a warmth through her and chipped away at the ice gripping her heart.

"But she's bound to that damn chair!" Papa pointed at her like a sharp stab in the chest. "How can she—"

"You're putting limits on your daughter and on God—" A trace of disappointment came and went on Gabriel's face "—that you yourself were not given. It's in the times of our greatest doubts that we're shown there is always a path, if we're brave enough to take it. Let your children walk the path and light the way for you."

Abuela sat on the edge of her bed, a soft sob escaping her lips. She turned to Lucia with such hope, even as her tears freely fell.

Papa twisted and faced Lucia. Abuela's cheerful bedroom had become somber, pushing against her outer shell. She forced her inner strength to fight for the truth she knew about herself. She sat up straighter, defiant in her stare, daring him to see something other than what God chose her to be... a guardian. His face fell as a shadow of shame crossed it like a fluttering curtain.

"I can't lose another child... I don't think I could survive... Sophia —" his breath hitched "—but I'll try to accept this... even though it claws at my heart." He walked towards Lucia and squatting before her. He took her hands and brought them to his lips, kissing them. When he gazed up at her, pain, confusion and love radiated from him. "I'm so sorry. *Te quiero, mi hermosa hija.*"

I love you, my beautiful daughter...

"*Te quiero,* Papa." She leaned forward. "Please believe in me... and Sergio. Together, we can do anything. But if you and Mama don't have faith in us, it will make it that much harder. We will fight for Manny and right that wrong—"

"No," he squeezed her hands. "You can't be a guardian with that on your heart. Sergio is already filled with so much anger and this need for revenge, I fear it holds him back and clouds his judgement. There's no changing the past. Manny is gone. But you, sweet Lucia... you can help lead Sergio away from this inner demon. I know this to be true." Dad slid his hands from hers and cradled her face. "You are the light he needs." She lifted and kissed each cheek, leaving a tingling sensation in its wake.

"Okay, Papa."

"Lucia, before we can have a ceremony for your guardianship, you must decide to accept the call. You've learned much more than past guardians because of your unique circumstances. This is more dangerous for you than anyone. After all you know... you can still say no." Gabriel's words hung in the air. Lucia glanced at Papa trying to shield the hope skirting across his face.

Do you want me to say yes or no, Papa?

Lucia swallowed past the boulder in her throat. Papa's fear couldn't sway her. His fledgling bravery was enough. She accepted his worry, because deep inside she understood his doubts... and his fears. But she wouldn't back down to his emotions or to her obvious limitations. She hadn't let the world define her so far and she wouldn't start now.

"I accept, Gabriel," Lucia said softly.

Papa's eyes closed briefly before he stood.

"*Usted una guerrera feroz.*" Abuela's voice, clogged with emotion, turned everyone's head. "Those were Manny's words that night, when we found your mark, and I shared with him the guardianship of Orion."

"*Si.* Manny was right. You are a fierce warrior, *Abuela.*"

"No, not anymore," she shook her head. "You, *mi nieta*, you are a fierce warrior and will be the fiercest of all." Her hand made a fist over her heart. "And I'm so proud of you." She released a shuddering breath, her eyes luminescent with tears.

"*Muchas gracias.* I won't let you down... any of you."

"Well, we're going camping tomorrow at Mt. Charleston," Javier announced, hands shoved in his pant pockets.

Lucia scrunched up her face. "Camping? Why—"

"Because we need a ceremony in your honor... to become a Guardian of Orion," Gabriel smiled, raising his eyebrows. "How does that sound?"

"Amazing!"

Terrifying, exhilarating, crazy...

"Until then." Gabriel left as spectacularly as he'd come... in a golden flash.

Until then... when my life changes forever.

CHAPTER
THIRTY-ONE

OLIVIA

A loud, yet muffled *woof* greeted her from the other side of Zach's front door. Olivia smiled at herself, knowing the sweet Labrador Retriever wasn't as scary as he sounded. She raised her hand to knock again, but heard hurried footsteps slapping against the tile floor.

"Hank, hush..." The door swung open to Rachel Paxton quizzical face peeking around the side while her other hand grasped Hank's collar. Her face lit up, and she released the dog. Olivia found herself swooped up in a hug from Zach's mom and a black mass wedging his way between them. Olivia laughed, returning the quick hug.

"Hi! It's so good to see you! Come on in... does Zach—"

"Who's here—" He paused on the landing when he saw her. "Liv." They locked eyes before he tore down the stairs like he was on fire.

God, he's cute...

The intensity of his gaze as he scanned her from head to toe brought a flush to her cheeks. She broke contact and bent over to give Hank the attention he wanted. She ruffled his fur, his tongue hanging out over the side in what she would swear was a smile of content-ment. Hank's brown eyes melted her heart. Her stomach fluttered when Zach stopped in front of her.

"I didn't know you were coming over. Is everything okay?"

Olivia stood, wiping her hands on her jeans. "Yeah... everything's fine. I should have called first, but I just got off work and was driving home so—"

"No... I'm glad you stopped." Zach's shoulders relaxed, slipping his hands in his pockets, but his gaze didn't let up. Olivia found herself tongue-tied, wondering why she hadn't resisted the urge to stop in front of his house like she'd done for every day since she'd told him she just wanted to just be friends.

Causing trouble for yourself...

The awkward silence didn't last long. Rachel tugged on Olivia's hand. "Come on inside... I just finished a batch of chocolate chip cookies. I need to run an errand, but I can make you lunch before I go?"

"No, but thanks anyway," Olivia giggled as she pulled her toward the kitchen. Hank's toenails clicked on the tile as he sped past them, tail wagging. He sat in front of the counter, his wet nose twitching in the air. The sugary scent of fresh baked goodies made her mouth water... and apparently Hank and Zach's, too.

"No cookies for you, buddy. They're all for me." Zach grinned at Olivia, popping a whole one in his mouth. He handed two to her before he snatched another for himself.

"Thanks." She took a bite of the cookie, giving her something to do instead of saying any words she'd regret.

"Well, I'm off. It was good seeing you again. Don't be such a stranger." She pecked Olivia on the cheek and landed a kiss on Zach, too. "I'll see you later." She waved and walked away, the garage door opened and closed behind her.

Taking another bite, Olivia examined the rest of her cookie like it was the most interesting thing she'd ever seen. "Your mom makes the best cookies." She glanced up at Zach. He was leaning against the counter, staring at her. He dusted his hands against his jeans, swallowing the last of his treat.

Zach tilted his head, examining her with those emerald eyes that stripped away her defenses searching for the truth he knew was hiding beneath it. "Yep, she sure does. Uhm... why did you stop by?"

Uhh... because I can't stop thinking about you since I touched you last night?

Yikes...

"Well... I... uh... was just wondering how you were doing since your hunt last night." She gazed at the faint thin line on his jaw before returning his stare. She caught the disappointment flickering across Zach's face. His finger reached up and ran along his jawline.

"Honestly, I was awake most of the night reliving it." His cheeks puffed as he exhaled a deep sigh. "I couldn't stop seeing the demon explode after I pierced its heart or the scared look on the girl's face. A fire burns in my gut when I remember the pimp's greedy face, his tattooed hand clutching the girl's small arm. She had to be our age. It makes me sick to think—"

"Don't do that to yourself," Olivia stepped closer. "Believe you've helped her instead."

He glanced at his feet, a frown puckering his brow. "I don't know. After I killed the demon, the pimp got this spooked look on his face before he turned and walked the other way. The girl peeked over her shoulder where I stood, as if she sensed me there. Her brown eyes were so big and her face was gaunt, like she hadn't had an actual meal in weeks." He ran his hands through his hair and scoffed. "And here I am... eating cookies that my mom made. It just really sucks." He closed his eyes, hands falling to his sides. "How can we kill the demons, yet leave the victims? It doesn't seem right." When he opened his eyes, he gazed at her with such sadness it broke her heart.

"I'm so sorry you hurt like this. The police came during my battle. One chased the dealers down the alley and the other cop took off after the car leaving the scene. I hope they got 'em." Olivia placed her hand on Zach's arm. "This may sound stupid, but after a battle, we can make anonymous calls to the police. We can ask..."

A flash of heat rolled off him, the color of his eyes shifted to a darker green. The air crackled between them. Zach pushed away from the counter. He lifted his hand and wrapped it around her neck. She wanted to step away, but the pull between them was too powerful. Zach's thumb reached up and touched her dragonfly earring. He lightly rubbed it in a circle.

"I've never seen you wear anything but this earring. Why?" he murmured, his gaze not leaving hers.

Olivia parted her mouth, surprised by his question. "When I was ten, Mom let me get my ears pierced. She gave them to me... said a dragonfly symbolizes beauty... of renewal, a positive life-force. All things that would encompass my life. It stuck with me, especially since my life was fragmented by Dad leaving us. I guess Mom was preparing me for my future.

"I like that. It's what I see in you... and more." Zach's gazed dropped to her lips. She froze as his thumb roamed from her earring and skimmed over her bottom lip, leaving a searing thrill where it touched. He inched his head lower, hovering over her lips.

Pull away...

But Olivia couldn't and if she was honest with herself, didn't want to stop. So, she closed the gap and ever so gently let her lips touch his, creating a spark that shot straight to her heart. Zach's chest rumbled with a low moan. He tilted his head and deepened the kiss, filling it with a sweet pressure that demanded no more and no less than what she gave in return. Her arms snaked around his neck, bringing him closer. Zach clasped his arm around her waist, bring their bodies flush against each other. The pounding of his heartbeat against hers, reawakening in her the powerful attraction between them no matter how hard she tried to deny it.

Zach pulled away, his excited breathing brushing across her face. "I've missed you so much, Liv." He leaned his forehead against hers, closing his eyes. "I'm so sorry for what I said... it was a cheap shot—"

She placed a finger on his lips. Zach's eyes flew open, dark with need, but worry etched lines in the corners.

"I'm sorry too. It made me mad, but I do have issues with my dad." They both chuckled, relief relaxing his face. "But you've shown me you respect my place, my equality in the guardianship. That's what I needed from you and for myself." She moved her finger away and kissed him again, tasting the chocolate lingering on his lips. Hating that she hadn't yet spilled her guts, she brought her hands from around his neck to his chest. She wanted a fraction of space from their need before it spun out of control for both of them.

He lifted his head. "But?"

"When I saw you last night after the hunt, my barriers for you dropped. You're a magnet, tugging at me. I couldn't pull away from it. I needed to touch you, to make sure you were okay... and that scared me—"

"Liv, I promise—"

"Wait..." Zach paused; his chest expanded like he was holding his breath.

"The three of us haven't been acting as a real team. We've been so busy concentrating on building our skills and figuring out our place in this destiny that we haven't been working together or... been honest with each other. After learning the truth about my dad's past, I realized that I need to work on opening up about my feelings. That's very difficult for me." Olivia bit her lip and took a step back. "But I will try, and I figured the best first step was talking with you. You do frighten me—" Zach shook his head—"not literally, emotionally."

She pushed against his chest and stepped away, giving her much needed breathing room.

"I understand that, too. I've never felt this way before about anyone. No matter what I'm doing, you're always there... in my mind never far away, a part of every thought. I need you—want you with me. It's like I'm half a person, and only you make me whole." The honesty and vulnerability etched on Zach's face as he spoke those words wrapped around her heart, healing her doubt and insecurity like a soothing balm.

Okay... that's amazing...

Olivia couldn't help but grin at him. "Wow—"

Zach ran a hand through his hair, his face flushed a sweet shade of pink. "I know that's a bit heavy—"

"It's perfect." Olivia turned serious. "And how it should be between two people who care about each other. But it's complicated for us because we're the Guardians of Orion. So, this is what I'd like us to do."

"I'm listening." Zach's stiffened as if braced for impact.

"I believe we're better guardians and people—" her mouth dried up "—together then apart."

"That's what I—" He reached for her, but she put her hand up.

"I'm not done. It will only be successful if you stand by the same earlier requests I made. I'll not have you treat me in any way different during training or in whatever circumstance we find ourselves. We are Guardians of Orion first and we leave this..." she waved her hand between them.

"Attraction?" Zach lifted his eyebrow. "Magnetism... L—"

Olivia slammed her hand over his mouth, aware his smile spread across her palm. "Don't you say that word, Zach. I'm not ready and neither are you." The humor left his eyes as he nodded. Her hand slipped from his mouth. "Can you do that? Can we keep the two separate?"

"Absolutely. We *are* better together." Zach hooked a lock of hair behind her ear, gazing at the dragonfly earring again. His mouth twitched as he stepped closer. "Can we seal it with a kiss before we go to the Magi?"

Smiling at him, the anxiety released she'd clung to for so long, the burden of it, sprung loose and opened a brightness inside of her.

"Wouldn't have it any other way."

He chuckled as his lips found hers, wrapping her inside his warm embrace.

Oh yeah... I've missed you, Zach Paxton.
Please don't let me down...

CHAPTER
THIRTY-TWO

LUCIA

Pine trees swayed above their campground, whispering through the branches and needles, their sweet tune of serenity. White, fluffy clouds glided in the blue sky, ducking between the canopy of rugged bark and clumps of green. Muted browns off the sloped mountainsides shifted with shadows of the clouds sliding across the sun's path. A hawk rode the updraft, circling above the tree line. Its hoarse screech echoed through the forest. Was its cry from pleasure or a warning? Either way, Lucia admired its raw beauty and envied its freedom.

The campsite was carved out of a slope next to the road located halfway up the mountain. The view of the valley below was dotted with empty campsites, pine trees and scrub brush. Crisp air stirred a shiver down her spine. She snuggled deeper into her jacket, wondering if the chill was only from the brisk breeze.

Tonight, she'd become a guardian. What that would entail they kept secret from her. She'd hardly slept these past few days, her imagination racing with possibilities and scenarios. Papa and Abuela evaded her questions and told her the answers she sought would be discovered soon. Her heart skipped a beat, knowing the ceremony would take place soon.

The waiting is killing me...

"Dinner's ready," Papa announced. He scooped the hamburger patties off the steel campsite grill, making a pile on the oval platter. "Get it while it's hot." Lucia was already seated at the end of the wooden picnic table, rereading her favorite fantasy adventure book with a heroine not afraid to take on the world. Her lips lifted in a sly smile.

I'll be as powerful and brave as she is...

The camper's screen door slammed shut after Mama and Abuela. Each of their hands held a bowl or platter brimming with sides dishes and makings for the hamburgers. Sergio emerged from the trees. He cast his head down at the pine needles strewn across the dusty path. He kicked a pinecone, sending it skittering out of his way while his arms remained stiff at his side. As he drew closer, Lucia could tell that the refreshing mountain air had done little to ease his sullen mood. The platters thumped against the wooden planks as Sergio slid into the seat next to her. He glanced over and smiled at her, but it didn't reach his eyes.

Papa placed the burgers in the middle of the table and sat at the empty seat at the end. The breeze carried their smoky, lightly charred aroma with it. Lucia's mouth watered, anticipating the garlic and spice explosion about to take place. They bowed their heads and recited the grace they've professed before each meal since Lucia could remember.

"Amen," the family chimed together. Eager hands reached for the dinner makings before them. Spoons and forks thudded against the plastic dinnerware. Lucia built her hamburger and added a generous scoop of macaroni salad and beans to her plate, all the while glancing over at Sergio. He raised his eyebrows and mouthed *"What?"* She patted his hand and shook her head, smiling at him. He shrugged and finished piling food on his plate.

"So, *mano*, find anything interesting on your hike?" Papa scooped up a bite of ranch beans.

Sergio chewed his food and kept his head bent. Lucia thought he wouldn't answer, but she turned to him anyway.

"Nah... just me and nature out there."

Neighing caught everyone's attention. A small group of wild horses roamed the small open pastures below the campsite. A paint and a black horse were closest, casting long shadows with the sun fading behind the mountains. Two brown horses grazed across the road, one of them neighing again. She was mesmerized by the black horse, its elegant stature surpassing the others. She marveled at its sleek, large, muscular body. Its silky mane swept forward as it chewed on the spiky grass. It raised its neck and gazed in their direction while its long black tail swished. She paused, not wanting to break contact or startle the magnificent animal. For a second, Lucia was sure the horse stared at her returning her gaze, but it shifted away, resuming its search for food.

"I still don't understand why I had to come on this surprise camping trip. I hate missing training with the—"

"Familia comes first, Sergio," Papa set his burger on the plate. "There's always time to train, but you need to balance that with family and friends. It will consume you if that's the only way you spend your time. Laughter, fun and nature are food for the soul." Papa leaned over and placed a kiss on Mama's cheek. Sergio rolled his eyes and took a big bite out of the hamburger. But it warmed Lucia's heart, seeing the love her parents had for each other still strong after all this time.

I hope I find someone who loves me like that...

Abuela nudged Lucia's hand. "Eat. We have a big night of s'mores and ghost stories by the fire soon." Sergio snorted, then popped in the last bite of his burger.

"What... are you too big now for scary tales around the fire?" Abuela teased.

He leaned across the table, a playful glint in his eye. "Yep... in fact—I may tell a story tonight that will—"

"I don't think Mama is up to listening to your adventures just yet. Besides, I have something new to share."

"Like what?" Sergio perked up, glancing around the table.

Papa chuckled. "Patience is a virtue. You should practice it." He winked at him. "Pass me another burger, *por favor*. I do love meat cooked on a grill."

Sergio handed him the platter, but not before he put a patty on his own plate. The table laughed. They were sounds Lucia welcomed and missed during meals since Manny's death.

Be with me tonight, brother... I miss you.

"We already have one foot in the grave!"

Howls of laughter echoed around the campfire when Papa finished telling his joke. Lucia had heard it a thousand times, but somehow the way he told the joke made it funny all over again. He wiped away the tears leaking from the corner of his eyes, his huge smile infectious. "I don't know why that joke cracks me up, but it gets me every time I tell it."

Lucia's gaze turned to the fire's flames licking at the fat marshmallow speared on the end of a thin metal rod. The fire burned low, crackling with orange and yellow, perfect for creating the first step in her s'more. She turned the wood handle in her hand, watching for signs of it burning over the greedy flames. The ends turned tan and bubbled, making her mouth water thinking of the hot gooey sweetness she was about to eat.

"It's ready, Abuela." Lucia leaned forward, swiveling the rod away from the flames.

"Si," She stood. In her hand laid half a large graham cracker with a square of chocolate placed on top. Lucia carefully put the marshmallow on top of the chocolate. Abuela placed the matching half of graham cracker on top of the hot marshmallow. She pressed down and pulled the creation off the stick and held up the prize for Lucia.

"That's perfect!" Lucia put the rod across the floral fleece blanket on her lap and accepted the treat from her grandma. Taking a bite, she closed her eyes as the sweet combination of melted chocolate and sweet marshmallow exploded in her mouth. "It's so yummy!"

"Nah, that's not how you do it!" Sergio raised up his rod with the marshmallow burning at the end more like a torch than a treat. He blew out the flame, pulled the charred remains off the end and popped it in his mouth. "Hmmm!" he groaned, licking his fingers as a wicked playfulness etched across his face. "So much better and faster too!" He stabbed another one and shoved it into the flames before Lucia could take a second bite.

"Eew," She rolled her eyes not understanding how a burnt marshmallow could taste anything but horrible.

"Don't eat too many or you'll be seeing that later," Papa teased. "And we wouldn't want to gross out our visitors."

Sergio stilled as his brows scrunched together. "What visitors?" He glanced around, not noticing his marshmallow sliding off the end of the rod in a burnt heap.

"Our guests will be here soon."

As if on que, a gold circle emerged behind Sergio. It hissed and snapped, widening out from the middle. It lit up the night akin to a golden halo. He spun around and stood, as did everyone else. Lucia's hands broke out in a sweat against the chilly evening air. She finished the s'more before gripping the blanket. Her body flushed hot with excitement, yet a snippet of dread lurked in the back of her mind.

Please accept me, Sergio...

Gabriel stepped through first, his wings half-folded behind him. The golden tips glistened as the firelight danced off them. Olivia and Zach stepped through, both pensive as they glanced at the firepit's occupants. Another ominous figure appeared; his black garb camouflaged the size of his body. His eyes twinkled with golden light against his dark-skinned face, partially hidden by a long black beard. A smile emerged when he gazed at Lucia, making her stomach flutter.

Balthazar.

Sergio gasped and turned back to Papa. "Why are they here? I knew this trip was sketchy. Is this some kind of intervention? I'm working on my anger—"

Gabriel placed his long, elegant hand on Sergio's shoulder. "You aren't in trouble, my child. In fact, this is an evening of celebration." Gabriel squeezed his shoulder and let go, turning to embrace Sofia in a welcoming hug. She sagged against him, winding her arms around his waist. Tears escaped through her closed eyes, and her head nestled against his chest. She looked so fragile and tiny, held by the powerful angel. Sofia opened her eyes, latching onto Lucia's gaze. Her heart lifted when her mama smiled and sent love and confidence through their connection. She stepped backward and stared up at Gabriel.

"Watch over her," she pleaded, head falling back to meet Gabriel's gaze.

He laid a simple kiss on her forehead. "Always. She has a deep well of wisdom and inner strength, just like her mama."

"Watch over who? What's going on?" Sergio demanded, looking at Gabriel and Balthazar. "Has something happened with Lucifer or the Mar of Sin?"

"No, brother. They're here because of me." He spun around, his mouth gaping at his sister.

"You? I—"

Lucia shrugged off her jacket. Her hands gripped the bottom of her sweatshirt and she pulled it off, leaving her bare except for a tank top. Goosebumps erupted over her skin when the cold night air wrapped around her. Gabriel waved his hands over the fire, the flames roaring and twisting as it heated the area and cast a brighter light around the campfire.

Sergio's eyes widened when he saw the mark of Orion on her chest. Abuela stepped back as he stumbled around the pit, his eyes riveted to the mark. He pushed her wheelchair back as he collapsed to his knees in front of her. He raised his hand and touched her mark, gliding his fingertips over the seven raised spots. Lucia lifted her chin when he locked eyes with her.

"How did this happen? I don't understand?" Sergio's chest heaved as he shook his head. "I'm the Guardian of Orion." His hand slapped over his mark as if checking it was still there. "There is only one—"

"But you are twins." Gabriel's calm claim reverberated around the group. "This has never happened before... having twins bear the sacred mark."

Lucia's hands grasped Sergio around his face. He tried to pull away, but she tightened her grip and leaned closer. "Two become one. That's us. We are different, but our hearts and mind have always been one. I know you, and you know me like no other. God wants us to be guardians together, too."

He yanked his head from her grasp and fell back onto his haunches. Confusion etched the lines on his face, so similar to hers, yet chiseled from grief since Manny's death. The muscles twitched in his jaw as he struggled with the revelation. "But you're in a wheelchair! She can't fight—she'll get hurt! That's not fair to put her through this!"

I'll show you brother...

"She'll receive an orb tonight, as you did," Balthazar said. "But her orb will be from Gabriel, not me. She'll become a guardian, revealing her role. You must have faith, Sergio."

"Please try to understand this. I haven't figured out how I'll be a guardian either, but I will do whatever it takes with the abilities given to me, to protect the Mar of Sin and kill demons. A Sloth demon attacked me the night you received your orb. It awakened the mark on me. I never want to be helpless like that again." Sergio gazed at Lucia with such uncertainty, it broke her heart. "You're scared and I am too, but I can do anything if you're by my side." Tears welled in her eyes as she ached for him to understand and support her... and their future.

Sergio's face fell as he stumbled back to her, wrapping his arms around her. "I will do everything in my power to protect you—" he whispered in her ear "—and help you be a mighty guardian."

Lucia felt the weight lift off her chest. "Thank you. I promise as well." She hugged him back, putting her love into the embrace.

Gabriel and Balthazar walked around the fire pit towards her. The flames grew larger, their ends snapping, leaning toward the noble men. Lucia's heart raced. Sergio stood up and moved next to her, laying a comforting, warm hand on her bare shoulder. Gabriel stopped and brought the blanket up from her lap and covered her body. Without speaking, Balthazar scooped her up from the wheelchair. He cradled her in his muscular arms. The warmth emanating from his chest cloaked her like a weighted cocoon.

"Are you ready?" His golden eyes glistened, with the flames, with awe and concern.

"Yes," she beamed at him, even though the tendrils of fear... of failure... or of death... gripped every part of her body she could feel.

He walked a few feet away and into the opening portal. "Then let's go to the mountain top."

CHAPTER
THIRTY-THREE

LUCIA

It's so quiet... so still.

Balthazar's arms cradled her against him, easing her nerves. But it was the serenity of the mountains and the blanket of stars which comforted her soul. Lucia exhaled her fears into the brisk night air, nipping at her cheeks. Looming trees encircled the small open area littered with chunks of stone on the pine needle floor. She followed the tree line up to the sky. The branches narrowed like arrows, guiding her to the expanse of stars bright enough to light the majestic scenery. Her mouth slipped open when she found Orion outshining the dazzling sea of stars. Having the constellation's mark on her shoulder humbled her along with the responsibilities that came with it. The three stars of Orion's belt shone brighter than the others and twinkled as if demanding her attention.

What are you trying to tell me, hunter of the sky? I want to understand the power of your light, Orion...

Footsteps crunched behind her as the portal snapped closed. Gabriel strolled in front of her and waved his hand over the ground. White flames erupted, throwing its much-needed heat over her body. Lucia sighed, welcoming the warmth and the illumination it brought with it. He faced her, glowing in his majesty of white and gold.

"Lucia... your grandmother has shared with you the mysteries of the mark of Orion upon your chest and your sacred lineage. The hunter graces us tonight, his belt awakened by our presence. The three stars are more than what meets the mortal eye. Humans see Orion and his belt, a sword hanging and the bow in his outstretched arm. But the stars of the belt hold a different meaning. Their dark portals are the antithesis of their shining light. It is called the Mar of Sin, the portal through which Lucifer and his Fallen passed through when cast from Heaven. It's a reminder of our free will and the cost of choosing to follow the path of sin. Soon, the guardians will learn more of the belt's secrets, but tonight, he watches us as you take part in the guardianship of Orion." Gabriel waved to the gathering. "Join us in a circle, please."

The tall pines swayed as low thunder rumbled in the distance. Blood pounded in Lucia's ears. The surrounding air swirled, rising around them in a dusty churning mist. The fire grew taller, the bellowing vortex shrouding them in the forest. Papa pulled Mama and Abuela closer; one's face frozen in distress, the other brimming with bold confidence. Olivia and Zach remained silent, but excitement radiated from their gaze. Lucia returned the gesture, hoping they understood the thankful twinkle in her eyes. Sergio stepped next to Balthazar. He and Lucia locked eyes, and for a moment she saw sadness float across his face. Lucia's heart raced along with the chaos whirling around them.

I need you, Sergio... and you need me...

His body tightened as if Sergio heard her plea. Escalating emotions played havoc on his face, but his shoulders relaxed. The turbulent air ruffled his thick hair, but his eyes were clearer than she'd seen them since Manny's death.

"I'll not let you down, Lucia," Sergio called out over the wind. He grabbed her hand out of the blanket and held it between his. "Two become one in the guardianship, but we're already one in our hearts." He kissed her hand and released it. Tears swam in her eyes. The reality of the moment stretched taunt between her and her twin.

"I won't let you down either," Lucia shouted, but the deafening vortex grew to its peak, sweeping away her promise.

Balthazar shifted her in his arms, positioning her as if in a chair facing Gabriel. "I have you, brave one. Do you trust me?" Her eyes widened when she turned back to the mighty stranger; a Magi, a stripped angel, her linage. She didn't know him, but she knew in her core she could trust him with her life.

"Yes." With that one simple word, Lucia's fears melted away.

Gabriel stepped in front of her. He was glorious in his white and gold fringed armor, glowing with a luminescence so pure yet powerful. He placed his hand over his heart and closed his eyes. His black lashes lay still upon his skin while his lips worked issuing no words. A bright golden flash blazed through his fingertips. Time stopped for Lucia. The steady beat of Balthazar's heart against her back and the quickening of her breathing was all she sensed as her destiny grew before her. Gabriel eased his hand away from his chest... gold sparkled between them like splitting atoms. He threw his head back, releasing a triumphant moan into the vortex. Turning his palm up, a brilliant gold orb hovered, crackling with energy. Lucia stared in awe at the orb inching its way toward her. Balthazar's arms tightened around her when she pushed back against his broad chest.

"Lucia, look at me." Her eyes snapped to Gabriel, but she frowned because his lips remained sealed. "Receive this and become one with me." The orb's energy swirled faster, as if it anticipated her answer. She licked her lips, knowing what was to happen, trying to shove away the doubts percolating.

I can do this... I've been chosen... Sergio...

"Yes!" Lucia's proclaimed in her mind.

Gabriel's golden eyes sparkled, and the corners of his mouth lifted. The angel's hand moved like a lightning strike, slamming the gold orb into her bare raised mark. Lucia's head flew back. She gasped at the surreal onslaught and the sensations exploding beneath the seven dots. Her nerve endings jolted alive, her vision cascading in white, like a waterfall, behind her closed lids. Balthazar held on tight while the orb's power coursed through her, sweeping her away... igniting her mind, her body, her soul.

Images flashed like a crafty magician fanning a deck of playing cards, then swept before her in a flurry. Mesmerized by their dazzling artistry, she tried to capture each one, wanting to soak in their majestic elegance. Snippets of people, animals and triumphant nature, woven in their fabric of life across time, played before her: a child's sweet kiss, a reunited couple collapsing in bliss, two hands aged by time clasped together, entwined as one. Joy and peace squeezed her heart as she absorbed the scenes before her.

But darkness tainted the new images, like film burning from the edges. Gone was love, now infiltrated with hate and horror. She cried out at the exposure of man's dark, twisted nature. She recoiled at its ability to inflict pain, suffering, bloodshed with delight, in the evil satisfaction, the humiliation and terror of their victims feeding their rotten souls. She squeezed her eyelids hard together, desperate to block out how evil and terror has thrived as long as man has been on Earth. The bombarding of hate pummeled her, shredding away her naivety. Tears leaked through her thick eyelashes while her mind weaved a new fabric of the realities of her fellow mankind.

"No... no more," Lucia begged. She shuddered; hands of various sizes touched her body. The images dimmed like a stage fading to black, but there was no mistaking the last picture lingering before her.

Balthazar!

But he was not as he was on Earth, but as he was in Heaven, before Lucifer's war.

His black skin glowed in his white armor fringed in gold. Four glorious wings fanned out behind him. Their tops blazed with golden light. His face was not all that rose above his massive shoulders; a lion's head faced right, an ox head faced left, and an eagle's head craned from behind his skull. They turned and gazed at her.

Her eyes flew open. Gabriel scanned her body but settled on her eyes.

"Balthazar—"

"Yes. You know him as a Magi in this world, but I know him as a Cherubim."

Lucia turned and stared at Balthazar. His eyes glistened with unshed tears. The pain on his chiseled face shredded what was left of her battered heart.

"My time in Heaven has passed... my devotion to you and the guardians is forever. I give you all I have." A tear slipped from the corner of his eye. She watched it trail down his cheek and slip into the course hair of his beard. So overwhelmed by what had transpired, she didn't grasp her legs slipping to the ground. Sobs of elation broke out around her as Balthazar stepped back. "And it's an honor to be at your service."

Realization hit Lucia before understanding. She stared at her feet, her vision traveling up her thin legs. She could barely remember how it felt to bear weight or look at people in the eye instead of up from the wheelchair. Gasping, she wiggled her toes. It was funny how she felt faint now that she could stand, but the people she loved would have caught her as they smothered her from every side. Chaotic questions rained upon her; they needed answers she couldn't give.

How can this be? Does this mean I can—

"Why don't you try?" Gabriel encouraged, silencing the cheers. Afraid it was a cruel joke, she hesitated in taking that first step.

"What if I can't..."

"You must try," Sergio urged with a gigantic smile. They released her and stepped away, but it was Sergio's hand she let go of last. "I know you can do it."

And she did... into the welcoming arms of her brother.

Lit by the night's brilliant sky, an empty meadow lined with pine trees raced beneath the beast's stride. Sharp claws tore into the soft ground driven by muscular legs aching for a reprieve. Sounds of grunting and harsh breaths exhaled through a large mouth filled with pointed teeth. Air rippled over the course fur as she charged toward the edge of the clearing. She glanced down, noting the front legs of white hair with black stripes slashed across them, ending in enormous paws made muddy by the run. Dragging air through its nostrils, her stride lengthened, straining to race faster. She reveled in its freedom and the power that came with it. But it wasn't the only beast it heard. Twisting her head from left to right, it wasn't the only beast she heard. A herd of wild horses ran with her, their sleek powerful muscles galloped while their manes whipped untamed. A roar boomed from her chest. The horses neighed, mirroring their flights of abandon.

Ahead the meadow ended, slowing the beast's pace as it entered the tree line. The horses turned away, some stopping to raise up on hind legs, kicking at the sky in a silent salute. As the herd disappeared behind the foliage, the night grew still. Only the crunch of gravel and fir needles created any sound. She lifted her nose and sniffed the air, pungent with pine, animal waste and... man.

The beast didn't fear mankind, but it understood the darkness that bloomed in some of their hearts, holding tight to its twisted promises. Whiffs of smoke from smoldering campfires made it cautious as it stalked the outskirts of the campground. It scanned the area, drawn to one place. Yellow streams of light broke over the mountain, setting its blood to race. It's stayed in the long shadows as it neared its destination. The familiar scent here soothed its wariness. It sat back on its haunches and stared at the area, uncertain what to do next.

The metal door flung open and slammed against the trailer's side. The bang echoed, causing birds to squawk and take flight. A young man stood in the doorway; his eyes wild with—

"Lucia!"

Excited voices cried out behind him. He froze when he saw what sat under the pines. Another man pushed him aside and stared at the beast, first in fear, and then in wonder.

"I have to get my—" Arms grabbed the young man who tried to push the other aside.

"Wait, Sergio," the man who grabbed him muttered. Familiar stirring swirled through it, unafraid of this man's approach. A low growl rolled from its chest as it fought an inner struggle whether to stay or escape through the trees.

"Lucia... it's Papa." He took another step and stopped as it rumbled at him again. "Lucia. Come back. Find your mark... shift back, *mi hija*."

Mark...

Papa...

Sergio...

Knowledge smashed her like a wrecking ball against the carnal wall of the beast's mind. Her giant heart beat at an erratic pace as she grappled with where she was and what she had become...

A white tiger.

"Remember your human form... find the memory and push it through to the mark." Papa's soothing voice helped her calm the animal inside her still wanting to run. A picture of her came to mind as she sought her mark buried in the white pelt. She imagined punching it—

Black shrouded Lucia's mind as she collapsed to the ground. She felt her muscles and bones morphing, surprisingly causing her little pain. Her vision returned in time to watch the beautiful white fur drift away like blowing on a dandelion. Uncontrollable tremors rocked her body as Papa scooped her up in his arms.

"Get a blanket!" He bellowed as he sat them down on the bench. "Sergio, start a fire."

Mama came out with blankets and Abuela followed behind her, whispering prayers as the rosary swung from her hand. But the commotion didn't faze her. Instead, she locked eyes with Sergio's.

"I'm okay... really." Lucia planted the message inside Sergio's mind. He bowed his head while his shoulders slumped. When he gazed back at her, relief had smoothed the worry across his face. He gave her a thumbs up, then turned to put kindling in the pit.

Papa held her close, rocking her against him. "What happened, Lucia? What do you recall?" His breath stirred the hair next to her cheek.

"I remember going to bed, but too excited to sleep from the ceremony. So I got out of bed, stood up, still amazed that I didn't fall. When no one woke up, I slipped out of the trailer. I just wanted to stare at the stars and Orion. I don't know how I became a tiger, but I remember running with the wild horses and wanting that sensation to last forever...." Lucia's words trailed off as she struggled to hold on to the fuzzy memories. "And then I was here."

"*Cambiaformas*," Abuela marveled as her fingers slid over to another rosary bead.

"*Si*." Papa agreed, his lips creating a thin line across his stoic face.

"What does that mean?" Sergio's hand stilled, holding a log over the budding fire.

"Shape shifter. This is her gift, but..."

"But what?" Lucia sat straighter; her tremors fading.

"The power rules you. And until you learn how to control the shift, you're in danger."

CHAPTER
THIRTY-FOUR

LUCIFER

Satisfaction pumped through him as his powerful legs strode through the winding stone hallway leading to his master suite. Lucifer's stride struck with authority and echoed off the barren walls, announcing his presence. He made the last curve, noting the two Wrath guards standing at attention, guarding his massive entryway. Fire sconces on each side flickered light over their stony faces, their eyes fixed on a point beyond him. He paused, his hand on the door.

"Has she left the room?" Lucifer lifted an eyebrow.

The guard on his right bowed but kept his hard gaze down the hallway. "No, my Lord."

"Good," Lucifer smirked. Needing nothing more from them, he entered his sanctuary. He closed the door, the dim room reverberated with the solid thump, announcing his arrival. His bedroom reflected the core of his being. The bed to quench his desires, the mirrors to inflame his vanity, and the windows to ignite his power. But Delilah stood in the middle of his room, her back to him; a lightning rod for all three. His fingers itched to entwine within the long flames of red hair raining over her ebony wings. Her black, skin-tight bodysuit allowed him to roam freely over every delicious curve. An ache to consume her drove him.

And he despised it.

227

Your pull is dangerous...

So, he dampened his urges and leaned against the door, irritated at her lack of acknowledgment.

"Did you not miss me, my sweet, or do you stare out into the Realm dreaming of another lover?" Lucifer didn't mask the underlying malice or the gauntlet he threw down.

It is time for you to unveil your loyalties...

Delilah's gasp of indignation humored him as she turned to face him, her eyes as fiery as her hair. "How dare you say that to me when you come in here reeking of her!" Her lips peeled back. "And keep me a prisoner here with your Wrath thugs now following my ever move!"

Lucifer threw his head back in laughter, releasing the cork on his urges. He snapped his six wings and took flight, grabbing Delilah before she could move away. He wrapped his arms around her, yanking her body against his. Blood boiled in his veins at how she incited all his passions; lust, rage, and... jealousy.

"Who is it you smell upon my flesh?" He demanded. She struggled to pull away, pounding against his chest. "Tell me!"

"Asmodeus! Her musky odor clings to you and chokes me with its vile message." She jeered.

"And what of the scent that lingers on you of late?" Lucifer changed his grip to around her waist and brought his free hand up to her chest. Delilah froze when she met his eyes. He traced his hand up her chest, nails digging into her flesh until it wrapped around her throat. "Did you presume I wouldn't notice or were you hoping I didn't care, because you are very wrong on both accounts."

"I—"

He cut off her words as his fingers tightened around her neck. She raised a hand over his, her sounds of choking mixed with his harsh breathing.

"I don't care for your lies or excuses. You'll stop meeting him, or I'll find him and brutalize the fool while you watch!" Lucifer gave her neck a last squeeze then tossed her to the ground. Air wheezed between ragged breaths while she heaved on all fours, shrouded in her hair.

He moved his neck from side to side, his chest heaving in his battle to gain control. He needed to keep her in her place, but walked a fine line retaining her allegiance. He needed this completely for complicated reasons he didn't want to fully explore. And didn't intend to.

"Get up, my sweet."

Delilah rose, lifting her chin, pressing her full lips together. Black lines ran up her chest, ending in an angry black imprint of his hand on her throat.

"I don't have to explain my actions to you, but I will this once. I met with Asmodeus to appease her needs... her desires. Lust is her Realm, so that's how we... let's say... communicate with each other. I meet with all my Princes in their Realms to partake in whatever delightful opportunity they grant me. They are ingenious in their entertainment. It honors them and allows me to watch them in unguarded moments. So, you see, Delilah, I have Asmodeus's musk trapped in every pore, but I learn something new about her each time and the way her wicked mind works."

He reached for her hand, bringing it near his lips. He peered at her green eyes, crackling with warring passions. To her credit, she didn't pull away when his tongue trailed a line over her hand, leaving a wet heat in its wake. Her pupils flared as he turned it over and kiss the valley in her palm. A lecherous grin cracked his hard face. "You're mine, and if my overprotection has driven you to make unwise choices, then I offer you the opportunity to clear the air between us and prove your allegiance to only me."

Lucifer's fingers felt the tension ebb from her body, but practiced words came from her lips. "I have only ever wanted to be yours. I'm eager to show my devotion to you and do whatever it takes to bring our plans to fruition. My actions were careless, but it was only to get your attention. Please forgive me."

Oh Delilah... you've begged for that one too many times.

"What is it you want me to do?"

"I grow weary of waiting. The drums of war pound in my head louder every day. It's time to capture the girl and discover the secrets of the portal. I can wait no longer for fear the Heavens may find out about my plans. You will bring her to me, but you must be careful. We don't know what kinds of protections surround her. It can't look like a kidnapping, so taking her in sleep or in front of others would show our hand. She must come to you unknown by her fellow guardians. Grab her, force her here and she will spill her secrets. When we've got what we need, you'll return her dead body with a Fallen and make it look like it killed her during a hunt. It must be swift, and no one can learn of our plans."

"It will be my honor to bring her to you," Delilah said, preening before him.

Excitement churned his blood as he thought of her spilling the mysteries and setting in motion his plans. "You are free to roam unwatched and portal to Earth. This is my show of trust. But take Zar with you. He knows the other guardians and the girl."

"He is the perfect partner, my Lord." She lifted on her tip toes, brushing her lips against his. He pulled her closer, deepening the kiss with his demanding lips. She pulled back. "Thank you."

He chuckled and released her. "Go... make your plans with Zar."

Delilah nodded and hustled to the door. He gazed out at the window into his Realms, pulsating with a malicious beat.

"Oh... and one more thing," Lucifer called out over his shoulder. Her hurried steps paused. "If you fail or double-cross me. I'll feed Tannin every delectable piece of you."

The door opened and closed behind him without a word spoken.
I'm so close.
The time is near when man will be my slave,
My entertainment,
Mine to exterminate.

CHAPTER
THIRTY-FIVE

DELILAH

E choing roar...
    Snapping jaws...
Spraying black blood...
Blinding pain...
Hot, inky water sucked into her lungs, dragged to the bottom of the pool...
I lose all and he wins.

The dark, winding hallway was as desolate as her fear; alone and ominous. Delilah's heart thumped against her chest as Lucifer's last words played a continual loop in her head.

I'll make sure Tannin eats every delectable piece of you.

How did he know his hideous serpent was more terrifying than a whip lashing the skin from her back? Or his beatings or any of his other twisted tortures?

Because he knows what makes you tick.

Well, so do I...

Power... and the fear of losing it.

Delilah didn't bother disguising the sound of her arrival. Instead, her footsteps announced her presence with pounding strikes against the stone floor. Her death loomed over her, but she was at least free to roam if anyone cared to notice. She shoved her revolting vision aside and replaced it with a single face.

Olivia.

Her life and the success of her plans hinged on this girl... her nemesis. Olivia's capture and demise would catapult her place and future in this world. Failure held the promise of a gruesome death and that was not an option... not the destiny she'd envisioned for herself.

Lost in the plan percolating in her mind, Delilah took flight off the perch at the end of the hallway. Heated air lifted her wings, smoke drifted off spiked feathers. She aimed for the mountain's entrance where she knew Zar rode his Degasus. By the time her feet landed on the gravel, she had the workings of a strategy that should meet Lucifer's requirements and her ulterior motives as well.

Ignoring the undulating membrane barrier, she focused on a faint light at the end of the tunnel. The Fallen crammed these creatures into their prison for future use during war. She could only image the horrid walls lining the mountains of the Seven Realms stockpiled with Lucifer's Damned.

Well, my Damned if all goes according to plan...

Flashes of vibrant colored wings, trailing fire, dashed across the pit's opening. The Degasus's neighing wasn't gentle as she remembered, but was instead laced with menace and aggression. Delilah stopped at the pit's edge and watched their dramatic flight, chasing each other like a choreographed dance between friend or foe. Some Degasus had riders, other flew free, stretching their soaring wings.

It wasn't hard to find Zar with his long, platinum hair whipping behind him. His face glowed with a cocky smile, aiming for his rival. With his legs gripped tightly to his mount, they dove with lightning speed. He lifted his mace and swung it, landing against the rider's back, knocking him off its mount. Zar raised his arms in victory, saying something she couldn't pick up in the winged bedlam. The Fallen righted its descent by expanding its wings and floating to the ground. Zar threw his head back in laughing. His Degasus made a lazy circle around the pit. A pang of jealousy hit her, annoyed by his freedom and his alluring power.

He's come a long way...

Stronger than before?

Zar's head whipped in her directions as if he'd overheard her thoughts. Eyeless pits stared at her. He couldn't see her, but she would swear he raked over her body none the less. She jumped off the pit's edge, following him to the bottom as did the other Degasus, departing to other black tunnels around the humongous pit. By the time she landed, only Zar remained with Cydanos. He stroked the creature's fiery mane and over its back, whispering into its pointed ears. Cydanos bowed its long snout as if it agreed with Zar's murmurings. It took flight as Delilah stopped a few feet from Zar. They both watched it ascend to its entrance.

"What's so urgent that it brings you here?" Zar faced her with a wary resignation she didn't appreciate.

She put her hands on her hips, cocking her head. "Well... sorry to bother you during your flights of fancy, but it can't wait. I just had the most interesting yet terrifying conversation with Lucifer and I'd thought I'd share it with you. But if you're too busy, I'll go find someone else." She turned to walk away, but he pulled her back with his firm hand latched around her arm. She yanked it from his grip, rounded on him as her pent-up fears exploded inside her. "I've been manhandled enough today," she sneered. "Keep your—"

Zar frowned and his posture tightened. "What happened with Lucifer?" His fingers fluttered with surprising gentleness over the fading bruises on her neck. "Why did he—"

Delilah jerked and spun away, hating he sensed her pain. "I'm fine. He came to me smelling like—" she swallowed the foul taste in her mouth "—Asmodeus. I got upset, but he turned the tables on me asking why I had an unfamiliar scent too... which I don't."

Can Zar detect it, too?

Shaking her head, Delilah turned, thankful he kept quiet. "But that's not why I'm here." She scanned the pit, looking for movement. "Are we alone?"

"Yes, but let's move out-of-sight to the tunnel." She followed Zar's long strides into the oppressive, black entrance. A chill ran down her spine. Her vision picked up nothing in the shadows, but the reek of despair and bloodshed hung in the air.

"What is this place?" she whispered, moving closer to him.

"They measure out discipline within the stalls." Zar's hair glowed in the dark. "Now what happened?"

Delilah let his lack of specifics slide, not interested in the gory details of the brutality against whom or what. "Lucifer said he's ready to capture the girl. He wants you and I to do it." His hiss surprised her. "What? Do you not want to help me? This is what I've waited for!" she seethed. "We've weaved our deceit among the Princes—"

"What if it's a trap... for you and possibly me too? The Army's not ready and none of the Princes talk of looming war," he hissed. "They're still gathering souls and going about the business of building an army as usual. Lucifer hasn't shared plans—"

"Why are you so sure of this? Maybe us getting the girl will put the plan in motion. He told me he's tired of waiting."

Zar crossed his arms. "Uhm. What else did he say?"

Delilah's pulse raced as Tannin's deadly teeth flashed in her mind. Her eyes narrowed, throwing daggers in the darkness. "He's given me free roam. No more thugs trailing behind me. It's his sign of trust and that you're also someone he trusts."

Zar snorted. "Great, Lucifer's given you just enough rope to hang both of us. And?"

She paused, exhaling through her nose. "That if I failed, he'd feed me to his disgusting pet, and I have no intentions of letting that happen."

"Swear to me you've told no one else."

Why does he keep asking me this?

Irritation rippled through her. "No... I haven't. I told you. It's just you and me. So, are you in or out?"

"Oh... I'm in. It's time for the girl to spill her guts... literally. Let's go back to my room and work on your plan. Let's hope you're right, that grabbing her is the beginning of his strategy." He pointed his hand at the entrance. "After you."

Delilah nodded and took a step, but Zar hesitated and faced the black abyss of the tunnel. "What... is someone there?" She stared into the gloom, as a wisp of air grazing her neck like an icy fingertip.

"No." Zar gripped her arm tighter and pulled her out of the darkness. He released her and flew away without glancing back.

But the open pit did little to dampen her unease. Delilah cast a last glimpse over her shoulder, frowning at the entrance.

No one better have listened to them talking...

Or I'm lunch...

CHAPTER
THIRTY-SIX

OLIVIA

Zach pushed open the heavy wooden door at the tunnel's end. Bright sunshine and the earthy fragrance of forest and grass was a welcome reprieve to Olivia. She followed him through the exit with Lucia and Sergio on her heels. Inhaling the refreshing air, she gazed upon the stunning, untouched landscape of the Magi's mystical world. Rushing waters from the chasm made a pleasant roar in the distance, another sign of the wild beauty surrounding her.

"Weren't the Magi meeting us here?" Sergio examined the green acreage.

Olivia glanced over her shoulder. "Actually, we're to make our way to the clearing over the rise."

Lucia stood next to her twin brother with wide eyes taking in the vast landscape. She turned to Olivia, her face lighting up with a smile. "I still can't get over this. It takes my breath away."

"As does your walking," She grinned back.

Sergio's face softened when he turned to Lucia. "Come on." He nudged her arm and jogged past Olivia to catch up with Zach.

"Wait up." She ran after her brother, leaving Olivia bringing up the rear. She sprinted after them, exhilarated by how her legs gobbled up the terrain with ease. It seemed like a lifetime had passed since her soccer injury.

I have a new life... amazing one... except for the rift with Dad.

She shook her head, not wanting to cloud her thoughts with pain and disappointment. She'd mended her relationship with Zach and with the surprise bonus of Lucia, her life as a guardian was how she wanted it. In her gut she knew she had to move past her parent's deceit, but how to accomplish that feat was too convoluted for her to unpack. Better for her to concentrate on the here and now.

The guardians reached the rise and stopped at the edge of the plateau before them. It was circular, like the mountain's top was sliced off leaving the perfect flat clearing. Thick luscious grass covered the ground. The forest treetops swayed in the breeze like flowing dancers surrounding a stage.

"Where are they? It's not like them to miss—" Olivia's words froze in her mouth when a loud screech pierced the air. Putting her hand to her forehead to block the sun, three dots grew larger on the horizon. A lower pitched shriek sent her heart pounding as the forms of three large flying beasts raced towards them. Their colorful bodies reflecting like prisms in the sky. Unique flaming colors rippled off their majestic wings flapping with light, powerful ease. A strident whinnying joined the cacophony of calls from the air.

"Pegasus?" Zach murmured. The beasts circled above them. "Yes... with orange flames!" he cried, pumping his fist, jumping up and down at the riders.

"That one with red flames is a Phoenix!" Sergio pointed his finger to the sky, his face alive with wonder and joy.

"You're right... see his long tail feathers?" Lucia nudged his shoulder. "Definitely a Phoenix."

Olivia picked out Melchior on an unfamiliar beast. His silver mane glistened in the sunlight along with the creature's golden flames rippling off its wings and chest.

A thrill shot through Olivia when the Magi, regal on their mounts, landed before them, hitting the soft ground and trotting to a stop before them. Rooted to her spot, she stood in awe of the spectacular creatures that once could only be imagined. But they were real, just like everything else in this land... and she wanted to ride one.

"Well, what do you think?" Caspar asked, a mischievous grin stretching across his face, green eyes alive with excitement. The chestnut's large hoof pawed at the grass, the breeze ruffling his orange dipped silky feathers.

"That you know how to make an entrance." Zach teased.

"No... but my friend here, Malik, certainly does. You remember him, don't you?"

"How could I ever forget? I can't believe he picked me after he saw my act during the training session."

"There's more than meets the eye to any creature... man or beast." Caspar ran his hand down over its lustrous orange mane. "He's an orange Pegasus from the Heavenly Virtue of Temperance. He's guided by self-restraint... unless he's flown into battle." Malik snorted, flaring his nostrils as if stating his approval.

The Magi dismounted, holding the reins in their hands. "Come, meet our friends." Balthazar waved to the guardians. "This is Sidra. She's a red Phoenix from the Heavenly Virtue of Forgiveness. Melchior's companion is Aureus. He's a gold Griffin from the Heavenly Virtue of Humility. They're creatures who lived in Heaven among us, honoring the Heavenly Host with their courage, wisdom and beauty." Balthazar smiled when Sidra nudged him with her hooked beak. He whispered to Sidra, her wings, long tail feathers, and plume shimmering red. Sergio approached the creature with an outstretched hand.

Olivia turned toward Melchior under the beast's watchful golden eyes. She took in its eagle head, chest, and front legs with powerful wings emerging from its shoulders. Behind the wings, the white feathers faded, and the body of a muscular lion appeared with its hind legs and tail still alight with a smoldering gold flame.

"He's spectacular," Olivia stopped next to Melchior, but couldn't pull her eyes away, feasting on every magnificent line. "I've never seen anything like him in books or movies."

"His kind is a unique creature," he chuckled. "He's noble like the lion and eagle; fiercely protective and a fearsome fighter... and Aureus has chosen you as his rider."

Olivia's mouth dropped, mind blank, trying to comprehend Melchior's incredible words.

"How... when did he choose me?" Olivia asked, turning to her mentor. "I have never seen him before."

"Aureus may be a grand creature, but he knows how to go unseen. He watched you train from the sky or peered at you from the forest. We are rarely ever alone here in our land. Griffins are very picky about their riders and don't often choose a guardian. But he senses in you a connection, a way for both of you to grow. I have my suspicions, but—"

"Tell me. If you don't, how will I know?"

Melchior laughed, shaking his head. "Well... it's not your patience he sees."

"Hey—"

"You'll find out when Aureus thinks the time is right. Until then, we have another urgent matter. Would you like to ride him to our destination?"

A fluttering sensation hit her stomach, a phenomenal expectation of riding on its back. "Absolutely!"

"That a girl." He nodded, handing over the reins.

Olivia glanced over at Sergio and Zach. Each had enormous grins, exuding the same excitement with a hint of apprehension.

"Shall we?" Melchior asked, sweeping his hand toward Aureus. The beast knelt down. "Stand behind the wing. Use your left hand and grab where it meets his shoulder, then jump up."

"You make it sound easy," Olivia scoffed.

"It is once you get the hang of it. Try it."

Olivia did as she was told. She landed with a not so graceful thud on its back and situated herself behind its wings. "I'll need to practice that a few times." Olivia's heart raced as she waited for Melchior to join her. When he crossed his arms, she cocked her head. "Aren't you coming?"

He shook his head. "Fly free, my friend. We'll meet you there. Aureus knows where to go."

"But I—"

"Yes, you can. Hold on to the reins and squeeze your thighs tight. Our friend here will not let you fall." He took a few steps back and raised his portal. "See you soon." He walked through, the crackling blue lights closing behind him.

Olivia turned to find Zach and Sergio gazing at her. She shrugged. "What's the worst thing that can happen?"

"My healing powers can't fix a broken neck?" Sergio snarky remark had them all laughing, releasing some of her jittery nerves. "What about Lucia?"

Balthazar put his arm around her shoulder. "She's her own magical beast, aren't you?" Lucia's smile beamed at him, her black hair lifting in the breeze. "We'll meet you there."

"Let's go!" Zach tapped his heels against Malik's side. The Pegasus galloped, its gorgeous wings expanded and flapped. Olivia gasped as Zach took flight. His cry of elation filled the air while orange flames trailed behind him.

"That's wicked!" Sergio tapped Sidra's side, and she didn't hesitate. The Phoenix took flight in a glory of red flames.

Olivia's sweaty hands tightened on the reins. She grinned as she tapped her heels against his side. Aureus took off in a run, his powerful muscles rippling beneath her, bringing back a familiar sensation, remembering the vision of herself in battle while she played a video game.

Was I riding you, Aureus, into battle?

The creature didn't reply, but a sense of absolute affirmation struck Olivia that he was the same one. Before she could contemplate it further, she was airborne. A giddy cry erupted from her, while her stomach dropped. Aureus climbed higher and chased the creatures in front of him, leaving streaks of gold flames across the sky. Her hair whipped behind her as the green ground grew smaller. Air whistled in her ears, and her shirt clung to her skin like her legs around Aureus. He turned, flying towards the river. Olivia leaned closer behind his head. His golden feathers fluttering in the magic of flight as he soared, one with the terrain and his nature.

She thought her heart would explode from the thrill, but Olivia sensed another heartbeat, slower yet stronger than hers, beckoning her to match its calm beat. When she exhaled and slowed her heart, it pounded with a unique beat, becoming one in heart... with Aureus. Olivia gasped, feeling the steady pulse of his blood, the motion of his wings thrusting through the air by muscles and bones made to fly.

Freedom...

Olivia's throat clogged from the beauty and humility of what this creature trusted her with... his heart and his body.

"Thank you, Aureus," she murmured. He squawked, barely loud enough for anyone to hear but Olivia. It was all she needed to know that he understood her.

Reaching the massive gray slate cliffs, he dove into the canyon. Sunlight and shadow grazed over their bodies as he flew low, skimming above the rushing water. Olivia whooped and hollered, every fiber in her body screaming with untold elation. The rocky walls blurred in her vision, her hands drenched in sweat from gripping the reins, but there was no fear. Unrestrained abandonment bathed her skin, sealing the sensation with every buffet and swirl of air they knifed their way through in their communal flight.

The canyon widened at the end of the ravine. A lush waterfall poured over the cliff's sides into a crystal blue lagoon. Zach and Sergio landed next to the pool. The Magi stared up at the sky at their approach. But it was the set of golden eyes from the huge white tiger that caught her attention.

Wow... she's magnificent... yet terrifying.

Glad she's on our side.

Olivia gripped tighter, expecting a hard landing, but Aureus transitioned into a smooth gallop, his legs absorbing the glide onto the ground.

Sergio and Zach's excited talk mixed with the loving strokes down Malik and Sidra's backs mirrored Olivia's bubbling emotions. She jumped off Aureus, letting her hand stroke against his course short fur. She walked around his folded wing and stood in front of him. His sharp hooked beak inches from hers, but there was no doubt, only a kindred spirit for this magical creature. His gold eyes sparkled with satisfaction, and she would have sworn a little humor.

"That was amazing," Olivia gushed. "To fly and be a part of you at the same time—" she swallowed past the lump in her throat "—well... I'll never forget it. And if we go into battle together, I'll be the bravest guardian there ever was with you leading me." Her hand glided over the silky feathers on his neck, tickling her palm.

"Olivia!" Zach ran up from behind, picked her up and spun her around in a circle. "Can you believe we were flying? This is the best day of my life!" He set her down and kissed her forehead, startling them both. He stared at her with a cocky smile. "I don't care, Liv. I expect everyone knows my feelings for you."

Sergio's arms wrapped around both of their necks, pulling them close. "Malik is amazing! Did you guys feel the heartbeat? Freaked me out at first, but—"

"Was that as thrilling as it looked?" Lucia asked, jumping into the fray.

"Oh yeah, but... I saw you when we were landing. A massive man-eating white tiger! Girl, you are leading the way during battles." A blush crept up Lucia's face as everyone grinned and jostled her around inside the group hug.

"I don't know about that, but I've a lot to learn yet, but it's a dream come true for me... as are you guys and the guardianship."

"Aw come on, don't get all serious!" Sergio nudged her. "Save it for Papa or Abuela... they'll eat that stuff up."

The guardians separated with the approach of the Magi.

"Did we become linked with them in flight?" Zach pointed at the majestic creatures.

"You did," said Caspar. "And the link will continue when you ride them. They're giving you their trust, and you must return that trust to them completely. They may not say a word, but their bodies and hearts will speak volumes. Heed them, especially in battle. You'll not only risk your lives, but theirs as well." Olivia nodded along with the others, sobering to the grave responsibility of their charge and duty.

"Come, we have something more of interest to share with you." Melchior's voice rose above the gentle crash of the waterfall against the rocks. "Follow me."

"More?" Zach eyebrows shot up as he flung his arms wide. "We just flew on heavenly creatures. What could be more interesting than that?"

"How about learning how to save the world?" Caspar crossed his arms, rocking on his heels.

Zach's arms fell to the side. "Uh... yep, that wins." He scoffed before setting off for Melchior.

Olivia glanced back at Aureus. His tail twitched, feather ruffling as he stared in return.

I have you, Aureus. What more could I need?

CHAPTER
THIRTY-SEVEN

ZACH

The waterfall towered before them, cascading like a wide shower of glistening rain. A rainbow shimmered at the edge of Zach's vision, the water frothing against the slick rocks edging the lagoon. He inhaled the rich earthy smell of the lush greenery while the roar of waterfall grew louder with their approach. His senses had awakened during his glorious ride on Malik. He was still in awe that the magnificent Pegasus had chosen him as a rider. The exhilarating rush of the unencumbered flight became a reality his imagination could never have touched.

Please Lord, help me be worthy of Malik's choice...

Zach released a cleansing breath into the misty air. The group neared the side of the waterfall. Walking among the intense beauty of the Magi's world, his senses normalized... that was, for a guardian. The outdoors was his domain, a place he was most at peace. The heightened awareness of his surroundings, given to him by Caspar, fed his soul as he communed with nature on a different level, especially the raw power of water... his element to command.

Confidence in his fighting abilities continued to grow, as did his feelings for Olivia. When she came over and they reconnected, tearing down the treacherous walls between them, his world was no longer tilted on its axis. He felt whole again... she was the missing piece to his spirit's puzzle.

Melchior stepped along the smooth rocks below the sheer cliff. He angled for the waterfall's edge and waved his hand in front of it. The rushing water parted like a curtain, revealing a dark cavern behind it. They followed him, single file, and disappeared behind the parted water. Mist sprayed over his body, refreshing on his warm skin. He glanced behind him and watched Balthazar wave his hand, closing the waterfall. Zach's breath caught as he gazed back through the waterfall. The sky and lagoon were a stunning scenery through the blanket of water... like looking at the landscape through shards of falling glass.

Zach's eyes adjusted to the cavern's dim lighting, the sunlight filtering through enough to light the cave. A small pool of crystal-clear water lead to a landing of pebbled ground, but the deep cavern opened wide around them. The water lapped while he scanned the cavern's high arched ceiling of smooth rock encasing them. Zach's hand trailed along the slippery rock, making his way around the pool until he took his first step on the pebble shore. His foot sank, the crunch of their footsteps echoed against the wall negating the silence. The air was ripe with wet stone and the pungent moss.

The group walked to the back of the cavern. A large cut-out in the stone, like a framed arched window, was carved into the far wall. Three ornate boxes sat on the ledge, but the Magi stepped in front of it before Zach could get a better look. Anticipation hummed through him as Olivia, Lucia, and Sergio lined up next to him. He glanced at Olivia, who shrugged, but a grin tugged at the corners of her mouth.

Melchior stepped forward, gazing intently at each of them. "We stand before you honored by your accomplishments and your bravery. Each of you developed your skills as demon slayers, honed your angelic powers and learned how to link with the Fallen. Because you passed these stages, you're now ready for the last piece. You'll fully undertake the role as Guardians of Orion. It's vital for a guardian to master the skills needed before this last step, but during this training, it leaves the Mar of Sin exposed... Orion unprotected."

Balthazar's fingertips brushed over where his mark lay hidden beneath his tunic. "While we train you, we can't spend our time linked with the Fallen or Orion. Instead we concentrate our efforts on the guardians. During this transition, we seek help from the Archangels, and in their infinite generosity, they comply. But it's your time to take over this responsibility and release them back to their duties in Heaven and on Earth." His deep voice echoed off the shadowy cavern walls like a steady drum beating its importance.

Glimmering orbs appeared and exploded, lighting up the dark corners in brilliant colors highlighting the grotto. Zach's pulse jumped, his instincts alert. Four webs came to life, each a distinct color; purple, orange, pink and red. His eyes widen as each crackled, exposing four glorious Angels. Even though he'd met Michael, Gabriel and Raphael, it never crossed his mind they would introduce them to more Angels. Overwhelmed by their beauty while their presences engulfed the cavern, a sense of tranquility washed over him.

Olivia's hand slipped into his. He squeezed it tight, reassuring himself as much as her. Zach glanced over her head when Lucia released a sob. She leaned into her brother, who wrapped his arm around her, the shimmering colors playing over their awestruck faces.

The Angel closest to him stepped forward. "My name is Sealtiel, and we are from the choir of Archangels. We're each infused with one of the Heavenly Virtues displayed by the color given to us. I belong to the Purple Kingdom of Diligence." Her ebony face glowed while her wise purple eyes scanned them. She clasped her hands in front of her, brushing against the pulsing purple sword at her side. But it was her wings Zach couldn't tear his eyes away from. Unlike the others who had traces of white feathers, hers were all iridescent purple... some so dark at her shoulders, they were like an opulent black sweeping in a rainbow of rich purple to lavender. They ruffled against an invisible swirl of air, catching the dazzling light of her fellow Archangels. Zach's throat clogged at never having seen something so exquisite. "It's been our privilege to serve all of you."

"I'm Jehidiel from the Orange Kingdom of Temperance." The Archangel next to Sealtiel acknowledged them with a slight bow. Bright orange sparked off the ends of his wings and off the tips of his short light brown hair. Two swords hung from his hip; the shiny metal alive with an orange glow. He grinned at them; the corner of his eyes crinkled but didn't dim the sparkle in his orange eyes. "It's a pleasure to meet you."

"My name is Barachiel and I'm from the Pink Kingdom of Chastity. Thank you for accepting your call." Her skin was so light, it was almost transparent, but her wings gleamed deep pink, fading to bright white ends. Her hair was a pale pink, her eyes a darker shade holding a steely strength that belied the softness of the color. A curved sword hung at her side; its hilt glowed deep pink while strapped to her other leg was a matching dagger.

A hush fell upon the cavern as all eyes turned to the last Archangel. He regarded them with a solemn stare, examining each of them with steady red eyes searching inside their every pore. A distinct energy emanating from him, coiled tight beneath the surface, ready to spring. Waist long hair shined like spilled black ink, draping around the edges of his dark brown face, highlighting the angle of a firm jaw marked with a deep cleft. But it was the scrolling red tattoo starting at the bridge of his nose and fanning out across his forehead that mesmerized Zach. His quiet stature reminded him of a picture he'd come across in a history book of a proud Indian chieftain. Zach waited with bated breath as the Archangel steadily measured the guardians. With his decision made, he lifted his chin and crossed his arms over his massive chest.

"I'm Uriel. I carry the color of the Red Kingdom of Forgiveness." As if on cue, a swirl scrolled up his heavy broadsword and the whip at his side awakened like an unfurling snake, while his wings' red feathers burned with flames. "It will be my honor to fight alongside you."

Zach stood in awe. His heart swelled at the Archangels' humility, yet they exuded a fearless warrior spirit. "We're the ones honored by your presence and for your help." His words felt silly, even trite, but Zach hoped they understood his sincerity.

"Orion's belt and the Mar of Sin have been linked since Lucifer's war... and the treachery of others." Caspar stepped in front, his lilt soothing Zach's amped nerves. "God created the Mar of Sin, the portal Lucifer and his Angels fell through and landed in Hell. But God also created two more portals hidden at the edges of Heaven. He understood this wasn't the last of Lucifer or those of his kind. Souls in heaven are in their perfect pure selves, just as the damned in Hell are their perfect evil selves. The second portal is vital for the war between the Angels and Fallen, but this war will take place on Earth. The portal's purpose is to release the souls, past warriors from Earth and Guardians of Orion, to take arms and battle the forces of Hell if Lucifer unleashes the Fallen and Damned upon mankind."

"Whoa..." Sergio murmured.

"The third portal is another Hell, a dank black pit of sorrow, bitterness and chains."

"A different Hell... worse than Lucifer's?" Sergio's eyes bugged out, shadowed with disbelief. "How can that be?"

Zach couldn't comprehend any place viler... more horrific than the one he saw.

"And who's there... what could they have possible done that was worse?" Olivia asked, glancing up at Zach.

"We call them the Watchers and their sins are more evil than Lucifer's."

"What—" But Caspar raised his hand before Zach could finish.

"In their beginnings on Earth, the Watchers were two hundred Angels sent to mankind. Their call was to guide and nurture humanity, which they freely accepted from God. But when they got to Earth, over time, they chose a different path. They decided on Earth, they could be gods... turn mankind away from their devotion to one unseen Heavenly God to many gods on Earth that man could bow before and serve. As part of the Watchers' sinister plan, they mated with women for the purpose of creating a new race. Giants, an abomination in God's nature for a child to be born part angels and part man. This offspring, called the Nephilim, terrorized the land and kept the people in fear and awe. God sent the deluge... the great flood... to wipe out the Nephilim... and mankind."

"The flood... you mean Noah's ark?" Lucia asked, disbelief in the pitch of her voice.

"Yes. The one and the same." Caspar nodded at her. "Unknown to the Watchers, the flood would not destroy them. Instead, God sent the Choir of Powers—warrior Angels, not to kill, but to capture the Watchers and bring them to Heaven. When these traitors were before God, Heaven shook with a fury. Their leader, Symedek, didn't turn from God's wrath even though the others did. He was defiant, not sorry for his heinous deeds in creating the giant offspring, polluting mankind and playing god to God's creation. But God didn't destroy them. He cast the Watchers through a portal with the warrior Angels, who shackled them in chains. They entombed the Watchers, made to exist in a damnation of their own making, sealed forever in an obsidian abyss with their sins. But if the time comes when the portals are opened, their final judgment will be at hand."

Zach had read the story of giants and the flood in Genesis, but he had considered it a tale... a fable from the bible. But these Watchers were real, awaiting their last sentence. The roar in his ears was from more than the waterfall.

"The universe sees these stars as part of the belt of Orion. But you're given the ability to initiate their purposes... as portals"

The Archangels parted, exposing the three boxes on the ledge. "When we left Heaven, God gave us these." Melchior waved his hand at the boxes. "Inside each box lays... Gold, Frankincense, and Myrrh." Caspar said.

Wait... did I hear him right?

"Like... what... uh... you presented to Jesus?" Zach stammered.

"Not with these boxes, but yes." Melchior's eyes twinkled. "We were told to present these to Jesus when He came to Earth as an infant. But these precious gifts are also used to show the portals in Orion's belt."

The Magi each lifted a lid. They reached inside and emerged with a silver necklace dangling from their hand. A small silver scrolled capsule swayed at the end.

"Inside each of these holds the gift you'll need," The necklace gleamed, hanging from Melchior's hand. "Inside mine is a nugget of gold. Its sign is for the royalty of Jesus and will shine upon the Mar of Sin... the gateway to the enemy of our Lord."

Caspar held up his necklace. "Inside is a piece of frankincense... for the divine nature of Jesus and will light up the portal for the Heavenly souls."

Lastly, Balthazar held up two necklaces. "And these each have a slice of myrrh... a sign of Jesus's mortality... his death. Each will illuminate the Watchers' portal whose actions brought death to man."

A heaviness spread inside Zach, his mind grappling with the truths being told to them. Everything that had happened to him, he'd been able to understand... and accept. But this—these same gifts given to Jesus were now a part of the guardianship? He swallowed the lump in his throat as his eyes locked onto Caspar.

How can I be worthy of this... my sins... my fears? Can I really do this?

"Yes, my friend. You are ready." Caspar's voice played in his mind.

"Wear each necklace for the duration of your guardianship." Balthazar's voice rumbled like the waterfall over Zach's taunt nerves. "If the time comes for the portals to illuminate, slice your palm and each clasp your hands together to share your blood, then reach up and hold the capsule inside your fist. Your shared blood dissolves the heavenly metal along with the gift. You must then place your palm against your mark. These three things; your shared blood, your gift, and the mark will show the portals in the Orion's belt. The Fallen will see the Mar of Sin in Hell. The other two will open in the sky. But only together will this work."

Zach glanced at Olivia, hearing her gasp.

The Magi approached them under the watchful eyes of the Archangels. Caspar stopped in front of Zach. He lifted the necklace as Sealtiel stepped next to Caspar. Zach's heart pounded as Caspar raised the necklace. The serpentine chain shimmered under the glow from Sealtiel. Caspar took the ends and wrapped them around Zach's neck, laying warm against his skin. Sealtiel's ebony hand reached behind him, her fingers trailing along his skin like a delicate breeze until they stopped where Caspar held the ends. Zach hissed as a flash of heat kissed his skin and zipped over his neck.

"It's now forged together... yours."

"Did my mom wear this?" Awe dripped within Zach's voice.

"She did." Sealtiel's full lips stretched across her face. "And the ones before you."

Zach should have felt the weight of the world pulling on him, but he found strength because his ancestors wore this same necklace.

"And closing the portals?" Olivia fingers glided over the capsule hanging in the middle of her chest.

Melchior nodded. "Once the portals open, past Heavenly souls who were once warriors or past guardians will rush to battle. The Watchers will be given a choice to make. We must allow for precious time so these events can come to their fruition. The Fallen that fly into the Mar of Sin will be met by Angels ready for battle at the gate of Heaven. You will see a sign and understand it's time to close the portals. Place your hand, still awakened from the mingling of blood and gifts on your mark. Call up the orb. It will release and hover in the palm of your hand... just as it did with us. The orbs will come together—" Melchior sighed, "—and close all the portals."

Release what was given... the saying on my talisman.

The heat of the token in his front pocket warmed a patch of skin on his thigh. Could that be what it means or is there more to it?

"But?" Zach pressed, blood rushing in his ears.

"If the portals not closed—"

251

"All Hell will break loose." Sergio groaned, running his hand through his black hair.

"Closing the Mar of Sin seals the gate of Hell, trapping the Fallen and damned forever where ever they are in that moment. If the gate is left open, unchecked for evil, it sets off a battle in Heaven and on Earth until the poison of evil is destroyed for eternity. A second war between good and evil. The battle for free will of Angels and mankind... the battle of souls... the living and the dead. In His infinite wisdom, He wants mankind to hold the key. To protect and fight for what they want... what He gave freely to them. Their free will. Their salvation. Therefore, you, Guardians of Orion, must be ready if the time comes. Life on Earth will change forever if Lucifer finds out the secret and can keep the gate open." Melchior crossed his arms. "Do you understand your duties?"

"Yes." Olivia, Zach, Sergio and Lucia chimed in unison, exchanging brave smiles. But Zach sensed their affirmation mixed with the same churning emotions inside of him.

Awe of duty.

Humility of choice.

Protection at any cost.

No pressure...

CHAPTER
THIRTY-EIGHT

SERGIO

He thrashed against the sheets. No matter how hard he tried to wake up from the dream, it kept Sergio locked in the visual torment with an iron fist.

Red sand crushing under his feet...

Black feathers slapping his face...

Gold web hissing open, dark bodies flying out...

Olivia's screams cut through the moonless night...

Sergio bolted upright, still unnerved by the familiar images. Was the dream trying to tell him something or was he worried about his fellow guardians? The landscape and players rarely changed, but the lingering affects haunted him.

I don't get to Olivia in time.

Sergio tucked his hand beneath the pillow, propping his head. He tried to decipher the nagging feelings that filtered like a mist inside his head. The ceiling fan circled above him; its swirling air cooled the beaded sweat on his forehead. Sighing into the dark of his bedroom, he focused on the day's events with the Magi and riding Sidra instead of frustrating himself about the cause of the repeating dream.

His hand rubbed the silver capsule resting on his chest. Sergio frowned, realizing he'd probably taken a pill bigger than this, yet it contained the contents that could save the world. The scrolling design felt familiar between his fingertips, but he couldn't place it. Overcome by his stomach's growling in its constant demand for food, he tossed back his bedcovers. A midnight snack sounded like the perfect way to take his mind off of Olivia and the capsule.

The house was quiet, his footsteps brushing along the carpeted hallway. But he wasn't alone in his midnight wanderings. His sensitive ears detected the melodies of a home; a fork scraping against ceramic plate, the air flowing through a vent, the heavy breathing of slumber. He sensed who was in the kitchen and braced himself for questions she might ask.

Lucia...

"Hey." Sergio muttered, walking through the living room.

"Hi." Lucia responded with a mouth full of food.

Sergio opened a kitchen drawer and grabbed a fork. His stomach growled again, the aroma of spices emanating from the casserole amplifying his hunger. He scooped up a big bite. The melted cheese draped over red sauce and chunks of chicken. He ignored the burning sensation in his mouth, sucking air through his teeth to cool the delicious food.

"Mom's enchiladas are the best." Sergio sighed as he dug in to the dish for another heaping bite. He glanced at Lucia, who gave him a thumbs up, swallowing her mouth full.

"I'm ravenous all the time." She chuckled at him.

"Yep. You get used to it after a while." He blew on his fork, leaning his hip against the counter. "It still catches me off guard... you standing next to me... watching you run and train." He popped the bite in his mouth, but it wedged against the lump in his throat. He forced it down, seeking control of his emotions.

Lucia placed her fork on the counter. Her large eyes sparkled with flecks of gold against the light filtering through the blinds. "I wake up and out of habit, grab my legs to pull them over the side of the bed and then I remember I can walk. I always wiggle my toes first. Just because I can. Sometimes it makes me cry or giggle... usually both out of complete and utter joy. I never thought—" But her lips pressed together, her chin quivered.

"Shhh, *bella*." Sergio reached over and brought her into a hug. He closed his eyes, sending a prayer of thanks for his sister. A piece of his heart stitched together, the quick prick of the needle nothing compared to the pain of his loss. He missed Manny every day. The anger and bitterness of it simmered within him, dangerous when needing an outlet. But Lucia! This miracle of her walking because she was a guardian had removed some scales from his eyes, bringing a scant ray of light into his darkness. He gave her a quick squeeze, then stepped back. "I'm just going to say that it's badass you shape shift into a tiger! Manny would have loved it." He smirked.

Lucia stared at him. He slammed his walls back up, sensing her probing within him. "Don't do that, Lucia." He hadn't meant for it to sound like a threat, but the hard edge tone held no humor or doubt. "My thoughts are my own. My business, so stay out of it. If I want to tell you something, I'll—"

"You hardly ever mention Manny's name to me." Lucia crossed her arms. "It's a surprise, *hermano,* when you do. You know I'm nosy by nature and I've always been able to read you better than most. I wasn't trying to intrude, but the link we share has enhanced on a different level. These abilities are new to me."

Sergio scrubbed his hands over his face feeling like a jerk, but his stomach tied in knots uneasy with her ability. "I'm sorry too. His death is still raw for me."

"For all of us."

Is she going to let this go or not?

"Yeah... well... you weren't there. He didn't die in your arms. You weren't the one Manny was trying to save." Sergio lashed out.

"So that's the root of your anger. Guilt?"

"That's only the tip of the iceberg, Lucia." Sergio sneered, the tightness in his chest growing. "There are others to blame in his death and I'll exact the consequences for their actions." Faces floated before him as he glowered at her. "Don't talk me out of it. Papa and Balthazar have already hammered away at me. So—"

"So... what? You're bullying me, too? I know you, like no one else. This hate. This darkness eclipsing the goodness... the brightness of your soul. It's not you. And I understand this because it's not me either. If you hold on to this, if you fulfill your desires for revenge... It will change you forever. Manny wouldn't want—"

Sergio got in Lucia's face so quickly, he caught the surprise in her eyes. "Don't you tell me what Manny would have wanted. I knew him best, what drove him to be a man. This is exactly what he would do!" He boasted to her face, livid she didn't understand and wouldn't let go.

"He was my brother, too. You don't own his memory or the pain of his death."

Her soft-spoken words might as well have punched him in the mouth. He backed away and headed for his room. He turned around, finding her rubbing the capsule between her fingers. "Two become one, Lucia. That's what we're supposed to do. But that's only with guardianship. Each of us gets their personal, private space. Honor that, and I will honor yours. I know you miss Manny, but don't compare our pain or judge how I'm dealing with it. I made a promise to Manny while his blood pooled around me, that I would avenge his death. Please don't get in the way of what I have to do." His head pounded; hands tingled in dark need.

"Okay. If that's how you want it. But I'm here, Sergio, alive, and I'll always have your back, even when you're not looking."

Sergio ran his hand through his thick hair and headed back to his room. He closed and locked his door. The pounding got louder, the need to hold the ax too unrelenting to ignore. He opened his closet and fished it out from the backpack hidden in the corner. His heart raced as he zipped it open, the frantic need like a drug addict getting his fix. The red scaled handle glowed, the half-moon shaped ax head sharp, ready to kill. As soon as his hand wrapped around the sinister handle, he closed his eyes as the swamp of relief washed over him. He dragged in a few deep breaths, calming him. The stronger he grew, the more compelled he was to find and kill Zar.

Gabriel...

Sergio clenched his teeth against the insidious roar of the sacred name. The ax shook in his trembling hands. He shoved the wretched images aside, disgusted with himself that such a horrific fantasy twists in his mind. It's different now with Gabriel because Lucia is a guardian. He's vital to her... been so good for—

But he was too late for you... for Manny.

No. Please stop.

Not Gabriel... only Zar... the Fallen.

Sergio doubled over, the ax cradled in his lap. He rocked back and forth, sickened by the war wagging inside of him. On some level he understood it was tearing him apart... comprehended it was despicable to crave death by his hands. But in his core, killing Zar was the only road he could see that led to relief... and peace. The only way he could forgive himself, or anyone else, for Manny's death.

Eye for an Eye...

Death to my enemies.

CHAPTER
THIRTY-NINE

DELILAH

F*ree...*
But is this my dominion... my place to rule?

The green web closed behind Delilah. She scanned her surroundings, knowing she was undetectable inside her invisible dome. Familiar scents of grass, fresh air and humans assaulted her along with a sun that shone too bright for her liking. She'd once found Earth so enticingly beautiful, God's creation perfect except where man's sins had cast a long shadow. Now the smells and sights repulsed her. The stink of humanity overwhelmed any beauty she'd ever adored.

Why had I loved this place so?
Conner and my love for him.

A vile taste rose in her mouth and burned like her hatred for him. But not just for him.

Mankind.

Delilah held no remorse. In fact, it vilified her, sure her decision to ruin God and his creation was her true destiny. She was the only angel, no longer blinded by the God's deceptions, courageous enough to take the fall after Lucifer. Her path she once thought was so crooked, murky and unyielding, was now straight and lucid with no twists or turns, perfectly set in place by her determination and careful planning.

And my new ally...

They all underestimated me...

Except him... he understands me, supreme in his power... more than any of them combined.

A wicked grin creased Delilah's marble-like face. Her fate now cast. Living under constant suspicion and heinous treatment under Lucifer's controlling thumb would all be worth it. Her smiling in victory, of retribution for all the wrongs done to her, would be their last memory before she killed them. The time had come to put her strategy into motion, exhilarated to be the wrecking ball starting it all.

Delilah lifted an eyebrow as she stared at Conner's house from across the street. Their daughter should be at school, but whether Conner and Stella were home was another matter. This care package was for Olivia only, but the urge flared to smash their love nest to bits. She quelled these desires, knowing the slow torturous path ahead for the love birds. Complete decimation of their hearts and souls, exacted by her hands, was well worth the wait.

You have no idea what's in store for you...

She chuckled as she made her way to the quiet house. Her senses didn't pick up Conner, his pathetic wife or any goon angels. She needed to peek through the window just in case. Stepping onto the porch, she gazed inside, but the looking glass flashed in a searing memory front of her.

Christmas...

Conner clutching Stella around the waist...

Home...

She sneered, finding her want for him empty. Hate filled to the brim validated her choices and her dreams. This family was just a means to an end, a steppingstone on her path to greatness.

Their demon cat jumped onto the back of the couch under the window, breaking the vision. He arched his body and hissed, exposing his sharp teeth. She scoffed at him as he paced, his guttural growl a warning.

"You must be the cat that attacked Zar. Should I take you back with me... be my pet? Would you like that?" Delilah grinned at the irate feline, provoking its agitation by running her nails down the glass. "Don't worry. You're safe for now, but I might come back for you later."

Delilah portaled to Olivia's bedroom. Excitement coursed deep with fiery need. She closed the door, hearing the cat bound up the stairs. Wasting time wrestling with it or killing it would only raise suspicion. Glancing around the tidy room, she found what she was seeking. The feathers leaning in a jar on her desk. She walked over and picked up a framed picture next to her prize. Olivia and two boys hugging around a fire pit, smiling with the carefreeness of youth against a backdrop of sloped barren red hills with red dirt powdering their shoes.

Perfect...

She opened the desk drawer and removed a notebook. Ignoring the cat's irritating pawing at the door, she ripped out a blank page. Delilah plucked a black feather from her wing. She twirled it between her fingers, inky and iridescent in light, as fine ash fell on the carpet. Closing her eyes, she drew up a memory of Conner. One that will certainly upset Olivia yet leave her wanting... demanding to know more. With the vision set, Delilah stabbed the end of her finger with the feather's razor-sharp end. Black blood oozed, throbbing to the beat of her pounding heart. She let it drip onto the desk, pooling like thick oil. Using the feather's end like a quill, she dipped it into the blood and scrolled her trap for Olivia.

The first I left
As white as snow
Turned black as I fell
Not long ago

Prick the end
And you shall find
A vision for you
So hellish divine

Want to know more
Come out and play
On this full moon
Where your picture displays

Courage you have?
We shall see
Dare to come alone
I hold the key

She let the feather fall from her grasp. The sharp end seeped the last of the bloody ink on the paper.

Click... The trap is set.

A smug smile crossed her lips. No way Olivia won't seek her out. The vision will, if nothing else, drive her out with a vengeance in a murderous rage. Delilah sucked on her finger, her blood tingling her tongue, delighted with her ploy.

She glanced out the window as she opened her portal. Comforting heat washed over her as the smells of sulfur and soot beckoned her home. One day she'll rule this horrid place filled with do-gooders and the saved. She wouldn't rest until the blue skies billowed with enough smoke to block out the sun mirroring its scorched earth.

And its inhabitants?

Dead or living as tortured slaves to their inner demons, driven by their destructive sins to satisfy the Fallen's every desire.

Her body hummed... fed by the power of her exploit, screamed for release and satisfaction. She bit her lip, thinking of the possibilities. Sighing, she stepped through the web, her day's deeds not quite complete.

A few more traps to set.

Then I'll decide who shall please me... Lucifer or my new ally.

Or why not both?

Her throaty laughter echoed as the portal closed on the hissing cat and cheery bedroom.

CHAPTER
FORTY

ZAR

Roars of adulation echoed around Zar from occupants reeking of blood lust. Fallen swarmed in the Main Hall's pit like a frenzied pack, anxious for their opportunity to be the next victor. He had no interest in entering the trench and prove his worth. He learned more by absorbing what made the mob tick. What incited them to fight and what controlled their basic instinct to destroy one another?

Power and pecking order...

He was working on both.

Delilah's musky scent crashed through his thoughts, but he'd trained himself to show no reaction to her arrivals. Delilah savored exposing another's weaknesses to exploit for her use. He'd already given her too many weapons. She wasn't his friend, even though he played along with her pretense. Considering her an enemy was safer for him... on many levels. She strutted over to him; her scent more overwhelming with each approaching step. Zar set his jaw, pounding his walking stick in approval as a Damned's shredded body flew out of the pit.

"Quite a lively crowd today," Delilah's hot breath breezed over his ear.

Chaotic yells reached a fevered pitch when a new Damned

paraded through the throng, parting for the massive opponent. Red slashes throbbed across his body, matching the beat of the throng.

"Looks like the Wrath Realm aims to rule the pit again." Zar admired how the new participant walked with a sole purpose, absorbing the crowd's energy. He stopped at the lip of the pit. The horde pushed unwilling participants over the edge, but this one sneered into the battle arena and jumped off, fists ready. Zar nodded in approval before turning to Delilah.

"I take it you were successful in your mission by your smug tone." He didn't need color vision to image her eyes sparking in a vibrant green.

"It went better than I expected. I left a delightful note for our little guardian to find along with one of my irresistible feathers. I have no doubt she'll take the bait and jump at the chance to rendezvous with us. The vision I left for her will leave her blind to any trap." Delilah's throaty laughter sent warning bells clanging in his head.

"I don't remember any talk of a vision, Delilah? What did you—"

"Oh, stop your worrying. It was a stroke of brilliance on my part... just some needed insurance that she'll show up as planned."

Zar seethed at her recklessness. "You'd better be right, or we have a date with Tannin for dinner." Her body stiffened.

Popped your bubble?

"Was anyone home?" he asked before she could jab him back.

"Just their hostile cat. He is a wretched little creature." Delilah laid a hand on his arm. "You remember him, don't you? I recall you returned with a few scratches?"

Zar scoffed, swatting her hand away. "Aw, yes... the demon cat. Did he get his licks in too?"

"No, I wasn't careless enough to tangle with him. I shut the door on his hissing face." She cracked a smile. "I considered killing it, but I think he'd make an excellent pet for me after we rid him of his owners. I appreciate loyalty in any form."

Zar turned to her, keeping his hard mask up against her obvious barb. "You two would form a perfect pair," he replied, sarcasm dripping in his tone. "Although, you don't strike me as the type who would enjoy a pet. They do require attention."

Delilah lifted an eyebrow, examining him from head to toe. "I know exactly who requires my attention and how to satisfy their needs."

"I bet you do." Zar muttered, but his reply drowned out by a vicious cry from the pit captured their attentions. He froze when he sensed Asura. She exhibited no outward sign of displeasure, but her body was taunt, poised to pounce.

"I tire of her presence. I find Asura's contempt for me droll considering all I'm doing to help the cause." Delilah tried to conceal her irritation, but her clenching fist betrayed her.

"You mean... all *we* are doing for the cause, don't you?"

Delilah put her hands on her hips and faced him. "Must you always correct me? I consider us as one."

Sure you do.

Is that what you say to the others?

Zar resisted laughing in her face. "Just checking. The pit is boring me. Shall we go back to my room and finalize our plans?"

"Hmm... no... but I'll be by later. I have a few things I must attend to first." Delilah licked her lips. He sensed excitement spiking in her body.

Where are you off to now?

I should follow you...

"More important than methods to kidnap—"

"Really, Zar... sometimes your questions are a true bore. I told you I'd come by when I'm finished." She waved her hand at him, shooing him away. "Go fly your Degasus or train with someone. Blow off some steam and wrap your mind around the next stage of the plan. That works for me." A wicked smile creased her face as she glanced at Asura. "'Til then."

I bet it does... pity the fool.

Delilah stepped aside, her wings expanding before she jumped into flight. He sensed her flying among the other Fallen, circling the pit. His pulse spiked when she exited through the massive arches leading to the Realm of Greed... Sonneillon's reign. He exhaled sharply, irked she chose to leave in that direction. Asura must have noticed too, because she stormed at him like it was his fault.

"Where is that viper going? Of all the exits she could have used, she goes through that one? I don't know how much longer I can stand to have her here. I'm following—"

Zar grabbed her arm before she could take flight. Asura yanked it back and rounded on him. "Don't ever try to stop me again." She leaned in closer. "You'll lose more than your eyes next time."

He held his ground and bowed slightly at her. "My apologies. But you can't forget your head when it comes to Delilah. Trust me, I've learned the hard way. I'm certain she did that for your benefit, hoping to get a rise from you, and it worked. She has become increasingly bolder in her actions... maybe she's more confident in her dealings with Lucifer." Zar kept the plan about kidnapping the girl to himself and his own compulsion to follow Delilah.

"She's up to something. I see it even though she thinks she's hiding her not-so-clever ways. She's not as cunning as she assumes." Asura sneered, gazing at the Realm of Greed's arches.

Zar's grip tightened on his walking stick, concern pounding in his head. "And if that's the case, Lucifer will take care of her... have no doubt. Now—" he gazed over the pit "—I'm off to ride Cydanos. Join me?"

"No." She turned to him; her ebony skin pulsated with gold scrolls. "But understand this. If I find out she's trying to seduce Sonneillon or is feeding him lies, I will skin her alive slowly, slicing chunks out of her with my dagger. I'll not feed her to Tannin, that's too quick. Introducing her to Astaroth's pit of snakes is more appropriate. I'll throw what's left of her in and she'll be devoured by those she emulates. Share that with her or not. I don't care. But I'm watching her." She placed her pointed nail under his chin. "And if I discover you've helped her? You will face the same fate," Asura promised, nicking his chin. She twisted and flew away, leaving him speechless. She exited through the Realm of Pride arches before he swiped away the blood dripping from his chin.

Zar stood there for a moment, sensing the crowd for any eavesdroppers. No one gave him a care, their focus on the blood splattered Red Wrath victor emerging from the pit. Zar envied him his easy praise from the Fallen with their cheers booming around him. He turned away, not wanting any part of the victory celebration. It sickened him how the Fallen gave their accolades so easily to the brute, failing to understand the value of a thinker. He walked instead of flying to ride Cydanos. He needed to calm himself before he rode his beloved beast.

With each step he took, he fought to contain a loss of control. Both Asura and Delilah complicated his life, yet he was chained to them, suffering their whims and rages. But the longer he roamed, he rebuilt his plan, molding it to fit the players while considering all the pitfalls and how to avoid them. This is how he'd improved as a Fallen. Strategy without emotion or care for anyone else but himself, portraying to everyone else their expectations of his behavior. He smiled to himself, secure in the knowledge that he wasn't the hapless puppet.

I will not be a meal for Tannin or tortured fool for Asura or Delilah.

I did that once.

Never again.

I will come out on top... and no one will know what hit them.

CHAPTER
FORTY-ONE

OLIVIA

Pain exploded across Olivia's lower back as her knees landed on the rough asphalt. She jumped aside before the Sloth demon could plant another vicious kick. Her hair was plastered to her head, heart pounding as she twirled to face her enemy. The Fallen swung his pulsating purple sword across his body, but Olivia met it with hers, the force jarring up her arm. The sharp clanging sound punctuated the desert night air.

"You fight well, human, but—" Olivia caught a movement in the bulge around his arm, "—you're no match for the two of us," he warned, his pale face breaking out in a hideous grin. What Olivia thought was part of his armor, slithered to life, uncoiling around his arm. The thick black snake raced down his arm, mouth open exposing its long purple fangs. It raised its triangular head back, aiming for her hand clutching the sword. She thrust against their joined swords, sending the Fallen's arms into the air along with the vicious snake.

"Not for long," she swore, watching the snake's body whip into the air like the end of a tattered flag. Olivia released her left hand and aimed it at the Fallen distracted by his snake. Calling upon her energy, she sought the dagger at her hip. She envisioned it flying from its sheath and embedding itself in the demon's black heart. She felt the tug at her hip, but her eyes never left the hideous snake as it fell, its fangs glistened with venom. The demon shrieked as she swung her sword at the snake, slicing it in two. The halves exploded and turned to ash. It caught in a gust of wind and blew away.

Olivia turned to the demon, ready to strike, but found oily blood evaporating and fading ash. She hung her head, relived the dagger had found its mark. She walked over to retrieve it; the blue flames had died down. She bent over and grabbed the handle, a smirk crossing her face. Exhilarated by her victory, she gazed around the park's lot, satisfied no other demon lurked with the group of kids lounging on an old park picnic table. One teen laid on the bench, his arm dangling over the side. He sat up, shaking his head as he gazed at his friends. Their muffled laughter and voices mocking his exit from the table floated to her. All eyes were trained on his back as he treaded away from them, oblivious to the danger that had stalked them. A warmth spread through her, nodding at the departing figure.

Go home or find a job...

Maybe he has a chance now.

But her purpose wasn't to judge or worry, only to kill the Fallen determined to ruin his soul.

Mission complete.

Her mark was dormant once more against her skin, but her concern still lingered on the teen as she opened her crackling portal.

Sweat drenched clothes clung to her body. Olivia couldn't wait to soak her aches and pains under the hot shower's spray. The blow to her back throbbed, but the effects were fading as the web snapped closed behind her. She paused, adrenaline spiking her system. Someone or something had been in her bedroom. The air was ripe, reeking of smoke. She sniffed again, checking it wasn't a lingering odor from the battle. A whiff of sulfur, fresh and pungent, hit her sensitive senses. Heart pounding, she turned in a circle, scouring the dark corners of her room. Nothing moved, but her mark tingled, reacting to whatever presence had invaded her sanctuary.

Thump, thump

Olivia whirled around and faced her closed door. Her brows creased as the soft thudding grew more insistent. Relaxing her stance, she opened the door. A blur of gray charged into the room and jumped onto her desk. She glanced into the hallway, lit only by the subtle glow filtering from downstairs. Muffled voices mingled with the rushing blood in her ears. Closing the door, she turned her attention to the mystery intruder.

Thunder's bushy tail swished over the side of the desk, perched to pounce. His deep guttural growl permeated the air. He crouched, his nose twitching over a piece of paper left on the desk. She flung her hand to the light switch, her finger flipping it up. Light radiated from above, illuminating what had riled her cat. A slash of black feather lay across an innocuous sheet of paper, mocking her sense of security. She swallowed, trying to gather some spit in her dry mouth. Thunder's growl lowered as Olivia ran her hand down his back.

"Did you tangle with another visitor? Hope you gouged their eyes out," she murmured.

She stared at the treacherous objects on her desk, wondering what the scrolling messages across the paper meant for her. Reaching out with a trembling hand, she skimmed her finger down the feather's spine. She paused at the sharp end laying in an inky pool. She leaned closer and sniffed, but jerked away, finding the source of the pungent odor.

Demon's blood.

Heat flushed through her body. She snatched up the menacing feather in one hand and the note in the other. No demons had been in her room since she suspected Zar had left the black feather for her when she'd been by her mom's side at the hospital a few months ago. Was it him again? Her eyes scoured the note. With each line she read, her hand clenched, crumbling the edge. Her anger burned inside her, ripe with indignation as the evil message seared her mind.

She digested the words a second time, confirming the wicked author and her intent left little doubt.

Delilah.

Prick the end...
A vision for you...
On the full moon...
Courage you have?
Come alone...

Olivia placed the paper back on her desk but still clutched the feather. She gazed at the frame alongside the mason jar. Three smiling faces stared back at her from the photo of Zach and Sergio with her at the Valley of Fire. This message, however, was personal and meant only for her. Thunder jumped next to her and pawed at the feather.

"I know kit-kitty. I wish I could throw it away, but I can't," she grumbled to him. "I have to find out what the vision is, even if it's dangerous." He sat on his haunches, staring at her with his big green eyes as if begging her to reconsider. But she couldn't. Warning bells clanged in her head. Apprehension clawed at her at the thought of what would happen if she pricked herself... and if she didn't.

What if its poison dipped like the dagger from her attacker or a marker for them to track her?

Poison she could fight, and they didn't need to mark her since they knew where she lived. If something happened to her, someone would discover the letter and understand who to blame. So why all the intrigue? There was only one way to find out.

Holding her breath, Olivia pressed the feather's pointed end to her fingertip, glistening with a fine sheen of sweat. She pricked her flesh, hissing between her teeth at the invasion of the brittle tip. A red dot bloomed, mixing with the dried evil blood on the feather's tip. She jolted like it had bitten her. A cold sensation rushed up her arm like an icy tentacle chasing prey for its hungry master. But as the tentacle swam up her arm, the feather's tip ignited in flame. Her heart pounded as sparks raced up feather's spine, ash falling on to her lap. Her eyes darted to the desk. A small green current sizzled across the pool of dried blood, catching the end of the dreaded note, consuming the paper in a flash. She fought her rising panic, fearing she'd calculated wrong.

It isn't a vision, it's a death trap.

Olivia gasped when the tentacle reached its destination and speared her brain. She tried to call out, but her thick tongue lay immobile. A white explosion of light erupted inside her head. She arched and fell back on her bed, hearing Thunder's meow next to her. Her body froze, victim to whatever Delilah had in store for her.

An unfamiliar alley bloomed before her, shrouded in the dim streetlight. Her pulse raced, realizing it was not through her eyes she was gazing through, but those of another. Banged-up trash cans lay knocked over; their ripe odor hung thick in the stagnant air. Stepping deeper into the alley, blue and pink lights flashed in the dark backdrop. The pace quickened, driven by a curiosity of the person trapping her. Two people battled in front of her, their grunts and clashes of metal familiar to Olivia. Recognition washed over her for the tall dark headed man swinging the sword, beheading a pink demon. Dad. His muscular back heaved as he sheathed his blazing blue sword.

"Conner..." He spun around, and surprise splashed over his face. "What—why are you fighting a demon? Where did you get that sword?"

He didn't answer, instead he ran over and gripped her arms. "Delilah! What are you doing here? You're not supposed—"

"I don't care about Michael's orders. I care about you! But I don't understand this! You just killed a demon... I—"

"Nobody can know about this—about what I do... not even you! Swear to me... promise me... you won't tell anyone." Conner gripped

her arms tighter, giving her a hard shake. "Promise me now!" He demanded through gritted teeth. Sweat still glistened on his forehead, but panic blazed in his blue eyes.

For a moment, Delilah didn't recognize the wild-eyed, desperate man begging for her promise. But even as uncertainty pounded in her mind, her need for him became something she would fight no longer. The infantile desire washed away, replaced by a deep-seated compulsion to own him... possess him at whatever the cost. He was more than the charge they had given her to guide in his walk of life. He needed her more than ever now... to protect him from his enemies and love him in a way only her angelic essence could.

Only I can do this Conner... no one else.

"I promise, but—"

"We must leave..."

Her dad's voice faded, as did the dark alley.

A fresh scene appeared, serene with sunlight fading over red rolling hills. Olivia's heart squeezed as she watched her dad walk up the trail alone from eyes not her own. He wore the same t-shirt Olivia had clung to coming down a similar pathway so many years ago. She railed against the voyeur for invading a time that was still precious to her. His scent of salt and dust enveloped her. The little girl in her wanted to cry out, beg him to return to the trailer...

Stay with me and Mom.

Delilah's heart swelled as she gazed at Conner, remembering the night they'd shared together, sealing them as one. He trudged up the red gravel path to where she waited for him in a shaded hollow nestled within the stark crimson hills. But his stare didn't return the same bliss or yearning. Instead they were icy blue, not the ones of her lover.

273

Conner stopped in front of her, but the space he left between them spoke volumes. She stepped forward, ignoring his unspoken wish. He raised his hand and shook his head.

"Don't, Delilah." But his words fell on deaf ears. She released a wave of her essence, bombarding him like waves on a rocky shore with the overwhelming emotions of want of him and desires for more. She watched the battle within the shifting blue of his eyes. They widen as she moved inches from him.

"I will never stop, Conner." Delilah whispered against his lips, brushing over them with the barest of a kiss. "You are mine. I know your secrets. I know your body. Forever, we'll be one. Mind. Body. Soul."

She entwined her fingers in his thick hair, bringing him into a deep kiss, silencing Conner's strangled groan. She'd make him understand. In the end, he'd see that she was his future... his life.

Olivia lay gasping for breath, the vision a fading haze in her tattered mind. Tears rolled down the side of her face, trailing down her neck. Bile rose as the memory of the deceitful kiss still lingered, smashing the last perfect day Olivia remembered as a family. It lay shattered, the shards piercing her heart. Was there a memory left of her family not tainted by betrayal, not shredded by lies? Her fingers clawed at her comforter, twisting in her hand like the memories yanking at her heart.

"How could you be so blind, Dad?" she muttered. Thunder's loud purr held no answer, but his presence comforted her as she rode the storm of her emotions. Slowly, her breathing calmed and nerves settled. She digested the new insight into Dad and Delilah. Olivia didn't want to admit it and she wasn't even sure her dad realized it, but he never stood a chance against Delilah. Her plan was to ensnare him no matter the cost. Delilah thought this revelation would inflame Olivia's hate for her dad, make her cry out in revenge. But that had backfired. Olivia was shown the truth. She saw what Delilah had done to him.

And that pissed her off.

You'll get the revenge you want, Delilah, but it won't be aimed at my dad.

I will avenge what you've done to my family.

Sitting up, Olivia grabbed her phone, wanting to text Sergio and Zach. Her shoulders slumped, the phone slipping from her hands to the bed. She couldn't tell them. She had to do this on her own or risk putting them all in danger. If Delilah wanted only her... fine. That's what she'll get. A cold knot formed in her stomach; struck by the fact she was committing the same sin she had damned her dad for; keeping secrets to protect those he loved. A kindling of understanding burned within her.

And she cursed herself for it.

CHAPTER
FORTY-TWO

LUCIFER

The wails of the damned flowed over him, bathing him with illicit power, cleansing him of any doubt about his rightful place as supreme leader of the Realms of Hell. Lucifer stood in the middle of the round stone room at the top of his tower, lording over his dark kingdom. Here, in his sanctuary, he wallowed in his wicked desires and calculated his plans of war and ultimate domination. No one interrupted him with their insipid demands or insufferable worries. He lost himself, free to live out his visions to fruition and unearth any potential traps. He absorbed the crescendo of cries, burned with the erupting colors of his Realms, pulsating against his body through the high-arched windows. His excitement grew as he thought of the girl—Olivia. She'd soon be here, under his control, bought to submission. He closed his eyes, imaging her hanging over the black pool, Tannin rippling beneath her. His whip licking at her flesh, red human blood dripping to his hungry serpent. Or might he chain her in the bowels of his tower and torture her slowly until she succumbs to his questions? He sneered at the image, her whimpering while his vicious ministrations ripped apart her mortal body.

"Our date with destiny is coming soon," he growled his promise to the fading picture. "And then my time to rule in the light and dark will finally come true." Lucifer paced near the windows, appreciating the kingdom he built since the day he'd left Heaven and brought his army of Fallen with him. He'd worked tirelessly to keep his vision the driving force behind their deeds, all the while on high alert for traitors who hungered for his power. Giving his most faithful Princes their own Realms to rule as a reward for their loyalty helped quench their thirst of any misguided desires to challenge his supremacy.

But one is a traitor...

He knew it to the depths of his black soul. Who would dare dream of dethroning him?

Delilah?

Zar?

They're not smart enough, or strong enough, to influence the Fallen. But do they have help?

He stopped and faced the Realm of Greed... Sonneillon's domain.

Would you conceive of such a plan, old friend, or did someone plant the seed for you?

Lucifer growled deep in his chest, seething at the possibility of Asura and Sonneillon betraying him.

Let's see what she has to say.

While Lucifer glared at the blue pool bubbling with a mutating soul of a Damned, he sought Asura through the link he created during the battle in Heaven. He probed the Realms; an energy tunnel winding its way until it found its target. She startled and turned to him, like he'd tapped her on the shoulder. He didn't need to speak, for she understood it wasn't a request. She flew out of the pit, dodging the Degasus circling the undulating walls.

He waited, gazing at the blue gurgling lava flowing into the black moat. Not a drop of lava retained its original color... always consumed by the black churning mass... his life blood.

Remember that, Sonneillon.

A knock on the door pulled him away from his Realm. "Enter," he said, turning to face the arrival of the Fallen who'd once been his closest confidant... and lover.

Asura entered the room, filling it with her ebony beauty. Her gold braided hair enhanced her wild nature. His blood pumped as he remembered their days ruling the Realm and nights tearing into each other until they fulfilled their wicked fantasies. But that time was gone. Her maddening power over him got out of control, so he'd cut her out of his life.

Maybe it's time to bring her back into the fold...

But as he followed her approach, he caught a glimpse of wariness flickering in her golden eyes. He reached out his hand. "Welcome back, Asura," he drawled as she placed her hand in his. Lowering his lips, he nipped her flesh. He placed a fiery kiss on her knuckles. She tried to pull her hand away, but he tightened his grip and stared at her.

"You remember our times together here... our hideaway? Entwined around each other as the Realms exploded like our passions." Her sharp inhale along with the flare of the gold swirls over her chest betrayed the weak indignation. This time when she yanked her hand, he released it with a soft chuckle. "I see you do."

"Our time together has passed. I hope that's not the reason—"

"If I want you back, you're in no place to deny me." His quiet statement belied his inner fire. Asura didn't reply, instead choosing to lift her chin in silent defiance.

"But you're right, I didn't call for you to quench my old desires—" he reached out and touched a thin braid, running his hand down its long length "—but you do ignite a fire in me, and I in you, even though you try to deny it." He let his hand fall, enjoying how she struggled for control of her want for him.

Yes... I think I will bring you back into my life...

That should inflame Sonneillon even more.

He smirked as she brushed past him. He let her go, inhaling the delicious scent she left in her wake.

"What is it you want, Lucifer? Did you call me here to play games or is there something more?" She turned to face him. The

Realm of Wrath's red flames glowed behind her, matching the fury bubbling below her surface.

"Testy, are we?" He chuckled. "I called you here for a task I've chosen just for you. Ever since you and Beelzebub came to me with your concerns of a traitor, I realized you still hold your allegiance to me above all else. In these uncertain times of war and my change of vision for the Fallen, I need fierce allies and trusted accomplices. You've shown me you are deserving of such a role." Asura's shoulders relaxed as she raised an eyebrow at him.

"I'm honored, my lord, but surely there are others—"

"You are unique in your place within the Realms. As a Seraphim, you're a rare breed here. You come from the most powerful Realm, yet your mate is a Prince of another. You also have the ear of Zar, whom Delilah trusts."

Asura sneered at the sound of Delilah's name. "I do not trust her, Lord. I fear she's not all you believe she is."

"Have no fear, I hold no illusions about Delilah. I know exactly who she is and what she wants... power. But this is where you come in. I have given her the opportunity to show her worth and where her allegiances truly stand. Soon she and Zar will bring the girl guardian to me. They've set the trap, but I need you with them when this happens, to keep a careful watch in case they decide to first take matters into their own hands." He clasped his fist behind his back, regarding Asura pace the room.

"What are you concerned about, my Lord?" She walked closer to him. He enjoyed observing the wheels turn on her exquisite face.

"Oh, come now. Don't be coy with me. If you were in her place and wanted the knowledge first, what would you do?"

She pursed, mulling over the scenario. "I'd kidnap her, take her someplace, and torture her to get the information. I'd then kill her and tell you she died in the fight before I could bring her back." She sneered.

"Yes. That is one of the many schemes I've devised. So, as you can surmise, I need you to be there so there's no opportunity for foul play."

"You don't trust Zar?"

His eyes narrowed as he lazily scanned her body from top to bottom. "Zar and I go back to the beginning. He's one of my chosen. I also know you have an affinity for him as well. But he has made poor choices under Delilah's spell. He paid for them but has not been put to the test since his punishment. Even if he is true to our cause, I would not underestimate Delilah's desire to kill him."

"Then why not kill her!" Asura pulled the dagger from its sheath, waving it in front of her face. "Or better yet, let me do the honor."

He stepped closer, the dagger's edge between them. "Your blood lust is intoxicating and admirable, but I need her alive for another purpose... one just as important as the guardian."

Asura sheathed her gold blade in disgust. "What could she know that's worthy of her drawing another breath?"

Lucifer closed the slight distance between them. Her nostrils flared as he ran his finger down her cheek, stopping under her chin. He lifted her face, ignited again by her scent. "I believe she is working with the traitor. I want to follow her trail of ash to his doorstep." He snatched her jaw within his hard grasp, bringing their lips inches apart. "I will kill the fool who betrayed me, and you can have Delilah to do with as you will." The gold crackled in her eyes as her lips parted.

Is your fire for me or for blood?

Lucifer brought his lips down hard, needing to taste again what once was his. The brutal kiss ground against her, splitting her lip where his teeth bit, so he could have a taste.

Fire

Passion

Blood...

Mine.

He stepped back as quickly as he had struck. Asura's chest

heaved; control and desire warred across her face. He turned, spreading his arms wide. His massive wings fanned out behind him.

"There is a traitor in the Realms—" he stalked in a circle, yelling at the windows "—one who thinks he can defeat me. But that will never happen." Lucifer stopped and faced his beautiful Fallen. "If you help me unearth him, you'll further your position within the Realm... and with me."

Asura lifted her sword. "I pledge to bring the traitor to you, my lord."

He bowed slightly, accepting her show of loyalty. "I'll tell you when the abduction is to take place. Keep a careful watch over Zar and Delilah. You'll be a last-minute arrival to the party, so they can't change their plans."

"I'm ready."

He let her make her way to the door before he called to her. "Asura." She glanced over her shoulder. "If this trail of ash leads to Sonneillon's door, I will kill him. If I find out you've double crossed me, I'll kill Sonneillon. If I link you to the traitor, I will also kill Sonneillon. If your loyalty is true, as is Sonneillon's, you both shall live."

"Why do you threaten such things, I've—"

"Because you know me well. You'd expect nothing less. But I also assume you've come to foresee that when I rule Heaven and Earth, I will take a queen. I name you... mated or not."

CHAPTER
FORTY-THREE

DARK
PRINCE

H e flew among the Lessors and observed them delivering their precious black orbs into the fiery pools, reflecting the sins that controlled their lives on Earth. Steamy updrafts pushed against his immense wings, lifting him above the Realms he would one day claim from Lucifer and rule with the deep-seated malevolent passion missing from Hell's current master. The Lessors had proved to heed Lucifer's demand for more souls to expand the army of the Damned. The Realm's black, ominous mountains bulged at the core, stuffed with the Damned yearning to be set loose.

He envisioned them pouring out of the bluff's exits, through the portals to Heaven and Earth. Their mutated forms devouring the fragile flesh of mankind brought a wicked sneer to his face. Humans were no match against these vicious souls and the Fallen. They would roll over in horror, ill-equipped to stop the horde overwhelming them.

Erased from the world...

At last...

During the battle, Lessors would continue to take black souls to Hell, generating an army for *his* new kingdom. Even when the Angels descended from Heaven, the Fallen would defeat them, leaving the Damned to crush the abomination of God. Those few humans who slipped through their grasp would become hunting sport for the Fallen. Each and every one wiped from the face of the Earth, not turned into slaves for entertainment like Lucifer wanted.

No.

We will live for eternity.

The Damned our slaves, not man.

His clandestine rendezvous went according to plan, his ally an eager accomplice, also impatient with Lucifer's maniacal hold and unstable rule.

You did well. The bait taken eagerly, but do not trust this one... only me.

"Yes, almost too desirous of our union," he muttered in agreement. "But, if I'm to know the guardian's secret first without raising Lucifer's suspicions, then I must—"

But there are others who can find this girl. Persuade them to take you to her now—

"No!" he growled at the ancient soul's voice, relentless in its interrogations, always challenging his plans. "Lucifer will suspect spies are lurking in his inner circle. No. Our mission works better if he stays in the dark with his new-world fantasies. Let him mount his new vision. Let him be the enemy receiving Heaven's blame. Let him lay down the groundwork and rattle their cages, and when the time is right, we will set ourselves free."

Yes... we will be one. Finally open to show our absolute power. We'll kill Lucifer and all loyal to him. The day will be upon us soon when the Fallen and Damned will bow and serve at our whim.

CHAPTER
FORTY-FOUR

OLIVIA

Full moon
      Tonight
   Is it a trap?
   Of course...

Olivia sprayed cleaner on the Defender's blank video game console. She wiped it with a cloth and caught her reflection. Memories of the battle she was a part of while playing the game played in her head. Was this a vision of her future set in stone, or could it change with her actions tonight by meeting Delilah? Her hand paused over the knob, body humming with excitement, as she remembered the beast she rode, facing a diabolical enemy she had learned how to defeat, including Delilah and her vile partner, Zar.

They will not win... I refuse to let that happen.

Olivia scanned her features once more, staring at eyes gleaming with hard determination. She wasn't the same girl who had played that game, even though it happened only four months ago. Her life had forever changed. She accepted that, along with the mixed bag of the good, bad and ugly along with it.

She'd also gotten used to her shorter hair, pulled back now in a light ponytail. Some people bemoaned her for cutting it. When asked why she did it, Olivia simply replied she'd been ready for a change.

But inside, she'd cut off the baggage with her dad in her anger after their argument and his final admission of his affair with Delilah. Hearing the truth cut deep, but it released a dam of misconceptions and cleared the slate to start over with him.

There was the added bonus that Zach liked the haircut too. Walking away from the game console, she smiled to herself, remembering the kiss they shared. Lord, her body tingled when she recalled his tender kisses and the peace his hugs brought to her. Such a simple act, yet the memories swirled with complicated emotions; the biggest of all, the word she stopped Zach from blurting out.

Am I ready to love him?

Am I even capable of the love he deserves?

And trust him completely with the fragile gift of my love?

"I remember when I used to go around with the same sappy smile," Callie grinned, winking at her.

Olivia stopped short before colliding into Callie, who stood in front of her with mugs dangling from her fingers and a playful grin.

A flush crept up Olivia's neck. "It wasn't a—"

"Girl, it was totally sappy!" Callie chuckled, cocking her head. "Who's the lucky guy? I sure hope it's Zach. Such a cutie with those green eyes, and that strong, silent type of mojo he's got—"

"Please stop before someone hears you!" Olivia covered her ears, the hot flush reaching her cheeks. "Sounds like he's your type." She quipped.

Callie rolled her eyes and gave Olivia a hip check as she passed. "He's all yours, besides—" she sighed, "—my ex may have wrecked me from ever loving again." She turned, giving Olivia a conspirator's wink. "Although, there is a certain brown-eyed, strong silent guy around here I'd like to know better."

"Joe?" Olivia gawked, moving closer while she scanned the cafe for her boss. "I had no idea... why didn't you tell me? You two would make a great couple."

Callie shook her head, placing the mugs on the wood shelf. "I shouldn't have said anything. I was just being silly, anyway."

"Right. Now it's my turn to roll my eyes." Callie snorted, glancing at Olivia. "Joe is an amazing guy. He'd be perfect for you—"

"Look... forget I mentioned it. I was being silly." A sadness floated over her face, but the fear in her eyes caught Olivia's attention. "I can't get involved with anyone right now. Just let it go, okay?" Callie laid her hand on her arm. "Please?"

"Fine. It's forgotten." Her shoulders relaxed as she squeezed Olivia's arm. "On one condition."

Callie's arm fell, her guard up. "What?"

"You promise to tell me if your jerk ex-husband hurts or threatens you or Chloe."

Callie crossed her arms. "Okay, but what could you do—" the door's bell jingled, halting her question, to Olivia's relief. She glanced over her shoulder and found Zach coming inside with Sergio in tow. Her heart skipped a beat when Zach grinned at her, showing off his dimple. Sergio lifted his chin. His shrewd eyes scanned the cafe.

"Speak of the devil," Callie whispered. "I'll cover the counter if you want to talk with them." She walked past Olivia, not waiting for her reply.

"Hey," Zach said, stopping next to her. "Not too busy in here today. Good time for a break?"

Olivia glanced at a beaming Callie serving a thin woman who handed her an over-sized red mug. She swallowed, needing moisture in her suddenly dry mouth. "Sure. You two want a cup of coffee?" She twirled the ring on her finger, orange and red glinting from the rays of afternoon sunlight streaming through the front window.

"Sounds tempting, but my body doesn't need the caffeine anymore." Zach shook his head.

"I don't either, but I can't resist the cookies," Sergio waggled his eyebrows. "You want one, boy scout?" He nudged Zach.

"Always. Thanks, man." Sergio weaved his way between the colorful wooden chairs. He waited for Callie until the whirr of the froth machine ended. Olivia didn't drink as much coffee as she used to either, but she never tired of the comforting earthy aroma. She inhaled, hoping to relax her nerves.

"Let's sit on the couch." Olivia sat on the sagging cushion. Zach plopped down next to her, laying his arm across the back. Her pulse kicked up a notch when their knees touched. But it wasn't the easy contact that caused the reaction. Knowing she was holding back the truth ate at her. Zach sat back, the leather squeaking beneath him. She squirmed under his watchful eye. His brow scrunched as his gaze turned intense. "What's up—"

Two large sugar cookies tucked in a white napkin shot between them. "Here ya go." Zach took the treats, but laid them on his lap, holding his stare.

"What brings you by?" Olivia's glance darted between the boys.

"Lucia suggested the four of us get a pizza and then see a movie tonight. She thinks we needed to act more like teenagers every once in a while. I guess some people from school have been asking where we've been. I personally don't care, but there's no need to raise any suspicions either." Sergio took a big bite of the cookie, tan crumbs falling onto his black t-shirt.

"So, how 'bout it? What time do you get off work?" Zach broke the cookie in half and put a piece in his mouth.

"Uhm... I can't go out tonight," Olivia protested softly.

Zach stopped chewing. His eyebrows shot up.

"I told my parents we could have a quiet evening together," Olivia continued. "You know—" she tugged on her dragonfly earring "—we're trying to mend fences and... move on... since Dad's back to stay and all. It's the best thing."

Stop rambling...

"But thanks." Olivia sat up, feeling as fake inside as the smile she had plastered on her face. "I'm sure you'll have fun."

"Cool. It's past time you mended those fences. The news will bum Lucia. She was looking forward to hanging out with you that didn't involve training or weapons." Sergio smirked.

Zach started chewing again, but whatever he was thinking, he kept to himself.

"I better get back to work." Olivia waved toward the counter. They all stood up, the boys dusting off their shirts. "Thanks for coming and inviting me. Have fun tonight." She turned to go, but Zach touched her arm.

"Good luck with your folks. If your evening ends early, text and we'll swing by and get you. I'm sure your parents wouldn't mind sharing you with us." His green eyes bore into hers as if seeking her hidden truth.

"I'll keep that in mind." She pledged, backing away from them. "Bye."

She turned and strode to the counter, her heart heavy with guilt. But she couldn't tell them. It was for their own good.

Especially if it's a trap.

Jeez, I hate myself.

The soft knock at the door startled Olivia, lost in her plans for tonight.

"Can I come in?" Mom's husky voice was muffled behind the closed bedroom door.

Olivia tossed the backpack in her closet. "Sure."

Her mom peeked through the crack before she opened it wide and stepped inside, leaving the door open behind her. Thunder jumped through and onto her bed, his tail swishing behind him. Olivia grinned at him and sat down to stroke her hand across his soft fur. He arched his back, all the while staring at her with his luminous green eyes.

"Thunder's been restless these last few days. I guess his evening escapades haven't been fruitful," Mom sat next to Olivia, joining her in petting the cat. "He hasn't brought me a present home for a while now." Mom chuckled.

Oh, how I'd love to lay Delilah at your door...

But Olivia knew the reason for Thunder's prowling around the house, but she wasn't about to share that with her. "The animal kingdom may have wised up to the predator lurking in our bushes." Olivia scoffed, sharing a smile with her mom.

"Hey. Dad and I are trying to decide what movie to watch tonight. We were thinking about something scary. I declared we each get our own bowl of popcorn. We'd love for you to join us." Her brown eyes looked hopeful as she stroked Thunder again.

"Um... how about a rain check? I've already told Zach and Sergio I'd meet them for dinner and a movie." Guilt tightened the knot in her stomach.

Mom's face fell even though her smile grew. "That sounds like way more fun than hanging out with your parents. I'm glad you're doing something else besides going on a hunt.

Gulp...

Olivia placed her hand over her mom's and brought it to her lap. "I miss hanging out with you. I loved those times when it was just us watching a chick flick."

"Honey—"

"I'm not saying that to make you feel bad. I'm sharing it because I miss you." Olivia glanced down at her ring with her fingers wrapped around her mom's delicate hand. "We've been kinda disconnected since you've recovered. I've been completely immersed with the guardianship. I'm worried you think I've abandoned you, but I haven't. Anyway... I just wanted you to know that I miss you and I love you. How about we make weekly dates... just us? We'll go shopping or get coffee like how it was before all this changed our lives." Olivia's throat clogged, her heart squeezed, realizing the depth of this desire to reconnect with her mom.

"That would make me so happy, sweetie." Mom said, raising her hand to cup Olivia's face. "I've missed our times together, too."

Olivia released a pent-up breath. "I also want the three of us to spend more time together. I know you've been giving me my space since I learned about Delilah. Thank you for that. I needed it, but I think I'm slowly coming to terms with Dad. All the training and time away, I guess I'm beginning to understand how a relationship can get complicated and drift apart."

Olivia watched a single tear slip from the corner of her mom's eye. "It's okay—"

"Please... let me finish. I'm not saying I've forgiven him or that I understand how he could have betrayed you... us... like he did with Delilah. I'm only saying that I'm ready to build the bridge between us we'd started before I learned the full truth. It might be rocky, but I'm willing to try."

Mom wrapped her willowy arms around her and brought her in for a hug. "We'd love nothing more than to be a family again," Mom whispered into Olivia's hair. She pulled away, eyes brimming bright with unshed tears and happiness. "Thank you." She patted Olivia's knee. "You better get going."

Olivia brushed the tear from her mom's cheek. "I love you."

"I love you, too. Have fun tonight." Mom stood up to leave. Glancing over her shoulder, her long wavy hair swept across her back. "Don't do anything I wouldn't do." She winked.

"Ha! Whatever Miss goodie-goodie!" They laughed as her mom shut the door.

The smile fell from Olivia's face. She replaced it with a jaw set in determination. She rose from the bed and pulled her talisman out of her pocket.

"Armor on," she commanded, closing her fingers around the token.

Olivia's sleek black armor materialized over her body. It started at her neck and flowed down her like tiny black dominoes falling into place. The snug fit enhanced her reassurance, having protected her from prior vicious hits during her battles.

"Weapons." Her sword, dagger, and throwing knives appeared in their sheaths on her belt. She retrieved her backpack from the closet and glanced at the door.

I'll be back, Mom...

Thunder's soft meow caught her attention from his perch on her bed. "Don't worry, Thunder. Delilah's not the only one who can set a trap," she smirked.

Olivia glimpsed the folded piece of paper she'd left for the boys, tucked under the silver frame on her desk.

She pulled up her portal. She hoped Zach and Sergio wouldn't be too late.

Please understand...

CHAPTER
FORTY-FIVE

SERGIO

Oppressive darkness seared him, like the black razor-edged feathers slashing across Sergio's skin, shutting out everything except the painful bites and rising panic in his chest. He was again trapped in the horribly familiar dream that haunted his sleep on occasions, it tormented him with the same dreadful ending.

Zar, in front of the gold portal, Olivia's body draped over his shoulder.

Even though Sergio understood that fighting inside his personal nightmare was pointless, he couldn't help himself from battling the evil forces working against him in his frantic need to reach Olivia. He summoned the essence of his mark. Putting his hands together, he created an orb between them. It crackled to life with its golden power. He threw the ball into the air. Shrieks ripped around him as the percussion wave exploded, knocking the demons away from him. The desert terrain came into view, brighter than it had been in previous dreams. But it only made the scene before him more horrifying. Unknown players emerged in his night's torment. Olivia was still draped over Zar, but a red-headed Fallen's shrill laughter of delight cut through him as she gazed at Olivia's limp body.

Delilah...

She hadn't been in the dreams before or had the dark-skinned Fallen with molten gold swirling over her body. Six massive wings burst out behind this new demon. Her golden eyes shifted to Sergio, igniting sparks inside them. She raised her golden sword as the smattering of Fallen turned in his direction. Sergio ran towards them, producing another air bomb in his hands. He recognized Zach's pounding footsteps, always next to him in his hellish dream. They raced in a matched stampede, their harsh breathing canceling out the words Delilah spoke to the gold Fallen. Whatever she said, it was confirmed with a sneer and a curt nod. The Fallen soldiers, most missing feathers and layers of skin from his air bomb, slipped into the portal's black abyss. Sergio nostrils flared, assaulted by the reek of sulfur and smoke oozing through the opening.

Knowing the dream's end was fast approaching, his panic overflowed. He released more air bombs, one after another. They sailed through the air, aimed for a direct hit, but the gold Fallen raised her hand. A golden blast of sizzling energy burst from her palm. Horror washed over him as it collided with his air bombs, sending electric sparks exploding in the air.

No!

Zach's water cyclone erupted next to him, splitting off into spinning shards aimed for the group.

But it was too late.

Zar disappeared through the portal, followed by a cackling Delilah. The gold web evaporated, sucked back with the evil who had raised it. The empty space stood as a devastating reminder of his failure to save his best friend from her fate at the hands of the malicious Fallen. He fell to the ground, howling at the bright moon, illuminating his defeat in an eerie pink hue. He turned to Zach, whose anguish matched his own.

"We've lost her." Zach's face crumbled, his arms wrapped around his middle, rocking back and forth.

"Why... Why can't we change the dream?" Sergio's voice broke, full of anger and disbelief.

"I don't know. We keep coming back to the same place ready to fight, but we never get to her in time. Why?"

Sergio shook his head, unable to come up with an answer. "Do you know if she's having the same one?"

Zach stood up, his face turning as pale as the large moon.

"She hasn't mentioned it to me if she has. I don't like this. We've never talked to each other before in the dream. I always wake up after she's through the portal."

Sergio's mouth became as parched as the desert air. "But this isn't real... it's only a dream." He glanced back to the spot where Olivia had disappeared, nausea brewing in his stomach. "It can't be real." He muttered as he stood up on shaky legs.

"What if it is... what if we are seeing into the future, linked somehow to Zar and Delilah's next move?"

"Or Olivia's—"

Sergio woke up gasping, wrapped up in his sheets, damp with his sweat. He blinked as stared around his unlit room, trying to get his bearings.

Only a dream... only a dream...

But the smell of smoke and the stink of his fear told him something had changed. This wasn't just a dream anymore.

Olivia's in danger...

He rolled over and reached for his phone, but it was already ringing. His pulse jumped, hoping it Olivia was on the other end. But the pounding rush in his ears increased when he recognized the caller.

Zach.

"Hey—"

"Did you have the—" Zach breathed hard through the phone.

"Yeah. Olivia's taken by Zar. You too?" Sergio raked his long fingers through his thick hair.

"Yep." Zach snarled over the rustling of his bed covers. "This isn't good, Sergio. I think she's in trouble."

Sergio closed his eyes trying to fight the terror seizing his chest.

"She's fine boy scout. Remember, she stayed home with her parents. She told us—"

"I think she was lying to us at the coffee shop. She was acting weird... distant... especially when we were talking on the couch. Her eye contact was off, and she was too antsy to get back to work when the place wasn't even busy."

Sergio let his statement hang in the air, recalling their quick visit with her. He hung his head, realizing Zach was right. "We need to go talk to her."

"Like now." The dire urgency in Zach's voice raised the hairs on Sergio's neck.

"Dude, what's going on? She wouldn't meet them without telling us—"

"Listen, this time was different. Think about it? The moon, Sergio. In all my dreams, it's a moonless night. But the moon was bright... too bright. It's a super moon, and there's one happening tonight."

Sergio scrambled out of bed and rushed to his window. He parted the blinds, then pounded his fist against the wall. The same moon mocked him as it did when he howled at it just a few minutes. It seemed like an eternity passed between now and his nightmare.

"We need to get to her house. Find out if she's home." Sergio growled as he turned away from the reality staring at him from the night's sky. He reached for his jeans he'd tossed earlier over the back of his chair.

"Wake up Lucia and meet me on Olivia's porch." The line went dead before Sergio could reply. He threw his phone on his bed and put on his pants, his mind racing with catastrophic possibilities. A soft knock on his door froze his hand gripping his t-shirt.

"Sergio," Lucia implored through the closed door. "What—"

"Come in," he said, muffled by the shirt he shoved over his head.

Lucia opened the door and walked in fully dressed. He narrowed his eyes at her. "Why are you—"

"I woke up with a start, my heart racing. I heard you talking about Olivia. Is it true?" Lucia's wide eyes searched his face for answers.

"I don't know. Zach and I have the same dream about her being taken through a portal by Zar," he shoved his feet into his sneakers. "But tonight, there was a full moon, and Zach and I talked to each other inside the vision too. Zach suspects it's the same moon as tonight. We're going to her house. Come on."

Sergio opened his portal, knowing Lucia was right behind him.

CHAPTER
FORTY-SIX

ZACH

*W*hy *would she go alone?*
I knew something was up...
I should have—

A gold web opened on the porch, interrupting his thoughts. Sergio and Lucia stepped out with pensive faces mirroring his own. Lucia walked to Zach, touching his arm. "Maybe Olivia's on a hunt. She wouldn't lie to—"

"I hope you're right. I'm worried Delilah lured her with information about her dad. She doesn't think straight when it comes to him. There's only one way to find out." Lucia stepped back, biting her lip as she glanced at the Drake's front door.

Zach knocked, rocking back on his heels. His stomach churned as he listened for any movement. Too impatient to wait, he raised his hand to knock again, but the foyer light flipped on as soft footsteps padded through the entryway.

"Who is it?" Olivia's dad called from the foyer. The front door couldn't muffle the gruff tone laced in his voice.

"It's Zach. I'm here with Sergio and Lucia. Can we—"

The door swung open. "Come in." Clad only in pajama pants, he scanned each of them before his keen eyes scanned the street behind them. He stepped aside, waving them in. Scratching his beard, he stuck his head back out through the entrance. "Where's Olivia? Didn't she come back here with you guys?"

Zach, Sergio and Lucia exchanged glances while her dad put his hands on his hips.

"Uh... we're sorry, Olivia said she was staying here tonight." Zach glanced at the others. "Is she here?"

"What do you mean is she here... she's been with you guys all night?" He cocked his head. "Wasn't she?"

Warning bells clanged in Zach's head. "No, sir. She told us she was having a quiet evening with you and her mom."

The room stilled as realization hit them like a rogue wave. Zach ran up the stairs with Sergio and Lucia in pursuit. "Hey, what's going on?" her dad bellowed from behind them. His heavy footsteps followed the group up the stairs.

Zach hit the landing at the same time as her mom opened her bedroom door. Her mouth fell open as Zach rushed past, opening Olivia's bedroom door. He flipped on her overhead light, heart thumping as he prayed to find a pissed off Olivia yelling at him from her bed.

"Conner. What's—"

But the bed was neatly made, untouched excepted for Thunder curled up in the middle. He raised his head as Zach walked into the room. A chill shot down his spine, the cat's vigilant eyes not the source.

She wasn't there.

Only the faint odor of electricity from the web lingered. She'd left from here without telling a soul where she went. His chest tightened, realizing she'd lied to them, increasing the odds that she was in danger.

"Oh no," muttered Sergio. He punched his leg and moved to check her bathroom. He flipped the light on, but no Olivia. "She's gone."

"Did Olivia say anything about going on a hunt tonight?" Lucia asked, turning to the parents.

"No... nothing." Olivia's mom shook her head. "She told me you guys were going out tonight for dinner and a movie. Conner—"

"She told the kids the same thing." He stared at Zach. "Spill it."

Zach exhaled, trying to calm his surging panic. "For the past few months, Sergio and I have had the same dream about Olivia, but we only just discovered that fact. It starts with us fighting demons. We fight back, but it's never in time to save her." Zach swallowed, forcing down the dry lump stuck in his throat.

"What do you mean *save her*?" His body froze, but a muscle in his jaw twitched.

"Zar has her flung over his shoulder and takes her through a portal. It closes before we can stop him," Sergio crossed his arms over his chest.

"Oh my God," her mom gasped, covering her mouth with a trembling hand.

"What else... tell me!" her dad stepped forward, fury brewing in his eyes.

"Tonight, Sergio and I had a dream at the same time, but it was different from the other ones we've shared. A super moon was in the sky, like tonight, and other Fallen were there." Zach lifted his chin. "I think it was Delilah, and another female Fallen... gold with six wings."

The room jumped as her dad's fist connected with the wall. Thunder scurried off the bed while Zach stared at the cracked imprint left by his huge fist. "Why would Olivia go to her? If Delilah has hurt her, I swear—"

"It's a trap, isn't it?" Her mom's voice cracked as she slumped against the door frame. "She coaxed her with the promise of telling secrets about her father to get her to come out, then torment Olivia before taking her away to get the truth about the guardianship."

"Why a trap, Stella?"

She turned to her husband. "Because that's what I would do if I were her. Torture our daughter's mind before I tortured her body."

The room's occupants absorb the harsh words spoken by the woman who loved Olivia the most.

"Can't we link with her... find out where she is?" Lucia placed her hand over her mark.

"The link through the mark only works if the person wants to be found, otherwise guardians might enter unknowingly into a hunt. Unfortunately, it's not a link like you and Sergio share. We have to wait for her signal or—"

"Alert the Archangels." Sergio blurted out.

Her dad rubbed his hand over his beard. "If they could find her in time. But don't forget, she's a warrior and this could all be in our imagination."

The blood rushing in Zach's head drowned out the words he felt in his gut weren't true. This wasn't a delusion. Olivia was in terrible trouble. His anger and fear for her warred inside of him. He shoved aside the nightmarish images of Olivia at the hands of Zar and Delilah that paralyzed his thinking. There had to be something—

"Maybe she left behind a clue." Zach blurted out, grasping at straws.

Please...

He scanned the room before locating the two feathers on her desk. His fear spiked as precious seconds ticked away. The room's walls closed in around him, amplifying his helplessness. He reached over to yank out the black feather when he glimpsed a folded piece of paper tucked under the picture of the three of them. A bubble of hope sprung up as Zach pulled the note out and unfolded it. His stomach dropped. Her neat writing in direct conflict to her careless written words.

If you've found this note, it means you're looking for me.
I'm meeting Delilah tonight at the Valley of Fire.
Go to the cave. I'm waiting for her there.
I had to first go alone. Don't be mad.
My choice.

I'm sorry.
Olivia

"Olivia's gone to meet her—" her dad snatched the note from Zach's hands, "—tonight. She's at the cave."

"Why would she do this?" Her dad's anguished question was one of many Zach would ask while he shook some sense into her. He passed the note to Olivia's mom. Her face paled as her shoulders slumped in defeat.

"Let's go," Olivia's parents stepped back when Sergio called up the portal. Darkness pulled from the other side while the familiar earthy red dust drifted through the opening.

"We'll bring her back. I promise." Zach's heart hammered as he turned away from her parents, praying he would not break his vow. "Armor on... weapons." The same utterances came from Sergio and Lucia, muffled by the waiting portal.

"God be with you." Filtered through the static noise, her dad's vehement prayer fortifying Zach's determination to get to Olivia in time and rid this world of Zar and Delilah once and for all.

We will need all the help we can get...

CHAPTER
FORTY-SEVEN

OLIVIA

The cave remained how she so vividly remembered, a time capsule for her and for others who for centuries had huddled here for wisdom, a rendezvous, or protection. For Olivia, it was all of these for her tonight. The rust-colored dirt floor was cool to her touch. Prehistoric stick figures, carved into the deep-red walls, gave her the sensation of being watched and sized up. Was she up to the task of facing the Fallen on her own? She rubbed her arms over the armor, which protected her from external blows, but it couldn't shield her from the internal war she waged with herself.

You've made your decision, Drake.

No turning back.

Olivia showed up early for the meeting to prepare herself mentally and to make sure an ambush wasn't already in place. Nothing was out of the ordinary... yet. She'd tried to decipher why she felt it was important for her to meet Delilah alone, at the risk of losing the trust of the guardians or her life. Her reflections came back to one simple fact.

It's personal.

She wished she'd discovered a better reason. A phrase more thoughtful in feeling or exciting in action, but it was crystal clear in the end. It all circled back to the beginning... when her dad left that fateful Christmas morning. Olivia stood in the middle of the fray, lost in the eye of the storm, since that day. It was now up to her to confront Delilah head on and make her suffer the consequences her actions caused under the guise of *love*.

Olivia now understood Dad's reasons for leaving. They sickened her, but her lens to the past was no longer warped by pain. Delilah manipulated him, forced a choice between his family and protecting the guardianship and her. He wasn't a saint, that was certain. His reckless actions had proved it, but he never stood a chance against an angel hell-bent on making him her possession. In the end, he made the hardest choice and lived with those consequences over the past ten years.

But Delilah's crazed desire for revenge brought it to another level. People Olivia loved were being hurt, hunted down, and even killed because... evil knows no bounds. Nothing more, nothing less.

It was time to put the blame where it belonged... on Delilah.

The sun faded to orange streaks cutting through the hills in the darkening sky. Tan-striped lizards performed push-ups in their territorial rite, sunning themselves on the last rays on vibrant red chunks of rocks. Dusk brought ominous anticipation of the full moon, and her date with evil.

And still she waited until the bright luminous moon glowed over the stark terrain. In the cave's cocoon, it was as if she gazed through a looking glass to a different planet, barren yet serene. Insects sang their tune to the moon. Other critters scurried to their hiding places across the desert floor, illuminated prey to the night's predators for an easy kill.

But not me...

Olivia embraced her angel-warrior side, ready to face any battle head on. But the human-side, the one uncertain about showing herself to her enemies, tackled a few personal demons of her own making, while she watched the day turn to night. She'd come to the meeting area early, not wanting to walk into an ambush she was certain awaited her. But as the hours passed, her resolve to attack

Delilah alone was fortified. Calling the other guardians now would only bring angst among them, breaking her concentration for her mission. She'd also concluded, in the cave where another epiphany had occurred, that she'd be a fool not to have someone watching her back. Delilah wouldn't come alone, so why should she? That conniving Fallen was banking on Olivia being driven by her tattered feelings for Dad, hoping her zeal for revenge would make her reckless. Fortunately, Olivia had the advantage of knowledge of Delilah's deceit, turning the illicit information to power.

She's underestimated me, but I can't underestimate her.

So as the moon rose above the horizon, blushing in the color of a pink full moon, Olivia decided she'd call for help.

Michael.

Olivia closed her eyes, running her fingers over the slight lump the capsule made under her armor. She stood up, stirring the surrounding dust. She envisioned Michael with his glorious blue tipped wings and blazing blue eyes which had always focused upon her with steadfast love.

"I need you, Michael," Olivia called into the cave, her voice echoing off the walls. The blue jewel nestled in the hilt of her sword pulsed. She cracked a smile as the air sparked with electricity like static building before a lightning strike. As if Michael had struck his hands together with tremendous force, a slap reverberated and he appeared, his sword already raised, ready if an unwelcomed scenario greeted him.

"What is wrong, my child?" His brow scrunched as he frantically scanned Olivia and the cave. "Are you hurt or—"

"No. I'm fine. I'm sorry if I frightened you." Olivia licked her lips, wondering how to begin. "I—uh... need to tell you something and you'll probably be upset with me, but please just remember I called you before all hell broke loose." Her smile quivered, not sure whether his smile or a frown would emerge next.

Michael lowered his sword, curiosity flitting over his face. "Whatever you have to say, I'm ready."

Olivia cleared her throat, wishing she didn't have to unearth the dirty truths. "You know about my dad and Delilah, right? And the fact that she's a Fallen."

Michael gave a solemn nod, pressing his lips together.

"Well... she—uh..."

Spit it out already

"She left a note in my room a few nights ago along with a black feather. She instructed me to prick my finger with the feather's quill and I'd see a vision." She exhaled, trying to expel the growing pit in her stomach as she recalled the vivid images. "So, I did it. One vision showed the night she found my dad locked in a battle with a Fallen and the other was of her... entwining him in her clutches saying she'd never let him go."

"I'm sorry she exposed you to those painful visions. Why would she do something so risky?"

Olivia felt the energy of cave amplify as if he knew grim news was coming. "Because in the note she dared me to meet her on the full moon so she could share her secrets about her and my dad. If I hadn't of found out the truth, I would be out of my mind wanting to hear her story. I think she's counting on that—because she wants to kidnap me to learn the secrets of the guardianship... and then... uhm... kill me." Olivia crossed her arms, waiting for Michael's reaction.

He delayed a beat before he replied, anger brewing in his eyes. "Did you tell the other guardians?"

Olivia shook her head and paced in front of him.

"You should connect with them—"

"I can't." She stopped and stared at him. "This is my problem, brought on by my dad. It's not their battle. I don't want them to get hurt and risk the guardianship even more. I left a note telling them where I am if they sense something is wrong. But I know I need someone watching me in case my fight with Delilah, and most likely Zar, goes wrong. So that's why I called you. I need you to watch my back... please."

Olivia started to fidget under Michael's probing gaze, seeking answers inside of her. She didn't shy away from him.

"I'm saddened you didn't share with the guardians your intentions. None of the Guardians of Orion are meant to bear their burdens alone. That undermines the purpose and power of sharing the mission."

"Michael, I—"

He put his hand up and Olivia clamped down on her bursting emotions.

"What's done is done. I'll not change your choice, but I dislike this plan of you seeing her alone. Get your answers. I can't stop you, but there will be no pleasure or healing found in the hateful words she shares."

"I understand that, but I need to hear it from her. Thank you, Michael." Her mark prickled against her skin. She turned and gazed out of the cave's mouth. Adrenaline hit her as Delilah emerged from a green web. "She's here. And alone."

"I doubt that holds true." He laid his hands on her shoulders. "Don't be surprised if I come in before you're ready. I'll not have another one die at her hands or Zar's."

"I understand, but Delilah is mine. You can kill all the others, but Delilah and I have some unfinished business to take care of."

"As long as you are safe, I'll not interfere. A word of advice. Leave your emotions in this cave or they too will be a weapon used against you. Now go." He squeezed her shoulders, sending an encouraging energy flow through her. "I have your back, Olivia... always."

"I know..." she whispered, relief swamping through her at having shared her intentions with Michael.

She raised her portal, knowing this was a defining moment for her.

I'm ready, Delilah...

CHAPTER
FORTY-EIGHT

DELILAH

Anticipation drummed through Delilah. Waiting on the long, stone bridge leading to the Realm of Wrath didn't ease her impatience. The red steaming lava flowed to the mouth's end, churning as the inky lava swirled around Lucifer's tower. She sensed Lucifer's presence from the tower, his life force boring into her back, reminding her of his threats if she failed to deliver Olivia to him. The thought of being Tannin's next meal sent a tendril of dread through her, but if she played her hand right, she'd emerge the winner in her shrouded, dangerous game. Still, worry nagged at her. Lucifer's exceptional knowledge of all happenings inside Hell never ceased to amaze her, leaving a shadow of a doubt that he could be a step ahead of her. There was only one way to find out who were her friends and who were her foes.

It's time...

Delilah turned to Zar. His platinum hair lifted with the updraft of steam from the lava river. The bleak, heavy air filled with lurid odors and ash matched the black pits marring his face, leaving a nothingness she couldn't decipher. The insidious holes kept his secrets, much to her chagrin. She'd always held true to the saying that the eyes are the windows to the soul... even dark ones. The many layers of evil entwined and mated in the fiery eyes of the Fallen, gave birth to their pure desires and motives, if only for a brief flash. She'd witnessed these careless peeks before their owners snatched away their treasonous emotions, thinking they'd kept their secrets hidden. But Delilah stashed these observations, remembering what inspired their deeds. This insight had kept her alive since she'd become a Fallen and it hadn't failed her... yet.

Zar laid his hand on the hilt of his sword. "Are you ready, Delilah, to impose the revenge you've been devising for so long?" His hard lips lifted with a sneer of pleasure, not disdain.

"Oh... I've yearned for this moment. It seems like nothing else has mattered except destroying Conner and his family, like he decimated me with his lies and betrayal." Her thick blood pumped faster at the prospect of all her plans coming to fruition.

"But revenge against Conner isn't all that matters, is it?" The approaching Fallen crossed the bridge, a backup in case the wretched girl brought friends. Delilah considered his question. Zar's eyes couldn't betray him, but his personal demons echoed through his voice deep and clear, laced with a bitter jealousy he found hard to mask.

"No. What matters most now is our rise to power. Tonight, we'll show we are deserving of this accolade. We'll set in motion a sequence of events that no one else here will see coming... not even Lucifer." Delilah placed her hand on his arm, delivering a jolt of her excitement through him as a warrior and a female. Zar's body tensed as the waves of her thrills traveled over him.

"Be careful what you ignite in me. I will not be denied if I come seeking what you offer so freely." She hid her smirk. His threat didn't concern her. She squeezed his arm and let her hand fall. Any tryst with him she'd endure... just another hook, gathering him into her web for further use.

Delilah lifted on her tiptoes and whispered in his ear. "We'll rule together soon. I expect nothing less than for us to share our reward, feasting upon each other."

Which will be the perfect time to kill you...

She preened to herself as she turned to face the ten Fallen, bristling with cold eagerness to kill, each one striking in their bright red slashes and swirls from the Realm of Wrath.

"When I open the portal, be prepared to fight our enemies. I want no angel spared," Delilah demanded. Vicious sneers and grunts answered her. They understood their job and reveled in it. Her concern turned to Olivia and getting the secrets from her. When she unveiled her surprise for the guardian, the mysteries would flow out of her like the lavas of Hell.

"Are you clear on your mission, Zar? No mistakes or... accidental deaths." Delilah's fingers tapped against the hilt of her sword.

"You do your part. I'll do mine." He smirked. "I won't deny you the satisfaction of his blood spilling over your hands."

"Perfect. It's time." Delilah raised her portal, the full moon's light a beacon for her destiny. A shiver ran through her like a finger shimming down her spine. She glanced over her shoulder, finding Lucifer standing in his tower room's window. His lone figure dominated the frame, his giant wings spread out behind him. Raising her perfectly arched eyebrow, she dipped her head at him, but would give him no more. Soon she would be freed from Lucifer's leash for good.

And him... the next feast for that vile serpent before I rid Hell of it, too.

It's glorious to be me...

She entered the portal, appreciating that her life would never be the same.

Zar

Delilah had stepped through her portal, but Zar waited until it was time to implement the plan's next stage. He turned his head, scanning with his senses for Lucifer in his tower window. Zar found nothing, but that didn't ensure Lucifer wasn't watching. No matter. Lucifer understood he was to follow Delilah after a period of time had lapsed, but the destination had changed. He'd opened his portal, eager to find his prey.

Unlike Delilah, Zar didn't like the light of the moon. Sightless, he'd grown used to moving in the margins of the shadows and murky corners of Hell. Here... the luminous light cast the shadows away, his vision map too bright as he walked across the backyard. The house was dark except for a single lamp in the living room. Two people sat on the couch. He smirked, remembering the scene from the kitchen window where he'd secretly peered and watched Delilah's splendid display of fury against Conner. His nostrils flared, breathing heavily in anticipation. The desire to ignore Delilah's wishes and kill the couple warred within him. But Zar had let his passions rule him before, and the punishment had served its purpose.

I'm a Fallen...

Master of my passions...

Not a slave to my flesh...

Zar raised his hand, waving it in front of the glass door. He charged through as the small shattered pieces of glass rained down on him. Startled, the couple turned and stared wide-eyed at him. But Zar was too quick. He backhanded Stella with a blow full of his malice for her, silencing the scream laying on her lips. She crumpled to the couch, blood trickling from her mouth. Conner's face twisted in fury, veins bulging in his neck as he launched himself at Zar. He stumbled back, the force of Conner shoving them against the counter. The barstools skidded apart, clanging on the floor. Connor's hands wrapped around Zar's throat.

"How dare you—" Connor's spittle hit his face, "—hit my wife!"

A cackle tore from Zar. He shoved his hands between Conner's arms and slammed them against Connor's bulging biceps. Conner grunted, the force throwing him backward, landing on his back.

"I will do more than hit your wife by the time I'm through with her." Zar straddled him and slammed his fist into Connor's mouth.

Blood sprayed over Zar's face, fuel to his rising fury. "I'm going to touch—"

Pain exploded in his thigh. He glanced down and found Conner's hand pulling out a dagger he'd thrust into Zar's leg. He raised it for another strike, but Zar grabbed his wrist and bent it back. A thrill zipped up his spine at the satisfying crack splitting the air. The blade fell from Conner's limp, twisted hand, his face pale with blood trickling down his beard.

"You'll never win..." Conner's comment was rewarded with another blow. The bones of his nose shattered against Zar's knuckles.

"You have no more say in this. You disgust me with your self-righteous words when you where the one who has forsaken your precious God with your sins."

"But—" Conner gagged on the blood pouring down his throat "—he'll forgive me." He coughed, spraying the floor red.

Zar stood and delivered a swift kick to Connor's side and another, satisfying his hunger to take out his fury on the man who'd been his nemesis. He bent over and grabbed Conner's hair, pulling his head off the floor. He scoffed at this once brave guardian. Zar leaned down and sneered, "I've done nothing I want His forgiveness for. 'Bye Conner." He slammed Conner's head on the floor, his body limp beneath Zar.

That should do it until Delilah comes for you...

Zar snickered as he walked over to Stella. A soft moan emanated as she rolled her head. He reached down and threw her over his shoulder. He'd wanted to smack her again, but Delilah wanted Stella awake. Whatever. He kicked Conner in the hip, his limp body jerking at the insult. He opened his portal, the desert's red dust greeted him.

Time for the show...

And collect my reward from Delilah.

CHAPTER
FORTY-NINE

OLIVIA

She'd be dazzling... if she wasn't pure evil.

Delilah's long red hair fanned like flames around her alabaster face, forged harder by the venomous hate pumping beneath her austere veneer. Olivia detected the edges of magnificence chiseled in the once serene angel created for good and love. How it must have awed her dad, weakening him to her twisted desires, masquerading in unabashed adoration for him. There was an allure to Delilah, a seductive impostor, posed like a statue, emanating the trite naivete of a martyr who wonders why she's the victim in the drama surrounding her. But she was no victim, and her charisma was as false and hollow as the smile stretching across her face.

"Olivia... finally we meet, although I've watched you from afar your entire life."

"Aw, so that was you I felt when an icy draft would snake by me. There was no need for your unwelcomed visits, as I'm sure you've surmised." Olivia tried to keep the simmering anger from her voice as her mark flared at the evil before her. "We were just fine without you."

Delilah *tsked* as she tilted her head. "Funny... that's not what I remember. You and your *mommy* slogging through your miserable existence, wondering where your *daddy* was as you cried yourself to sleep, asking why he'd abandoned you. Truly pitiful, as I recall."

Olivia shifted her weight, readying herself for Delilah's next move. "Let's not play any more games. I know who you are, Fallen angel. My dad told me all about you and your tortured illusions of having him for your own. Disgusting. An angel—"

Delilah threw her head back, laughing into the cool night air. "You know nothing about me or my love for Conner. The notion of true unadulterated love, so complete and all consuming, a human would never understand. Only I could protect him... love him... like God had intended. We were meant to be a team, unstoppable in our conquest to fight evil and make him pure in spirit. I was created for Conner! He was given to me—mine, not Michael's, not Stella's, and not yours—mine!"

"He isn't a possession. He's—" But Delilah's tirade spewed uninterrupted, blooming like a black mist churning over an angry, black sea.

"That man spurned my love after our shared night of passion. He told me he loved me and then shoved me aside in his guilt and shame! I can't forgive his utter disregard for me... for us. I gave him everything—even my choice to forego being an angel—but my generous gift wasn't good enough for him, a guardian on his own mission from God. So I wanted to damn Conner, make him as lonely and tragic as me. It was the only way forward in my own wretched existence. Even then, at the moment of his accepted banishment, something broke inside me. A bleak chasm I couldn't forge a bridge across. Deep down, a seed planted in my heart and burrowed with thick roots, compelling me to plunge into the Mar of Sin. I couldn't be an angel stuck in the middle, never serving the purpose of my creation." Delilah's chest heaved, her eyes narrowing on Olivia. "So I waited—" she sneered, "—as time drifted past me in my hellish limbo... waiting in hopes he'd come to his senses and realize we were meant to be together... that I am the only one he needs. I would help him in the guardianship. But he wanted you and your weak mother—"

"My mom is not weak!" Olivia interrupted. "She's a fighter, fierce in her love for me and Dad. She carried the burden you heaved upon our family with grace and true love... something you would never have accepted." Olivia withdrew her sword; its blue stone ignited and sent a flame down the blade. "You'll not speak of her that way. She's an innocent—"

Delilah shrieked, releasing a green sparkling crack of energy, hitting Olivia in the chest. The blast lifted her off her feet, hurling her from the ground and landing in an impact of red dust. Olivia rolled to her right and jumped up, dodging another blast. Delilah had also unsheathed her sword of black metal, throbbing with a green pulse.

"She's *not* an innocent! Conner whined the same words to me as he begged me to spare her. But you see, she always stood in our way, just like you do now, protecting the ones you love even when your heart is shredded from betrayal! You're just like him and you can't even acknowledge it!"

Delilah's words cut through her as if the blade had split her in two, exposing her thoughts of being a mirror of him. Yet, Delilah's words, spewed in hate, spread an unexpected warmth and pride through her, filling up the hollowed part of her heart, once crammed with her pain. She found this truth, a thunder stuck moment of enlightenment, she'd never expected to receive. Let alone from the Fallen creature which had originally stoked those fires of hate and resentment.

Olivia held her sword to the side, placing her fist over her heart. "I want to thank you." Olivia's smile appeared as radiant as the joy exploding inside her.

Delilah froze, a statue created in her disbelief. "Thank me? Why—"

"Because in your reckless zeal to destroy my dad with your vicious petty words, you're intent backfired. I didn't think I was anything like him. My conflicting pain and torment burned my psyche. It was always in my way like an immoveable boulder. But you moved it for me. Your hateful tale revealed a man... human, with sin and virtue... stuck between two forces pulling at him because he is innately an honorable man. He's brave, loyal... to God most of all... and loves to a fault. What you see as weakness in your distorted view, is a strength that you twisted and used against him because you are the weak one—the one who can't give what you assumed you did, love unconditionally. Because if you had, you would have done what every other guardian angel did when it was time to step aside... set the ones you love free."

Delilah's sword vibrated in her hands, the flames in her hair billowing larger in her reflective fury.

"So, now I realize it was okay Dad made Mom and me second to God and his calling to protect His kingdom. I guess this is part of me growing up. Understanding the people I love have failures helped me recognize and own mine as well. I lied to my fellow guardians about tonight and it may very well cost me my life, but you will pay the cost, too!"

Olivia charged, filled with a dauntless courage she'd not embraced before tonight. She shot out her hand, releasing a fiery blue flame while she summoned her dagger to fly free from her hip. The flame hit Delilah's chest, spreading down the front of her. She screamed as she flung herself to the ground and rolled, causing Olivia's blade to fly over her. Delilah jumped to her feet, grabbing her sword. Olivia swung across her body, but Delilah blocked the sword with hers. The thunderous clang split the air. They pushed away from each other, but Olivia spun and brought the blade around, hitting Delilah across her arm below the shoulder. Inky, foul blood sprayed Olivia. Delilah shrieked as she stumbled back, making a circle with her hand as blood squirted from her open wound. Olivia ducked and rushed forward, missing the wild energy surge from her talon-tipped hand. Raising her sword, she aimed for Delilah's long white neck to deliver the deadly stroke. But a portal emerged next to Delilah, catching Olivia off guard before she delivered the blow. Delivering another blast, it hit Olivia's sword, tearing it from her grip. She cried out as the painful vibration zipped up her arm.

But all pain and anger came to a screeching halt.

An instantaneous thud of fear struck her as Zar emerged with her mom slung over his shoulder, pounding against his back.

A smug grin stretched across his chiseled face. "I think that's enough fighting, unless you'd want to watch me slit your mom's throat... hmm?"

"Put her down." Olivia pointed at Zar. "If you've hurt her—"

"Oh, please, with your threats. She's fine. Your dad, on the other hand—" he shrugged "—is not doing so well. He's not so tough now that he's passed on his powers to you. But he's not dead... yet... Delilah wanted those honors." A low rumble blossomed from his chest as he tossed her mom down at his feet.

Olivia lurched forward, but Zar's sword stopped her.

"Why did you bring her here?" Olivia demanded. "It's me you want, not her. I'll go with you—just leave my mom alone."

"We can't do that." Delilah reached down, entwining her hand into Olivia's mom's hair, yanking her head back. Mom cried out, her fist hitting against the arm wrenching her scalp. "You see, I need information from you before I take you to meet Lucifer. I figured the best way to get you to talk was to bring *mommy* here... quicken the process." She sneered as she released her head, shoving it into the ground. "You will answer all my questions or Zar will start removing body parts from your precious—"

Delilah's words were cut short as a bright light streaked toward them, followed by two more. Zar snarled, realizing who swept down from the sky.

Michael!

Relief flooded through Olivia as her sword glinted within reach. A sizzle split the air behind her. Delilah and Zar sneered at the emerging the portal.

"You're not the only one with a plan, Delilah." Olivia summoned her sword, needing to kill the two Fallen who'd been bent on destroying her family. Elation surged through her as the sword leapt into her grip. "I'm not the fool you think I am."

But Olivia's upper hand was short lived. A gold portal erupted next to Zar, blasting her with smoke and noxious heat. Red slashed Fallen poured from the portal, the ferocious beating of their black wings knocking her back, swooping to meet their nemeses. The last to emerge was a fierce golden Fallen with thin gold braids whipping behind her. ...

And then Heaven and Hell broke loose.

CHAPTER
FIFTY

ZACH

The bright moon illuminated the red shifting desert terrain as it had in Zach's dreams. They'd watched Olivia and Delilah from the cave's entrance, anxiety whipping through him, helpless until Michael gave the word to attack. But when Zar arrived with her mom, the reins were released, and they flew into action.

About time...

He charged through the portal ready to confront the Fallen, with Sergio and Lucia at his side, determined to reach Olivia before they whisked her away. Adrenaline coursed through his veins, his armor, both a shield and a comfort in the battle which lay ahead. The portal had barely closed before Zach raised his sword, training kicking in as a growing swarm of red Fallen flew towards them. Three bright lights streaked down from the corner of his eye. The sight of Olivia, clutching her sword, ready to fight with the odds stacked against her, swelled his heart with pride while his fierce protectiveness of her threatened to undermine his control.

We're here... I'm here...

Snarls of anger filled the air. Massive flapping wings disturbed the cracked desert ground. Swirling red dust mingled with the ash cascading from the sharp inky feathers diluting his vision. But the guardians didn't need their sight to fight their enemies. Clangs and grunts around him matched his own. Zach slashed his sword, whirling with the green light of his water element. The vicious vibration from metal meeting metal surged up his arms. Their weapons hung together before he pushed away.

"I will enjoy shredding you after I free you from your head." Silvia dripped from the Fallen's black twisted teeth; its mouth yawned open, ready to bite before she killed him. Red sparks flew from her sword, arcing through the night's sky. Zach ducked under the swing. Pushing up from his legs, he leapt, aiming his sword at her chest. He plunged it into her heart. Her red eyes grew wide as her agonizing shriek pierced his ears, skewered by his blade. Her body erupted in blood and ash, spraying him with the putrid oil-like gore of the Fallen. He celebrated in the fetid smell because it meant victory over his enemies.

"Not today," he yelled. The field in front of him cleared. Black blood sprayed over him as Lucia and Sergio slayed their opponents. One of the bright lights peeled away, heading towards them. Zach raced for Olivia. An air bomb released behind him, and Sergio's yell of delight erupted as a Fallen's limp body ejected from the melee. Gold wings of Gabriel blurred over him in flight as Zach's legs pumped, eating up the distance between them. His stomach dropped as Olivia raised her sword, blocking a move by Delilah.

Hold on...

Michael and Raphael battled the warrior Fallen who held back, their swords a dazzling blur against the darkness. Zar sneered, his eyes locking with Zach's. The gold Fallen turned away from the losing battle and stared at Olivia. Her eyes narrowed, homing in on her target. She jumped into the air. Zach's heart skipped a beat as he created a cyclone between his hands and threw it at the gold Fallen.

"Asura—look out!" Zar shouted in time for her to dodge, but not miss all the spinning blades. They slashed against Asura's right side, shredding her armor. Chunks ripped away along with ebony flesh;

her black blood spray lost in the night. She shrieked, clutching her injury, falling to the ground in a heap.

Zar launched himself at Zach, who stood a few feet away from Olivia, sensing the fight between her and Delilah. The pounding footsteps of his fellow guardians and the roar of a tiger mixed with Zar's snarls. He charged at Zach, leaving Olivia's mom unattended.

"Now you die!" Zar raised his sword high. Zach went to block the attack, but Zar spun and lowered his blade. He struck Zach's exposed side, knocking him to the ground. Clenching his teeth against the pain, his hand flew to his side. He felt the warm blood ooze between his fingers, his skin stitching together like ants running up his side. Zach rolled, hoping to miss Zar's next blow. But when he stopped on his back, Zar's black pits locked on him with his sword held point down, aimed at Zach's heart. Time slowed for Zach. He heard Olivia's grunts as she fought against Delilah's energy blasts and Sergio yelling *no* somewhere behind him. But all that faded, amidst the fear of Zar's evil face being the last thing he'd see.

Zach threw his hand out, green energy exploded from his palm. He pushed with all his might against the downward moving blade. The sharp end sparked as the clash of powers held the sword only a foot above its deadly trajectory to his heart. Zar roared, thrusting harder with all his strength, his power overwhelming Zach. The sword slipped closer, Zar's cackle assaulting his ears.

I'm sorry I failed you...

Olivia

"No!" Delilah's blood-curdling cry aimed at the Archangels hurtling towards them, sprung Olivia to act. She swung her blade, hoping to catch Delilah off guard, but she jumped to the side, avoiding the blade. Olivia cursed herself for her inaccuracy. Delilah stared wild-eyed at her as they circled each other in a warrior dance.

"You should have left my family alone and stayed in the black pit. You'll never win. You've played your hand." Olivia jabbed at her, baiting her to make a bad move. Delilah jumped back but continued to shrewdly circle Olivia as her eyes darted to the chaos taking place around her. Olivia kept moving towards her mom, desperate to get her away from Zar and the gold Fallen.

She heard Zar cry out a warning, but she didn't dare take her eyes off Delilah.

"You know nothing about our plans... the future of the Realms of Hell. There are things set in motion that you and your insignificant guardians will never stop." Delilah released her grip from the sword and shot a thunderbolt at Olivia. It hit her left shoulder, sending an electric charge through her arm, but Olivia's armor absorbed most of the energy. Delilah laughed, her evil glee pissing her off even more.

"Till next time." Delilah took flight, aiming for the portal sizzling open like a hungry beast. Olivia raised her hand, shooting blue flames at the fleeing figure. They struck Delilah's wing, licking over the black feathers. She arched, crying out as she fell from the sky, landing with a dusty thud.

Olivia knelt down next to her mom, smoothing back her hair. A sob of relief caught in her throat as confused, angry brown eyes greeted Olivia. "Are you all right? We have to get you—"

Mom groaned as she sat up, glancing at the surrounding chaos. "Don't worry about me. Go fight—"

"No! I'm staying here with—"

Raphael landed next to them; his soothing luminance washed over her. "I've got her." His heated voice belied his calming essence. She turned, stunned by his ferocious face and green eyes inflamed with outrage. "I'll get her home." He scooped her up and jettisoned away. Relief flooded her as she professed a *thank you* into the night.

A flash of blue and gold blurred not far away. She gasped at the flurry of movements Michael and Asura created. Their battle flew through the sky and over the ground; a fight of light and dark displayed on a stark canvas under the watchful eye of a luminescent moon. But Olivia turned away, knowing she would be no help to Michael. She had her own battle to wage.

Olivia gripped her sword and stood, needing to finish off Delilah before she tried to escape again. She caught movement out of the corner of her eye, flaming red hair and smoking wings charging at her. Olivia spun around, but she was upon her; wild-eyed and brandishing her sword overhead. Olivia swung up, igniting the blue fire in her blade. She snarled in fury, releasing the anguish Delilah had unleashed upon her. The fiery blade caught Delilah's arms in their downward motion. The blue flaming metal sliced underneath her right arm, beneath her shoulder, and embedded on the side of her face. Blue fire traveled over Delilah's severed arm, falling to the ground. The stump left behind pumped black blood, leaching over the battle worn ground.

Olivia pulled her sword back. Delilah shrieked, dropping her blade as her hand flew to the angry slash running from the side of her head down her jawline. Delilah staggered back and gazed horrified at the blood spraying from her arm. Shock replaced her vicious veneer. Dropping to her knees, her chest heaved as her hand searched for her sword. When her fingers found what was left of her arm instead of the hilt, her hand retracted like her own flesh had shocked her. A macabre sneer, formed by hatred, flared in her malicious glare.

"You'll pay for that." Delilah shot out her hand, sending another bolt of energy crackling towards Olivia. She returned with a burst of power, hoping to deflect it, but it missed the stream and hit Delilah's chest. The green blast slammed against her launching Olivia into the air. Her body went into spasms, this energy more potent than the last. She hit the ground with a hard thud, knocking the air from her lungs. Her head swam, the energy enveloping her only, absorbed so much by the armor. It was as if tiny insidious whips lashed against her flesh.

Her vision tunneled as she gazed upon the moon, which had lured her here. Large enough she yearned to touch it... to run her fingertips across the cratered surface and feel the precious dirt shift between them. Instead, Olivia's hands scooped up the dry dusty earth. The red soil lodged under her fingernails, as she clawed against the darkness closing in around her. Panic grew as she succumbed to the inky world, unable to assimilate if the vicious roar shattering the air and the arms reaching beneath her were friend or foe?

CHAPTER
FIFTY-ONE

ZAR

G reen energy pulsed from the end of Zar's sword, wrapping around him in a cocoon of heat. He grunted as he pushed down, straining to plunge the blade through the guardian's heart. Zach's body trembled beneath him, losing the battle between them. Zar thrust harder, sensing his victory was near. Reflective green lights flashed and sparked over Zach's sweat-drenched face, while the roar of their powers clashing bombarded his ears.

Almost have you now...

So lost in his determination, he'd tuned out the chaotic world around him; Delilah's losing fight with Olivia, Michael and Asura battling across the night sky, and the Fallen's demise at the hands of their enemies. But one sound penetrated his concentration. A deafening roar and a heavy pounding stride heading for him. Too late to dodge the white blur jumping for him, pain ricocheted through his side as claws gripped into his armor. The force slammed him to the ground, freeing the sword from his grip. Red dirt flew up around them. Panic tore at him when he perceived the open mouth of a white tiger, saliva dripping off its razor-sharp teeth coming down on him. He howled as they ripped into his shoulder, piercing his flesh, seeking to rip out a chunk of his body.

No... not this way!

Zar arched against the pain, freeing his other arm enough for his hand to reach for his dagger. He slipped it from its sheath, desperate to kill the animal, its weight crushing him. Thrusting up, aimlessly seeking its vulnerable underbelly, he hit his mark. He felt the blade slip through the course hair, the hilt stopping at the fur flowing over his hand. The jaws of death released his shoulder, its agonizing roar boomed. The tiger jumped off of him, the dagger still in its side, blood pooling around the wound, staining the fur red.

"Lucia!" A dark-haired guardian leaped to the tiger; fear etched in the silent scream hovering at his lips. He pulled the blade out of its belly, flung it aside, and turned to Zar with hatred burning in his golden-brown eyes. Zar struggled to his feet and grabbed his sword in his good hand while his other arm fell useless and bloodied at his side.

"I hate you! You steal everyone I love away from me!" he wailed as he swung his sword blindly at Zar. He met the wild swing easily, blocking it with his own. Zar jumped into the air, putting his energy into his wings. In his retreat, he slashed the guardian on his back in a glancing blow, but it gave him enough time to land and retrieve his dagger. The guardian had run back to the wounded tiger now struggling to its feet. He sheathed his sword and grabbed the dagger, its size easier for his damaged arm to manage. His nostrils flared as he flew at the guardian on his knees, his back to him soothing the tiger.

"Not as deeply as I loathe you," he seethed. Landing behind him, Zar wrapped his long fingers into the thick black hair and yanked his head back. "You're coming with me," Zar raged into the guardian's ear, placing his wicked blade under his chin. The guardian gasped as Zar pulled him to his feet. The tiger roared, snarling at him, the wound in its belly no longer spurting blood.

"Stay back—," Zar threatened, "—or I'll slit his throat!" Pain throbbed in his shoulder, his body healing the mangled flesh. Zar shuffled backward toward the portal, crackling somewhere behind him. He staggered under the weight of the guardian struggling in his grasp. Zar nicked at the exposed neck, drawing blood while he hastened for his escape. "Stop moving or I'll finish what I started." His captive stiffened in his grasp.

"You'll never get away—" he sputtered and for a moment Zar thought he might be right. Gabriel landed before them in a streak of golden wings.

"Let him go, and you can walk away with your life." Gabriel raised his sword, taking a step toward him.

"Get back." Zar hissed. He pushed the blade deeper into the flesh, the portal close enough that he could feel the heat pouring over his back. "He's coming with me and you can't stop it." Euphoria surged in him as he took flight, clutching the guardian close to him. His powerful wings, rippling green among the black feathers, pumped for the portal.

Delilah...

His senses found her stumbling, her severed arm jerked aimlessly on the ground next to her as if seeking to link and not be left behind. Asura, bruised and bloodied, grabbed Delilah and shoved her through the darkness inside the portal, her flaming hair devoured by the smoke and ash before Asura jumped in after her.

Zar frantically scanned for Michael in hopes he lay dead somewhere. He couldn't detect him, the path clear for his escape. His thick blood pumped harder as he flew with his hostage for the portal. He shifted as he pierced the portal's core, but his blood, which pumped hot, turned cold.

"No! You can't enter!" Zar wailed. His certain victory extinguished by the large translucent hand gripping the guardian's ankle.

Gabriel.

His golden wings exploded in his mental mapping, glistened against the portal closing behind them. Determination and fury radiated from the Archangel, glowing blindingly luminescent inside the opaque walls of Hell.

The web crackled and snapped closed. A bright light exploded around Zar; his mind awash in a sea of white, his hopes of victory doused in black.

CHAPTER
FIFTY-TWO

SERGIO

L ucia...
So much blood.

Searing pain sliced across his neck. The dagger dangerously embedded in his skin, he waited for the final thrust from Zar to finish severing his flesh. Panic rippled through Sergio as their flight neared the portal where his certain torture and death awaited. Smoke billowed through, burning his eyes while the overpowering odor of sulfur assaulted him. The moans of the damned mixed with the cries of Hell, a place haunting his dreams, producing a cacophony of horror tearing at his soul.

Disgust for himself swelled, realizing he had only himself to blame for being trapped in Zar's grip. He'd been reckless, lost in despair, when Zar's dagger punctured Lucia. Instead of attacking Zar, he'd rushed to Lucia, so paralyzed by the thought of losing her, too. Instinct and all his training flew out the window when Sergio heard her pain filled roar. It shot through his heart. He should have known the wound would heal itself and killed Zar when he'd had the chance.

But he failed... himself and the guardians.

I can't die

I haven't avenged Manny

Manny...

His sob lodged against the blade as memories of Manny sped through his mind and heart, gut-wrenching snippets of times with his brother who had molded him... inspired him... loved him. Bitter tears formed at the loss of him, but a revelation struck home. The only positive outcome of his death would be reuniting with Manny in the afterlife.

But I'm not ready to leave my family and friends
There's so much more to do...

Anger welled against the Fallen threatening his life. This evil being the catalyst for his brother's death. If Zar wanted to kill him, then he'd fight like hell with all his skill and powers to kill Zar and fulfill his promise to Manny.

A hand grasping his ankle jolted Sergio out of his dire images. He raised his other foot to fight off who'd latched on to him, but a reassuring warmth coursed up his leg. Looking down, Sergio found Gabriel, sword in one hand, his ankle in the other, brilliant in his fierceness. Hope ignited in Sergio as he basked in Gabriel's unabashed determination. He turned his torment into resolve, matching the courage of the Archangel, who Sergio had so foolhardily blamed for Manny's death. The portal slammed closed behind them, sealing their unknown fate in Hell.

"I've got you," Gabriel cried, a bright light exploding from his chest. The dank corner of evil's pit was no longer cast with lurid shadows and caustic colors of death, instead it shined with a pure illumination of unselfish bravery and devotion. "Fight!"

Yes!

Urgency burst inside Sergio, stimulating his powers. He raised his hand and gripped Zar's, clutching the dagger's handle. Pinpricks ran along his cut skin, trying to heal the wound oozing blood down his neck. Sergio sought his mark and ignited the energy within it. Electric gold webbing erupted from his palm and spread across Zar and his blade. He drove more energy into Zar's hand, forcing the grip to loosen. Zar cursed as the dagger was ripped from his control.

Sergio punched his power against Zar, shoving himself free from his captive. Gabriel yanked Sergio against him, suffering the brunt of impact when they struck a stone surface. Sergio searched for Zar; sure he wasn't far. He found his sprawled body on the other side of the long massive bridge where they'd landed, leading to a black looming tower he'd seen in his nightmares.

Lucifer's lair

"Thank you, Gabriel," Sergio panted, jumping to his feet. The churning black lava below them gurgled and spit like a beast who demanded to be satisfied. "Can you get us out—"

The Fallen's battle cries, like nails on a chalkboard, cut him off. Their footsteps thundered on the bridge. Streaks of vibrant colors marked their black armor, swarming their way. Others took flight and circled the murky sky. Left with only his dagger and throwing stars, Sergio raised his hands. He created an air bomb, launching it at the threatening horde. The percussion wave struck the first line of Fallen, sending them careening over the side of the bridge, devoured by the lava. He raced against time, his heart thundering to the same beat as he raised more bombs in each hand. He threw the swirling golden globes into the ashy skies and at those who charged across the bridge.

Gabriel's bright light kept some Fallen at bay, but the six winged Fallen seemed oblivious to the light almost upon them. Sergio's pulse rushed in his ears as he desperately tried to ward off the enemy that would soon overtake them. But their looming approach wasn't what caused Sergio to falter. A malevolent roar split the air, its blood chilling boom terrifying, raising the hair on his neck.

"What is that?" Sergio twisted to the source. In the roof of a building adjacent to Lucifer's black tower, two enormous doors yawned opened. He froze at the sight that would be forever burned into the memory of his short life.

A monstrous black scaled dragon, wings of iridescent black flames, burst through the open doors. It launched into the steamy air, rising with the smoke choking the black sky. But it was not the only form with wings. A huge six-winged rider rode on its back, hands gripping the horns running down the serpentine spine. Only one villainous being was powerful enough to ride the dragon—Lucifer.

What seemed like a lifetime had only been a minute since they'd landed in Hell. The sight of Lucifer and his horrifyingly magnificent ride had stunned not only Sergio. The inhabitants of Hell stopped for one precious moment, mesmerized by the dragon circling above them. Its jaws opened, roaring as red fire glowed inside its belly, like a furnace billowing to life. A fire ball surged through its ribcage and into its neck, glowing with a malevolent promise of carnage. Its mouth gaped open, spewing a blast of swirling fire. The Fallen cheered, aroused by the duo turning for the bridge.

"We have to leave—now!" Gabriel didn't stand thunder stuck by the evil heading their way. He raised his portal as others gawked, grabbing Sergio's arm. The dragon's wings pumped, surging closer in a dive, headed straight for them. Gold webbing opened, crackling the oppressive heavy air. Its presence lifted the Fallen from their fog, inciting their riotous race toward them. Sergio's mouth turned dry, his cry stuck in his throat as the dragon's mouth yawned wide again, fire percolating in the rear of its black abyss. Gabriel shoved Sergio through the portal. Fire streamed past its spiked black teeth, shooting at them like a wildfire plummeting down a parched hillside.

"Go!" shouted Gabriel. The fire's heat licked at Sergio's armor. The red desert, refreshingly clean and barren, stretched before him with the guardians and Archangels standing near the opening. Their mouths fell open as Sergio hurdled through, expecting the dragon's flames to set him on fire.

"Sergio—" Olivia wailed, but the earth-shaking explosion from the dragon's fiery blast shattered their world.

He landed with a thud, the flames never scorched his skin, the heat hadn't disintegrated his armor. He dared a glance back and then wished he hadn't. Gabriel's face twisted in agony; his glorious wings were being devoured by heinous red flames. Moving as a shield for Sergio, he'd absorbed the dragon's fury to protect of all of them.

"Zach! Watch out—" Olivia shouted. Sergio gazed in horror as tendrils of fire lashed out through the portal. A flame licked across the back of Zach's neck and armor, like a fiery whip. Olivia pushed Zach to the ground and then rolled him in the red dirt. Zach's groans were laced with pain, whiffs of smoke swirling from beneath him. Raphael raced to Zach. He rolled him over and laid his healing hands on his red, blistered neck and the sizzling crack running down his back.

Sergio turned back to Gabriel, a sight that shocked him and shattered his heart. Michael hovered above Gabriel. His wings were a battlefield of blue dipped feathers clashing with the sparks of red flames. White light emanated from him into the portal, his blue sword shooting a bolt of blue flames directed into the bowels of Hell at the beast and his rider. An enraged screech pierced the night. The dragon's fire stopped after it turned away from Michael's attack.

But Gabriel...

His head hung forward, his white armor casting a luminescent glow against a black backdrop, void of his wings.

Oh my God...

I have to do something...

"Close the portal!" Sergio screamed. He shot up and ran back to Gabriel. Sergio grabbed Gabriel's chest. The hot armor seared his hands, but Sergio couldn't let go. His pain minuet compared to Gabriel's. He yanked at him, willing him through. "Now—"

Gabriel raised his head and peered at Sergio with eyes glazed over in agony. His fingers fluttered, slamming the portal shut, silencing Hell's outrage. Gabriel took two steps and then they collapsed. He lay face down, his wings gone, the back of him burnt black but for a few sparse places where his battered armor remained. A pressure built in Sergio's chest like someone squeezed his lungs. His breaths came out in harsh gasps. His trembling hand reach out and touched Gabriel's lifeless body.

"No—please no—" Hot tears trailed down Sergio's face as he rocked next to him. "You can't die. I need you... you can't leave me, too."

Streaks of green and blue landed next to Gabriel. Sergio glanced up at Michael and Raphael, their anguish reflected in luminescent tears, but anger boiled over in their eyes. Raphael knelt down and took Sergio's scalded hands into his. A cool sensation washed over the angry burns on his palms.

"You showed great bravery, young guardian." But Raphael's approval didn't sooth Sergio's aching heart. He yanked his hands away, his throat constricting as desolation enveloped him.

"No! Help him, not me... this is my fault. He came after me and then the dragon—" Michael placed his hand on Sergio's shoulder, sending a warm peace that couldn't reach the cold pit in his stomach.

"This is Lucifer's work. Not yours. Take Zach to the Magi—" Michael glanced behind Sergio, "—all of you... go... go now. Gabriel is ours."

The Archangels bent over, each taking a side, and lifted his crumbled, ruined body off the ground. "Make haste. The Fallen might return seeking to continue their fight." They streaked up into the night sky, once so beautiful with its bright moon. Now the stars glistened as if weeping along with Sergio.

"Let's go!" Lucia barked as she opened her portal. Elation flooded him to see his sister alive and moving unencumbered in her armor. He dragged himself up from the desert floor. Lucia grabbed his hand, pulling him to a world safe from evil. Zach leaned on Olivia. Pain etched on his face.

Sergio and Zach exchanged a quick glance before leaving the scene where their shared nightmare had played out. No victorious gleams in their eyes, only the dull acceptance and guilt of warriors turned survivors bearing their injuries as they walk away from the field soiled with blood.

They had saved Olivia, but the cost an unimaginable toll.

CHAPTER
FIFTY-THREE

OLIVIA

The church opened up in front of her, the large solitary dark cross hanging on the back wall. Light filtered across the floor, flecks of dust sifting through the air, seeking a place to settle. The golden sparks from the portal disappeared, leaving them in the muted room. Zach groaned; his weight heavy as she led him to a wooden pew. She guided him, easing him onto the worn bench. He sighed and flung his hands over the pew in front of him, hanging his head between his arms. Olivia gasped, the extent of the burns along the side of his head, neck and the slash down his back. Angry red skin shriveled in the burnt away edges of his armor. She reached out her hand to sweep away the frayed ends of Zach's hair around his ear, but paused, afraid her touch would only add to his pain, not ease it.

"Olivia!" Melchior's voice boomed as light flooded the church. The door slammed against the back wall, echoing against the bare walls. The Magi tore through the dark doorway, feet pounding against the wooden floors. "We saw the battle—"

"Please help him. He's badly burned—" Olivia caught the sob in her throat, stuck like an invisible hand squeezed around her neck.

"Let me see." Olivia stepped back as Caspar rushed forward and leaned over Zach. He hovered over him, his soothing voice asking questions Zach answered in one-syllable replies. Olivia's muscles quivered while her heart pounded, the horrific turn of events played over in her mind like flashcards raised by a sadistic hand.

Mom crumpled at Zar's feet
Oily blood spurting from Delilah's severed arm
Sergio and Gabriel lost behind the gold portal
Black dragon spewing fire
Gabriel's wings ablaze
Zach's screams as flames licked at him
All because of me...

Olivia shivered as the consequences of her actions tore her in two. "What have I done?" she whispered.

Sturdy arms enveloped her and brought her to his chest. Melchior's earthy scent wafted over her. She heard his heartbeat steady beneath his tunic. She closed her eyes wanting to stem the tears threatening to fall.

"This is not the time to search for blame. What's done is done." Melchior pulled back and ran his hands up and down her arms. "Come, let's sit, while Caspar aids in Zach's healing. Raphael and Balthazar are with your mom and dad—"

Olivia's stomach dropped. "How is he... Mom—"

"Raphael got her back safely and helped heal your dad. Zar's brutal attack left its mark, but he did not intend to kill... Delilah wanted to return and finish him off as a final part of her revenge. He'll be as good as new in a few days. Your dad is a strong man." Olivia sagged against the weight of her actions. The adrenaline had long left her system, leaving her knees weak and mind numb. He led her across the aisle where Sergio and Lucia sat huddled in a heated exchange.

"Gabriel will be fine. He's—" Lucia placed a hand on his shoulder.

"You don't understand. I did it again... I jumped into a fight with my emotions driving me instead of letting my training take over. When I saw Zar stab you, my mind went blank and then it filled with mindless rage and panic. I attacked with no plan and allowed Zar to take me. I should have never—"

"We were all acting on our fears. When I saw Zar on top of Zach, I could only think to jump. Maybe If I'd shifted back, I would have had my sword—"

"Both of you acted as we trained you. You attacked the Fallen swarming out of the portal and defeated them because of your training and skill. Even hardened warriors can succumb to their emotions when their comrades are hurt." Melchior guided Olivia into the pew and slid in next to her.

"How do you know?" Lucia's brow rose into her dark hairline.

"We watched through meditation. When you and Gabriel vanished into Hell, we readied ourselves for battle, but then you and Gabriel returned, and Michael sent you here." Melchior's tense shoulders belied his soft voice.

"Will he be all right... Gabriel?" Sergio asked with a hollow gaze.

"We'll find out soon enough. He's in God's hands." Melchior patted Sergio on his back. "You fought bravely... all of you. The Fallen underestimated you. That will not happen again. You survived their treachery. They will not make the same mistake again."

"That is my fault. I should have killed Zar." Sergio's nostrils flared. "I can't believe I let him get away."

"I didn't kill Delilah either. It all happened so fast." Olivia glanced over Melchior's shoulder. Zach sat up, his face pale against the burn, now pink as it healed. All heads turned as Zach stood while Caspar stepped aside. "If I had told you Delilah wanted to meet—"

"You all right, boy scout?" Sergio called out as Zach approached them, but Sergio's eyes weren't as carefree as his remarked sounded.

"Why didn't you tell us? I thought you were hiding something. If Sergio and I hadn't realized we had the same dream... you'd be dead."

A vision... I should have known.

Olivia swallowed and lifted her chin at Zach's harsh, but accurate words. "I was wrong not to tell you... any of you. Delilah's message to me was personal... hurtful, meant to draw me out alone. I wanted to face her and my demons about my dad on my own and not put you guys in any more danger because of my dad's past. At the last minute, I told Michael in case it turned bad. I left the note, too. I guess a part of me felt you'd figure out if I was in danger." Her eyes ached with unshed tears. "I was so very wrong not to share Delilah's note and that I was worried about walking into a trap. I've probably ruined the trust—" she scoffed, "—that I always demanded from you guys. I'm so sorry." A tear slipped, running a lone streak down her dusty face.

Zach's shoulders sagged as he sat behind her, but he remained tight lipped as he examined her with dark green eyes. Caspar sat down, leaned over and wiped away her tear. "All the past guardians have struggled, in one way or another, with how to let go of their pride... of feeling like there are times when it's justified to work alone or keep a secret from their fellow guardians. It is the human condition." He smiled at her as he leaned back. "This enlightenment... this forgiveness you are asking of your friends, it is one of the many reasons why God so loves his creation. He gave you free will. You'll make more mistakes than excellent choices, but it's what you do with the mistakes you make that allow wisdom and growth to flourish."

"I forgive you." Lucia's soft voice came from in front of her. Olivia turned and found the twins so similar in look and heart. "I would have done the same thing if I thought it was the only way to protect my family and friends."

Sergio took Olivia's hand, his long brown fingers entwining with hers. "I've never been able to stay mad at you and I'm not going to start now. God knows I've been a pain in the butt and you've always stuck by me. I didn't have my best day either." He smirked as he shook his head. "I get you, girl. We're good." Sergio gave her hand a last squeeze before he let it go.

Relief flooded Olivia, easing the knot in her stomach. But an ominous silence thickened the air behind her, making her wonder if Zach could ever find it in his heart to forgive her after everything they've been through.

How do I make it up to you, Zach?

"Liv." Zach's strangled voice broke her heart. She turned around, fearing that whatever he said might ruin the fragile relationship rebuilt so new. Holding her breath, she found Zach staring at her with conflicting emotions, each warring for control, but not winning. "What you did today scared me... wrecked me. You and me... us...—" his Adam's apple bobbed up and down, "—I mean... I thought you trusted me completely. It hurts that you didn't, but I get it. I really do. Your relationship with your dad... well... you have to fix it. It can't rule you anymore. We were damn lucky today. But if we keep more secrets from each other, and someone goes off on their own again... one of us will die. I can't be a guardian with you... any of you... if we can't be completely honest. If you promise me, you can from this moment forward, I'll grant the forgiveness you seek."

Olivia took in his handsome face, still marred with pink spider webs like creases along his jawline. How she had screwed something up so badly and he could find forgiveness while still healing from a fire blast from Hell, amazed her. "I promise you—" she sniffed "—that I'm done fighting my feeling for my dad and that I will never jeopardize the guardianship with secrets again."

Zach nodded; a lopsided grin accentuated the dimple bumping up against his wound. "That's a deal."

"That's good," Melchior said. "Because you'll need each other more than ever. Lucifer played his hand tonight by going after you. Delilah didn't do this on her own and Lucifer knows it."

"Why? What happened?" A tendril of dread trailed down her spine.

"Michael called me to the cave after you left. He told me to link with the Fallen and stay as long as I dared to find out what I could. I found Lucifer standing in his tower. When Delilah passed through the portal, he signaled Asura, the gold Fallen, with a single nod. He exuded a primal excitement. His evil overwhelmed me... sickened me. When Asura and the red Fallen disappeared through the portal, he became enraged. Yelled sporadic words about betrayal and killing the traitor. He flew down the spiral staircase and into his throne room. His facade changed as he grew in size, his armor in place. Lucifer stopped in front of his throne and stood gazing at it. For a moment, I thought he'd sensed me, so I began to pull back. It wasn't me his stillness was for. It was for the massive stone dragon throne that guards the room.

"'The time has come, Abaddon. Time for you to rise and take me to my enemies!' He bellowed as he raised his arms in the air, the ground rumbling beneath him. He punched his hands in the air and shattered the black granite of his throne. A maniacal laughter rose as the dragon roared, stretching itself to its full length. The last thing I saw was the ceiling doors opening while Lucifer climbed up its leg and onto its neck. The dragon's body shivered, its black scales all reflecting the colors of Hell exploding through the windows."

"That's crazy that an actual dragon was his throne, waiting for Lucifer to awaken it. That's bad news for us." Sergio slouched against the pew's side.

"Yes, it is." Melchior shook his head. "Abaddon was the most magnificent of all dragons in Heaven and Lucifer's only to ride. If he has waited until now to rise it from its slumber, it must mean he's ready to make his move... to strike out and implement whatever plan he's concocted."

"War is ahead for all of us. In the Heavens and on Earth unless you the guardians along with the Angels can stop him." Caspar's words hung in the air as if the weight of his statement stopped time for a precious moment.

"We won't let that happen. Lucifer and the Fallen can't win. We'll do whatever it takes to defeat him." Olivia glanced at her fellow guardians. She put her hand out, palm down. "Are you in?"

"Yes."

"Absolutely!"

"Oh yeah!"

Each guardian laid their hand on top of hers, followed by Caspar and Melchior.

"The time for his reckoning has come."

CHAPTER
FIFTY-FOUR

LUCIFER

A baddon's flames scorched the air where the portal once lay opened. Lucifer's legs quivered against the dragon's hard scales flexing beneath him as it flew toward the black tower. A guttural roar tore from Lucifer, his veins bulging in his neck. Abaddon answered his cry with a one of its own, shooting a stream of fire into the smoke riddled skies. The dragon's massive wings flapped, dominating the Realm, its sweeping turbulence sending any demon who dared to be near, tumbling in its wake.

They were here.

So close I saw the fear in them...

Wretched Gabriel ruined it...

But we made him pay... hopefully with his life.

Lucifer's fury pumped his thick, black blood, burning inside, needing release for the failure of his strategy. He sent a call through his link, demanding all meet at the Main Hall. Fallen and Lessors scurried and flew from the Seven Realms, swarming the arched entrances from all sides. Lucifer circled above while the violence inside of him spilled over, creating a plan of punishment for the failures handed to him. His hands gripped Abaddon's horns, maneuvering it toward the waiting horde. The dragon roared as it landed, jaws opening, fire percolating at the back of its cavernous throat. The

Fallen scattered from the entrance, parting as its horned feet thundered against the floor. Its claws clicked on the stone until it stopped in front of the pit. Hot air snorted from its flared nostrils; black reptilian eyes glared into the crowd.

Lucifer scanned the hall, glowing and undulating with the colors of the Seven Realms. The Fallen positioned themselves in front of the entrances leading to their lairs, their magnificent Princes stationed before their Realms. Lucifer stared at each section. Their specialized skills at infiltrating man and inciting their sins had built the army of the Damned because of him. These are the angels that followed his vision, wanting to thrive under his rule of self-indulgence and wickedness. Their service to him was absolute. He let his stare linger upon each of his Princes. But among the enraptured faces, traitors had wormed their lies into ears too deaf to understand the consequences of their betrayal.

Let the lesson begin.

"My fellow Fallen," Lucifer called out, the excited murmurings fading. "Today our Realm was invaded by one of our enemies who fought against us in Heaven: Gabriel, the Archangel from the virtue of Humility, messenger of God to mankind—the abomination that split our kind. He dared to enter here to rescue a mere human. But not just any human. This unique one has knowledge we need to conquer God and all his Angels, leaving humans for us to destroy and use for our many whims and pleasures. Because of this intrusion into our world, I awakened the mighty dragon, Abaddon, from his millennium in slumber. He fought gallantly... his fire breathing flames destroyed Gabriel's wings, extinguishing his life as they sought escape from their certain doom." The Hall exploded with vicious cries of affirmation, pounding their chests and stomping on the stone floor. Their pleasure boomed around him, feeding the rage boiling beneath his armor.

Lucifer raised his hand, quieting the crowd crammed into every corner of his enormous hall. Those standing around the lip of the empty pit, gaping in the middle, were the high-ranking soldiers of the

Princes positioned in front of them. He narrowed his eyes, leaning closer over Abaddon.

"But there's another reason why this human and Gabriel slipped through our grasp. They need to atone for their failures." The undercurrents of excited rumbles sent a shiver over the sinuous body beneath him.

"Saxem. Bring me Delilah. She languishes in my chamber, defying me." Saxem flew out of the Realm of Wrath's arches to answer his Master's request.

The pounding renewed, like the slow beat of a war drum. The Fallen's anticipation of Lucifer's punishment ignited the horde's blood lust.

"Zar. Come before me." A skirmish broke out in the crowd, but Zar flew from those clawing at him. He landed before Abaddon, his face a chiseled mask, lips sealed together in a hard line. Lucifer matched the growl rumbling in Abaddon as it leaned closer to Zar. He stepped away from the dragon, his brave facade slipping.

You should be very afraid...

Lucifer let the violent air brew amongst the Fallen, wanting their underlying frenzy to unleash in the hall. He needed their complete attention while he fulfilled their depraved desires, even if it struck one of their own. He unfolded his powerful body and stood, commanding their adulation on Abaddon's back. Raising his arms, he turned in a circle until he faced the Realm of Pride. He found Asura. Her ebony face gave nothing away, but the gold swirls on her armor blazed. She stepped forward under the watchful eyes of Beelzebub. Asura shook her head at her Prince when she strode past him, but ignored her mate Sonneillon, whose fists clenched at his side.

"Asura. Never one afraid to meet her fate."

Saxem swooped into the hall carrying Delilah. Her only arm wrapped behind his neck. What was left of her other arm protruded from her shoulder. No sympathy rose when he dumped her next to Zar. She glared back at Saxem, the angry red slash down the side of her face only highlighted her indignation. Delilah stood, not the

341

brazen beauty Lucifer had first encountered when she'd first taken the fall.

No.

Bitterness and fear warred over her face. The enticing decadence he'd first tasted now held no appeal... at least for satisfying his wanton pleasures. Lucifer dropped his arm, silencing the impatient crowd. He felt his heart beat steady and strong... eager to implement his punishments.

"The three Fallen before me, I sent on a vital mission. Their failure was not an option and yet... fail they did. There's no place in our Realm for failure or disobedience. Zar—step forward."

Zar did as commanded, lifting his black soulless pits to the voice calling him. "You and Delilah were instructed to bring a specific human to me. Not only did you fail, but you brought a different human instead... and an Archangel, too. Along with this failure, your counterpart was maimed, but Delilah's defeat in battle doesn't fall on you. Long ago, I gave you one of my cherished feathers. A sign that you belonged to me, under my protection and given special consideration. The feather also holds a precious power to heal. So... you have a choice. You can give the feather to Delilah. The angel you encouraged to become a Fallen and brought to me, signaling your loyalty. It will grow back her arm. Or... return it to me as proof of respect and penance for your failure."

Zar sneered as he turned to Delilah, her plea for the feather blatant in her gaze. "She is the reason for the failed mission. Her desire for revenge and power outweighed your command to bring the human to you. I tire of getting caught in her web of lies. I'll not waste the feather for her flesh." He plucked the treasured black feather from his wing. He raised it between his fingers to Lucifer. "My allegiance has always been to you, my Lord. I don't deserve to be a chosen one—my failure to you is my greatest sorrow."

"Liar—" a force struck Delilah across the check, knocking her head back.

"Do not speak!" Spittle flew from Lucifer's mouth. His harsh rebuke echoed in the hall. Black blood trickled down her chin. Terrified eyes stared back at him.

Lucifer raised his hand. The feather jumped from Zar's grip, twirling through the thick air. It stopped, suspended before Lucifer's palm, and burst into flame. The ashes fell onto Abaddon and disappeared between the inky scales.

"It is done. You choose wisely, Zar. The courage to stand alone among the Fallen far outweighs the weakness of aligning with a traitor." The horde pounded their feet with approval. Lucifer turned to her, a sneer lifting to his face.

She stared at him in horror. "Delilah... the only angel to have taken the fall after us. You came to me with knowledge and vowed to serve only me to aid us in our quest to bring down our enemies. But your actions today proved you are a liar—your deceit clear in disobeying my instructions. You came here to be a part of us, but only to implement your own agenda... to use your beauty and half-truths for your own devious purposes. You deserve to die." Excited growls and snarls filled the hall, eager for his discipline.

"No—"

"Silence!" Delilah choked on her words. She clawed at her neck, trying to fight off his force pressing against her airways. "Alas, I won't kill you. That's too easy a consequence for you. For I believe you still have knowledge hidden inside your warped mind I can use against our enemies. I shall enjoy breaking you... humiliating you... to gain this information. But for now, you're an example of what happens when a Fallen betrays me." Lucifer released his choke and grabbed the whip at his side, raising it in the air. The horde moved like a pit of agitated snakes, their demand for violence palatable. Lucifer tossed the weapon at Zar's feet. He froze as he stared at Lucifer's whip, crackling with black energy at his feet.

"Pick it up, Zar. As a reward for your renewed vow to me, you will be the master of Delilah's punishment... the vile angel who tricked you—the cause of your torture and the loss of your eyes."

Delilah turned to run, but Lucifer shot out his hands—black

swirling ropes erupted from his palms, lashing around her wrist and the shorn arm. She fought, kicking and screaming, but her efforts were useless.

"Please... Lucifer... listen to me!" Delilah begged.

"My time for listening to you is done." Lucifer stretched her arms until they threatened to tear from her body. He lifted her, feet dangling as her sobs increased. A wicked thrill coursed through him as she rose above the crowd, her hysteria complete... her demise total. His hands fell to his sides, the ropes suspended by his unseen powers.

"Your flesh, shredded by Zar's lashes, will heal slowly and painfully. The scars never to fade completely as a reminder of your betrayal... never again able to use your beauty against another."

Zar picked up the whip, his excitement shared on the humorless smile stretched across his hard face. He cracked the lash at the floor below her feet. The crowd rippled with a fevered frenzy, needing fulfillment matching Lucifer's.

"Please..." Delilah whimpered before the first long lash licked across her thighs. She screamed and arched against Lucifer's ropes that bound her. Black blood oozed from the wound; her armor was slashed, exposing her torn flesh. Zar struck again across her face, opening a slash from her temple over her nose to her jaw. Her mouth hung open, frozen in a macabre yawn. Zar paced around her, aiming the whip's tip over the front and back of her, marring her coveted beauty forever. Her head lolled back, eyes closed as her blood dripped on the floor, splattering on him with each strike. His chest heaved as he paused, sightless pits gazing up at her mutilated form. The whip fell from his hand, but he remained standing in the pool of her blood spreading around his feet.

You did well.

Lucifer jumped off Abaddon. The hordes blood thirsty cries magnified; eyes now fixed on him as Delilah hung suspended by his ropes. He strutted around the dragon, dragging on the anticipation of his next move. Strutting past each Prince, he displayed his massive, more powerful form, mightier than any of them combined. He grinned as he passed the other traitor.

Your time will come soon...

He kept up his steady pace until he faced Asura. She lifted her blazing gold eyes to him. Whatever fear or anger burned inside, she kept well hidden. Lucifer raised his hand, stroking over the wild braids surrounding her. He moved down her cheek until he cupped her jaw. The room quieted, except for the drip of Delilah's blood, hungry to hear his words.

"Asura. My Asura. Once my mate. Still one of my fiercest warriors as shown today in fighting off Michael and thwarting Delilah's plan. I called you forward not to punish you, but to reward you... and free you of the chains that truly bind you."

Confusion played over her ebony lines. "Free me... I don't understand."

"You will soon, my queen." Lucifer slammed his hard lips against her, the crowd erupting in cries of approval. He pulled away as quickly as he'd struck, leaving her stunned.

"Asura is my mate." Sonneillon stepped forward from his snarling Realm. "The bond approved by you."

Lucifer turned to Sonneillon, the Prince from the Blue Realm of Greed, a mighty Seraphim. His blue marbled chest heaved, agitating his six black wings dripping in sizzling cobalt blue. He glared at Lucifer with eyes blazing with angry defiance.

"You're right. I gave Asura to you long ago, when treachery and deceit did not simmer in one of my Princes. But you see... times have now changed and so has our future. A traitor... once a loyal prince... has come to my attention with his acts of subterfuge and power grabs." Lucifer's eyes narrowed as Sonneillon's widened.

"My Lord, you cannot think it is me. My devotion—" The rest of his plea lost when Lucifer sent a force, punching him in the chest, launching him high over the crowd. His body flayed until it landed with a thud on the pit's unforgiving dirt floor.

A hand grabbed Lucifer's arm. Asura stepped in front of him.

"He's not the traitor, my Lord. I swear! I would be the first to tell you—"

"You're blinded by him and his lies... no more!" His wings erupted and with a mighty thrust, he was gone, leaving Asura's pleas behind him. He circled above the pit, spiraling down until he flew just above the rocky lip. He glared at Sonneillon, who shook his head and fell to his knees.

"I swear I'm not the traitor you seek!" Sonneillon struck a fist over his heart, sparking a blue wave across his chest. "We fought side by side against God. Someone has poisoned you against—"

Lucifer landed a blow to his face, sending him back to the ground. He landed in the pit as Sonneillon rose and spit black blood into the dirt. "I know what you've been doing, the secret meetings you hold... the Damned you whip in the dungeons... spouting your madness."

The room ducked when Abaddon took flight, his wings seeming to touch the sides of the wall as it circled above them. Lucifer glanced up at the magnificent beast, catching sight of Asura and Zar at the pit's edge.

It's good to have you back Abaddon... it's been too long.

"Those lashings aren't what you think—" Lucifer struck him again.

"Don't tell me what I *think*... what I *know* is wrong. I have led the Fallen since the beginning and I will again lead them into our greatest battle ever. And we will be victorious... because I have exposed all my traitors. Farewell."

Lucifer flew from the pit. Abaddon dove closer, its body rippled when Lucifer landed on his back. He raised his arm, pointing his long damning finger at the shocked face of Sonneillon. A burst of fire erupted from Abaddon's mouth, covering Sonneillon in a wall of flames. His tortured wails fuel for the thunderous chaos above him. The ground shook, walls vibrated with impassioned sound and color.

"This is what happens to traitors in my Realm." Lucifer warned the Fallen, pointing to what lay left of Sonneillon's burning body.

"Our destiny to rule Heaven and Earth is soon approaching." Lucifer throbbed with the power surging in him, having finally freed himself of the traitor.

Nothing can stop me now...

"We will rise up and decimate the Angels—" The noise was deafening, their rabid zeal intoxicating "—and cast God out of Heaven and rule Earth with our Seven Realms destroying mankind with our weapons and their sins!"

"Who is with me and my chosen queen, Asura!" The Fallen's cries reached a fevered pitch he'd never stirred in them before.

Triumph!

Abaddon swooped near Delilah. Lucifer cut the bonds; her body falling to the floor, crumbled and broken, drenched in her own pool of blood. "Take her to the dungeons. Make sure she lives." He sneered, exiting the hall for the Fallen to celebrate as they please.

"Fly, my friend, to the Throne Room. We have a war to plan."

CHAPTER
FIFTY-FIVE

DARK
PRINCE

Abaddon flew overhead, Lucifer's exit from the hall a complete show of domination, power... and ignorance. The Prince stared down into the pit at Sonneillon's remains. He seethed at the waste of a supreme Fallen at the hands of the fool no longer aligned with the desires of the Realm.

My comrade
My ally
My cover...

Killed because Lucifer is so blinded by the desires of his flesh, yet so delusional he can't see the supreme power in front of him.

His body quivered as it fought against the ancient soul ignited by the violence; awakened by the Prince's rage. Oh, how he wanted to set the ancient soul free and show the Realm the face of the true leader who would bring their foes to their knees in submission while the Fallen obliterated the Angels and man.

Set me free. Let them see you in your full glory. Strike now before Lucifer can poison them further with his deluded plan for the Realm!

Not now... I have to find another prince—

The Prince scanned the hall, sizing up the others as potential conspirators ... and opponents. Berith's Realm of Wrath, eager for war, vibrated in their red slashed armor, prepared to attack at this very moment. Other Princes turned to their Realms, fanning the flames of Lucifer's insinuating claims and actions. The Prince turned as well, lifting his sword high in the air, pounding his chest as in a display of false unity. His Realm wouldn't conceive that his display was for anything else but acceptance of Lucifer's vision. But it was his own vision causing his heart to pound, his black blood to course in his veins with the promise of killing the true traitor... Lucifer.

Look at them. They worship you. They will follow you, not Lucifer, when the time comes.

The Prince unfolded his magnificent wings, ready to lead his Fallon back to his Realm where they built the army of the Damned. He launched himself toward the exit, but another Prince came into view as he also returned to his Realm. He watched the mask slip from his face when he thought no one observed, the flat eyes of disgust, the sneer thinning his full lips.

Would his ears be open to my words?

No... that Prince is too dangerous... too close to Lucifer. You don't need anyone but me. I am your counsel, the only one you can truly trust. Together—

The Prince growled at the voice crowding his thoughts. He breathed in deep the open air of the Realm, leaving the Main Hall's suffocating atmosphere, ripe with the odor of Lucifer's delusional will in the death and useless torture of what he'd left behind when he rode out in assumed glory on the magnificent Abaddon.

No one cares about Delilah... she had it coming.

Zar has always been a lap dog... although his whipping of her was entertaining.

Asura... she'll never be his submissive queen. She's probably planning Lucifer's death now.

Sonneillon...

You didn't need him... you have me.

And what is it you want, ancient soul? Your forked- tongue whis-

S.L. RICHARDSON

pers words of only our devious desires, but I sense in you a need to dominate me. That will not happen.

Never would I—

Silence.

The Prince landed in his Realm, his pool churning in need of the black orbs clutched in the Lessors talon's circling overhead. He didn't stop at his throne, his mind in need of clearing, his body in need of violence. He walked toward his mountain where a dungeon room lay dug out of the black unforgiving rock. There he would find the release his malignant soul sought, feeding his vision of the Seven Realms under his rule.

While *he* flew over his conquests on the back of Abaddon.

CHAPTER
FIFTY-SIX

OLIVIA

The doorbell rang as Olivia closed the refrigerator door. She put her mom's yummy potato salad on the counter, wondering who could be here. The Paxton and Mendes families had all arrived for Mom and Dad's BBQ. They'd wanted to get everyone's mind off the horrible events from a few days ago. Dad opened the sliding glass patio door, his sizeable frame turning sideways to step into the den. Laughter and raucous talk filtering in behind him. He walked across the carpet where he'd laid broken on the floor; unconscious and badly beaten at the hands of Zar.

Don't think about it... we survived... hopefully Zar and Delilah didn't.

"The doorbell just rang. Did you invite someone else?" Olivia asked, as she walked past him. His eyebrows shot up, warily glancing at the door. He reached out his hand, grabbing her elbow.

"I didn't. I'll get the door."

"My mark isn't tingling." Olivia pulled her arm away. "I'll see who it is. Besides, you don't want those burgers to burn."

"Right." Dad chuckled. "But I thought that's how you liked them... like a hockey puck!"

She laughed, stepping into the foyer, sensing his gaze on her.

"But not everyone else does," she replied, reaching for the door-knob. Butterflies fluttering in her stomach when she turned it and opened the door.

A tall, rugged man, with salt and pepper hair, stood a few steps back from the entryway. A smile tugged at one corner of his mouth. Bright blue eyes misty as he openly stared at her. Olivia cocked her head. A sense of familiarity washed over her.

"Hi. Can I help you?" She asked, her heart pounding. Another couple emerged behind him, holding hands on the pathway leading to the porch. Both smiled with a spirited energy, like they enjoyed the surprise of their appearance. They stopped short of the concrete steps, lingering with a twinkle in their eyes.

"Olivia—" he stretched out his hand, "—it's so good—"

"Who is it?" Dad called from behind her. She stepped aside, the man's tanned hand returning to his side.

"I don't—" Olivia stopped when she glanced at her dad. He stood frozen in the foyer. His hands still inside the dishcloth wrapped around them. A flush crept up his neck, eyes narrowing at the visitor.

What the heck?

"Hi, Conner. Can I come in?" His lips twitched; hands palm up in front of him. "I know it's been awhile, but—"

"Are you sober?" Dad's flat voice had her turning back to the man, peering at the stranger in a new light.

"Is that anyway to say hi to your old man?" The man said. "Just celebrated five years... sober." Dad's lips thinned

"What?" Olivia gasped, her head whipping back and forth between the two men.

"I'm your grandpa, honey. My name's Sam... Sam Drake." The once misty blue eyes shadowed with sadness. A stunned silence enveloped the porch. She understood now why he looked familiar. The eyes staring back at her were a carbon copy of her dad's... and hers.

Olivia stretch out a trembling hand. "It nice to meet you—"

"Sam." His warm hand engulfed hers. She smiled, a flush of her own blooming on her cheeks.

"Please, come in." Sam glanced at her dad, who waved him inside and stepped aside. A smile filled with relief spread over his face. He stepped through as a couple who had watched in silence, approached the door. Olivia tried to hide her surprise, noticing the red-haired lady was missing her left arm above the elbow. No sadness or wariness encompassed the couple, only joy shined in their smiles.

"We're David and Helen Paxton, Zach's grandparents."

"Please, come—" Olivia waved the couple through the doorway, dizzy by the surprising and confusing introductions.

"Why are you here?" Her dad scowled at Sam. "I haven't seen you since Mom's funeral... what, going on ten years now?"

A quirky half smile spread on Sam's face, but his body deflated under Dad's harsh words. "It's been too long. A birdie told us there was a party." Sam stepped toward the sliding door. "And you know I hate missing out on a party." Zach's grandparents followed, oblivious to the low growl emanating from Dad.

"What's going on? Why would he just show up unannounced?" Olivia pointed to the procession that had just passed her.

"I don't know, but I don't like it. I'm going to find out why." Dad muttered, hurrying after his dad. Olivia grabbed the salad bowl, then darted after him, concerned the fireworks between them was about to start.

Sam stood on the concrete deck, off to the side of the door. A wave of laughter rolled through the entrance as Olivia rushed out, making her way next to Sam. He gazed over the backyard crowd, his Adam's apple bobbing inside the creases of his neck.

Sergio's grandma held a plastic bowl filled with salad. Her grey floral scarf fluttered in the gentle breeze. She glanced over at the door. The salad bowl slipped from her hands, spilling lettuce across the table, landing with a *thunk*.

"Sam—" she gasped. She raised a trembling hand over her heart, startled as if she'd seen a ghost.

"Camilla." Sam spoke her name with a thickness; his chin quivered as they stared at each other as if they were the only ones there.

"Mom... Dad!" Rachel sputtered, popping up from her seat. Whatever passed between Sam and Camilla got lost in the pandemonium that ensued. Rachel, followed by her family, wrapped her parents up in a big, group hug. The Mendes family also stood, exchanging curious glances. Olivia watched her mom's slow approach toward Sam. She stopped in front of him, tears welling in her eyes.

"You're just as beautiful as ever," Sam said, shifting the weight on his feet.

Mom chuckled and threw her arms around his neck. "Still a charmer, I see." She released him after a quick squeeze.

"And you're still a hugger," Sam laughed, scratching his chin.

Olivia's heart warmed at the easy teasing passing between them.

"I have to say... this is quite a surprise." Mom glanced nervously at Dad, who still stood in the open doorway. "Uhm... Conner... the burgers?"

"Damn!" He jumped out of his stupor and ran to the grill.

"I'm sorry I didn't call, but—" his words tapered off as Sergio's grandma took tentative steps towards him. Mom glanced over her shoulder. Her grin grew when she gazed back at Sam again.

"Well, it doesn't matter. We're glad you're here and just in time, too. We were about to eat. Soda and water are in the cooler. Help yourself." Mom worked her way over to Dad, their whispers too low for Olivia to catch.

"I have to say, Sam Drake, you were always one for surprises." Camilla stopped in front of him, head bent back as he was a good foot taller than her.

"I hope it's a pleasant one." The playful note in Sam's voice belayed the somberness on his hopeful face.

Camilla lifted her two hands towards him, like a welcoming bridge between two old friends. "You are a sight for sore eyes, *mi amigo viejo.*"

"Who you calling old?" Sam chuckled, taking her hands in his. "I've got plenty of pep left in my step." She threw her head back in laughter.

"I bet you do." She turned and hooked her arm through his. "Let's get you something to cool those flushed cheeks down. How have you been...?" Her words faded as Sam's head leaned closer to hers. They once again seemed to have forgotten the surrounding people watching with eyes of varying emotion. Some cautious, others curious... and one with simmering anger.

"What is going on here?" Sergio surprised her from behind. "Abuela is acting weird, and your grandpa shows up out of the blue?" Olivia turned to him with a furrowed brow.

Zach came up next to them. "My dad reminded me that Sam was a guardian and so was my grandma, Helen. She's super cool and so is Grandpa. Her story was she lost her arm in a car accident, but I wonder now if there's more to it." Zach stared at the families now sitting in camp chairs, laughing at his grandpa's animated gestures.. Her fingers itched to trace down the faint web of scars etched over the side of his neck, disappearing under his collar. Zach's wound had healed as far as he would let it. He wanted the scars to stay as a memory, a constant reminder to stay vigilant.

"But why are they all here?" Lucia tossed her soda can into the recycle bin, before stopping in front of them. She shook her head. "Just seems odd, don't you think? Showing up... unannounced—"

A hiss and crackle erupted, startling the crowd. The backyard's skyline blurred with a clear, protective film spreading into a dome around them. Olivia's heart raced when the three Magi emerged from a blue portal.

"I bet we get our answers now," Sergio muttered.

"But will we like them?" Zach asked, lifting an eyebrow.

Another reunion ensued as the three older guardians greeted the Magi. Olivia marveled at the scene, wondering if this would be her future. Waiting for cherished moments to see the mysterious Angels who'd forever changed her life.

Melchior stepped forward. "We're sure you all are curious about this clandestine appearance, so I'll get straight to the point. After the recent events at the Valley of Fire, we came to a conclusion we hope will meet with your approval. The safety of the guardians and their families are in peril. We've come up with two choices. Each one has its pros and cons. The decision is for you to make. We will not impose upon your free will."

Nervous clamoring peppered Melchior, but he raised his hand, stopping the questions. "We're sure Lucifer knows about the guardians and who you are. That makes the families easy bait. The first choice is the easiest one. You all go to a place Lucifer knows nothing about. All of you will come and live safe in our world."

Olivia's heart raced, excited for herself, but nervous about the ramification for the families.

"The second is your lives go on as they are right now, except there will be some changes. The guardians will spend their days *and* nights with us. If they are followed or linked during a hunt, there is no way they can be traced back to us. School has a month left. You will portal to your house, drive to school and back home, all under the watchful eyes of the Archangels you met in the waterfall cave. The families will stay in their homes here with the grandparents, also under the same protections as the guardians. If your lives are in danger, the past guardians here will have a way to escape."

Gasps raised across the yard, hands jerking up in surprise. Sam, Camilla, Helen, Conner, Javier, and Rachel stared at their palms.

"What is this?" Javier asked, gesturing his hand at Melchior.

"These are talismans, each created for you. They will open a portal to our world if you need to leave."

"I've missed you in my pocket." Dad murmured, closing his hand around the token.

Balthazar stepped forward. "This plan is not perfect, filled with opportunities for the Fallen to attack. And they will strike again."

"What do the Archangels think we should do?" Olivia called out.

As if on cue, a green light flashed. Everyone cheered at the angel who emerged.

"Gabriel!" Sergio shouted, running full speed until he slammed against the Angel's chest. He threw his arms around him. "I thought—"

"It will take more than the flames from an evil dragon to end my days." Gabriel smiled down at Sergio. "We still have much to do, my friend." A sob escaped Sergio when Gabriel extended his wings, as glorious and vibrant as ever, covered completely in gold.

"Yours wings... Abaddon's fire burned them—" Sergio ran his hand over the gorgeous feathers.

"Yes... they did burn, but I happen to know someone who performs miracles." The crowd laughed, easing the mounting tension. "Abaddon was the most magnificent dragon in Heaven. My heart is heavy to learn the creature will be used to kill instead of glorify."

"So, these plans—" Rachel wrapped her arms around Kaylee, bringing her daughter closer, "—they meet with your approval?"

"Yes. The Magi approached us before taking it to you and your families. The choice is yours."

"I don't like the idea of being chased from my home by the Fallen I've spent my life fighting." He glanced at Sofia, who nodded at him. "With angelic protection and the talisman, we will stay."

"As will we," Rachel said, Matt's hand slipping into his wife's. "And my parents are here with us. We are always stronger together."

Dad and Mom put their arms around each other. "I'm not leaving now after all we've been through." His gazed turned to Sam. "You're welcome to stay." Sam's lopsided grin quivered as he nodded back at Dad, then broke out into a smile when he stared at Mom.

"We will assign Angels to you. They'll go unseen, but you'll sense their presence. All precautions will begin now until we feel it is safe again. Lucifer is erratic, supremely dangerous, and unpredictable. He may strike at any moment. If at any time you feel the need for change. Contact us. Are we in agreement?" Gabriel asked.

All heads nodded along with solemn affirmations, even Zach's sister still wrapped in her mom's arms.

"Good... and thank you. We shall go now and make preparations." With that, the Magi and Gabriel left, leaving the backyard in stunned silence.

"Anyone want a burger?" Conner lifted a forked prong holding a patty too burnt for even Olivia to gag down. Snickers rained upon him. He shrugged, grinning as he tossed the charred patty back on the grill.

But his joke did the trick. Nervous chatter started, but the food went untouched.

"I can't wait to live with the Magi. It's better than any book I've read and way more exciting. I'm relieved knowing our families will be safe while we hunt and protect Orion." Lucia peered at the blue sky. "It's even more vital now that Lucifer knows about us."

Sam snuck up behind Lucia and squeezed her shoulders. "I wanted to introduce myself to you, Lucia. I'm Sam, and you're one of the reasons for my return." He glanced up at Dad, then passed over to Olivia. He winked before turning back to Lucia. "You see... I'm a shifter too."

"What? That's amazing! What do you shift into?" Lucia's eyes sparkled at Sam.

"A grizzly bear," he smirked. "An old gnarly one if I could still change, but I will help you navigate your transitions and harness your powers."

"Yay!" Lucia threw her arms around him. "I'm so relieved and thrilled to have your guidance, especially after I got stabbed. I don't want that to happen again."

"Good! We'll start tomorrow." He walked back to Sergio's grandma with pep back in his step.

"Well, I guess that's that," Zach remarked, gazing out into the backyard.

A shiver passed over Olivia's spine as flutters of excitement grew in her belly. Was it from the thrill of living with the Magi in their magical land or the dread of Lucifer's knowledge and his wanton intentions to find out more?

Probably both, if she were truthful with herself. They were all lucky to have survived that night. She pushed away the horrid images still haunting her; Sergio disappearing, a dagger in Lucia's side, Gabriel's wings on fire, and Zach's body burning—his wails piercing her heart.

She slipped her hand into Zach's. He peered down, grinning at her as if the same thoughts circulated inside him. She wanted to reach up on her tip toes and give him a kiss, but—Olivia did it before she chickened out. Her lips grazed over his, her eyes open, looking at his stunned face. She pulled back smiling and squeezed his hand.

"Why did you do that?" Zach whispered, his emerald eyes darkening with pleasure.

"Because I'm not hiding my feelings or keeping secrets anymore. So, when I wanted to kiss you, I thought I'd let you in on it," she arched her eyebrow, enjoying her newfound freedom to be herself.

"I like it," Zach told her.

"You like what, boy scout?" Sergio came up to them like the weight of the world had been lifted off him.

Zach turned to him. "That I have you, Lucia, and Liv on my side when we battle the Fallen."

"They will train our butts off in Magi-land," Sergio grinned. "And I can't wait."

"Magi-land? Is that what you call it?" Zach chuckled, nudging him.

"Yeah... it's like Disneyland, but way better!" Sergio laughed.

"I'm using it. It could never be named anything else now." The guardians all guffawed in agreement with Zach, who just shook his head at Sergio's beaming face.

"Come on, let's eat. We got a lot to do before we go." Olivia released Zach's hand and walked toward the table full of people she loved and would fight to the death to protect.

The fight is coming...

We haven't seen the last of the Fallen who hate us either...
Delilah.
Zar.
Lucifer.
We'll be ready, I promise you that.

PLEASE WRITE A REVIEW

Thank you so much for reading *Light of Orion!* I hope you loved reading this book as much as I enjoyed writing it! I would like to know what you think about the book, as would others. Reviews breathe life into an author's spirit and help others in their quest to find their next entertaining book. Please write your review on Amazon and/or Goodreads. Thank you so much!

Amazon:
https://www.amazon.com/S.-L.-Richardson/e/B07ZN9M8K2

Goodreads:
https://www.goodreads.com/author/show/
19692005.S_L_Richardson

DON'T MISS OUT!

Never miss any future sneak peeks or updates on any of your favorite characters, happenings or my upcoming books! Go to my website at www.slrichardson.com and sign-up for my newsletter full of fun and intriguing insights about the *Guardians of Orion* series and my writing life. I'd also love it if you'd drop me an email on my *"contact me"* page with questions or what you think about my books. I'll get back with you. You're the best!

Hunt for Orion
Guardians of Orion Book 3

Olivia, Zach and Sergio's epic journey concludes in the last install-ment of the *Guardians of Orion* trilogy, *Hunt for Orion!*

Having escaped from Lucifer's clutches in his scheme to kidnap a guardian of Orion, Olivia, Zach, Lucia and Sergio must now live in the land of the Magi to protect themselves, their families, and the secrets of the mystical portals. Will this plan be enough to keep them safe from Lucifer and the Fallen determined to destroy them?

Lucifer is enraged by those who let the guardians slip away and by their continued betrayals. As his maniacal Army of the Damned grows under the ruthless tutelage of the Seven Princes of the Realm, Lucifer tries to uncover the prince who is bent on his demise. Who can he trust to lure out this traitor while he diabolically plans his destruction of Heaven and become ruler over mankind on Earth?

As the guardians come into their fullness in power and enlighten-ment with the help of the Magi, Guardian Angels and past guardians, their need to defeat their inner demons becomes even more critical if they are to eradicate the evil threatening them and humanity.

Are the guardians ready for the ultimate battle for who shall rule over Heaven and Earth? Or will their free will, and those of man, shatter the chances of their survival and forever change the world in which they live?

Don't miss out on the final book in the trilogy,
Hunt for Orion!
Coming Soon!

ACKNOWLEDGMENTS

Writing a novel is done in solitude. Stolen moments of time for me on the weekends or while my husband is at work and my son in school during the week. I need quiet to work. No music or TV, just me madly tapping on the keyboard the movie reel my muse is playing for me in my head. Sometimes, I read back what I wrote, and I'm amazed by what is on the page. I don't necessarily remember writing it or I think *Wow... that's crazy cool* or simply *that's wicked!* Whatever is going through my mind, I know to my core that this gift is from God... He's awakened my muse.

Thank you, God.

My family is my sail. They breathe life into me every day and set me free to write across the blank computer screen in my office. My husband's unending support, loving guidance, and brilliant edits drive me to *do better*. Our children are fabulous with their encouragement, love, and understanding of my wacky days. Love you to the moon and back...

Mom... my biggest cheerleader... I can hear her imaginary pompoms over the phone as she listens to my concerns or gives me her edits, for which she always feels so badly about! Thank you, Jim, for supporting our efforts and for printing off reams of paper so she can sit in the sunroom and pour over the book. Orin, thank you for your sweet phone calls and asking questions that always give me food for thought. I promise you get to be the casting director... haha! Auntie Marie, your generous soul and courageous words always mean the world to me. Daddy... my firewall... during my 50 plus years of life, and for helping to make this book as perfect as it can be before publishing. My gratitude to all of you is as endless as is my love for each of you.

Thank you to some very special friends who have been a shoulder of support over the phone, zoom, or over a glass of wine. Mary, Barbara, Lisa & Paige, Jen, and Teresa. You always make me laugh, even when you can't see it though those damn masks! Love ya!

Thank you, Natalie from Original Book Cover Designs, for your mentorship and stunning work. Thanks to my editor, Rebekah, who helped me polish the book and for your positive encouragement. Final thanks to my formatter, Melissa at Bookly Style, for your patience and making the printed word so lovely on the page.

I'll leave you with the prayer to the archangel, St. Michael. He is a warrior and will fight for you. Pray to him for his intercessions, on your behalf, to our Lord to aid in your battle against whatever you face. St. Michael has certainly helped carry me across the finish line.

Prayer to St. Michael

Saint Michael, the Archangel,
defend us in battle.
Be our safeguard against the
wickedness and snares of the devil;
May God rebuke him, we humbly pray, and do thou,
O Prince of the heavenly host,
by the power of God, thrust into hell Satan, and
all the evil spirits who
prowl about the world seeking the ruins of souls.
Amen

ABOUT
S. L. RICHARDSON

When you don't find her reading the latest YA fantasy or thriller or running her high schooler to his various activities, she is at the computer writing the next book in her trilogy, *Guardians of Orion*.

Being an author has been a dream of hers, but like running a marathon, thought it would never happen. After hitting 50, she chased the dream (not running a marathon, but writing), and released her first two books of the trilogy, *Mark of Orion* and *Light of Orion*.

When she's not writing, she loves cooking, gardening, going to Houston Astros baseball games, and walking her German Shepherd (or maybe he walks her).

She lives in Texas with her incredible and supportive husband and is blessed with four amazing children.

CONNECT WITH S.L.
Visit my website:
www.slrichardson.com

Get my other books:
Amazon: https://www.amazon.com/S.-L.-Richardson/e/B07ZN9M8K2

Join the fan page:
Facebook: https://www.facebook.com/slrichardsonauthor

Follow me on:
Instagram: @authorslrichardson
Twitter: @_slrichardson
Pinterest: authorslrichardson
Goodreads: https://www.goodreads.com/author/show/19692005.S_L_Richardson
BookBub: https://www.bookbub.com/profile/s-l-richardson

Made in the USA
Las Vegas, NV
24 August 2024

94391145R00215